ALL I EVER DID WAS
LOVE A MAN

SHARON DENISE ALLISON-OTTEY

God Is Love —
Share Him!

HILTON PUBLISHING COMPANY • CHICAGO, ILLINOIS

Hilton Publishing Company
Chicago, IL

Direct all correspondence to:
Hilton Publishing Company
110 Ridge Road
Munster, IN 46321
815-885-1070
www.hiltonpub.com

Library of Congress Control Number: 2005936514

Printed and bound in the United States of America.

ALL I EVER DID WAS

LOVE A MAN

DEDICATION

I have truly only loved one man during my life and I know that this love will last through eternity. This book is dedicated to the man of my dreams, Colin Carlton Ottey, M.D., my beloved husband. Thank you for being my inspiration, my cheerleader, my soulmate, my high priest, my covering, and allowing me to just be Sharon. I love you. It's all I ever did.

ACKNOWLEDGMENTS

First and foremost, I want to give all praise and honor to God for his grace and mercy. I know that without Him, I can do absolutely nothing but with him I can do all things. I would also like to acknowledge the steadfast prayers of my family and friends. This book is dedicated to my beloved husband, Colin Carlton Ottey, M.D. While it is impossible to name everyone that has walked with me through this journey, I certainly must formally thank my parents, Thomas and Guerleane Allison, for always standing with me and pushing me forward. I'm grateful for all of my siblings and must particularly thank Darrell and Roderick Allison, for their prayers, assistance, advice, and patience during this time of "birthing" in my life.

I am grateful to my other family members, who include a host of aunts, uncles, cousins, nieces, nephews, and others whom are priceless to me. I would be remiss if I did not specifically thank my "other" mother, my auntie and one of my best friends, Cleo Washington, who is one of the most phenomenal women I've ever known. I am grateful to have been blessed with another "father," my uncle, Carl Allison, who never forgets that I am his first born. I must also acknowledge the support and prayers of my Pastors, Revs. Dr. Grainger Browning, Jr. and Dr. Jo Ann Browning. I want to particularly thank Pastor Jo Ann for her walking with me through this process in prayer, and her continued encouragement to me and women across the world.

I am blessed to have many dear friends that have supported me and continued to drive me forward. I thank all that have touched my life in any manner and know that you were divinely placed for such a time as this. A special thanks to my "other husbands," Christian Foster, the best Public Relations man in the business, Dr. Barry L.

Harris III, Dr. Garfield Clunie, and Dr. Randall Maxey. I must thank the women that keep me grounded, including Deena Currie, Jacqueline Alexander, Dr. Patricia Hart, and Dr. L. Natalie Carroll, as well as the "Don't Hate Me Crew" that began with us being starry-eyed students, but continues as we have become "older" women. We are all forever sisters, Dr. Octavia Cannon, Dr. Victoria Holloway, and Dr. Rachel Villanueva. My heartfelt thanks to two of my mentors, Dr. William Hines and Dr. Andrew Best, for their "time in" and molding of me. I must thank our role models for Godly marriage and my spiritual mentors, Drs. Mark and Myra Wade, for their undying love, prayers, and support. True friends are a treasure and I am blessed with many. As we age, the circle becomes more closed and dear. However, I am thankful for the love and deep friendship of Rev. Kevin and Elder Terry White.

Finally, I thank the staff of The COSHAR Foundation and COSHAR Medical, with particular thanks to my long-time assistant, Cassandra Denise Smith, for her enduring loyalty, love, and support. I would end with thanking the following for their very kind professional advice, assistance, encouragement, and new friendships throughout this process; Dr. Renita Weems, Valorie Burton, and Jucinda Fenn-Hodson. I would certainly like to thank my editor, Karla Dougherty, and the entire staff of Hilton Publishing for the opportunity of letting the world hear this story.

This book is a journey and my first fiction novel. However, fact is often more startling than fiction, and it is in this vein that I acknowledge the countless women who find themselves in a similar situation as Sabrena—looking for the love of their lives and finding pitfalls, challenges, heartache, and pain. I'm thankful that where there is life, there is hope that runs eternal, and if you accept the love of God, yourself, and your family, often the other love that you so desire finds you. To women around the world, I salute you and offer you hope of a better tomorrow that will begin on today. Although this book is one of fiction, there was indeed a "real" Sabrena from which this book is very loosely based. She changed my life and made an impact that will now last for an eternity. I know that I'm a better woman because she touched my life.

Thank you, the reader, for spending a little time with me, and hopefully your life will be touched.

PART I

CHAPTER ONE

Once again she was waiting, which seemed to be her new state in life—waiting for Steve to pick her up for another apology date. She had caught him in yet another lie. Worse yet, she had checked the voice mail on his cell phone and heard a woman thank him for a great weekend. He had told her he was going to a mandatory training session in Atlanta that weekend; he had even brought back T-shirts for the girls. Steve had of course denied the woman's call and even said it must have been a prank—after all, he only loved her. Sabrena was sick of it all. She felt as if she had wasted the last three years of her life on yet another worthless man. Unfortunately, she couldn't simply let go. Each time she tried, he drew her back into him, and then disappointed her again. Sabrena had thought she was in love, but, lately, she wondered if it really was love for Steve or just her fear of being totally alone.

"If he doesn't get here in ten minutes, I'm not letting him in," Sabrena swore to herself. "I'm not calling him again; he should be waiting on *me*!" She paced the floor and looked out the window.

So she could have a quiet time with her man, she'd sent the kids to stay at her friend Rachel's house. She loved her girls, but she needed a break every now and then. As she thought of Deena and Renee, she smiled. They asked if "Uncle Steve" was going to be their new daddy—over and over again. They adored him, and who wouldn't? That man could charm the panties off a nun. He would enter the room, grab each girl and twirl her in the air, putting her down gently with a gift or candy pressed into her little hands. The worse his crime was against Sabrena, the better he treated her girls. These moments were priceless to her daughters, and, because their father wasn't in the picture, Sabrena couldn't find it in her heart to break up with him, as hurtful as it was to her.

She and Steve had met at the grocery store. It had been an embarrassing moment for Sabrena, because she didn't have enough money to pay for her groceries. Her daughters couldn't understand and looked at her with pleading eyes as she put back two of their treats. But that still wasn't enough, so she looked for more to put back.

A tall, chocolate brother appeared out of thin air. "May I help you?" he asked.

She was embarrassed and mumbled some excuse about not having her checkbook. Sabrena could barely look at him, but noticed his nicely polished shoes and the perfect cuff on his pants. He raised his voice a little and gently asked again, "May I help you, Miss?" He smiled and lightly touched her hand.

"No, I don't think so," Sabrena responded. "I didn't bring enough cash or my checkbook, but I'll work this out."

The nice man whispered something to the cashier, who pointed to the register and answered, much louder than was necessary, "She's $38.72 short and I need to go on break." The fine-looking man stuck out his hand and smoothly spoke to Sabrena, "Hello, I'm Steve Addison, the store manager, and you're . . . ?"

Sabrena was becoming more embarrassed by the moment and felt her face flush as she meekly offered her hand to meet his. She noticed how nice his hands looked and particularly noticed that there was no wedding ring. "I'm Sabrena . . . Sabrena Collins." The man wouldn't let go and she felt something in her palm. She quickly retracted her hand and found two folded twenty dollar bills. She was speechless. Steve winked at her knowingly. She pretended to look again in her purse and told the cashier that she had "found" the rest of the money. The cashier couldn't have cared less as she took the money and completed the transaction.

Her rescuer walked to the back of the store. Sabrena hadn't even had time to thank him. Deena and Renee were getting restless and already pulling their goodies out of the bags. Sabrena decided to leave the store, whispering thanks to God. She warmly smiled as she thought of the tall, handsome, kind man.

"Steve Addison," she had thought. Gosh, he was fine, with that dark chocolate skin and piercing, deep brown eyes with flecks of light in them. His hand was strong, and his lips . . . mmmm . . . his lips were perfectly full, with the ends turned up as he smiled. Sabrena had only glanced at him, but she'd noticed how smooth his skin was—

there weren't any razor bumps or flaws of any kind on his face. He had a dimple in his right cheek; Sabrena had never seen anyone with a dimple in one cheek and not the other. Sabrena guessed that he was in his early forties; he looked mature with just the right amount of gray at his temples. She also noticed his body—it was tough not to. He certainly was in shape and probably worked out several times a week. Sabrena guessed he was about six feet two inches.

For Sabrena, though, it was his kindness that struck her most, and she was thankful. She decided to send a thank-you card to him. She would make sure that she put her phone number and address in it—not expecting him to call, but just being sincere in expressing her thanks to the decent brother who saved her from embarrassment and from that ghetto-fabulous clerk. She was sure a man like that wouldn't be interested in her, but felt she at least owed him a card.

"Hmmph, that was years ago . . . his $40 cost me hundreds of hours of misery. I should have never fallen for this player," Sabrena thought. She began to undress and settle down with a bowl of Breyers™ butter pecan ice cream. She felt tired, disappointed, and angry, mostly angry with herself for once again believing Steve. She wondered what it would be this time—working late? Caught in traffic? Mom sick? Oh, there was the "fire in the store" a few weeks ago that of course was a lie. Steve treated her like crap and she continued to take it. Why?

Sabrena knew that she was attractive; she'd been told that she was "pretty," even "beautiful." She didn't know about all that, but she knew she was certainly not ugly. She always felt that beauty was really only skin deep and faded quickly; she'd met very pretty women whose personalities were so evil that it overshadowed any semblance of attractiveness. Sabrena tried to keep herself together; despite having two kids, she'd maintained her figure. She was medium build, like her mother, and stood five feet seven inches in her bare feet. Her weight fluctuated depending on the time of the month and how many Krispy Kreme™ doughnuts she ate the week before, but she was usually about 140 to 145 pounds—although she felt like she may have lost a few pounds in the last few months. She rarely got on the scale but used her clothes as a measure of where she was with her weight; she was usually a perfect size 10, and before Renee was born she was a size 8. She wasn't too big but not skin and bones either, and she noticed that most men looked at her twice.

She kept her face up and with just a little eyeliner, powder, and lipstick on most days. Although she had gone through several "makeovers" during her lunch hour at the cosmetics counter, she liked simple makeup unless she was going out and even then not too much. Sabrena twirled her hair a lot; a habit she shared with her mother, whose hair was naturally curly and at times hard to manage. She was too busy to fuss with it so she wore a nice bob just to her shoulders that complemented her round face.

Sabrena glanced at herself in the mirror in her living room. Her eyes were red. Her Momma had always told her that she had the "eyes of an angel" (although she didn't see anything special about her too big brown eyes). She held the rare compliment from her mother close to her heart.

Sabrena had two girls with no father in sight, so she lived on a tight budget and couldn't afford to spend money on herself. She did her own hair, except for her perms, and bought maybe four or five outfits a year for herself. She was grateful for her Bloomingdale's employee discount and advance sales notice that allowed her dollars to stretch further in taking care of her girls. Sabrena believed that Renee and Deena shouldn't have to pay for her bad choices in men. So, as long as there was no daddy in the picture, Sabrena had the responsibility to save money for a rainy day, but she also tried to spoil her babies at least a little bit.

They were good girls and they were going to have a life better than she ever had. They were very smart and absolutely beautiful. She smiled. She remembered that when they were very small, people would stop her and go crazy over them. Even now, when they went out, people commented on how well-behaved and pretty they were. Sabrena's pride was wrapped up in her daughters, and she had vowed that, no matter what, she was going to take care of them.

Deena, at seven, was the oldest. She was definitely a "girly-girl" and loved playing with her dolls and in Sabrena's makeup. She had mocha skin and jet black hair that was soft and easy to braid. She loved ribbons in her hair and took pride in how they looked. Deena had Sabrena's eyes—big and questioning—and a bubbly personality. She never met a stranger who wasn't taken with her, and Sabrena was always trying to keep her from being too friendly. Deena was old enough to vaguely remember when Sabrena had left her father, Carlton. She used to ask Sabrena where her daddy was, but one day she just stopped asking.

Unlike Deena, Renee was usually quiet around strangers and at school. She needed time to warm up to people and was very clingy to both Sabrena and her big sister. But just like her sister, Renee was a beautiful child. She had honey-colored skin and brownish hair that was hard to manage, but when Sabrena pressed it, it was thick and strong. Renee had eyes like an old woman's—big, deep brown saucers full of wisdom. Renee loved to just be near Sabrena. Even at age six, she sometimes still cried in the morning when she had to leave her mommy. She had just learned to walk when Sabrena left Carlton.

Sabrena was still amazed that it had taken her so long to leave him. Their years together were filled with insults and verbal abuse, and he had actually hit her once in the heat of an argument when he said that she disrespected him. She had been shocked and afterwards begun to pack her clothes. He ran after her, was apologetic, and actually called her mother. Her mother brought up the fact that this would be Sabrena's second failed marriage and talked her into staying. For a while, things actually got better. She stayed for her daughters. Carlton was a good provider and, although he wasn't home a lot, she believed that, in his own way, he loved his family. Most days, Sabrena figured that stress at work was the reason he always told her she was stupid and lucky to have him.

The end came when he began to yell at the girls. One day, when Carlton came home from work, three-year-old Deena ran to show him a drawing she'd done at day care. Carlton paid no attention to her and, when she pulled at his arm, jerked it away and called to Sabrena, "I don't have time to be bothered with this nappy-headed girl today. That's your job—get her away from me." Sabrena saw Deena's tears. Although Deena probably didn't understand every word he said, she knew that her daddy didn't want her around. Sabrena made up her mind to leave, feeling that even a homeless shelter was a better place to raise her girls than such a loveless, hateful environment.

Something changed in Deena after that. Although she was just a little girl, she did not want to be around Carlton. It was like the fire had gone out of her. Sabrena noticed that Deena listened in a corner when he berated her mommy. Once, when Sabrena had gotten sick of being called stupid, a whore, and a failure, she went into the living room and started crying. Deena followed her and whispered, "Okay, Mommy, okay Mommy, okay Mommy." She rubbed Sabrena's leg gently and said, "Bye, bye, Daddy." Sabrena looked at her baby and decided that she couldn't let her girls see her like this ever again.

Sabrena began to plan to leave. For months, she took a few dollars a week from the grocery and bill money—Carlton watched every penny like a hawk. However, she wasn't as dumb as he thought she was. Sabrena knew enough to go to the bank and ask for a list of all of the accounts. She discovered that he had a savings account that had both their names on it, but the statement was being mailed to a Post Office box. Sabrena figured out the statement dates and asked for a copy of everything. That account never had withdrawals from it and seemed to be a little "nest egg" for Carlton. Sabrena opened her own account in her own name, using her best friend Rach's address, and began to look for an apartment or house. Rach lived about two hours from Sabrena, and that was perfect.

Within a few months, with scrimping and saving, Sabrena stashed away several thousand dollars. She also managed to get two credit cards with high limits on them by using Carlton's name. She had convinced him they should make extra payments on her car so he could get the BMW he wanted sooner rather than later. He agreed, put most of his bonus check towards paying off her car, and began to look at BMWs. Sabrena knew that looking for the new car would create a diversion for him and that he would never suspect she would leave or was strong or smart enough to take money. She told him little lies, like that day care was increasing by $50 a week for both girls. Sabrena asked the bank for an increase on their credit card limits, with overdraft protection linked to their checking account. She was very careful with the timing, knowing the new bills wouldn't come before she left. Carlton was none the wiser. Sabrena purchased two receipt books and wrote receipts for "bills" that had to be paid in cash, $20 here, $29 for something else, and other amounts that slipped under the radar. These dollars added up and helped build her "escape" fund.

Carlton had crossed the line, and no matter what she thought of herself, she couldn't let him mess up her daughters' lives. Sabrena also knew that once she left he would be as mad as a pit bull. Under it all, he was very insecure. He only put her down so he could feel better, but he was still tough enough to really hurt her.

She planned her escape well. He was working on his company's annual report and had to travel out of town for three days. She told him that she needed to have the carpets cleaned and get both the cars tuned up while he was gone, so she would need some extra money. She told him cash would be better for the mechanic, as she could probably get a discount. He agreed, which surprised Sabrena, because although he made a good salary, he was tight with the dollars. He constantly reminded her that he was the only one who really worked and that whatever they bought with her money was a waste. Sabrena did work as well, but, of course, she made nowhere near the money he made, and her salary was, to him, an embarrassment. That's okay, she thought. My embarrassing job is helping me get my girls away from him. Sabrena waited for the perfect time to leave.

She remembered the day well. She had taken him to the airport, even kissed him good-bye. Unfortunately, the night before, he had wanted sex, and she had to endure yet another 90 seconds of unenthusiastic huffing and puffing. He didn't even look at her, never kissed her, rolled over afterwards, and then ran to the shower. She didn't know how she had ever gotten pregnant—he was definitely *not* a Casanova. Deep down, Sabrena believed that he had been a virgin when they started dating, because he just didn't know how to touch a woman. Years before, she had resolved that this would never be a good area for her and Carlton and decided that she would have to put up with it if he was good to her girls. But being a horrible lover *and* a horrible father was just not going to get it.

Once she'd dropped him at the airport, she took the girls and met Rach. She had to pack and get moved. She could always count on Rach to help her when she was in trouble. She met the movers at the house and took some of the furniture—just the living room, a guest bedroom set, the girls' beds and dressers, and the kitchen dinette. She left the expensive artwork that she knew Carlton loved to show off to his friends. She sent the movers on to her new home and went directly to the bank.

Sabrena withdrew all the money from the private savings account, except for $100 to keep the account open. She couldn't believe that Carlton had put close to $10,000 in an account she had not known about. She also took all the money out of the other savings account and $11,600 from the checking account, with a little help from their overdraft line. She didn't want to leave Carlton without any money, but she needed enough to pay rent and bills for at least eight months. She took the maximum advances on all of the credit cards and sold her wedding ring. She also put some clothes that he had bought for her, which she hated, into a consignment shop under Rach's name and address. Fortunately, the car was in her name and was now paid for in full. She hadn't told a complete lie: before she left, she charged a tune-up, brake check, and full inspection of her car to his credit card.

It took Sabrena two days to get everything done and to pack up the clothes that were left. She wrote Carlton a note and gave him the phone number of the lawyer who would handle the divorce. She had been smart enough to find a lawyer and tell her everything about her plan. She also told her that she didn't want anything else from Carlton as long as he gave her sole custody of the girls with no visitation. She had paid the lawyer with their American Express card and hid the bill—he would find it soon enough. When Sabrena walked out of the house, she had over $78,000 in cash and $22,000 in certified checks that she immediately put into her new bank account. She figured she could make it for awhile on that money, and get started again without bothering anyone, including her mother. She didn't call her mother to tell her she was leaving. Let Carlton call.

For the first night in the new house, she'd left the girls with Rach so that she could set up. In the quiet, she just sat in the middle of the living room floor and cried—not tears of sadness, but of freedom. She looked around and felt lonely, but knew that she'd done the right thing. She had been lonely with Carlton, and, although she had loved him, she had never received his love in return. Sabrena had pulled her girls out of an environment that would have hurt them. They needed to know and feel love, and Sabrena would give them enough love for both mother and father, no matter what the cost.

Now, as ever, the girls were the center of her life, but she felt she needed something just for herself. She wanted to be in a relationship with a man unlike Steve or any of the other men she'd known before. Steve, when he was around, made her laugh and made her feel beautiful. He treated her differently than her first husband, Kevin, or Carlton had. He knew how to work her, and a piece of Steve was better than nothing at all. Did she love him? She did, but his part-time love wasn't enough for someone who loved so much. She wanted a man who loved her as much as she loved him.

CHAPTER TWO

Tears welled up in Sabrena's eyes as she realized that Steve didn't have any plans to take her out—another set of empty promises. She ran a bath, poured some wine, and lit some candles. At least she would take advantage of her quiet time. She needed a break; between work, the girls, and trying to keep everything together, she was just tired. She had been tired a lot for the last few months and feeling burned out. Sabrena hadn't been sick at all since she had the flu a few weeks after leaving Carlton. She figured that she had been run-down with the move. Lately, she felt even more rundown and wondered if she was coming down with something. It didn't help that she kept getting yeast infections and, unless she was imagining things, fever and hot flashes at night. All of this and life challenges were wearing her out.

Sabrena didn't want to cry. She vowed after the last time that she wouldn't shed any more tears over Steve. But as she cleansed the makeup off of her face, she couldn't stop the tears—how foolish could she be? Steve only wanted her at night and only when his other women weren't available. She knew that there had been other women in the past and possibly were even now. During their first year together, one of Steve's women had even come to her house confronting her about messing with her fiancé. Steve denied everything and said the woman was crazy. However, Sabrena knew that he was lying and that the woman was another sister who was a fool for him. To make up for that big fight, Steve had taken Sabrena away for the weekend. He had bought her daughters new dolls and paid for their babysitter for two weeks. Sabrena thought he must love her to do all that just to keep her. She had let herself believe that Steve loved her, at least for the moment, and that things were good, until the next time.

The story was always the same: call, disappear, and reappear; sweet talk, lies, and then passionate sex. Sabrena thought that if she could satisfy his sexual cravings, he would be hers, and he was—for that moment. Sabrena pulled herself together and violently shook her head as if to rid herself of the memory of Steve. She had to call her daughters before they went to sleep. No matter how bad Steve—or any man—was to her, she knew her girls loved her unconditionally.

"Hi Rach, are the girls still up?" Sabrena asked her dearest friend.

"Girl, yeah—they have worn me slam out—what happened to just playing with the Barbie dolls? The girls have run me ragged with the Barbie fashion show, makeover, and Friday night party. I haven't seen this much drama since college."

"I know, they're a handful. I'm so thankful they have Auntie Rach!"

"How is your date with the rat, oops, Steve?" Rach asked, dripping with distaste for her friend's so-called man. She told Sabrena over and over again to leave him. Rach had even seen him hugged up with a woman from Sabrena's neighborhood at a club. He laughed when she confronted him and told her that Sabrena would never believe her and to mind her business. She had the last laugh when she saw the woman in the restroom and gave her some "secret" sista girl advice. She told her that Steve had given her and several other women herpes and that he became very violent when women rejected him so she should just sneak out the door. She watched from a distance as Steve continued to look for his date for the rest of the night. The stupid, arrogant fool would never think that a woman would leave him standing. That had made her night, and when she told Sabrena, they had a good laugh about it. However, a few days later, Sabrena told her they were back together. She said she just couldn't get him out of her system.

Rach couldn't understand—Sabrena was a great person on the inside and out, but she just wasn't able to see how bad Steve was making her look. But Rach was cut from a different cloth. She could do badly all by herself and let any man who was even remotely interested know that she didn't need or necessarily want to be bothered. Rach knew that this was the key for men to keep swarming around her—she could always have a date on the weekend if she wanted one. However, she wasn't going to be anyone's fool; her man had to be righteous and worthy of her love. Barry, her "friend," was good to her and she knew that he loved her. But Rach could only let this go so far. She wasn't going to be a fool for any man—she'd done that before and she had vowed that she would never be stupid again.

"Oh, its fine," Sabrena lied, "He's in the bathroom now, so I can't talk long. Where are the girls?" Sabrena couldn't bear to hear Rach tell her *again* how bad Steve was. She knew, but she wasn't like Rachel. She needed a man and a piece of a man would have to do for now. The girls came to the phone sleepily. Sabrena chatted for a few minutes, then ended their day the same way she had begun it, saying, "I love you, my princesses," and blew a kiss over the phone. As she hung up, she felt guilty for not going to pick them up. However, she really couldn't face the questions and needed time to just think.

The wine had made her sleepy. She walked back into her bathroom and put mineral salts into her running bath. When she glanced at her bed and saw lingerie that she had splurged on for tonight, her eyes watered. Good thing she'd left the tags on; she would take it back tomorrow. How could she be a fool over and over again? Steve was like virtually every other man she had known in her life: her father, whom she barely knew, was always making promises he didn't keep; Kevin, whom she married a few months after high school with hopes of the white picket fence and fairy tale life, abandoned her; and Carlton, who was even more of a nightmare. At least with Kevin, she could claim that it was a mistake of her youth.

The reality was that Kevin wanted her and a few other sisters at the same time. She had stayed in that relationship for almost two years, knowing he was cheating on her, but staying because she didn't want to be alone or to prove her mother right. She knew that Kevin was no good, and at the end they barely saw each other—he would leave for weeks at a time, but she was always there waiting for his return. One day he left and never came back. She received divorce papers in the mail about a year later that she just signed without thinking. His cousin told her a few years later that he had remarried, graduated from trade school, and fathered three sons.

Hearing that Kevin had three sons hurt, because when they were together he always told her he didn't want any kids to tie them down. What she realized now is that he *did* want a family, just not with her. She'd been young and hopeful—maybe in love and maybe not. She really had just wanted to be a grown-up and get out of her mother's house.

Her mother had no sympathy for Sabrena when she told her that she and Kevin had split up. "I told you your stupid butt should have never gotten married." Her mother had almost laughed into the phone. "Oh, but you were just hot in the pants and went with that boy. Well, whatcha gonna do now—you certainly ain't coming back to my house."

In her greatest time of need, those were the words of Mrs. Jennifer Lorene Collins. Despite her dire straits, Sabrena would have lived on the street before going back to her mother's house. She experienced pain during her relationship and marriage that was unlike any other in her young life. It was her first broken heart. Fortunately, her best friend from high school, Rachel, was in college and had her own apartment. Sabrena moved in and helped pay the bills while she figured out her next steps. She worked at a department store to make ends meet, and it wasn't a bad life.

Sabrena loved to cook and made these fabulous meals on the weekends for Rach and her friends. It was during one of her throw-down cooking sessions that she met her second husband, Carlton Wilson. He was a senior in college when they met, majoring in accounting. He was funny and she was flattered that someone like him would ask her out. Although she never felt real sparks when he kissed her, Carlton was smart and that was attractive to her; he was always giving her books to read and telling her about interesting things. She felt safe with Carlton; he wasn't the pretty boy type who would fool around. With each passing day and interesting date, with her listening to him talk, she fell in love. Soon, Carlton was the most important thing in her life and she was totally committed to making him happy. Looking back, Sabrena should have realized how things would end up. Carlton always thought he was the most interesting person in the room and that never changed, even when he had a wife and two daughters.

She remembered meeting his parents at his graduation and, sure enough, he looked like his dad and acted like his mom. His whole family seemed to hang on his every word. Carlton had graduated number one in his class and gave a valedictory speech. Sabrena laughed as she remembered the dry, boring speech—even the Dean looked utterly bored. But his family seemed to think he was the Reverend Martin Luther King, Jr., reincarnated. Despite his less than rousing speech, Sabrena had been proud of him and to be with him.

It was after graduation that she told him she was pregnant with their first daughter, Deena. Carlton hadn't even hesitated proposing and they were married before she was even three months along in her pregnancy. Lord, marriage with Carlton happened so quickly and was a complete nightmare.

When they first started dating, it had been great to hear him talk all the time, but once they were married, she realized that she never got to say a word. It was fine until he started talking about how dumb she was, how fat she was getting—he apparently didn't know that women got bigger when they got pregnant—and how bored he was with her. He belittled her at every turn, both privately and in public. The only joy for Sabrena came with the birth of her daughter, whom they named Deena after his mother. Despite her namesake, she was Sabrena's daughter completely. Carlton's family doted on Deena and constantly tried to tell Sabrena how to raise her. He would be attentive when his parents or family came to visit, but that would end as soon as they left. Carlton wasn't interested in Sabrena or their daughter, and it was always about the magnificent, wonderful, brilliant, legend-in-his-own-mind Carlton.

As if she sensed her dad's disinterest, Deena would scream when Carlton came to pick her up. This frustrated him no end. When Sabrena's first daughter was born, she felt helpless in her marriage, but when her second, Renee, came along, she felt trapped. But she loved them too much to imagine raising them alone, so she endured. Sabrena shed many tears over Carlton. She had loved him enough to make his dreams her dreams and to be molded into his life. Even though her love and respect were not returned, she tried to make it work. She only realized she had to leave him when she saw that his actions were poisoning her daughter. She loved no man more than she loved her girls—not even herself.

Sabrena never asked for child support or anything from him and he certainly didn't try to find them. He simply went on with his life. Her lawyer said he was more concerned about his money than Sabrena or his daughters. Sabrena changed her name back to her maiden name in an attempt to wash any trace of Carlton from her life. It was odd, because even his family never tried to see the girls—it was as if that part of his life had never existed.

After Carlton, there had been one or two other men who came into Sabrena's life, but she refused to give her heart to anyone, until

Steve. He just came to her like a rushing wind, and for the first few months, it was great. He was her dream: caring, considerate, taking care of her, and spending time with her and the girls. He brought her flowers and gave dolls to her daughters. They spent days in the park, and had romantic getaways. Sabrena felt refreshed for the first time in many years. Steve rubbed her feet after she had been working all day and he always brought her groceries from work.

Simply put, Steve was handsome, considerate, safe, and stable. Once Sabrena had given up her heart, it was easy to fall in love and into bed with him. He was a sensitive and caring lover who made her feel complete. Thinking of being with him gave her goose bumps. After years with Carlton, she felt like she had been awakened from the dead. She remembered the first time they made love: she'd wept softly afterwards as she looked at him and knew that she had fallen in love again. Steve was everything Sabrena wanted and needed and she tried to be all that he needed, too. She constantly cooked his favorite meals, told him how wonderful he was, and did things for him that every woman should do for her man. They spent hours talking on the phone and just lying in bed. They shared their dreams and aspirations and shed tears about the past. Sabrena felt valued with Steve. For once, her opinions mattered.

After the first few months, she sensed Steve pulling away. He took phone calls in the other room; she went to his store and he told her that it was unprofessional for his girlfriend to hang out at his job; he became busy on the weekends and felt more tired than usual. Steve, who had once taken her everywhere, now just wanted to sit at home with her. When Sabrena confronted him about his behavior, he denied any problems, but stated that he needed to be free to come and go as he pleased. Their lovemaking went from wonderful and emotional to late night "booty calls" that were sexually satisfying but often left her feeling used.

Now she was alone again in an empty house.

"Well, what do I do now?" Sabrena screamed aloud. Boxer, their cat, was startled and ran to the other room, knocking over his litter box—that uncivilized cat—they had found him going through their trash and the girls had insisted on keeping him. Sabrena yelled again as she eased into her bath, alone. She was tired of thinking about, worrying about, and crying about Steve. She was tired of the mess and of being a doormat. Yet, despite her resolve, she almost expected Steve to come in (as always) and make last minute proclamations of love.

"You're the only one for me," he'd probably say, "One day, you will be my wife." He had told these lies dozens of times during their courtship. Of course, there was never any ring, any real proposal, only excuse after excuse.

"Wait until I become district manager, then I'll have more money to take care of you and my girls," Steve once said when pressed for real commitment. Sabrena's protest would be muted by his hugs and kisses and she would promise herself to ask again in the morning. She couldn't hurt his manhood, she thought, and he did want to do right by her and her daughters.

Steve would say, "Sabrena, I have to be the man; I have to make the decisions; I have to feel that I can give you something. Let me do this the right way."

His words now sounded so hollow in her head, but at the time, Sabrena swore that his eyes had been filled with tears. Time had taught her not to worry about Steve—she used to fret about him being in an accident, or some other terrible event that held him up. Sabrena smiled as she remembered the time she called the police, telling them that her boyfriend was missing. Her smile was just a mask for her pain—she had grown up and wised up—or had she? Sabrena shook her head and tried to focus on some good memories of Steve and, strangely enough, they came pretty fast. But for each quiet dinner, there was a phone call from another woman. For each bouquet of flowers, there was a weeklong disappearing act.

Once, he'd actually accused *her* of cheating on *him* when, after a routine well-woman visit, she'd told him the doctor had found chlamydia. Her doctor had told her that it was sexually transmitted and, since Sabrena had only been with Steve, she knew he had given it to her. He accused her of stepping out on him and even went through the pretense of being upset. Shoot, after Steve got finished— Sabrena had to really think if she had cheated on him—he was just that convincing. In her mind, she resolved that this infection was from one of her previous relationships and just hadn't shown up before this Pap exam. She actually told Steve they needed to use condoms until she finished the medication so that *he* wouldn't have any problems.

Funny, usually she depended on the men in her life to make the decision about whether or not to use condoms, but only when she needed to protect Steve did she insist on their use. She was nearly 40 and had never purchased any. Sabrena and Steve initially did use condoms, until they both agreed they wouldn't see anyone else. During the same conversation, Sabrena told Steve that because she'd had her tubes tied, she didn't use birth control. Carlton had persuaded her after Renee's birth that they could not afford any more children and she had reluctantly agreed. Sabrena had been afraid to tell Steve earlier in the relationship because she'd thought he would want to have children when they got married. Sabrena remembered practicing how she would tell him and even printed out information from a web site on how to get the procedure reversed. She thought he was so understanding when she told him, because he said "their" daughters would be enough—he even said all he wanted was Sabrena. Looking back, Steve appeared relieved.

CHAPTER THREE

Sabrena silently wept as she finished her bath and dragged herself to bed—thinking of all the days and nights wasted on Steve. Boxer came to bed, as if on cue, and nuzzled her. She hugged the cat and rubbed his fur, thinking this affection would be the only love she'd have tonight. She thought of how she was going to finally kick Steve out of her life for good. She knew it would hurt, but she was hurting now, so what was the difference? She lay in her bed and willed herself to sleep. She actually tried counting sheep and considered drinking another glass of wine or taking some Tylenol® PM, but eventually, as in hundreds of nights before, her tears wooed her into a deep sleep.

She heard a loud thumping at the door and at first she thought she was dreaming, until she heard a male voice loudly calling out her name. She looked at the clock; it was after three in the morning.

"Sabrena, wake up! Wake up—they're going to get me!" she heard the male voice scream. "Sabrena, open the door! Hurry!" Once she'd shaken off her sleepiness, she recognized Steve's voice. She walked slowly to the door, careful not to take off the safety chain, and looked at him. He was sweaty, appeared scared, and was begging her to let him in. Sabrena pulled together her courage and just stood at the door. This was the stand she should have made years ago. She was resolved that she and Steve were through, no matter what crazy excuse or lie he came up with.

"Steve, what the hell are you doing here at three o'clock in the morning?" Sabrena hissed.

"There was a break-in at the store and these guys held me hostage while they tried to open the safe. I got away when one of them went to the bathroom. Let me in—they were after me."

"You must think I'm an even bigger fool than I've been—go *home*! We're finished. I don't want to see you, hear your lying voice, or know you anymore—*go home*!" Sabrena screamed as she slammed the door shut. She heard Steve slump to the floor and continue begging.

"Baby, please open the door—I'm really scared. No matter what happens with us, please help me now. You don't want me to die on your doorstep, do you?" he pleaded. "They were following me and they have my wallet, so they know my address. I don't have any money or credit cards—they took my wallet. Come on, Sabrena—help me—just treat me like anyone else. I swear that I'm scared. I won't talk or anything. I just need to get out of sight." She swore she heard him crying and she opened the door. She would just let him in to call the police and then send him home.

"Thank you, baby, thank you. I hope they didn't see me come in here. I couldn't stand it if anyone tried to hurt you," Steve said as he jumped into the house, looking out through the crack of the door and out the windows. She noticed a scratch on his forehead and went to get some rubbing alcohol.

"Steve, don't lie to me," she said quietly. "I'd rather you sat there like a deaf mute than for you to open your mouth and lie." She wiped his forehead.

"Baby, I'm not lying—all I could think about was how you were gonna be waiting for me and that I couldn't call you," Steve said as he hung his head. "I knew that you wouldn't believe me, but it is true—you know how bad the neighborhood is. These three guys came in right before I closed the store. One of them bought some beer and the others just stood around. Cindy rang them up and then they walked out. I let everyone else go home and was going to lock the safe, but I heard something in the storage room. When I went back to check it out, this guy grabbed me and put a knife to my throat. He must have been hiding in the storage room—I didn't see him come in, but he opened the back door and the other guys came into the store. They asked for money and for me to open the safe. I told them that the safe was on a timer and that I couldn't get back in. They didn't believe me and began punching me. I told them that I hadn't cleaned out all the registers, so they went up front and got the cash. The guy that had the knife to my throat took my wallet and pushed me in a corner. All I could think of was getting back to you, but they wouldn't let me move or anything. Baby, I was so scared." Steve began to visibly tremble and put his head in his hands and sobbed, not wanting her to see him cry. Sabrena reached for Steve and began to hold him. She didn't know what to think—what if he was telling the truth? "All I could think of was that I let the love of my life down again—but I had no control. They even smashed my cell phone, baby." Steve continued sobbing like a three-year-old on her chest.

"Thanks for letting me in. I know you don't believe me and are probably going to break up with me. But I want you to know that I'm not lying and that I love you with all my heart. But you do what you have to do." He continued to sob and hold onto her. She didn't know what to do or believe. She saw that he had been roughed up, the cut looked deep on his face. The store *is* in a bad neighborhood and had been robbed twice in the last two years before they put in the alarm system. They'd even had to hire a security guard, not that he'd done any good that night.

"We need to call the police," she reminded him. "We need to call right away so that you can give a full description and they can catch them." She pushed further.

"Baby, I'll call in the morning. I'm just too shaken up right now—I just need you to hold me. I know that a man isn't supposed to get scared or cry, but I thought they were going to kill me." He sobbed even louder and held onto Sabrena even tighter, with his face buried in her breasts.

"Okay Steve, just be quiet and rest. I'll get you a drink and run a bath for you. We'll talk more about this in the morning." Sabrena figured that she would at least help him through the night and then get her head cleared before she made any major decisions. She got a glass of wine for him, ran a bath, and pulled out his robe and slippers from the closet. She put on some jazz and led a still shaky-looking Steve into the tub. "Don't leave me alone, Brena," he pleaded, holding onto her arm. He looked like a frightened little boy.

"Just relax and I'll get the bed ready for you," she said, attempting to comfort him. She noticed that he had some blood under the nail of his index finger—he must have tried to fight. He looked so scared and like he couldn't get himself together. She owed him the benefit of the doubt; she would give him tonight and just see what happened. Sabrena went back to her door and made sure that all the locks were on. She looked out her window to see if anyone had followed him. The streets were empty; after all, it was close to 3:30 in the morning. She heard Steve getting out of the tub. When she turned to look at him, all rage flowed out of her. All she saw was her fine chocolate man. She shuddered as she thought of someone hurting him, worse yet killing him. She shook her head violently, couldn't bear the thought. With all of his mess, she still loved him.

"Is there anything you need, Steve?" Sabrena asked, as she made sure the pillows were fluffed behind his head.

"Yes, I need you to kiss me and make it all better." Sabrena kissed Steve's forehead and got into bed with him. She held him and continued to kiss his entire face slowly and methodically.

"Is that better?" she asked, as Steve began to caress her body. Her body willfully betrayed her.

"Yes, but there are some other places that need to be kissed and held," Steve told her as he began to remove her gown. Sabrena knew she should make Steve sleep and wait until later in the morning to sort this out, because, after all, she didn't know 100 percent whether he was lying or not. She weakly tried to push him away. "Brena, I need you, you're the love of my life; I need you tonight." He moaned and slowly caressed her breasts.

"Steve, we really should try to sleep—you've been through a lot." Sabrena tried to protest, but her words fell on deaf ears. Her body was on fire, and she slowly gave into him as she felt her body respond to his touch. Sabrena loved this man with her whole heart, even if her head was telling her that she was a fool.

The ringing phone woke Sabrena up from her sleep—she felt as if she had just dozed off.

"Hi, Mommy" the girls said in unison. "Can you come get us later? Auntie Rach is gonna make pancakes for us." Deena took the lead in coaxing Sabrena. Sabrena smiled as she thought about the last few hours with Steve and how she wanted to spend a few more in bed with him.

"Well, good morning, how was last night? Were you both good?" She asked as she slipped out of bed and walked into her bathroom so she wouldn't wake Steve.

"Yes, Mommy," Deena said. "Renee started crying right before we went to sleep, but Auntie Rach let her sleep in her bed." "She was good, though, and so was I. Can we stay?"

"Let me speak with Auntie Rach." Sabrena couldn't believe that her friend was going to attempt to make pancakes; this was a new one on her.

"Hey Girl, what's up?"

"Nothing much—still in bed. The girls said that *you* were going to make some pancakes. Is that right? From scratch? Who has taken my friend?" Sabrena chuckled at her undomesticated friend.

"Yes, I am making pancakes, thank you very much! Me and Aunt Jemima's frozen specialty; they won't know the difference. I'll let Deena microwave them."

"Shoulda known. Look, I can be there in about an hour. I don't want them to take up your whole day." Sabrena walked into her closet and began looking for her favorite white shirt and her jeans. "Thank you for last night, but I know they can be very active and can wear out even the best Auntie."

"Bre, we're fine. Actually, we're gonna play house, which is a good way for me to get my clothes folded and some cleaning done. Take your time, get them sometime this afternoon, or I can bring them home." Rach smiled as she looked at the girls standing next to her, listening intently with their fingers crossed. "They're fine. Now, we gotta go."

"Okay, I'll talk to you later. Thanks, Rach." Sabrena heard the girls cheer as Rach hung up the phone. She was grateful that she had Rach and, more importantly, that the girls had her as their Auntie. So much for loving Mommy—she smiled as she thought of them and made a mental note to pick them up no later than two.

Sabrena looked at Steve, who was sleeping quietly. She walked back to bed. He looked so innocent, like a little boy. The scratch on his forehead was closed now and looked much smaller than it did last night. She looked at his beautiful curly eyelashes and full lips and thought how lucky someone like her was to have such a man. He loved her, he told her all the time—last night he said that she was the love of his life.

All couples have problems and it was hard for Steve—managing the store and answering to others. He was under a lot of pressure on several levels, especially now with another break-in. It was odd that the security guard wasn't in the store with him last night when this happened or that the alarms didn't go off when the thieves started messing with the safe. She would have to ask him about these things when he woke up, but for now she would make him a big breakfast before he called the police. She liked it when Steve was in the house; it made her feel complete. Unlike a lot of the women today, she liked cooking for him and doing his laundry. She loved him, and just as he helped her out with the clothes for the girls, piano lessons, and other things around the house, she liked doing things for him. He was her man and she was his woman. They were a team with problems, but still they were together.

"Whatcha cooking, Babes?" Steve asked as he walked naked into the kitchen.

"Just a little breakfast for you, honey, all your favorites—grits, eggs, bacon, and French toast," she replied, making sure to kiss him good morning. "Why don't you take a shower, and by that time I'll be finished and you can eat before we call the police."

"Okay, I need to get to the store to see how bad things are. I probably should have gone back last night," he replied, and walked into the shower. Sabrena wondered if he had left the doors to the store open as he ran away from the burglars. Did they take all the food or merchandise? If he just left it and they vandalized the place, the District Manager was going to be mad and wonder why Steve hadn't reported the break-in immediately. She said a silent prayer for Steve, his job, and any problems that might be brewing as a result of the burglary.

"Steve, your breakfast is on the table," Sabrena yelled. Steve came into the kitchen and began to devour the food. She wasn't hungry and figured she would pick up something later.

"Are you okay? How is your head?" Sabrena cautiously asked, afraid that she might evoke bad memories from the night before.

"Yeah, I'm okay—still a little shaken up; but I'm straight. I'm going down to the store in a few to check on things and do a report," Steve said, gulping down his orange juice. He seemed nervous and Sabrena chalked it up to his still being shaken up.

"Okay, do you want me to drive you down or go with you to file the police report?" Sabrena pressed. "I don't need to pick up the girls for another couple of hours, so I can help you or give you some support."

"No, this is something I've got to do by myself. I'll be okay. I'll call you later or if I need you," he said, and kissed her on the cheek. She noticed some bruising on his neck—must have been from one of the guys choking him or something, because it looked like a thumb print.

"Bye, honey. Why don't you come over tonight and hang out with us?" She asked, trying to be supportive and loving, while allowing him to have space.

"Okay, I'll see what happens, but I really may need to just clear my head—may need some time alone." He kissed her on the cheek again before he walked out the door.

Sabrena understood and had pretty much decided that she believed Steve. It all made sense and she knew what type of neighborhood the store was in. She felt angered by the possibility of someone trying to hurt him. Steve was a good man at heart; some problems, but who doesn't have them? He was smart, handsome, considerate of her girls, and a great lover who would make a good husband one day. He never put her down like Carlton had and, while he had faults, he did make her feel worthwhile when they were together. She loved him, and that had to be more than enough to make this relationship work. All the drama from last night, and the lovemaking, had left Sabrena drained. She wanted to take a nap before picking up the girls. She might even take some vitamins to get some pep. She had been worn out for weeks.

CHAPTER FOUR

Sabrena awoke a bit refreshed and ready to see her daughters. She thought she'd surprise the girls with some snacks, so she headed to Steve's store. She figured she could pick up the treats and see how he was doing. When she entered the store, she saw Janine, one of the assistant managers.

"Hi Sabrena, how are you?" Janine was always nice to her.

"Hey, I'm doing good. What about you? Do you know where Steve is?"

"He's in the back, I'll tell him that you're here."

"Thanks. How was everything this morning?" Sabrena asked Janine as she pulled out a basket. "It seems to be pulled together. I hope Steve doesn't get into any trouble."

"Everything was fine; another day, another headache." Janice looked a bit puzzled, but began to walk back toward the offices. Janine lived only a block from Sabrena, and their daughters were in the same school. She was nice and they often talked while waiting on the girls.

Sabrena headed for the produce department and saw Steve walking toward her.

"Hey, Brena—what are you doing here?" Steve asked, appearing a bit irritated to see her. She couldn't believe that this was the same man who had passionately made love to her just a few hours ago.

"I came by on my way to pick up the girls from Rach, but needed to get some of their snacks. I also wanted to check on you."

"I'm fine, just very busy and a little nervous—you never know who's looking," he replied, while looking over her shoulder. She figured that she was just being paranoid and tried to shake off her feelings.

"Okay, well, I'll see you later—are you still coming by tonight?"

"Huh, oh right, I don't know. I may need some time alone, yeah—I'm going to go home, have some beers, and order a pizza or something. I'm really tired and sleepy. I don't want the girls to see me shaken up, although you know that I can hardly resist your cooking. I'll just suffer for tonight—maybe I'll come over tomorrow." He hurriedly said good-bye, without even a hug or kiss.

She wondered what was going on and if he needed to talk about it. She quickly picked up some fruit and ice cream bars for the house and went into the express lane, where she was greeted by a pretty, young new clerk in the line. She had a beautiful smile and nice figure. She almost glowed and this made Sabrena smile. She greeted Sabrena and was very pleasant—smiling all the time like she had a secret. Sabrena knew the look well: the look of love.

"What a pretty smile you have," Sabrena told the younger woman.

"Thank you very much. I just try to make the best of the day—it's easier to smile than to frown," the girl replied. "That'll be $18.42."

"Thanks, this little stuff sure does cost a lot—but my kids will enjoy it, so it's worth it. How do you pronounce your name?" she asked, looking at the girl's name tag.

"Kiara, like Tiara but with a K."

"That's nice. I haven't seen you here before. Are you new?"

"Well, I worked here about a year ago, then I left. I started working here again about six weeks ago," Kiara replied.

"Oh, well, I can see why they rehired you. Thanks for being nice. Have a good day and keep smiling," she said with a wink. She swore that she saw Kiara start to blush.

Sabrena thought she'd seen Steve from a distance looking at her in the line, but he didn't come over as he usually did to help her with the bag. He must be busy, she thought, as she walked to the car. His cell phone was smashed last night, so she couldn't call him—she would call him this evening at home.

The girls ran out to meet her as she drove up. They had only been gone overnight, but it felt like an eternity.

"Mommy, Mommy, you're here," the girls sang in unison. They jumped up and down and squeezed her so hard she could barely breathe.

"Hey, princesses, where's Auntie Rach?"

"In the house, Mommy. She's getting our stuff," Renee said as she ran ahead of Sabrena into the house.

"Hey, girl," Rach said as Sabrena came into the house. "You could've come to get them later. We're having fun. The girls tore up my kitchen making some cookies—Lord, I know why I don't have kids." She laughed. "How was your night?"

"It was nice," Sabrena replied, not feeling like talking to Rach about Steve today. "I'm just a little tired, but last night was cool."

"I bet you are. I ain't even gonna ask what time you went to sleep!" She elbowed Sabrena.

"Girl, I don't have time for your stuff today. Let me get these girls out of your hair." Sabrena laughed with her friend. "I went to the store, but I completely forgot to get some Monistat®. Do you have any?" She and Rach were just that close to talk about infections and personal hygiene that would usually embarrass another person.

"No, sorry—you got another yeast infection?" Rach asked. "You need to stop messing with that whorish Steve—he's probably passing it to you from his other women." Here we go, just what Sabrena didn't want to hear—another day of Steve-bashing.

"Whatever. I just asked the question. I'll pick some up myself—no lecture today, okay?" Sabrena was getting annoyed with the ever judgmental Rachel. She didn't need to hear it; what she did with Steve was her business. Sabrena *was* tired of getting these infections. She usually treated them herself with over-the-counter medications, eating yogurt, and drinking enough cranberry juice to drown in. However, they never really seemed to totally go away. She had received a reminder card from her doctor's office telling her that she was overdue for her Pap smear; she would call for an appointment. For now, she'd just head to the drugstore and pick up something over-the-counter.

"'Bye, Rach, I'll call you later," she yelled, as she put the girls in the car. She was looking forward to making them a home-cooked meal, taking another nap, and calling Steve.

Sabrena had a tea party with her daughters in their room. They were so prim and proper; they wanted to drink with their pinkies out and had the napkins in the right places. It was funny, she had even more fun than they did as she watched them play hostess. After the tea party, they wanted to play Twister®. Great combination: prim and proper while putting your butt in someone's face and trying not to fall. She always lost, but today she was worse than usual; she felt dizzy as she bent down. Sabrena made a mental note to tell her doctor when she went in for her visit. She had been getting light-headed a couple of times a week. She and the girls made dinner and their special treats—ice cream sundaes. They were ready for bed after all of the excitement. Sabrena kept them awake just long enough to help them bathe, before tucking them in and reading to them from their *Children's Bible Story* book that Steve had bought them.

"I love you, Deena. I love you, Renee. You're Mommy's little princesses," she said, as she always did before she kissed them goodnight. "Sweet dreams and know that Mommy is always here." The girls fell right to sleep and Sabrena watched them from the doorway. She did love them with all of her heart. Their father, Carlton, was trifling, but they were worth all the heartache she had experienced with him. She needed to tell them all the time how special they were, because she didn't want them to need to hear it from someone else as they grew older and be fools like she had been. Her girls were special, with hearts of gold and beauty inside and out. They had a sweet innocence that was precious. Sabrena could be at her lowest point, and a hug from either of them would immediately lift her spirit. They were everything to her. It was worth all the sacrifices, all the penny-pinching and extra work, just to see her girls happy.

As she cleaned up the kitchen, Sabrena tried to reach Steve, but there was no answer at his house. She thought of taking some food over to him, but reconsidered. She couldn't wake the girls and would never leave them alone. She would call again first thing in the morning. She wondered where he was and if he was really okay. Yesterday had been a wild one for him.

Sabrena crawled into bed feeling exhausted. She felt warm and tired—she just wanted to get some rest. She put on one of Steve's T-shirts; she needed to stay cool, since she was getting those hot flashes at night. Lately, although she was just 38, she felt like she was going through the change of life. She would have to talk with her mother about this during their monthly phone call. Maybe it was because her tubes were tied and that was causing her to go through the change earlier. She'd just sleep in the T-shirt and open the window, which should help her from sweating through the night.

PART II

CHAPTER FIVE

Sabrena hated doctors' offices. She dreaded the appointments, especially when they were for female things. The only times in her life she had welcomed doctor visits were when she was pregnant. She had been faithful with her appointments. Carlton had accused her of being a hypochondriac because she called her obstetrician with the least little question during both of her pregnancies. Outside of those times, she had to work up the nerve to go, especially for Pap smears. Sabrena did not like anyone looking at her private parts or asking all those questions. In the hopes of getting rid of some of her anxiety, she always wore pink, her favorite color, when she had to see the doctor; it always made her feel a little more relaxed.

She did like her doctor, Dr. Gwendolyn Scott. She was a sister and very down to earth. Dr. Scott was an internal medicine doctor who also did regular female exams. Her staff was friendly like she was, but Sabrena hated all the questions, the cold room, and especially the stirrups. What could you say? Small talk just didn't cut it when a person was looking in your vagina. Sabrena always became anxious as she waited for the doctor to come into the room. The nurse had taken her blood, weight, and blood pressure, and Sabrena had left her urine sample in the bathroom—it was such a task to pee in that little cup. The nurse said she had a little fever of 100.1 degrees F and had lost about 18 pounds since her visit seven months ago, when she had come in with bronchitis. The weight loss is fine, Sabrena thought. It seemed like when she wasn't trying to lose weight, she did—maybe that was the trick.

Sabrena had noticed that her clothes had gotten a little looser—not her butt, though. Steve always commented on how he liked a woman with something in the back and she had no problem in that department. Oh, well, she liked how she looked. Sabrena mentally went through all the things she wanted to talk with Dr. Scott about. For one, this darn yeast infection that wouldn't go away. She also wanted to talk to him about feeling tired. She hoped that she didn't have fibroids—she'd heard she could get low blood from them and that would make her tired. Rach had two small fibroids, but they only caused her to have some pain around her period. She also needed to talk about menopause. She had been curious about getting her tubes untied, in case she and Steve got married and he wanted more kids, but she didn't need to talk about that today.

Where was Dr. Scott? Sabrena was getting cold in the stupid paper gown and she needed to get out in time to pick up her kids. Lucky for her, she had a good job with benefits and she was able to take a half day off with pay to come to the doctor. Her job at Bloomingdale's was okay; it paid the bills and took care of her and her family. She never thought she would still be working there, but with the job market what it was, she was grateful to have her job.

"Hello, Ms. Collins, how are you today?" Dr. Scott asked as she walked in the room.

Now this was one sharp-looking doctor. Her hair was nicely styled and she wore a modest amount of makeup, tastefully applied. Sabrena looked at her shoes, which she knew were Dr. Scott's passion, as they had discussed many times. Once again they were *bad*— she knew they had to be Jimmy Choos or Manolos. The pumps were flashy for a doctor's office, but they were toned down with a simple blouse and skirt.

"Hi, Dr. Scott. I'm fine. You look nice today as always—I'm lovin' those pumps!" Sabrena said, as she smiled at her.

"Thank you, and you look nice yourself, as usual. What brings you in today? Is this for your annual well-woman exam or are you having some specific issues?" Dr. Scott asked as she looked at her chart.

"Well, I need to get my annual exam, but I'm having another yeast infection and I just can't get rid of it. Also I'm more tired than usual," Sabrena said.

"How many yeast infections have you had over the last few months and what have you been using?"

"I don't know if there are different infections or if it is the same one that has never really gone away. I have used two different over-the-counter medications and once your office called in a prescription for Diflucan®, but nothing has seemed to make it completely go away. I always have some itching," Sabrena said, trying to give as much information as possible. "Also, it's a little different kind of discharge—sometimes it's white with some yellowish discharge that is thicker and smells fishier." This part really got to Sabrena. Even though she liked Dr. Scott, this was just too much information.

"Ms. Collins, I'll take a look, but first tell me about your energy level. How long have you noticed a problem? Have you been sleeping well? Are you under any more stress or working more?"

"Maybe a little more stress," Sabrena answered. "But nothing out of the ordinary. My sleep is all right, but I get hot flashes at night. I have to sleep in something light or I'll just sweat through my night clothes." She tried to give as many details as possible.

"Let me examine you and then we'll try to put all this together," Dr. Scott said as she rubbed her hands together to warm them before she touched Sabrena. This was a simple thing, but important for Sabrena, because the other doctors she had seen before treated her like a science project—with little care as to how she felt. Dr. Scott talked to her as she examined her, asking her questions, and even remembering her daughters' names.

"Is your throat sore?" Dr. Scott asked as she looked in her mouth.

"No, not really, but sometimes when my sinuses drain I get hoarse and maybe a little sore."

"Have you felt these bumps under your chin and on your neck? Feel here." Dr. Scott guided her hands to the small pea-sized lumps. Dr. Scott called them lymph nodes. Sabrena had no idea where they had come from. Dr. Scott checked everything, and then began the dreaded Pap smear. Sabrena was still self-conscious about this part of the exam, but Dr. Scott made it easier. Sabrena just looked at the ceiling, which had a poster right above the exam table and provided a nice distraction.

"Ms. Collins, when is the last time you had sex?" Dr. Scott asked her while doing her pelvic exam.

"About two weeks ago." Oh, how she dreaded the personal questions.

"How many sexual partners do you have? Do you use condoms?" Dr. Scott continued to probe, gently.

"Just one for the last three years, and no, we don't use condoms. My tubes are tied," Sabrena answered, hoping for no more sex questions. "Is there a problem?"

"Well, I just need to ask the questions. I'm almost finished, and then I'll let you get dressed while I make a slide and take a look at it." Dr. Scott told Sabrena to sit up, gave the equipment to her nurse, and stepped out of the room.

"Why was Dr. Scott asking all those questions today?" Sabrena asked the nurse.

"Oh, you know she's very thorough. She'll come back and talk to you about it. She just wants to make sure that you're okay," the nurse assured her. "I'm going to step out so you can get dressed. Dr. Scott will be back in to speak with you."

Sabrena was glad that the examination was over and tried to remember if she needed to tell Dr. Scott anything else. She reminded herself to ask her about the change of life and if she thought she was going through early menopause. As she sat, she realized that she had seen Steve only once during the last two weeks and that they hadn't had sex since the night of the robbery. He was really busy and trying to prove himself to his boss; he was working later hours and had little time for anyone. Sabrena had seen him briefly when he dropped off his laundry at her house and took the girls roller skating. They had talked on the phone on most days, but often the conversations were rushed, and whenever Sabrena asked him to come over, he was busy. The weekends had been their time; now he was working late or was too tired to do anything. She was going to call him tonight and set a date to just hang out—maybe she could get Rach to watch the girls again. Her thoughts were interrupted when Dr. Scott came back into the exam room.

"Hello again," Dr. Scott said as she sat down. "We have a few things to talk about and there are some more tests that I want to do. You do have a yeast infection, but you also have another type of infection, something called trichomoniasis, which is probably why you noticed the yellowish discharge and the fishy smell."

"Where did this come from? Am I using the wrong detergent, not drinking enough water or cranberry juice?"

"No, the infection is caused by a parasite called Trichomonas, that is usually transmitted from sexual intercourse." Dr. Scott said this as nicely as possible, but to the point.

"What? So my boyfriend gave this to me—what about the yeast infection?" Sabrena asked, with wild thoughts rushing through her head. "Can I give it to my daughters? We're always eating and drinking after each other. Does it have to be passed on from sex?"

"Well, the yeast infection actually can be due to a number of things and we need to talk about other tests. However, since you keep getting it—it can be passed from you to your partner and back again and that's why it hasn't gone away fully." Dr. Scott continued, "I'm also concerned about this low-grade fever and some weight loss since I saw you last. On your exam today, you had some enlarged lymph nodes under your neck and also a few in your groin area. You also complained of feeling very tired and having a sore throat a few weeks ago. Have you ever seen the white patches on your tongue?" Dr. Scott asked. She looked seriously at Sabrena.

"What do you mean by white patches? No, I don't think so—sometimes my sinuses drain and I'll get a little white mucous on my tongue, but that's about it. I have a real problem with sinus stuff and I don't think the cat is helping." Sabrena tried to remember the last few months. Dr. Scott gave her a mirror and pointed to the spots on her tongue with a tongue depressor.

"These small white spots," Dr. Scott said.

"Oh, I've noticed them before, but I thought that was phlegm. I usually see them when my throat is scratchy and sore and I feel stuffy," Sabrena added, looking into the mirror.

Dr. Scott wrote all her comments in the chart and pulled out some papers. "Sabrena, I'm not sure what exactly is going on, but in addition to your regular blood tests, I also want to make sure that we test you for diabetes—which could be contributing to the yeast infections. However, I also would like to test you for HIV, which you probably know stands for Human Immunodeficiency Virus. To do this, you will need to sign a consent form. Is this okay?"

Sabrena's mouth dropped open and she needed a few minutes to compose herself. Did Dr. Scott think she had HIV? She had been tested about four years ago for her insurance policy, about a month after she had left Carlton and she had started her job. She already had the results when she received a call from Carlton's mother out of the blue. His mother said she'd called to thank her for leaving her son, so that he could be with someone who deserved him and not someone who had trapped him by becoming pregnant. Mrs. Wilson also said the only reason she had been with her son was to gain some respectability and get their money. She ended the rampage by saying that Carlton still had the last laugh, as he had been seeing "his equal" the entire time they were married. Rach had suggested that she get tested for HIV at that time, but Sabrena told her that her most recent test was negative.

Sabrena had only been with Steve in the last three years, and although she had her suspicions, Steve swore that he hadn't slept with anyone else.

"Dr. Scott, I just don't know—my boyfriend doesn't have HIV, or at least he doesn't look like it. He has been my main partner since I left my husband several years ago. Could my ex-husband have given me HIV? But, after I left him, when I started working, I had a negative test."

"Ms. Collins, first of all, we don't know that you have HIV, so let's not jump the gun. We are going to do the test. I don't know any of the specifics of your sexual partners and their risk factors, but you must remember that you have had chlamydia in the past and now have trichomoniasis, both of which you can get from unprotected sex, just like HIV." Dr. Scott handed her a brochure on STDs.

"Does this tricho stuff only come from sex?" Sabrena asked Dr. Scott. She was becoming more confused by the minute and wanted to bolt out of the office.

"More than likely, yes, it's sexually transmitted. However, there's also a chance that the infection was from another source, such as going to a spa and using the same towel as someone with trich. Your daughters are more than likely fine, because you can't pass this on just by casual contact." Sabrena was going to read the brochure that Dr. Scott gave her and, of course, she'd take the medication.

"I'm writing a prescription for you and your partner. He'll need to take this as well, so that you don't pass the infection back and forth."

Sabrena tried to ask more questions, but was stopped mid-sentence, when Dr. Scott began to talk with her about the HIV testing.

"Ms. Collins, I certainly understand your questions about the diagnosis and can understand how you may be feeling about your partner. However, I must tell you that this is bigger than just a case of trich. I'm very concerned about your energy level, swollen lymph nodes, the sweating at night, and the unexplained weight loss. We really need to fully investigate any and all possible causes, which include several medical conditions. You have known me for a long time—you know that I'll work to get to the bottom of this and get you feeling better," Dr. Scott told her as she patted her on her hand.

"Thank you, Dr. Scott. This is a lot to take in, but I'll agree to the testing and anything else you think is necessary." Sabrena trusted her.

"Good, make a follow-up appointment in two weeks and we'll go from there. Do call me if you have any problem with the medication, and don't drink any alcohol while taking it, as it could make you sick to your stomach. Ms. Collins, if you have sex, use condoms until we get all of this sorted out. Really, it's what I recommend, unless you're in a totally monogamous long-term relationship and both have been fully tested for every type of STD."

Sabrena walked out of the room armed with prescriptions and brochures. She couldn't explain how she felt; it was overwhelming, and she had a lot to think about. She was too old to listen to a doctor talk about sexually transmitted diseases and the like. Changes had to be made in her life, beginning today.

CHAPTER SIX

Sabrena usually got her prescriptions filled at the pharmacy in Steve's store, but today she decided to go to the drugstore in the same building as Dr. Scott's office. She didn't want his employees to see that she had a medication for an STD. Sabrena told herself it wasn't 100 percent certain that it was an STD, but, all the same, Steve's employees didn't need to be in their business. As she waited for the medications, she read pamphlets and picked up information on other things like low blood counts and menopause.

She was convinced that she was going to have to confront Steve about the infection. Last time, with the chlamydia episode, he had denied everything and made her feel guilty. This was a little different, in that Dr. Scott said it didn't always come from sex, so she didn't want to make any accusations when she may have picked it up somewhere else. Sabrena knew that she hadn't been with anyone else— except for an innocent kiss over a year ago when she broke up with Steve for a weekend. She had known that Steve would find out about her date and she'd wanted to make him jealous. Sure enough, he'd been waiting at her house when she got back from her date, and they'd been together ever since. Sabrena knew that he loved her; otherwise he would have just easily walked away from her when another man entered the picture.

Sabrena's mind began to turn. She was going to make some calls; she needed to get to the bottom of some things. She wondered if she could have gotten this thing . . . this parasite . . . from kissing somebody over a year ago. Sabrena was worried about her visit with Dr. Scott and all the questions, tests, and doctor stuff. She was just going to have to wait it out . . . she was glad to get the medication for the yeast infection and the other thing—the trich. Maybe once that cleared up, she would be better.

She looked at the vitamin section, thinking vitamins might help her energy. She decided to start walking in the evenings with the girls. They could all use some exercise. She briefly thought about the HIV test, but she wasn't worried. Her tests before were negative and she wasn't the type to sleep around or use drugs. Besides Steve, there had only been one other guy since Carlton. Francis was a stupid mistake that she had made when she was feeling lonely, but that was just twice and he used condoms both times.

Steve was fine: he didn't do drugs or certainly sleep with men—more importantly he looked healthy and was in good shape. He may have flirted a lot, but Sabrena felt he hadn't slept around—at least not in the last year and a half. But did she really know? How could she?

Although she wasn't worried about HIV or AIDS, she was concerned about the other things Dr. Scott had told her. What if she had cancer or something? What about her girls? What about work? Sabrena shook her head to get the thoughts out of her mind—she would just wait until she got her results; she probably just needed some rest and had gotten run down. She paid for her medications and popped a vitamin in her mouth—may as well start living a healthier lifestyle now. She had to focus on her mind, body, and soul.

"Hey Rach, how are you?" Sabrena asked.

"Fine, what's up—is everything all right? You never call me at the office."

"Yes, I'm fine, but I need to know if you can pick up the girls. I have some unexpected business I have to take care of, but I shouldn't be more than an hour or so." Sabrena had some calls to make and a few stops that were important on the way home—it was time for her to stop taking things at face value. She was going to have to take a cake to her neighbor, Janine.

Sabrena parked the car and checked her eyes again to make sure she looked okay. The day was long, but necessary. She forced herself to smile as she got out of the car and walked to her door. She was greeted by Deena, with Renee not far behind. They were full of energy and they never failed to lift her spirits. They loved their Auntie Rach and her other friends; they adored their Uncle Gerald, her older brother, and Uncle Steve, but their hearts belonged to their mommy.

"Hi, Mommy, where were you?" Deena asked, as she hugged her waist.

"I was running late, but I'm here now. How was your day, how was school?" Sabrena began the evening ritual. It did not matter what she was facing, her job was to be there for her girls, and each day she was. She helped them finish their homework while Rach finished a conference call for work. Sabrena gave them a treat from the snack box and told them to go play with their dolls, so that she and Rach could talk. They were good girls, strong and healthy, and really they had never been sick, even as babies. Sabrena was grateful to God for her girls. She knew she had to shake whatever it was that was making her feel tired, so she could be ready for the summer with them.

Rach walked into the kitchen and helped herself to some of Sabrena's infamous lasagna. "Girl, you put your *whole* foot in this lasagna," she said with a mouthful of her favorite dish. "This is good!"

"Thank you much. Take some home with you. I can't cook just a little of anything," Sabrena said as she put some in the microwave for herself. She did love her special lasagna. It was the first dish she'd made for Steve and he had been hooked every since. "Did Renee eat some salad and lasagna? She hates vegetables and leftovers."

"Yeah, but I didn't force it with the salad. I didn't give her a choice with the lasagna, I just put her plate down and that was it."

"You let them get away with murder. Renee will pick at her dinner and still be allowed to have cookies," Sabrena said. Her little one had never had much of an appetite, unlike Deena. However, she was not complaining because they were both healthy.

Sabrena started sniffing in the pantry. "What is that smell?" It was a strong odor; she looked down and saw Boxer's litter box. "If these girls don't start changing this cat's litter box, he's gonna end up back on the streets." Sabrena cleaned up the mess.

"So, what did Dr. Scott say?" Rach asked, still stuffing her face.

"Oh, it's nothing—I have another yeast infection, but overall I'm fine. It was time for my gyn exam and some blood work," Sabrena said, trying to sound unconcerned and light about the situation. She knew that if she hinted of a problem, her friend would know. Rach was like a sister to Sabrena—they had both been through tough times together and always took care of each other. Sabrena remembered Rach's breast cancer scare; she had been right there with her for the biopsy and the results. They had cried in each other's arms when the doctor had told them it was just a cyst. The following Sunday they both went to church; something Sabrena knew she needed to do more often. She would eventually tell Rach about the visit, but today she just needed to relax. No need in getting her upset when this was all probably nothing. However, this episode was an eye opener for her—just enough to nudge her into some detective work.

"Has anyone called since you've been here?" Sabrena asked, looking at the answering machine. There were no messages waiting—she wondered if she had turned it on.

"No, not at all, but we got here about thirty minutes before you."

"Okay, I'm tired . . . I hope you didn't give the girls sodas—they're gonna have to go to sleep tonight. You know how much I hate going to the doctor, even though I like Dr. Scott," Sabrena said with a yawn. "Girl, she had on some bad pumps today!"

"Oh yeah—she's always sharp. I saw her one weekend at the mall—she can do some damage. Even on the weekend she had it together with her little Chanel slides and sunglasses." Rach smiled as she thought of her doctor and remembered first meeting her when she was having bad migraines. After talking to Dr. Scott, she realized that her headaches were coming from her then no-count boyfriend, Alex. Funny, because when they broke up, her migraines stopped. Dr. Scott kept it real and she liked that—cool, classy, but warm and caring.

"Sabrena, why don't you take a long shower? I'll take care of the girls and you can go to sleep. We'll be fine," Rach told her friend as she poured a glass of wine. "I'll stay here tonight and just go home after work tomorrow. It's better this way since I'm closer to the office and can sleep later."

"You don't have to do that, but since you offered . . ." Sabrena was grateful for her friend, who often stayed over to help her out. Sabrena turned on the shower and found her favorite nightgown. She loved the feel of silk on her body. Even if she was just sleeping alone, she liked to feel and smell good when she went to bed.

As she got into the shower, she thought of Steve. He knew that she'd had a doctor's appointment and was a little surprised he had not called. Oh, well, maybe he was busy. Or maybe he just didn't give a damn. She needed strength to figure out this relationship, or lack thereof. He said she was going to be his wife, but there was no ring, and he really only brought it up when she threatened to leave him. She wanted the old days back when he called her every day, tried to see her all the time, and sent flowers. More than that, she just wanted to feel his strong hands hold her and tell her everything was going to be all right. Steve could just hug her and she would feel the strength of his arms ease her worries. She needed to know that someone out there other than her daughters and Rach cared about her.

CHAPTER SEVEN

Sabrena wasn't stupid. Sometimes she did stupid things, but she was getting wiser by the minute. She thought about all the lies and junk that came with Steve, but reminded herself that sometimes you have to take the bitter with the sweet—especially if the sweet was Steve on his best behavior. However, now the bitter wasn't just bad behavior. It was affecting her health. She didn't know how to begin talking to Steve about Dr. Scott's diagnosis. Sabrena's eyes teared and her cheeks got warm. She felt confused, lonely, and a little scared. She needed some rest and she needed to talk to Steve, but tonight she wasn't going to be the one to track him down. She would demand to see him tomorrow, give him the medication, and confront him with the truth. Then she would just go from there. It's amazing what a simple store-bought cake and a gallon of ice cream can do to open the door for information. She had a few more calls to make, but she was on track to catching a weasel.

Sabrena went to kiss her girls good-night and she remembered to take the medicines for the infections. Before getting back in bed, she did something she hadn't done in a long time. She got on her knees and prayed.

"Our Father, who art in heaven, hallowed be thy name.
Thy Kingdom come, thy will be done, on earth as it is in
    heaven.
Give us this day our daily bread. And forgive us our tres-
    passes,
as we forgive those who trespass against us. And lead us
    not into temptation,

> *but deliver us from evil. For thine is the kingdom, the*
> *power, and the glory, forever and ever.*
> *Lord, please help me to be a good mother, keep me healthy*
> *and strong for them. Guide my steps and bless Deena*
> *and Renee, keep them safe and from all harm. Thank*
> *you for them and for the blessings they are to my life,*
> *even when I don't deserve it. Thank you for Rach. God,*
> *please give me the courage to take the proper steps in my*
> *life and give me the wisdom to know what to do with*
> *Steve. Lord, I need your help and I thank you in*
> *advance. Amen."*

Sabrena climbed into bed and fell quickly into a deep sleep.

Then Sabrena awoke well rested and ready to face the day. She needed to go back to work this morning and could only imagine what the day would be like since she had left early yesterday. She had worked in retail for years now and was the assistant manager in women's clothing at Bloomingdale's. It was a good position, and she only worked in the mornings or early afternoons during the week, except during the holidays. The hours were flexible and she could come and go as she needed for the girls. She and her boss, Vivian, worked well together and they usually covered each other. The girls were still sleeping so she took the time to enjoy a cup of tea and took the vitamins that she'd bought at the drugstore. She went to pick out her clothes for the day and put a load of laundry in the washing machine. The girls would be up any minute so Sabrena tried to get as much done as possible before hurricanes Deena and Renee blew through.

"Good morning, Bre," Rach was still yawning as she walked into the kitchen. "I smell my coffee—you know how to treat your nanny."

"I sure do, but I ain't paying you and you better not be beating my kids," Sabrena replied and laughed as she looked at her friend in her gown that was two sizes too small for her. "You need to lose some weight! Why are you in my gown?" Sabrena asked while going into the room for a robe for her.

"I don't need to lose no weight; my man likes me with some meat on my bones. Heck, even if he didn't, I wouldn't care" Rach said, sticking out her chest and butt. She was a full-figured sister, but she was confident and just knew that she had it going on. She never worried about getting or keeping a man. "You could pick up a few pounds," she said, walking around Sabrena. "You're looking like a white girl—what happened to your butt?"

"Oh, my booty is still there—I'm just toned up—whatever!" Sabrena laughed, and then remembered that Dr. Scott had told her she'd lost 18 pounds since her last visit. Ahhhh, this morning she didn't want to think about the visit—she just needed to get up and out with the girls. Time would work this out.

"Rach, you're gonna be late for work, you can't use the traffic as an excuse today. Do you want some cereal or toast?"

"Toast is fine and I'm going to take a shower. Do you have a shower cap? And don't I've some pants here from last time?" Sabrena helped her friend get dressed and got the girls together.

CHAPTER EIGHT

Sabrena was out the door in the nick of time. She hurried to work and was glad to see Vivian in the employee lounge doctoring her coffee.

"Good morning, Vivian? How're you?" She asked pouring a cup of coffee for herself to help get her through the morning.

"Hey, Sabrena. I'm fine. What about you? How was your appointment?"

"Oh, fine—the usual," Sabrena replied with all of the enthusiasm she could muster. She didn't like people in her business, especially people she worked with. She really only talked to Rach and one or two of her other girlfriends. She liked Vivian and they were a good team for work, but she didn't talk with her about her personal life.

Vivian always talked to her about her kids and husband and a lifestyle that was very different from Sabrena's. Vivian was 56 years old, had four kids, and had been married for over 35 years. Her husband owned a car dealership and they had some dollars, but she wanted to keep her independence, so she worked. All of her children were grown, with her youngest in her first year of college. Sabrena suspected that Vivian was bored at home and that's why she worked. She had met Vivian's husband at a Christmas party and he seemed nice enough. Sabrena had also met her oldest son, Vance, who came to take Vivian to lunch at least once a month. He was a looker, not that Sabrena got into white men—but he was handsome and nice. She knew that he wasn't married and when she had asked Vivian about it, Vivian had quickly brushed it off.

Vivian was an attractive white lady, who dressed very conservatively, but was stylish. She wore her hair in a twist with very little makeup. However, looks were deceiving. Although Vivian was professional at all times, she had a terrific sense of humor and a big, boisterous laugh that snuck out sometimes, usually when Sabrena told a good joke. Sabrena and Vivian had gone out to dinner a few times after work and always went "shopping" through the new clothes as they came in. They were friends—sort of. The bottom line was that Vivian was still Sabrena's boss and Sabrena would only let her get so close.

Vivian had been with Bloomingdale's for about two years; Sabrena remembered when it was announced that she would be the new manager for her department. Sabrena had been hurt that she didn't get the position and had been very cool to Vivian. However, that really wasn't her style, and, after getting to know Vivian, she realized that she was mad at the wrong person. One day, out of the blue, Vivian began talking to her about being the assistant manager and asked why she thought she had been overlooked for the manager's job. Sabrena initially told her she thought it was because she was black and didn't have a college degree. However, Vivian told her she hadn't been to college, either, and had worked in retail since she was 17, with the exception of time off with her children. Vivian also told her she knew what it was like to be overlooked. She'd left Nordstrom because she wasn't given the store manager position, although she was clearly the most qualified and had been there the longest. She told her how bitter she was for months. That bitterness was killing her spirit, so one day she walked in and gave them her two-weeks notice. She didn't have another job lined up, but called all the major stores and sent out dozens of copies of her résumé. Vivian described how she checked that the HR departments had received her résumé, then called and asked for the manager of each of the stores, making it clear that she was still employed by one of their competitors. She spoke to the manager of Bloomingdale's to make sure that he had a copy of her résumé and then invited him to lunch in their employee lounge. She told him that even if nothing else happened, he could see the competition close up and in person.

Sabrena couldn't believe that Vivian had been so bold, but then she really could understand. In the end, Vivian was offered a job and Sabrena's old boss was moved to another area. It always struck Sabrena as odd that Vivian told her all the details, even about being overlooked for the job at Nordstrom. Vivian also said that when she was hired she asked a lot of questions about Sabrena and was told she was a great employee. She'd even asked why Sabrena hadn't been promoted, and found out that the only concerns management had were that Sabrena sometimes was late for work and often took days off because of problems with child care. Sabrena listened and, since Vivian had come to her store, had missed only one day of work, was always early, and, if she was needed, stayed late. Sabrena was rewarded with an increase in salary and bonuses throughout the year. It was easy to like Vivian and to work with the others in the department.

Sabrena kept looking at the clock, counting down the hours until her lunch break. She had called Steve and told him it was urgent that she see him today. He agreed to come during her lunch break and kept asking her what the problem was.

"Is it the girls? Has that lying Rachel been talking about me again?" The questions kept coming, but Sabrena just told him that it was important. She went through the morning in a fog. Since the usual cashier hadn't showed up, Sabrena had to ring up purchases and do more hands-on work with the customers. Everything worked out, because being on the floor and busy kept her from thinking about Steve, the office visit, and just life in general. She was able to take a few minutes to finish her calls, and now she was armed with something that Steve knew little about, the truth.

She saw Steve coming down the aisle, a little earlier than expected. He looked nervous. When Sabrena went to greet him, she felt him pull back from her. They went to an Italian restaurant in the mall. After they had ordered, Sabrena tried to find a way to bring up the subject.

"Here Steve, you have to take this medication," she said bluntly, and handed him the bottle.

"What? What's this and what's it for?" Steve asked, appearing totally confused.

"My doctor said that I've an infection called trichomoniasis and that it could be sexually transmitted so my partner would need to be treated, too," Sabrena said in one long breath. She barely let it sink in before continuing, "It's not transmitted only through sex but in the majority of cases it is. Steve, I need to know—for me, my health, my kids, and my sanity—no jokes and please God no more lies— have you been sleeping around?" Sabrena surprised herself by the frankness of her question. She looked at him intently, looking for any hint of the truth.

"Brena, you drop this on me with little or no explanation, hand me some pills, and then ask *me* about cheating?" Steve hissed in a low voice, looking around the restaurant. "Come on—slow down—do I have this infection? I feel fine, I haven't had any problems with peeing, no itching or seeing anything on my penis. Do I need to go get checked?" he asked. Sabrena noted that he didn't even ask about her, which just reinforced the reality of his selfishness.

"Yes, if I were you I would get checked, but Dr. Scott gave me the prescription for you and I filled it when I filled mine. Steve, I just need to know from your mouth, no mess, no lies. Just yes or no. Have you been messing around?" Sabrena demanded to know and she wasn't backing up this time.

"Sabrena, I love you and wouldn't do anything to hurt you or the girls." Steve grabbed her hand as he spoke. "I know that you had reason not to trust me before but that was a long time ago. You can trust me now. I'm too old for all the games." He looked directly into Sabrena's eyes. "Now, I need to ask you—is there someone else? Have you been sleeping with someone else?" Steve asked, already knowing the answer. Sabrena was loyal, definitely not a wandering woman. And heck, it had taken him four months of wining and dining before she would sleep with him. She wouldn't let him meet her daughters for over six months after they were dating.

"No, Steve, you know that's not my style. Please don't go there again." She totally dismissed the question because she knew that it was a ploy to change the subject. She wasn't falling for that again. "What happened a few weeks ago when you came to my house in the middle of the night talking about a robbery at the store? What's the truth?"

"Sabrena, I told you what happened. Don't bring that up again—I got into a lot of trouble at the store because of that." Steve pulled his hands back and looked disgusted.

At that moment Sabrena knew that she had to walk away. When she came to lunch she had no idea how it all was going to play out, but now she knew she was ending this relationship. She had all the information she needed: Janine and her other sources would have no reason to lie.

"Steve, you don't have to lie anymore. It's not worth it and it really doesn't matter to me now. A police report was never filed—I actually went to the station. I called the store's district office and asked if there had been any robberies at your store. They said there had been none in the last eight months. I spoke with the security guards at your store and they said that there had been some shoplifting but no break-ins." Sabrena kept on talking, even though Steve looked at her with disbelief, scrambling to put some lie together. "I also know that you have not been to any training sessions for the last six months, so those little weekend sessions were a lie as well. Steve, you think that I'm stupid, but that's a big mistake. I've been foolish but never stupid. I loved you and still do love you but I love my girls and myself more. Some things I've just ignored or they have been too painful to really confront, but I've not been stupid. I have really gotten tired—mentally and physically—and now it's time to just move on." Sabrena had put everything on the table and waited for Steve to catch his breath.

This latest incident with the infection was really the straw that broke the camel's back. Sabrena was finally ready to say good-bye to Steve. She knew she still loved him, or the "him" she thought he could be, but she needed to be loved and respected.

"Steve, you don't have to say anything. And don't waste your energy trying to make up some lie. It's too late for that," Sabrena said, and pulled her hand away. Their food came and Steve began to eat—saying nothing, but looking intently at her face. Sabrena sipped her Pepsi and nibbled at her food, but felt like getting as far away from him as she could. In her heart, she knew that this was finally over, and, although she loved him, she had to leave him alone.

With little emotion, Sabrena said, "Steve, please don't call me or try to contact me in any way. Please don't come over to the house. If you want to say good-bye to the girls, I'll let you, but I'll tell them about us. This relationship, or whatever it was, is over. I'll get your stuff from my house and I'll drop it off at the store."

Steve asked quietly, still eating his lunch, "So it's like that, Sabrena? Three years of my life just disappears. *You* decide that you don't want me and that's it—no discussion, no nothing? You're just going to drop my stuff off and that's it?" He actually sounded sad. Sabrena knew he cared for her, but she also knew he had a taste for women and enjoyed wielding his power over them. Once, she'd overheard him say to a buddy that no man likes having the same meal every night and she was sure what he meant was, "No man likes sleeping with the same woman every night." Well, now he could do whatever he wanted, with whomever he wanted.

Steve's mind raced. How could this be happening to him? He was usually the "dumper" with women. He wasn't going to be trapped by any woman; he knew how that looked. All his life, his father had been controlled by his mother. His father had no life, she knew where he was at all times; he had no desire, no get up and go. Steve really believed his dad was scared of his mother. After watching years of this, seeing his strong dad reduced to a yes man, Steve had decided that this would never be his lot.

Steve's heart felt heavy, and it started pounding in his chest. He looked at Sabrena. He knew he was caught and sensed that Sabrena was really finished with him. Steve loved Sabrena, as much as he could love any woman. Being with Sabrena had been the closest thing to a real relationship he had ever experienced but although he did love her, he couldn't let her control him. He did see other women—one in particular had his undivided attention now—but he saw Sabrena as his main woman. She was consistent and nurturing. She was a lady, and, more than anything else, he knew that she loved him. Sabrena believed in him—even when he doubted himself. She was always telling him how smart he was, how he would one day be a district manager. Steve could confide his hopes and dreams in Sabrena, and, no matter what, she wouldn't stomp on them. Most important of all, Sabrena challenged him to be a better man. His friends were always telling him how lucky he was and he knew that a few of them secretly wanted her. He was careful not to discuss too much of their relationship; Sabrena was his and his alone.

He also loved Deena and Renee as if they were his own daughters and he tried to help them out as much as possible. Steve knew they loved him back unconditionally—and even if he hadn't been around in a few weeks, they were always excited to see him. They never asked any questions, but just ran to see "Uncle Steve." In their eyes, he could do no wrong, and that was a great feeling. The girls were listed on his insurance policy at work and in his will prepared by his brother-in-law. As he thought about the possibility of not being with them anymore, he felt a deep sense of loss. Panic rushed over him.

It was a perfect situation—except for Sabrena. Yes, he loved her; yes, she was a good woman with a big heart. Yes, she was pretty, warm, and loving, a good fit. Yes, she was a giving and always willing lover who never nagged. But she wanted more of him than he could give any woman. He had thought of marriage over the last few years but it always scared him, and, though he dangled the promise out there, he was afraid to propose. It was hard to live up to her expectations—something inside him held him back.

Was Sabrena serious? They had broken up before, but this time was different—she was calm and collected. Perhaps it was because of this infection thing. He made a mental note to go see his doctor. Hopefully, Sabrena was just mad and this would blow over. He knew Sabrena would never cheat on him; she wasn't that kind of woman. He probably had picked this up from one of his other conquests, but he was an old player and there was only one thing to do—deny, deny, deny.

He usually used condoms during first encounters, and, depending on the woman, would go bare after a few times together. Of course, with Sabrena, he didn't use condoms, because they were a couple. He didn't like how condoms felt unnatural and restricting. He'd had a vasectomy, so he wasn't worried about kids; but he had not told anyone, not even Sabrena. He looked at her sitting quietly across the table. She was a very attractive woman and he still got lost in her eyes. He was surprised that she had checked out his story, since she usually believed him at face value, unless that Rachel got involved. Steve couldn't figure how he could get out of his lie now.

Steve smiled inwardly as he thought of that night and the impromptu picnic in his office. Mmmm, that hookup ran late. He had to think up something to tell Sabrena and it had to be good because he had been caught in another lie and that night was supposed to be the makeup date. Shoot, he really worked that story, even scratching his pretty skin to try to look believable, and he thought that he had made it; especially after making love to her. He might be getting older, but he still had it in that department: two women in one night; he didn't need any Viagra®, although he had a little stash, just in case. Looking back, it was a lie in which he was easily caught. Maybe he'd let her cool off, and it would be just like before. In a few days she would miss him and he would play the humble puppy. He would call her, spend some time, send flowers, make some weekend plans, and get things back to normal. Why didn't women understand that he couldn't be caged in?

Steve was jerked back into reality with Sabrena's frankness.

"What do you mean no discussion?" she asked. "We've had this discussion a million times. You've just never heard me." Sabrena amazed herself with the conviction of her words. After taking a few minutes to digest what she'd said, Steve started to nod his head.

"Brena, I love you, but maybe you're right, maybe we need to part. You obviously don't trust me and I'm sure you doubt that I love you," Steve said, trying to sound sincere. "I won't call and I won't come over, if that's what you want. But I do need to talk to the girls. I have to see them. I love them no matter what happens with us."

Sabrena knew that Steve was very protective of them and he would have a hard time not seeing them. "Okay, that's not a problem; you've always been good for them," Sabrena said, and started to get up from the table. Steve grabbed her hand gently with what she swore was genuine pain and sadness.

"Sabrena, I'm sorry for everything. Baby, I do love you, but I don't know if I can love you the way you want me to. This is as close to the real thing as I have ever come and I just . . ." Steve choked up and then seemed to catch himself—he hugged her and let her go. Steve's emotions had surprised even him. Somehow, in the pit of his stomach, he knew that this time was different for them. He looked at the medication bottle and swallowed a dose of the tablets. He wondered who else was going to tell him they had an infection. He hoped not his new interest. He would just have to wait. He would have to wear condoms more often.

Sabrena walked back to work, feeling more free and stronger than she ever had. She was glad she had talked to Steve during her lunch—less time, no major drama, and they weren't near a bed, so there was no temptation. She knew that the next days, weeks, and months would be hard. She was through with men, and her girls were going to have to be enough.

The rest of the day went by in a flash, and before she knew it, she was walking out to her car. She had about two hours before she had to get the girls. Since she had some energy, she would go home and pull together Steve's things and put them in the trunk of her car so she could drop them off on her way to get Renee.

It only took a few minutes to pick up the clothes and toiletries Steve had left at her house. She looked at the TV he'd bought for the girls, but she decided that it was a gift. The TV reminded Sabrena that Steve paid for cable and the girl's piano lessons. She would have to make some real adjustments so the girls wouldn't miss anything. Sabrena's tears fell as she put Steve's things in her trunk.

"God, please help me stay strong and fully walk away from Steve," she whispered as she drove to Steve's store. "I love him and the girls love him, but I know this is right. Lord, help me to be stronger and better. Give me guidance and help me heal from this pain. Amen."

"Hi, Chester," Sabrena said. She'd always liked this security guard.

"Well, hello, pretty lady. How are you today?"

"I'm fine, but I need a favor. Can you take these to Steve? I'm in a bit of a hurry." Sabrena handed the box to Chester and jumped back into the car. Chester looked a little puzzled, but he smiled and took the box inside.

"Thank you," she called. "See you next time."

"Good-bye," he said. "I'll see that Mr. Steve gets this."

As she was driving away, she had a flashback to the times she and Steve had made love in his office. In the early days, Sabrena would often bring him dinner when he was working late, and these precious moments kept the passion in their relationship. She laughed aloud as she remembered getting caught by the night security guard when they had gotten just a little too loud. They'd thought they were alone, but had been jolted into reality by the flashlight in their faces. But those days were long gone. Lately, Steve had scolded her for coming into the store to see him. She wondered how many other women were just coming by, but that was no longer her problem.

CHAPTER NINE

It was good to get home. The girls were tired and actually went to sleep in the car after she picked them up. They had gotten so big that there was no way Sabrena could carry them both into the house, so she woke the little sleepy heads and walked them in. She'd picked up some Chinese food so she didn't have to cook and fortunately the girls didn't have homework. Sabrena fed them and watched their favorite video with them before putting them to bed. She ended the day by tucking them into bed and lightly kissing their foreheads. "I love you, my princesses," she said.

Sabrena would kill for her girls. She wanted them to feel secure in who they were and to really know love. She thought of Steve and tried to figure out how she was going to tell them about the breakup. Sabrena had been so careful that they didn't meet a lot of men or see men come and go. She had girlfriends who exposed their kids to every new man in their lives, but Sabrena didn't think that was good for her girls. She didn't want them to continually have to lose "uncles" and Sabrena knew that such short-term relationships set a bad example.

That being said, she was still a woman and there was certainly a kind of love she desired that she couldn't get from her children. She wondered why she had never received the love she gave with Kevin, Carlton, or Steve. Francis didn't really count; she'd dated him briefly and discovered he too was unfaithful. She really hadn't been passionately in love with Carlton, but she had loved him and was committed to that marriage. When she'd found out from his crazy mother that he'd been having an affair, it further wrecked her self-esteem.

Maybe she attracted the wrong type of men, maybe she slept with them too soon, maybe she needed to go to school and work on herself. There were so many maybes, but no concrete answers. One thing was for sure, she had closed the book on Steve.

In times like these, her large garden bathtub was her luxury. She lit candles and played music, and in this little room Sabrena often found herself solving her problems, meditating, and enjoying the solitude. Tonight she thought of her next steps and of how she was going to just cool out socially and swear off all men! She was going to be busy in the upcoming weeks with end-of-season sales and getting things ready for the store fashion show. Sabrena was lulled to sleep by the smooth voice of Oleta Adams, but she woke to chilly water and wrinkled skin. She jumped out of the tub to reach for the ringing phone.

"Hello, hello," Sabrena said, out of breath

"Hey girl—what's up?" It was Rach. "What took you so long and why are you breathing hard? Tell me that Rover, I mean Steve, isn't there."

"No Rach, he's not and guess what? He won't be," Sabrena replied. It was time to tell her friend what she'd been waiting to hear for three years. "I broke up with Steve today and if you love me like you say you do, you won't kill me with questions." Although she wanted to share with Rach, Sabrena wasn't in the mood tonight.

"Hmmpppphhhh, I'll bite my tongue, but *hallelujah*! is an appropriate word in this instance. I just hope that this is for real. Anyway, how are you doing?" Rach tried to sound nonchalant but Sabrena could hear her smiling through the phone. She hated Steve, and even more than Steve, she hated who Sabrena became with him. She remembered the slick, conniving Sabrena who took Carlton to the cleaners before leaving him—that was her girl! For her to regress to this passive, gullible female was difficult for Rach to watch. She was proud of her friend, but also knew it would be hard for her. She made a mental note to get her a card in the morning and take her to dinner.

"I'm okay. Actually I'm good. I just got out of the tub and am going to bed early," Sabrena replied, hoping to get Rach off the phone, so she could curl up in bed.

"Okay, I'll call you in the morning. I need to come to Bloomingdale's. This girlfriend needs the discount, so I'll call before I come. Let's do something tomorrow evening, okay?"

"No problem, it's a date. Good night, girl," Sabrena said as she hung up. The urge to pray drew her to her knees.

She said aloud:

"Dear God, I really need your help. I need you to heal my heart and give me strength to stand. I love him but I can't be with him. Please help me to really get Steve out of my soul. Lord, forgive me for my sins, and please help me to be a better mother. Bless my babies and don't let any hurt or harm come to them. Bless Rach, and God bless my family. Amen."

Sabrena felt better and went directly to sleep, with Boxer curled up at her feet.

CHAPTER TEN

The next several days went by swiftly for Sabrena. She had tried to occupy her time and, fortunately, between work and the girls, there was little time to think about her life. She had actually seen Steve once; they had arranged for him to take the girls out for pizza.

"Uncle Steve!" Both girls screamed and ran into Steve's waiting arms. They hadn't seen him in over a week; you would have thought that it had been years. Their little arms were holding him so tight; Sabrena thought they would cut off his breath.

"Hey, my little ladies, how ya'll doin'?" Steve put the girls down, but held onto their hands as he walked them to the table.

"Fine, we miss you, whatcha bring us back?" Deena asked. They were used to Steve going on trips and always having something for them. Sabrena watched their interactions and she was sad that they would be losing Steve. No matter how he had treated her, he had always been there for the girls. They loved him, much like a girl loves the first love of her life, their father. She couldn't take that away from them. She remembered her life after her father left.

"Of course, I brought my ladies something." Steve said. He pulled out two silver bracelets with heart charms, engraved with each girl's initials. His eyes misted as he put them on their tiny arms. He gave the boxes to Sabrena.

"Oh, Uncle Steve, it's so pretty. Does Mommy get one?" Renee asked.

Steve was getting choked up. "No, these are just for you two. I need you to make sure that you don't lose them and that you don't forget Uncle Steve."

"We never forget you, Uncle Steve. Can you come to our house and play after we eat?" Deena asked as she looked at her bracelet.

"Uncle Steve has plans already, but you know that you'll see him and you can call him tonight if you like. Uncle Steve may take you to piano practice on Saturday, if he's not working." Sabrena couldn't deny the love that was shared between her girls and Steve. He mouthed the words thank-you to her as the girls began coloring their placemats.

After eating, they talked briefly and Steve handed Sabrena an envelope which he asked her to open when she got home. Sabrena hugged him for old time's sake. When she got the girls settled at home, she opened the envelope to find twenty one hundred dollar bills—she was shocked. There was also a letter which read:

Dear Sabrena,
I know that I'm not worthy of your love or affection and understand the breakup. I thought that this would be like all the other times, but your eyes always give you away. I know that this is it and that I've really messed up this time. I'm not asking for any more chances or anything right now. However, I want you to know that I do love you and loved you the best I could—right or wrong. Baby, Deena and Renee are as close as I've ever come to being a father. We've been together for a few years and I couldn't love them more. I love them with all my heart and no matter what happens to us, I want to be there for the girls. I've put enough money in this envelope to cover their cable and piano lessons for awhile, with extra for their special treats. I hope that you allow me to still come get them once in awhile. They're my heart and I need them, just as much as they need me. Funny, the girls don't expect me to be anything but me—Uncle Steve, their buddy—and I need to be somebody's buddy. If you or they need anything, just let me know—I mean it.
With all the love that I can give,
Steve

As she lay on her bed reading the letter, Sabrena wept softly. Had she done the right thing? What about her daughters? Was Steve sincere? What was next? Sabrena's thoughts whirled around her and she realized she wasn't necessarily crying over losing Steve, but rather over having had another bad relationship. She wouldn't deny her girls their Uncle Steve, but she had to move on. She called Rach and read the letter. She was momentarily speechless.

"Girl, I gotta give him props; that Negro is good. I bet you're laid out crying," Rach said.

"Rach, you have to admit that he has always taken care of the girls. My daughters aren't his children and he has genuinely cared for them and helped me with them."

"Bre, you're right. That's the *one* thing that I can't dog Steve out for. He does get credit for that. However, he loses all points, because he has continued to treat you like dirt. You deserve better and I am glad that he's out. I have never been one to tell you how to run your life, but the best thing that you can do is say good-bye to that doggie." Rach and Sabrena chatted for a few more minutes before signing off. Sabrena drank a glass of wine and went to sleep holding the letter in her hands. She had a full day on tomorrow. She had to take cookies to school with Deena and she had a doctor's appointment.

CHAPTER ELEVEN

Sabrena sat patiently in Dr. Scott's office. The nurse had taken her vitals and more blood.

"Denise, I gave blood the last time I was here; why do you need more?" Sabrena asked as she saw the hated needle being unwrapped.

"Oh, you know how Dr. Scott is; she has more tests that she wants to do," Denise said, as she tried to quickly and painlessly take Sabrena's blood. She liked Denise. In spite of having so much blood taken on the last visit and now today, Sabrena actually felt better. She had been taking vitamins daily and trying to get more sleep. Since her breakup with Steve, she felt that a huge weight had been lifted from her shoulders. Of course, she had some tough days and it would definitely take time to get over the breakup, but Sabrena felt stronger than she had in a while.

"Dr. Scott is running a few minutes late, so take this magazine and I will let you know if it's going to be more than ten minutes or so." Denise handed Sabrena the latest *Essence* magazine and closed the door. She took a deep breath and whispered a prayer on her way to get the doctor.

Dr. Scott took the chart from Denise, and looked over Sabrena's information again. "How does she look?"

"Good. She did ask me why I was taking more blood. I just told her that you asked for it and that you would be talking with her." Denise patted Dr. Scott gently on the back. "You'll be fine and she'll be fine, but I know how hard this is for you."

"If only I didn't care so much. But I do and hope I never stop. This is never easy. " Dr. Scott sighed and took a few more sips of her jasmine tea. "Did you make sure there's tissue in the room and another chair? I will need the information pack that I put together."

Denise nodded as she walked out of the room. She knew that Dr. Scott would need some extra time with Ms. Collins and had rescheduled the two other patients who had appointments before lunch. Unlike some of the other doctors Denise had worked with, Dr. Scott actually cared about her patients. When Denise had gotten Ms. Collins's test results, she'd called the lab to make sure that there was no mix-up and then gave them to Dr. Scott. The doctor sank into her chair and tears trickled down her cheeks. Denise had been deeply touched, as well. The few times she had met Ms. Collins let her know that she would have a hard time hearing this news. It was hard for anybody, but all too common these days.

Dr. Gwendolyn Scott was an internist by training, with a special interest in women's health. She was married to Darren Foster, a well-respected city councilman, and they had hopes of starting a family in the next year or two. Gwen, as her friends called her, was passionate about her life—all of it—God, her husband, her family, her patients, and her friends. She also loved to laugh and didn't take herself too seriously; she was just another sista who was trying to make it. Her girlfriends, a few of them doctors, were a big part of her life. She found that as she continued on her professional journey, new friends were hard to come by and she knew that the old ones stayed with you and by you.

At 41, she had to trust in her instincts and commit time to nurturing her friendships. She had a large practice that was doing well; it would be doing better if only she could get rid of the managed care headaches. She loved her job and looked forward to coming in on most days. It was important for her to connect with her patients, to know them, and to try to help in any way. Often she felt that she was more of a psychologist than anything else, but that was okay; the mind, body, and soul were so connected and she had to address all three. She tried to connect and certainly cared for her patients on all levels, often to a fault. She was guilty of taking their problems home with her to Darren, and this sometimes caused a strain on their marriage.

Gwen prayed for her patients daily and sought God for guidance in giving them care. Her morning devotion had centered on Ms. Collins for the last two days. She knew her well and knew how hard it would be for her. Although Gwen knew the advances that had been made in the recent years, she also knew this diagnosis would initially be devastating for her patient. In her case, she would have to deal with it immediately. Gwen thought of Sabrena's daughters, whom she spoke of at every visit. She had a Christmas card with pictures of the girls on her wall, along with hundreds of other photographs of her patients' children, and she could see why Ms. Collins doted on them. Gwen knew that they would be Ms. Collins's first concern. She sighed again and began to pray:

> *"Father, I come right now asking for your strength to do what you have called me to do. Please help me talk with Ms. Collins; give me the words to say and the knowledge to apply for her good. Lord, bless her now. Let her feel your power in the room and keep her strong. You can heal in any way that you choose. Heal miraculously, heal using me and my colleagues and medication—but Father please begin the healing process even right now. Lord, help me to stand. Amen."*

Dr. Scott lifted her head and put her best face on, making sure to wipe her eyes before she walked into the exam room.

PART III

CHAPTER TWELVE

Sabrena was in a daze. She couldn't believe what Dr. Scott had told her—she just couldn't believe it. Not me! She walked to her car and began to drive. She didn't know what to say or do; she just kept hearing Dr. Scott's words over and over again in her head. She had to go somewhere and just sit. She needed to be alone.

"Aghhhhhhhhhhhhhh, no, no, this cannot be happening to me," she moaned. Sabrena heard herself screaming in her car and she couldn't stop. She saw a Holiday Inn on the right side of the street and made a frantic U-turn in the four-lane highway.

"I need a room for the night," she announced to the clerk. He looked at her oddly, seeing that she had no luggage and appeared to be spaced out.

"Are you okay?" the clerk asked as she handed her the key.

"Yes," Sabrena answered. "I just need to lie down. Thank you." She felt like she was on the outside looking in on her life. As she went into the room, she put the "Do Not Disturb" sign on the door and called Rach at work. "Rach, I need you to pick up the girls and keep them tonight. I hate to ask you, but I really need you to do this for me." She spoke in a monotone, hoping to avoid a lot of questions.

"Sabrena, are you okay? What's up?" Rach asked, questioning this odd behavior from her friend.

"Yeah, I just have something that I've got to deal with alone. Rach, please trust me on this and just help me out—okay?" Sabrena pleaded, trying not to break down on the phone.

"Of course Sabrena," Rachel said, knowing Sabrena just wanted to get off the phone. "I'll take care of it—where can I reach you?"

"On my cell, but I'll be busy for a while. It's best if I just call you—I'll call the girls before bedtime. Thanks. Good-bye, Rach."

Sabrena looked around the unfamiliar room. Her head was pounding and her heart was racing; what on earth was she going to do? She kept hearing Dr. Scott saying over and over again:

"Ms. Collins, there is no easy way to talk to you about this," Dr. Scott had said as she sat down next to her in the exam room. Funny, Sabrena hadn't noticed the extra chair before the doctor sat down.

"Dr. Scott, just tell me. It's okay. What is it, Dr. Scott? You're scaring me now. I took the medications and am taking multivitamins, so I'm feeling a bit better. I also gave my partner the medication. I dumped him first, but I did give it to him," Sabrena said. Dr. Scott, who always seemed calm, appeared very uneasy.

"Ms. Collins, your tests came back and there are several areas that were abnormal."

"Which areas? What's wrong with me?" Sabrena asked.

Dr. Scott took her hands.

It took a moment before he spoke through quivering lips, "You're HIV-positive, Sabrena. The test was positive for the HIV virus."

Dr. Scott squeezed her hand. He looked at her intently, compassion in his eyes.

Sabrena thought that she was dreaming or that she hadn't heard her correctly.

"Dr. Scott, what did you say? I don't understand, could you please repeat that again? I didn't get that."

"Sabrena, your blood test for HIV came back positive" Dr. Scott said slowly, still holding her hand. "You're infected with the virus that causes AIDS."

Sabrena didn't hear anything else her doctor said. She felt the room spinning and growing darker, and then she heard nothing. She awoke on the exam table with Denise and Dr. Scott standing next to her and a cold compress on her head. Good, this had been a dream; she'd fallen asleep while waiting for Dr. Scott. What a nightmare. But Sabrena didn't remember getting up on the exam table; she had been sitting in the chair. Oh, my God, she thought, could this really be happening?

"Ms. Collins, are you all right? You passed out. Are you okay? Do you need some water?" Denise asked, fanning her. She unbuttoned her blouse.

Sabrena was still dazed, but made herself focus on Dr. Scott. Without hesitation, she asked, "Dr. Scott, were you just telling me about my blood work? Did you tell me that I was HIV-positive or was I dreaming? Dr. Scott, did you tell me that I have HIV? Please tell me that I was dreaming!" Sabrena grabbed Dr. Scott's hand and shook it violently.

"Ms. Collins, please, let's take this slowly. Yes, yes, you're HIV-positive. I'm sorry to have to give you the news, but we must begin to plan for how you're going to handle this. You have to handle it and not let it handle you," Dr. Scott said, trying to find the words to give her the full picture.

"What about my babies, what about my girls—what about them? What am I going to do? They need me!" Sabrena began to sob and felt a sharp pain in her chest as the room started to spin again. She felt as if she was being choked; she couldn't breathe.

"Please try to calm down, Ms. Collins; I'm right here and we'll talk about all of that. You still have a life to live." Dr. Scott held Sabrena in her arms and gently rocked her.

The rocking calmed Sabrena and she tried to muffle her sobs. She heard Dr. Scott whispering, saying a quiet prayer.

"Denise, please get some water for Ms. Collins." Dr. Scott now took Sabrena's head in her hands and looked into her eyes. "Sabrena, you have to and we will get through this. I can only imagine what you're feeling, but I'm right here and we're going to take care of you." Dr. Scott took a tissue and began to wipe Sabrena's face. Sabrena bolted off the table and into a corner.

"Don't touch me, don't touch my tears—can't you get it?" Sabrena cried. "Oh God, what about my girls? Have I given it to them?" Her knees felt weak and she leaned against the wall.

Dr. Scott slowly walked over to her and hugged her again. "Shhhh, Ms. Collins, more than likely your girls are fine. Let's talk about you for a minute." She sat down with her again and held her hand as she explained the diagnosis.

Once again holding Sabrena's hands and looking at her intently, Dr. Scott said, "You're HIV-positive. The tests were checked and rechecked. It is important for us to talk about what that means and what the next steps are. You do have symptoms of the disease and your other lab tests were abnormal, so we have work to do to get a handle on this. I must tell you that I've treated and continue to treat a number of patients who are HIV-positive and have AIDS. There are so many advances in this area. But often how well people do depends on *what* they do; specifically, how they handle the diagnosis and treatment plan."

Sabrena could still not believe this was happening to her. "I'm just so confused, so shocked. Why me? I don't do drugs, haven't slept around a lot. I have children and I'm responsible. I don't know why this is happening to me. Dr. Scott, how and why did this happen to me?" Sabrena pleaded for an answer from her doctor, and began to cry again.

"I don't have an answer for you, but HIV is on the rise in black women and many are infected by their partners." Unfortunately, there were few words that Dr. Scott could give her patient. It was always difficult to break the news, and the patients usually needed time to digest the information.

The rest of the visit was a blur. Sabrena felt overloaded with information and needed to get out of the office. Dr. Scott made her promise to come back tomorrow and had asked for her cell phone number. Sabrena's head throbbed as she remembered Dr. Scott's closing words: "Ms. Collins, I'm sorry to have to tell you this but I need to be clear that you understand the full picture of where we are with this disease process. You're HIV-positive and you have symptoms of the disease caused by the HIV virus. Ms. Collins, you have AIDS. Do you understand that this is what I meant when I talked about your symptoms before?" Sabrena looked at Dr. Scott as if she were speaking a foreign language, mumbled, and ran out of the office. When she was outside, she felt the earth spinning and quickly got into her car.

CHAPTER THIRTEEN

As she lay on the hotel bed, the scene played in her head repeatedly: she had AIDS. What in God's name was she going to do? She knew a little about HIV/AIDS, but never in a thousand years could have imagined that she could get it. She had so many questions, so many thoughts, and so many fears. What about her girls? What about them? All they had in this world was her. She sobbed as she thought of Deena and Renee; what would she do, how could she get through this? Her head was throbbing and her heart was beating fast. She just wanted to wake up from this nightmare.

Sabrena was startled by the ringing of her cell phone. She looked around the strange room and slowly realized where she was. The clock read 6:10 P.M. She must have fallen asleep, but she didn't feel rested at all.

"Hello," she said.

"Hello, Ms. Collins. This is Dr. Scott. I'm just calling to make sure that you're okay." Sabrena was shocked to hear Dr. Scott on the phone and then the events of the afternoon came rushing back to her.

"Hi, Dr. Scott. I'm okay—confused, scared, and messed up but okay." Sabrena tried not to cry again. How could she have any more tears?

"Are you at home?" Dr. Scott asked.

"No, I needed to be alone. I stopped at the Holiday Inn near your office. I'm going to stay here tonight. I hope my head will be clearer tomorrow."

"Just remember that you have everything to live for. Life is rough, but not hopeless. I'm worried about you and just wanted to check on you. I know this is probably the most difficult news you've ever heard, but we have to face this challenge head on. I do want you to come back to the office tomorrow. You left without making an appointment. Why don't you come here before any of my regularly scheduled patients in the morning, about 7:30? I'll come in early to meet you." Dr. Scott hoped Sabrena would be up to seeing her again. Often patients began to avoid her after she gave them the diagnosis and precious time was wasted. Dr. Scott also wanted to make sure that Sabrena didn't feel like she had given her a death warrant. She knew that the emotions of the day were running deep with Sabrena and that she had been taken totally by surprise. Dr. Scott would come in early or stay late to help her patient through this and get her the best care possible. They had to discuss all her results; she wanted to recommend starting medications right away.

"Dr. Scott, I don't know—maybe I need a few days; I really don't know what to do or say," Sabrena said, not really wanting to hear anymore about the diagnosis.

"I know, Ms. Collins, but I need to answer your questions and help you face this. I promise that it will help. Trust me. Tonight you're going to have thousands of questions and concerns going through your head. I'll be here to answer them and to put things in perspective. You're right around the corner, so just come by tomorrow and we can finish our discussion. You're not in this alone."

"All right, Dr. Scott, thanks for everything. I'll be there at 7:30." Sabrena hung up the phone and then called her job. Fortunately, Vivian hadn't left the department.

"Hey Vivian, how are you?"

"Fine, just walking out. How 'bout you—you sound horrible, are you feeling well?" Vivian asked with concern.

"Actually not, I don't feel good and won't be in on tomorrow. I'll let you know about the next day. I'll have a doctor's note," Sabrena said, trying to end the conversation quickly.

"Is there something that I can do? Is everything okay?" Vivian was becoming more worried by the minute. She knew Sabrena must be really ill not to come in. Sabrena was guarded about her personal life, even though they had worked together for years and were friends.

"No, I'll be all right. It's just a bug. I'll speak with you tomorrow. Good-bye." Sabrena hung up the phone and lay back down. She didn't have the strength to call Rach yet; fortunately, she knew the girls were in good hands. The thought of her daughters brought tears to her eyes.

Sabrena found a vending machine at the end of the hall and bought a Coke and a bag of chips. She felt numb, like she was walking through a dream with Dr. Scott's words booming in her head. She didn't know what to do with her body or mind, didn't know how to shut out the words. She was just lost, It was good she was here, since there was no way she could let her daughters see her like this. What would happen to them? Would she be alive to see them get married or see her grand-kids? Would she even live long enough to see her girls graduate from elementary school? Sabrena's tears rolled down her puffy face. What would she do? Who could she turn to? What if people found out? How would her daughters be treated at school or by their friends? How would her own friends treat her? What about work? How long would she be able to work? What about money, what about anything?

Her life was over. Sabrena didn't know what her next steps would be. She only knew she was in hell and that somehow she had done something in her life so terrible she deserved this punishment. She didn't want to live with it, but what could she do? She couldn't end her life; that could scar her daughters. She just had to figure it out. Dr. Scott said that they would talk and get a plan together. What kind of plans could help her now—burial plans?

Sabrena didn't know much about HIV/AIDS, but she had heard that black women were getting it more than any other group. She thought that women who did drugs or were prostitutes had the biggest risk, not a person like her. She thought of all the men she had slept with—compared to her friends, not a lot. Sabrena counted on her fingers and there were only six men she had ever had intercourse with, and two of them had been her husbands. Why her? Why now? Who gave it to her? The only guy in the last three years had been Steve. He had given her chlamydia and trich—could it be him? How long had she had it? How long did she have to live? Had she given it to her girls? What about all their friends? How were they going to deal with her? Would she get sick and lose a lot of weight? All these questions kept spinning in Sabrena's head. She took off her clothes and lay back on the bed. She couldn't keep the tears from flowing; she thought she had cried herself out but they just kept coming. She looked at the clock and it was after midnight. Where had the day gone? She hadn't called her girls to tell them good-night. This would be the first time in their lives that they hadn't heard her voice before going to sleep. Was this a sign of things to come?

CHAPTER FOURTEEN

Sabrena jolted up in the bed, hearing her own screams. She was sweaty and her heart was beating fast. She frantically looked around the room. She thought she was having a nightmare but as the memories of the day flooded back to her, she realized she was living a nightmare. She decided to take a cool shower and found the basic toiletries in the hotel bathroom. It was after 5:00 A.M. and she would try to pull herself together. She felt a bit of peace from the water beating down on her body. She looked at her full breasts and flat stomach, felt her rounded bottom, and wondered what would happen in the days to come. Would she look like the pictures she had seen?

Her cousin Edward had died of AIDS. Sabrena remembered it well, though it was over 10 years ago. He was gay and had lived in New York for a while. She always liked Edward; they listened to music together and he was sort of a big brother. She remembered that when his mother brought him home from New York, he was thin and had an oxygen tank. Everyone whispered about him. No one really ever said anything to his mother, but they all knew that it was AIDS.

One of Sabrena's friends, Theresa, was a minister, and when they talked about it, she said that God was punishing Edward for his lifestyle. Sabrena didn't agree and she always took time to go see him once a week. Sabrena enjoyed their talks. Often, she would just hold his hand and try to feed him. She laughed at a passing memory of him asking her to get him a rum and Coke. Sabrena had protested, but he insisted, saying, "What, it ain't gonna kill me, and if it does— so what!" Edward did have a sense of humor right up until the end.

She remembered the day he died: just an ordinary Tuesday, but it rained like she had never seen it rain before. It started early in the morning with some lightning, and then, as if on a timer, at 11:00 A.M.

it stopped. A few minutes later she got a call about Edward's death. Sabrena remembered the whispers, the family members who refused to attend the funeral, the hard time they had finding a mortician. She remembered her auntie, his mother, and the sadness that followed her for the rest of her life. Sabrena didn't think his mother ever got over Edward's death; she died about three years later.

Sabrena thought of her mother and brother. How could she ever tell them? Her mother would surely disown her for good. She shook her head violently, trying to erase the memory of yesterday and the thoughts of today. All she could do was just go see Dr. Scott and take one step at a time. She had been in the shower for only an hour, but it seemed like an eternity. She still had an hour before she had to leave to go see Dr. Scott. After that appointment, she was going to go home. The girls would be at school and she would have the house to herself. She decided to write down some questions for Dr. Scott to try to get a better understanding.

Gwen fought the urge to stay in bed longer and it didn't help that her husband Darren reached for her playfully. "Hey, babes, what about just hanging out with me for another thirty minutes? I could keep you nicely occupied." He smiled mischievously and began to kiss her neck. "The best time to exercise is in the morning, you taught me that."

"Oh, I would love to, honey, but I'm meeting a patient at 7:30 and I've got to get myself together before I see her," Gwen said as she kissed him on his forehead. "You know, I told you about her last night. This is rough."

"Don't make me beg. . . . Please don't make me," Darren said, as he began to remove her silk gown. "Think of me as a patient, I need you; I mean I *really* need you right now, its an *emergency*!" He begin to nuzzle her again, and as he lifted her nightgown over her head, her protests fell to the wayside. Gwen moaned as she thought, I'm the doctor, but that boy must have taken some anatomy classes!

Sabrena stood outside Dr. Scott's office door. It was 7:45 A.M. and no one was answering the door. She didn't see Dr. Scott's car in her reserved space and wondered if she had gotten the time wrong. Just when she had decided to leave, she heard heels clicking on the linoleum floor and soon saw Dr. Scott rushing in the back door. Within a few minutes, Dr. Scott had opened the front door and led her into her private office. "Hi, Ms. Collins, I apologize for being late. Do you want some coffee or tea?"

Sabrena had never been in any doctor's private office but she was sure that they didn't all look like this. The office was mauve with fresh flowers, nice African-American artwork on the walls and all of Dr. Scott's degrees. There was also a large picture of a very handsome man on her desk; Sabrena assumed that it was her husband.

"No, thank you, I am fine, Dr. Scott. Thank you for meeting with me this early. I have so many questions and am just a wreck." Sabrena then launched into her list of questions.

"What is the possibility that I have given HIV to my daughters?" This was her greatest concern.

"Well, HIV is passed by intimate contact like sexual intercourse, sharing needles, and in very rare cases now, blood transfusions. It is extremely unlikely that you passed the virus to your daughters. If you want to be one hundred percent certain and ease your mind, you can get them tested." Dr. Scott understood Ms. Collins's concerns and she tried to reassure her as best she could. Sabrena breathed an audible sigh of relief.

"Ms. Collins, I need to repeat a few things for you and I can answer as many questions as you have. You are diagnosed with Acquired Immunodeficiency Syndrome, which we know as AIDS. In order to have AIDS, your body must have been exposed to the human immunodeficiency virus, which we call HIV, the virus that causes AIDS. The first stage is usually being HIV-positive. We determine a diagnosis of AIDS based on your symptoms, your test results, and something called CD4 or T-cell counts." Dr. Scott was careful to speak slowly and to use the pamphlets in her office. "Are you with me so far?"

"Yes, I think that I am, but what is a CD4 or the T cell?" Sabrena was trying to follow all of Dr. Scott's words.

"Simply put, these are the cells that tell us your ability to fight infection. The whole big picture with AIDS is that your body cannot fight off infection like it should because your immune system, your natural fighting system, is damaged. Because your body lacks the ability to fight off infections, even the common cold can become a problem if you have AIDS." Dr. Scott pulled out another pamphlet with diagrams.

"Your CD4 count is 133; we diagnose AIDS whenever this count falls below 200. I'll give you a pamphlet that talks about these numbers in more details. This morning, I don't want to overwhelm you and I know that this is very hard. Is this helping? "

"Yes, doctor—I understand a little better. How long have I had AIDS or HIV?" Sabrena knew that her last test was negative, but that was years ago.

"Well, I really can't pinpoint the date of your infection. It usually takes about ten years after being infected by HIV before people develop AIDS, but a small percentage of people could develop AIDS within fewer than two years after exposure to the HIV virus." Dr. Scott continued, "We need to get more test results, which include a viral load, that may or may not give us a better idea of when you became infected."

"I'm confused; I had a negative test a few years ago. Doesn't that mean that I became infected after that test?" Sabrena remembered the test for her life insurance and she hadn't worried about HIV since that test was negative. She had not really worried about it before, because she didn't think she was at risk for the virus.

"You could've been in the very early stages of viral infection and your body may not have formed the antibodies to HIV. When we test for HIV, we are looking to see if your body has been exposed to the virus. If your body has been exposed to HIV, it makes natural substances called antibodies, in response to that exposure. It usually takes between two to eight weeks for the antibodies to show up in your blood tests. About ninety-seven percent of people will develop antibodies within the first three months of the time of infection. However, in some cases, it can take longer to develop the antibodies to HIV." She asked about any drug history, number of partners, and if any of Sabrena's former lovers had been bisexual or gay and if she had ever slept with any former prison inmates. Dr. Scott also talked about blood transfusions. Sabrena was confused and answered as best she could.

"Dr. Scott, do I need to tell everyone that I've ever slept with?" Sabrena asked.

"Well, that's certainly up to you. However, you should definitely talk with your most recent sexual partners, so that they can get tested. This is especially important if you didn't use condoms with them." Dr. Scott warned Sabrena that this conversation might be difficult, but assured her that her testing was confidential and that she would be happy to test any of her partners. Sabrena could already feel even more anxiety as she thought about how she was going to tell her family and friends.

Sabrena had been in Dr. Scott's office for over an hour when the nurse, Denise, came in to tell Dr. Scott that her first patient had arrived. As if on cue, Dr. Scott began to talk to Sabrena about the things she would have to do immediately. She was going to give her a lot of information to read and suggested that she pick up a book that would explain more. "Ms. Collins, it's important for you to know that the diagnosis is not a death sentence. We have to work to keep you healthy."

No matter what Dr. Scott said, Sabrena had known people with AIDS, and even though one infected person in her neighborhood seemed to be doing well, Sabrena couldn't help thinking of those who had died of AIDS. She finished her list of questions and asked when she should come back to the office.

Dr. Scott wanted her to read the information and to come back in three days. She also gave her information on types of medications that she might be prescribed.

Sabrena was still in shock, but she realized that, though things weren't great, the end of the world hadn't yet come. She was going to have to learn all she could about the disease so that she could live for her girls. Sabrena still had so many questions swimming in her head, but she knew Dr. Scott had to go and had given her a lot of time already. Sabrena knew more than she had twenty-four hours ago, but was a bit confused by some of the terms and "doctor talk." Dr. Scott was better than most doctors in breaking things down. She had drawn her pictures, circled information in the brochures, and given her places to get more information.

"Ms. Collins, I want you to take it slow. You will undoubtedly go through a lot of emotions in the upcoming months. I am here for you and will help guide you through it all the best that I can. You can start by reading this book by Dr. Eric Goosby, an expert in HIV. Just read a few pages at a time. I find that it helps patients learn more about this disease."

Sabrena looked at the book titled, *Living with HIV/AIDS: The Black Person's Guide to Survival*. She quickly put it in her purse. She didn't want anyone to see her walk out with it, but was grateful for the information.

"Thank you, Dr. Scott; thanks for everything." Sabrena felt awkward, but was quickly warmed by Dr. Scott's hug and reassuring pat on her back.

CHAPTER FIFTEEN

Sabrina was glad that the girls weren't home, but Boxer came out to greet her. The house looked like a tornado had come through. She loved Rach but she was certainly no housekeeper. When they lived together during Rach's college years and right after Sabrena's first divorce, they had to have a heart-to-heart on cleaning and living. They agreed that Sabrena would do all the cooking, because Rach was horrible cook, and all the cleaning. Rach was a bit of a slob, but agreed to pay more of the rent. Everybody won.

As Sabrena surveyed the damage, she said to herself, "Hmmpppphhhh, I have my work cut out for me this afternoon." She started to wash dishes and took out some chicken to thaw. She had all day with no interruptions and she would use it to make the girls and Rach a nice dinner. Maybe that would take her mind off her mess of a life. Boxer came and rubbed against her leg, letting her know that he was happy to see her. Funny, how the little things bring you pleasure: the warmth of the cat reminded her that she was still human and needed to be touched and loved. Sabrena turned on a local radio station. She listened for a few minutes to the latest rap and hip/hop songs, and then turned to a soothing Gospel station. She continued to clean the kitchen, season the chicken, and cut up potatoes for dinner. The girls loved her fried chicken and so did Rach. She only cooked it once or twice a month because she worried about clogged arteries. She laughed to herself at the irony of it; she worked so hard to eat right and stay in shape, but now she was HIV-positive and no amount of push-ups or salads could fix that. She had tried to protect her heart, but she hadn't thought or acted seriously about protecting her body.

In the midst of her laughter, the tears came again. Then one of her favorite songs came on the radio. It was "Stand" by Donnie McClurkin.

"What do you do, when you've done all you can and it seems that it's never enough," he crooned.

Sabrena sat on the couch and sang along with the song, "When you've prayed and cried, cried and prayed . . . you just stand; let the Lord see you through, just stand. . . ." By the end of the song, Sabrena was sobbing to the point of no control. A voice inside her repeated the words, "prayed and cried," and she sank to her knees. Yesterday and even this morning, she couldn't pray. She felt like God didn't want to hear her and that this was His punishment. On her knees, she began to talk softly to God. The words she'd learned as a child came first:

> *"Our Father, who art in heaven, hallowed be thy name, thy kingdom come, thy will be done—God, is this your will? Is this your will for my life? How can it be? Am I that bad of a person that you would curse me like this? How can I ever believe that you love me when you have done this to me? Do I deserve it? What did I do—I loved, that's it—I just loved and now my heart is broken and my body is infected. Lord, forgive me, but I don't understand. How can I stand this? How can my babies stand this? How can I make it through this? Please help me, please help me, please make this go away."*

Sabrena realized that she was screaming by the end of her prayer. She wiped her eyes and stood up. She tried to finish making dinner.

"Hey Rach, can you come over for dinner?" Sabrena found Rach on her cell phone.

"Yeah, you know that a sista likes to eat. What's up?" Rach tried to lighten Sabrena's tone, but she knew that something heavy was going on with her friend. She hoped that it didn't have anything to do with that troll, Steve.

"Nothing, I'm okay but need you to pick up Deena and Renee."

"No problem, you get some rest."

Sabrena could always count on Rach in a tight squeeze and loved her for her strength. She went into her room and hid the book and pamphlets in her nightstand under a stack of papers. She would read them after making dinner; she had been saturated with information today and just couldn't take another thing. She heard the phone ringing and glanced at caller ID. It was her job.

"Hello," Sabrena answered.

"Hi, Sabrena, this is Vivian. How are you doing?"

"Oh, I'm okay. I don't know about tomorrow yet, though." Sabrena assumed that Vivian was calling to see if she would be coming into the store.

"I don't care about you coming to work, I care about you. Is there anything I can do? You know, I'm off tomorrow. I'll come in for you and I can drop off some food or something if you need it." Vivian responded with her usual caring, almost motherly tone.

"No, I'm fine, but I may need a few more days off."

"No problem, it's done. Sabrena, I know I'm your boss and we work together, but I would like to think that we're friends. If ever you or your girls need anything, just let me know. I really mean it; you don't sound good and I'm worried." Vivian liked Sabrena, saw how hard she worked and how caring she was to everyone. Sabrena touched people and she had certainly touched her life.

"Thank you so much, Vivian, and I know we're friends. I'll talk with you tomorrow," Sabrena replied and quickly hung up the phone. She wondered how Vivian and her other co-workers would react if they knew she had AIDS. "Oh my God. I have AIDS," Sabrena whispered aloud, feeling the free-flowing tears stream down her cheeks again.

CHAPTER SIXTEEN

Sabrena awoke at the sound of the alarm she'd set before taking a nap. She wanted to give herself plenty of time before the girls came home to get herself together. She had nearly finished dinner and decided to take a quick shower and put on some makeup. As Sabrena looked at herself in the mirror, she realized that she was going to need more than makeup to get rid of her puffy, red eyes and she started the hunt for some Visine. She found it, and a couple drops later, her eyes looked much better. Too bad they didn't make Visine for faces, she thought, as she poked at her puffy face. She gave up and just combed her hair down, put on some makeup, and tried to appear as normal as possible. She put on one of her lounging velour jumpers and went to the kitchen to finish the salad. She soon heard the girls running through the door.

"Mommy, Mommy," Renee and Deena sang in unison with Renee holding up her arms to be picked up and Deena hugging her at the legs. Sabrena was so glad to see them. It felt like it had been years rather than just a day.

"Hi, my princesses, I missed you." She squeezed them tightly and she felt tears welling in her eyes. She kissed them on the forehead. She made sure to keep her mouth tightly closed. "I made dinner, go wash up." Rach stood near the door and walked slowly into the kitchen, watching Sabrena intently. She knew her friend well and knew that something was very wrong.

"Hey girl, what's up?" Rach asked as she picked up a chicken wing and began to nibble. She knew the routine. She'd ask, Sabrena would say "nothing," Rach would give her a few minutes, and then Sabrena would let it all out. They were sisters of the soul.

"Oh nothing, we'll talk later. How's the chicken?" Sabrena turned her back to Rach; she knew that if she looked in her face she would burst into tears. She had to talk with someone, but she needed to get her girls fed and prepared for tomorrow before opening this up.

"Okay Bre, but you know that I know you, and I know that there is something very wrong. Whenever you need me, I gotcha," Rach said, using her childhood nickname, which she reserved for only the most serious occasions. Sabrena shrugged her shoulders and fought back the tears but she needed a hug and reached for her friend. Once she felt Rach's embrace, she began to cry silently into her shoulder, trying not to make any sounds for the girls to hear. She quickly pulled away, not wanting her tears to touch Rachel.

"Rach, Rach, I don't know what to do," Sabrena whispered, "This is too much for me to bear."

"Bre, just relax. Go to the bathroom and wipe your face before the girls come out. We'll have dinner and then talk. There's s nothing too big for the dynamic duo!" Rach said with a smile. Inside, Rach was worrying more and more by the minute. Was it money? Was it that no-good dog Steve? What could be causing all of this bizarre behavior? Sabrena had never unexpectedly not come home like yesterday and she had never, in all the years that she had known her, failed to call to tell the girls good-night. Shoot, Rach remembered keeping Deena when she was about eight months old and Sabrena called from Cancun to say good-night to her. Even though Deena had no idea what a telephone was, she did know her mother's voice. Time would tell, and no matter what, like always, they would be there for each other.

After dinner and playing the soul train line with the girls until they were ready for bed, Rach sat Sabrena down on the couch.

"Bre, tell me what's going on?"

"I can't tell you, I can't tell anyone yet. I have got to get this straight in my mind first," Sabrena told her beloved friend.

"Bre, we've known each other all of our lives—what is so hard that you can't tell me? You have to know that I love you and only want to help you, but I see that there is something really wrong and I can't stand to see you like this." Rach grabbed her friend's hands and put them in hers. She looked Sabrena in the eyes. "There isn't anything or anyone that can come between us. There is no problem that we can't figure out together. I'll not have you hold this in, I can't do it." Rach saw the tears in Sabrena's eyes and she reached to wipe them off her cheeks. Sabrena quickly turned her head and moved from the couch.

"Rach, I know, but I just need some time to pull this together. Trust me, okay?" Sabrena pleaded with her friend and Rach understood not to go any further.

"Well, I'm staying over here tonight. There is another chicken leg that has my name on it. You know I only love ya 'cause you can cook." Rach tried to lighten the moment but Sabrena was deep in thought.

Sabrena lay down and tried to sleep but felt like the air was being sucked out of her lungs. It was late, the girls were in bed, and Rach was asleep in the guest room, which they also called Rach's room. She had tucked her girls in and had read to them until they both fell off to sleep. Sabrena had taken the glass of wine Rach had offered her in hopes of it helping her sleep, but she continued to feel uncomfortable. She decided to read one of the pamphlets that Dr. Scott had given her and locked the door. After a few moments, though, all the terms and information overwhelmed her and she put it back in the drawer. She decided to go sit on her porch. She needed to find some peace.

As she looked into the sky, she had flashbacks of her first night here and how she had felt alone and scared. At the time, she hadn't known how she was going to make it, but she'd vowed that she would and that her girls would be taken care of. Sabrena hadn't faltered on that promise and they were doing okay—until this. How could she ever recover?

She hated herself for crying again and felt like such a weakling. Her mother had always told her that she was weak.

"Mommy, I fell down and hurt my leg," Sabrena remembered, crying to her mother when she was about Deena's age. Her mother had looked at her and hissed, "Sabrena! Stop that crying. What's that gonna do? Stop it *now*! Big girls don't cry, they just take it!" Sabrena would then run into her room and sit in the closet. She saw the evil in her mother's eyes and she was so afraid. She really started crying then. Her big brother, Gerald, eventually came into the room, opened the closet, and hugged her and told her not to worry about Mommy. "She loves you," he would say, "It's just her way." Sabrena remembered her brother wiping off her knee and kissing it.

She loved her brother and could always depend on him to be her savior. As she grew up, no one messed with her, because they knew that Gerald would beat them up over his baby sister. She remembered when she finally left Carlton. Gerald came to see her one night and she told him everything. He was very quiet the whole time and then told her he was going to see a friend. Later, she found out he had driven two hours to see Carlton and had told him that he would kill him if he ever came near his sister or his nieces again. They had a special bond, which made it all the harder to think about telling him her news. What could Gerald do now? What could anyone do?

Sabrena felt chilled and went inside. She couldn't resist the urge to go into Rach's room.

Rach was sound asleep. Sabrena lay down next to her friend. "Rach, Rach, are you awake?" Sabrena whispered.

"Huh, what?" Rach responded in a daze.

"Rach, wake up, are you awake?"

"Well, I am now, even if I don't wanna be."

"There's no way to say this but to just say it." Sabrena took a deep breath and went on, "Dr. Scott told me that I'm HIV-positive and that I have AIDS." She searched Rach's eyes for a reaction, but she only found shock and disbelief.

Rach sat straight up in the bed and said, "What, what did you say, Sabrena? What? Tell me again." Rach put her hands on her head and massaged her temples. "Now, repeat what you said. Bre, please repeat it."

"You heard me right. Dr. Scott said that I have AIDS." Sabrena dropped her head in shame and began to sob. She felt Rach's arms around her and they cried together. It was Rach who broke the embrace.

"Sabrena, there isn't anything too hard for us. I'm here for you and you're gonna be all right. I don't care what the doctor says, you're going to be all right. Do you hear me?" Rach was crying, but firm in her conviction. Her mind was racing, but she knew that she had to be strong for Sabrena. She was the closest thing to a sister that she had ever had and she'd be damned if she was going to wimp out on her.

"Sabrena, we're going to make it! No pity party, only positive thoughts. We've got to handle our business."

Sabrena looked at Rach and partially believed her. Rach was the rock on the outside, but inside she was warm and frail. Sabrena was shocked that she didn't ask her the questions that she would have wanted to know—the who, what, when, where, and how. She knew that they would come, but for tonight, she was just going to be her friend, her sister. Sabrena hugged Rach again and they lay down holding each other as they both wept silent tears.

Rach's snoring woke up Sabrena. She looked at her best friend sleeping. She was so thankful for Rach and knew that it would be this friendship that would buoy her through a mess. Sabrena eased out of Rach's bed and went to her room. She looked into her backyard and wondered what the rest of her tomorrows would hold.

Rach looked at the clock next to the bed and was amazed she was awake so early. She was a late sleeper and had an unforgivable habit of being late to work and everywhere else. But she was wide awake. She looked around the room. Suddenly, all of the previous night's conversation came rushing back.

"Sabrena," she whispered. She didn't really know what else to say or do. They had both known people with HIV and even AIDS, but this was just too close to home for Rach. She thought of all of the drama that Sabrena had survived and now this. What was going to happen? What about Rach's goddaughters, Deena and Renee? Thousands of thoughts flooded Rachel's head. As she looked for a robe, she knew that she would have to be strong for Sabrena and that it would be as it always was, them against the world.

Her mind wandered back to when she was a freshman in college and got pregnant; she couldn't tell her family or the father. She'd been seeing a basketball player, Everett, and was crazy about him. He hated wearing condoms, so she had gone to the school clinic and gotten fitted for a diaphragm. She and Everett were inseparable, or so she thought. Rach had used the diaphragm, but decided that all the messy foam/spermicide wasn't always necessary. A few months later she had missed two periods, but was in denial about a pregnancy. Rach called Sabrena. They talked about it, and Rach had decided to wait until spring break to get a pregnancy test. She remembered telling Sabrena that she couldn't go to her doctor because she was on her mother's insurance and her mother would kill her if she ever knew. Rach smiled as she remembered coming back to her dorm and seeing Sabrena in the lobby waiting with a large bag. Sabrena had bought every type of pregnancy test that there was and had Rach drink two Cokes to help her pee enough for all the tests.

The tests were positive. As Rach struggled to come to grips with the pregnancy, Sabrena took charge. Sabrena, armed with her credit card, made an appointment for her to see a local doctor. She paid for everything, although she really didn't have the money. Rach was terrified and Sabrena was her rock. She decided to have an abortion but didn't want to tell Everett, because she was scared he would leave her. Rach still cringed at the memory. She cried through the whole procedure and clung to Sabrena's hand. Somewhere in that room, Rach grew up. She decided she was going to make *Rachel* a priority. Funny, Sabrena never asked how Rach had let herself get pregnant, and she never judged her. Afterwards, they only talked about it when Rach brought it up. Rach chuckled as she remembered the cheap little hotel room that Sabrena had rented for her so she wouldn't have to go back to the dorm. Her friend had come to her rescue and carried her through one of the roughest periods of her young life. Every once in awhile, Rach thought of the child that she had aborted, the baby who would have been about three years older than Deena.

Fresh tears misted Rach's eyes. She loved no one as much as she loved Sabrena. She needed no one as she needed the safety and comfort of their friendship. What would Rach do now? How could she do anything but just be there for Sabrena? Their friendship had been solid for so long. Rach remembered the relationships, Sabrena's marriages, and her scare with breast cancer. They had gone through it all. Now that they were almost 40, and ready to embrace their womanhood, how could they embrace this diagnosis? Rach felt her back stiffen as she tried to hold back her tears. She couldn't fall to pieces; she had work to do with Sabrena. She knew that she couldn't go into her office today. There was no way that she could leave Sabrena alone.

Rach was glad to see Sabrena stirring in the kitchen and thought that she smelled bacon cooking.

"Hey, that sure smells good. I was going to cook this morning," Rach said. She tried to sound as normal as possible. She could tell that Sabrena had been crying, just as she had.

"Yeah, right, who in this house was going to eat it?" Sabrena said, laughing. She began making eggs and grits to complete the breakfast.

"What are those?" Rach noticed that Sabrena was cracking the eggs with plastic gloves on her hands.

"Oh, I just wanted to—" Sabrena stammered and stared off into space.

"Just wanted to—what? Have you lost your mind! I hope that ain't for me or the girls. Fool, I'm gonna take you to the psych ward!" Rach said, as she forcibly removed the plastic gloves from her friend's hands. Rach knew that Sabrena would go totally overboard on this and it was up to her to keep her from the edge.

"What the heck are you doing with those gloves? You look like you're trying to poison me for sure!" She then burst into laughter and grabbed her friend in a bear hug. They heard the underarm seam rip on the tight robe, which led to even more laughter.

"Girl, I gotta lose some weight, your little stuff isn't fitting me at all." They laughed so hard that tears were running down their cheeks. Rach quickly and intentionally wiped Sabrena's face and held it between her hands.

"Bre, we're going to be fine; I know about this a little and what I don't know, what we don't know, we'll learn. Let's not go overboard. You can't walk around like the boy in the bubble," Rach said and began laughing again as she thought of that stupid John Travolta movie.

"Okay, I just want to . . ." Sabrena started to explain.

"Shut up and cook my breakfast. I'm hungry and I'm sure that we've woken up the two little monsters." Rach laughed again as she thought of the girls. They were great, but boy, were they a handful. As if on cue, Deena came walking into the room.

"What ya'll laughin' at?" Deena asked as she climbed on the kitchen stool.

"Oh, nothing, pumpkin, did you sleep good?" Sabrena asked as she kissed her on her fat cheeks.

"Yes, Ma'am. Renee is still 'sleep and I think that she wet the bed. The room smells funny."

The morning was in full swing. Rach showered as Sabrena got the girls ready for school. When Rach came back into the living room, she noticed that Sabrena wasn't dressed.

"I'll take the girls to school. Why don't you take a bath and relax. We'll talk when I get back."

"Thanks," Sabrena said. "Come here, girls, and give Mommy a kiss. Auntie Rach is going to drop you off." Sabrena hugged her girls tightly and kissed them on their foreheads as she walked them to the door.

CHAPTER SEVENTEEN

Sabrena was grateful that today was her scheduled day off and that she could use the time to try to get herself together for work tomorrow. As she sank into her tub, her mind began to drift back to when the large garden tub was installed. It had been a present from Steve early on in their relationship. The first night she'd slept at Steve's, she'd squealed when she saw his garden tub. Steve had come running into the bathroom as if something were wrong.

"What happened, Sabrena—are you okay?" Steve asked.

"Yes, I'm in heaven. I didn't know that you had a garden tub. I love to soak in these." Sabrena ran the water and found some dishwashing liquid to serve as bubble bath. Steve had seen her smiling and watched how happy and tiny she looked in the tub—like the country mouse in the Taj Mahal. A few weeks later, Steve had asked Sabrena to hold the entire day open for him and he took her all over the city. Little did Sabrena know, she'd been set up. When she and Steve got back home, the house was empty and Steve had asked her to show him where she kept the towels in her bathroom. Sabrena almost got annoyed by the silly question; Steve knew how to find the towels. She walked into her newly remodeled bathroom with the huge tub and separate shower. Sabrena smiled as she remembered the day. No one had ever done anything like this for her. They had "christened" the tub that night.

"It's over, especially now," Sabrena whispered to herself. Had Steve infected her? Did he intentionally infect her? How could he have put her and her girls at risk? Dr. Scott said she couldn't pinpoint the time she was infected. She said something about it being within ten years. She had slept with only six men in her whole life. Why then did she have HIV? She climbed out of the tub and toweled off.

She began to cry. She looked at her body in the full length mirror and thought she looked good to be almost 40, but how long would that last? She touched her breasts and wondered if she would ever feel a man's hands again. How could she? She was damaged and contagious. How could she ever feel the warmth of a man's lips on her body? Ever feel a man inside her again? Who would ever want to even be seen in public with her?

"How could I even think about it? That's what got me into this mess!" Sabrena screamed and fell in a heap to the floor. Her tears were flooding her face. She saw a bottle of aspirin sitting on her counter and in that fleeting moment she wondered how many she would have to take for all this to be over. "No, I can't do that. My girls can't have a mom who killed herself." Sabrena grabbed the bottle and threw it against the wall. The bottle was child resistant, so it just bounced to the floor. She began laughing at the site of her naked body and the rolling aspirin bottle. She continued to laugh as tears rolled down her cheeks.

"Sabrena, are you okay?" Rach's voice startled Sabrena, who hadn't heard her come in. She quickly wiped her eyes. "Yeah, I'm all right. I'll be out in a minute."

They spent the day watching TV and talking but mainly just sitting as they always did in troubled times—together.

Sabrena made sandwiches for lunch. "Rach, what am I going to do?" she asked.

"I don't know," Rach said, "but we'll make it." Rach noticed that Sabrena had seemed to age in the last few days. She knew it was from worrying. "We should go get some books and read everything Dr. Scott gave you. We have to know what we're facing. I also want to go with you to your next appointment, if you don't mind. I think that it would be good for you to have someone there with you."

"You know, I'm not so worried about me. I am, but you know what I mean. I am worried about the girls. I'm all they got. . . ." Sabrena felt a headache coming on and the gravity of her situation had her glued to the floor. She felt so dirty, so low, and helpless.

"Deena and Renee will be fine. Let's not start talking about you not being around and that crap! I'm serious, Bre, you know that I love you like a sister and I'm hurting for you. But I also know that this isn't a death sentence. The new medicines have really turned this thing around. Look at Magic Johnson. We just have to make sure that you get the best treatment possible, get your rest, and live your life in spite of this. Sabrena, you can't die before your time. I'm not trying to sound all together. This is hard for me, too, but I just know that this is going to be okay. When its not, then we deal with it." Rach spoke firmly to convince both of them. She couldn't be a part of a death watch.

Silence passed between them as they forced themselves to eat, deep in thought. The silence didn't last, though, as fortunately, something stupid was on Jerry Springer that they could laugh over together.

"Who should I tell?"

"Well, me—of course and after that, who cares?" Rach said lightly. "What did Dr. Scott say?"

"She said that it was up to me, but that I could give the health department the names and addresses of my partners, if I have them. They would contact persons anonymously, but I don't remember all that she said." Sabrena didn't even want to think about calling or telling anyone. "What about Steve and Francis, those are the only people who I've been with since the time I took the HIV test for insurance. However, she said that I could have been positive at that time, but it may have been too early to detect. If that's the case, and if I need to go back ten years, that would include Carlton, right?"

"Hmmph, I think we should talk with Dr. Scott and not make any sudden moves," Rach said, thinking all the while about that dog of a man Steve, he had to be the one. He was never 'bout anything anyway; trying to be all suave and nice but Rach had seen his kind over and over again. Bre managed to always pick the same kind of guys, self-centered men who didn't appreciate her. She'd not had much luck with men at all so it really could have been any of them, even that control freak Carlton whom Rach had introduced to her.

"Girl, you slept with that guy Francis? I forgot about him, did you tell me that?" Rach asked. She remembered that fine but rather thuggish brother they'd met at one of her sorority functions.

"I don't remember. Believe me, it was uneventful and only happened twice. He was seeing me and everybody else," Sabrena told her friend. Francis was a distant and rather unpleasant memory. She was glad she hadn't gotten too involved with him but regretted giving her body to him. She had been lonely and that was that. "Let's change the subject, Rach. Have you heard from Theresa? What's she up to?" Rach took the hint and filled Sabrena in on the latest family gossip. They caught up and spent the rest of the afternoon reminiscing about the past. They enjoyed just being together. Rach left to go home and Sabrena went to pick up the girls. She took them to Chucky E. Cheese as a treat, but it was a treat for Sabrena, too. She loved seeing them laugh and run loose. Deena was so protective of Renee, and Sabrena was glad they were so close. They reminded her of herself and Gerald; he had always taken care of her. As she thought about her brother, she wondered how she could even begin to tell him what was going on.

CHAPTER EIGHTEEN

Sabrena felt herself becoming sad again, but instead of letting herself cry, she just whispered a prayer and watched the girls play. They fell asleep in the car on the ride home; Sabrena woke them long enough to get them in the house and put them to bed. She watched them sleep and kissed each of them on the forehead. For the first time in days, she thought how lucky she really was to be their mother.

Sabrena had a glass of wine and called her mother before going to bed. In order to talk to her mother she often needed some wine. Sabrena asked, "Hello, Mom, how are you?"

"Hey Sabrena, well, how are you? Glad to know that you're still alive. You ain't called me in over three weeks." Her mother was in her typical negative mode.

Sabrena bristled at her mother's tone. The phone did work both ways, for heaven's sake. God forbid that her mom ever just called her. "Sorry, Mom, the girls have kept me running. How're you?" Sabrena tried to redirect the conversation.

"I'm okay; your brother Gerald called yesterday and sent me a ticket to Los Angeles for July Fourth. At least *he* knows how to treat his mother." The stream of negativity was endless, but, over the years, Sabrena had become immune to the venom.

"Good Mom, how's my big brother?" Sabrena asked. She made a mental note to call him later on today. Sabrena continued to talk to her mom about the girls and just engage in some small talk. Afterwards, she felt as if she had done her duty with her. She did have to admit that her mother really seemed to love her granddaughters and they loved their Grammy. The girls spent several weeks in the summer with her, and she always sent a big box with clothes and toys for their birthdays, Easter, and Christmas. It amazed Sabrena how a woman who had been cold to her since she could remember could be so warm to her girls. Sabrena loved her mother but refused to open her heart again to her. She had learned a long time ago that it would only lead to disappointment. She really didn't know why her mother treated her with such coldness. . . . Maybe it was because she looked like her father—whom her mother despised.

Sabrena remembered the day her father left them for good. He and her mother had been separated before but he always seemed to come back. As a little girl, she adored him, she loved to jump into his arms when he came home. Her father always made her feel special, usually had something in his right pocket for her, and was the only one who would sit and play dolls with her. One day her father just left and they didn't see or hear from him for several months. She was only eight years old and kept waiting for him to come back through the door, but he never did. One day, when she was crying to Gerald after she'd been scolded by their mother, she told him that she couldn't wait until her daddy came home. Gerald had been the one to tell her that their father wasn't coming back, that he and their mom had gotten a divorce.

She didn't hear from her father until she graduated from high school. Out of the blue, she spotted her father in the audience, sitting next to a woman with a little girl. He was still a tall, handsome man, but now had salt and pepper gray hair that hadn't been there when he left. George Collins wore glasses and when Sabrena looked into his eyes it was like looking into a mirror.

"Hello, my little Brena, I'm so proud of you, my oldest girl, graduating with honors," her father said. He hugged her and introduced his wife, Loretta, and Sabrena's half sister, Kenya. Sabrena was surprised to see him and even more surprised that her heart skipped a beat.

Her mother quickly interrupted their reunion. "You so proud—why? I've been the mother and the father to Gerald and Sabrena. What are you proud of—Mr. Father of the Decade?" her mother said, pulling Sabrena away.

Sabrena wondered about her father and his other family, and the little girl who looked so much like Sabrena had at that age. She had not spoken to him since that day. The only contact she'd had with him was when he sent her a card with a $500 money order when Deena was born. The envelope had no return address.

Shaking herself out of memory, she knew she needed to speak with Gerald. For all practical purposes, he'd been her substitute dad for most of her life. She remembered her first dates and everybody being afraid of him. Even when she left the first semester of college and married Kevin, Gerald had been the buffer between her and her mother. He had always been there and he'd be there for her now. She took a deep breath and dialed the phone.

"Hey Big Bro, how ya doing?" Sabrena smiled when she heard her brother's voice.

"Hey Brena, what's going on—how are you and the girls?" Gerald asked.

"Oh, I'm fine. The girls are terrific. What about Sheila and those nephews of mine?" Sabrena smiled as she thought of Gerald's twin boys, who looked just like him. "When you coming back to the East Coast? The girls are forgetting what their Uncle G looks like." Sabrena knew that she could get to Gerald just by mentioning the girls. "I heard that Mom is coming out in July. Hope Sheila is ready."

"Oh, she'll be ready. Mom is gonna have to stop trippin' or Sheila will have her back on the plane in a heartbeat. I'm gonna talk to her when she gets here." Gerald was torn between both women; his mother was hard, but underneath she was just a lonely woman who was empty inside.

He and Sheila had been married for nine years and had four-year-old twins. The boys were the joy of his life, a gift from God. They had lost three babies before the twins were born and it had been rough. When Sheila became pregnant with the boys, they had decided to wait until she was four months pregnant before telling anyone—except Sabrena. But the boys were his little miracles. Sabrena was there when they were born.

But before the twins, when Sheila had her second miscarriage, Sabrena had flown to LA to comfort her. Sheila had carried the baby for five months and she and Gerald were utterly devastated. Sabrena called one day when things were really bad, about six weeks after the miscarriage. Sheila was unable to make it through a sentence without crying. Sabrena had never been to see them in LA but showed up suddenly on their doorstep. Gerald's baby sister had been the one who brought his wife back to him, and he was eternally grateful. That was his baby sis; she had a heart of gold and always took care of everyone. Gerald had always tried to take care of her, especially after their dad left.

Now Gerald said, "Sis, don't try to play the nieces' card. I'm coming to Washington in a few weeks and I'll see what I can do to get a few extra days." Gerald sensed a need to see his sister and made a mental note to make time in his schedule. It would be good to hang out with her and the girls. They talked for a few minutes and then Sheila and Sabrena ended up on the phone for over an hour. He was grateful that they got along so well; he loved them both and smiled as he heard Sheila telling Sabrena about the boys. Maybe at Christmas they could all be together.

Sabrena hung up the phone and curled up in her bed with Boxer, who soon snuggled around her feet. She refused to cry herself to sleep tonight. Tomorrow she would see Dr. Scott again and take the next steps in this journey. She was afraid and confused, but for now she just had to take it one step at a time. It was too early to tell Gerald and certainly she couldn't tell her mother. She was glad that Rach was picking her up from work and going with her.

CHAPTER NINETEEN

The phone startled Sabrena out of her deep sleep. She sat straight up in bed and looked at the clock: 2:14 A.M.

"Hello?" She answered, disoriented and half asleep.

"Hey, Baby. It's Steve."

"Steve, are you all right—why are you calling me this late? The girls have school tomorrow and I've to work. What's wrong?" Sabrena was now wide awake, surprised and annoyed by Steve's call.

"I just needed to hear your voice. I have tried to stay away. I really needed to hear your voice . . . I'm sorry for bothering you," Steve really didn't know why he was calling, but he just felt empty without Sabrena. He missed her, and although he didn't want to admit it, he really felt incomplete. He was tired of the game and had suddenly realized that he was an old man—not too old, but old enough. These young girls were crazy and he was tired of them. The last few weeks had been a rude awakening for him.

"Okay. Well, Steve, I've to get up in a few hours. You need to go to sleep. Have you been drinking?" Sabrena asked. Steve wasn't a heavy drinker, but she couldn't figure out why he was calling her. She hoped that this wasn't a ploy to try to get back into her life. She had no time for him. However, she knew that she would have to talk to him about her recent mess. Sabrena was conflicted, because part of her smiled when she heard his voice, but another part, that part close to her brain, was sounding all the alarm bells.

"Baby, I mean Sabrena, I'm sorry for bothering you. I just missed you tonight. Hell—I've missed you for a while. This whole game of playing women isn't what it's cracked up to be. I really miss you. I miss the girls. How are they?" Steve asked.

"They're doing well. They miss you, too. Even Rach asked about you this weekend," Sabrena said. She decided not to go into all the details. "Steve . . ."

"Okay, Sabrena, I know it's late, but I want you to know—Sabrena—I love you and I'm sorry I hurt you. That's all, I'm sorry," Steve said with heaviness in his voice. Sabrena knew that he meant every word—as much as he could mean it.

"Goodnight, Steve. I'll tell the girls you called." Sabrena hung up the phone and tried to go back to sleep. Just when she thought that she would be getting a real rest, he would have to call. Sabrena had bigger issues to deal with than Steve, and she needed her strength.

Steve sat looking at the phone after he hung up with Sabrena. He really hadn't wanted to call but he was so messed up inside. He missed her more than he thought he would. He also wanted to see the girls. Funny, he thought he loved the game and the women, but the last few weeks had taught him that he had outgrown the foolishness. He needed stability and not some fly-by-night booty call. Steve thought back to his date this weekend; he had been at a club that Kiara had chosen and left feeling like an old man. Kiara was fine and sweet, but a real freak at heart. Steve had been seeing her for a few months. He remembered their "sexual reunion." Ironically, it was the night that ultimately led to Sabrena's breaking up with him. He should have been more careful, but she had worn him out and they had fallen asleep. He hadn't expected that she would be that easy again; after all, they had messed around when she worked at the store before, and when he saw her application, he knew that it was her way of getting close to him again.

Kiara changed after he slept with her again. She started demanding things from him: better hours, money, the use of his car. She wanted to live it up on his dime. Once, he heard her refer to him as her "Sugar Daddy" to her friends. Kiara was pretty—that smile and booty were a knockout, and the sex was good, but he got tired of all the drama. Fortunately, Steve didn't have to make up something to get rid of her or to fire her like he did before. She just didn't show up for work one day and didn't answer his calls. Usually he did the dumping, but he was actually glad to be rid of her. He knew that he wanted Sabrena back; she was a lady, settled and always looking out for him. He wondered if it was too late. Sabrena sounded different, stronger on the phone. He would have to just wait and see.

CHAPTER TWENTY

Sabrena heard Renee calling her name and she quickly got out of bed to find her.

When she walked into the kitchen, Renee squealed, "Mommy, look at what Deena did—I'm all wet." Deena had tried to make cereal for them and had accidentally poured the milk in Renee's lap. Fortunately, the milk stain didn't upset her too much because she was still eating her cereal. Deena was trying to clean up the milk, and as Sabrena stooped down to help her, she felt the room spin. She grabbed the legs of the bar stool and steadied herself, hoping the girls wouldn't notice. She quickly got the girls cleaned up and saw that she was running behind schedule. She couldn't believe she'd slept so long on a weekday.

Sabrena ran through the Bloomingdale's parking lot and went directly to her department. Vivian had left a message on her machine reminding her that the buyers would be in this morning to show them the summer line. Sabrena hadn't been back to work for almost a week, and she needed to catch up on everything. The morning flew by. Sabrena enjoyed looking at all the bright colors for summer and talking to the display team about how they were going to set up. Before she knew it, lunch had passed, and she was starving. She ran to the machine to pick up some chips and a soda and went to eat at her desk.

"That's not lunch, is it?" Vivian said as she passed her desk.

"Yeah, I'm trying to catch up and work on schedules for next month."

"How are you feeling? Are you better?" Vivian asked, pulling up a chair. Sabrena wasn't in the mood to talk, or even to think about her health. She couldn't talk to Vivian about her personal life.

"Oh, I'm doing much better—it was just a bug. I hope it wasn't a problem for you," Sabrena replied, never looking in Vivian's eyes.

"I was just worried about you—having coverage in the department is my least concern. Sabrena, I'm just asking as a friend if there is anything I can do. I'll be glad to, shop, cook, watch your girls, or whatever." Vivian seemed to get the hint from Sabrena and went to her office. Sabrena quickly finished her snack and the schedules. She went to the floor to complete the new markdowns.

Sabrena was happy to see Rach walking through the doors. For once, she was early.

Sabrena asked, "Girl, when have you ever been early—anywhere?"

"I got off early to pick you up and decided to look for some sales before we left. You could at least hook me up with your discount," Rach said as she picked up one of the bikinis for summer. "Girl, can you imagine my big butt in this—Lawd!" They both laughed and Sabrena went to get some items that she'd put on hold for Rach. She wasn't getting off for another 45 minutes and wanted to tidy up her desk and rearrange a few of the sale racks. Rach found several new outfits and ran to the shoe department before coming back to get everything rung up. Sabrena got Theresa, a sales associate, to ring up the items using her discount.

"Girl, don't ever stop working here. The 30 percent off on top of the sale is fabulous!" Rach said as she tried to pay with her credit card. Sabrena intercepted and gave Theresa her Bloomingdale's credit card.

"I got this, Rach," Sabrena said as she pushed her hand away.

"Take my credit card, you already hooked me up with the discount. I'm gonna pay for my stuff."

"I told you that I have it. It's a new policy that in order to get the discount the employee has to pay. Ain't that right, Theresa, who needs next Friday off and I haven't done the schedule yet," Sabrena winked at the young associate and began helping her pack up the clothes.

"Now, why are you lying and then trying to get this girl to lie for you? Okay for now, but I'll get you back. Thank you and don't be jealous of me pulling out my new stuff this summer." Rach laughed as she took the bags. Soon they were en route to Dr. Scott's office.

"Okay, Bre—I wrote down some questions. I read a lot about some new drugs that are really supposed to help people stay well. We also need to ask about what tests you had and what you need to get done. I looked on the state's web site and you don't have to contact anyone you've been with about being positive. However, you can tell the doctor, who can send the names to the health department. The health department can contact them anonymously if you want, but it is up to you." Rach began to rattle off a list of things that they needed to remember when they saw Dr. Scott. She had spent the last several hours online and calling the HIV hotline to find out more information. Before she came to Bloomingdale's to pick up Sabrena she stopped for a cup of coffee and picked up some books at Borders. She was determined that they were going to be armed with the best possible medical information and that Sabrena was going to be fine.

"Okay, Rach. I wrote down a few questions as well, but I left them in my nightstand, so I'll have to wing it." Sabrena was angry with herself for being so stupid but with the mess of the morning she had rushed out without picking up her sheet of paper. However, she knew that she wanted to know how long before . . . She couldn't even think the words. Sabrena was hopeful Dr. Scott would just talk to her and calm her fears. She was glad that Rach was with her. She was smart and would be a second set of ears.

Dr. Scott was running late, which made both Sabrena and Rach more anxious.

"This reminds me, I need to make an appointment for my Pap, got to keep my stuff together," Rach said as she opened the cabinets in the exam room.

"Rach! Stop being such a snoop and sit down. What if she walks in?" Sabrena was already nervous, but her noisy friend was making her even more so. "Sit down or go back outside."

"Who exactly are you talking to? I'm R-A-C-H-E-L. You must have me confused with R-E-N-E-E, your six-year-old. Dr. Scott was my doctor before she was yours, so shut up," Rach said, pursing her lips and sitting down nicely. Just then, Dr. Scott walked into the room.

"Well, hello, Ms. Washington. I haven't seen you in a while," Dr. Scott said.

"Hey, Doc. I know, I know. I'll make an appointment for myself when we leave."

"Okay, good. Let me just get over one formality. I need to let you know, Ms. Collins, that your medical records, care, and everything else is strictly confidential. However, if you would like for me to speak openly about your care with Ms. Washington, I would ask that you put that in writing so everything is in order. Today, I'm writing in the chart that you brought Ms. Washington with you to the visit and that I've gotten your permission to speak freely about your care. Is this okay with you?" Dr. Scott, always the professional, wanted to assure that they were all on the same page.

"Yes, Dr. Scott, Rach is my best friend. She's really a sister to me and she knows everything that we've talked about. She's already on the records as the emergency contact. I'm fine with you talking openly and if ever that changes, I'll let you know." Sabrena was secure with Rach and knew that if she could trust anyone, it would be her.

The visit took over 30 minutes and Dr. Scott patiently answered all the questions, just as she had done before. This time, Dr. Scott wrote down some specifics like her CD4 count, which was 193 and her viral load which was 31,500. This was still all Greek to Sabrena, but Dr. Scott patiently explained that the CD4 count, also called helper T cells, was what her body used to fight infection and that the viral load indicated how much of the HIV virus she had in her system. Dr. Scott again told her that she met the criteria for AIDS, due to her counts, and that her viral load was high. Rach took notes as Dr. Scott went over her lab results.

Sabrena was relieved to know that her syphilis and hepatitis tests were both negative. She also talked about her Pap smear, which had been fine the last two years but which now had some abnormal cells. Dr. Scott called them "atypical" cells which could have been the result of inflammation from the infection. She would repeat the Pap in three weeks and then they would go from there. The last time Sabrena had been in the office, the nurse had tested her for TB. She had to come back to get her arm looked at, and today Dr. Scott told her that everything was fine with that test. Sabrena was just overloaded by all of the medical talk and she just wanted to run out of the office. Rach, however, was really into the conversation and was taking notes like she was in class.

"Dr. Scott, I want to know what I should do about the men I've slept with. Rach read that I could give you their names and that the health department could notify them without my name being mentioned. What do you think?"

"I'm glad that you will give the names and contact information. You don't have to, but it is, in my opinion, the right thing to do. I'm proud of you for doing right by these men. Hopefully, any other women or men they have been with will be notified. Unfortunately, I can't tell you exactly when you became infected, so we'll have to decide how far back we need to go." Dr. Scott had plenty of patients who didn't want to tell anyone or have anyone notified. Many of them became angry and said that if they could get HIV, so could everyone else. She knew that Sabrena wasn't that cold and uncaring.

Rach asked a few more questions, and then Dr. Scott told Sabrena about the vaccinations she would be getting at the end of the visit. This surprised Sabrena; she didn't know she needed vaccinations as an adult, but she was willing to do whatever.

"Ms. Collins, I have discussed your case with one of my colleagues. His name is Dr. Grier, and he's an infectious disease specialist. He agrees that we should start medication right away. I'm actually going to refer you to him for evaluation, so that he can help us keep you healthy."

"But, I don't want another doctor. I thought that you were going to take care of this, why are you giving me away?" Sabrena panicked at the thought of changing doctors. She liked Dr. Scott and felt that she could talk with her about almost anything.

"No, I'm not going to give you away," Dr. Scott chuckled. "Just like if there were a problem with your skin and I wanted a second opinion, I would send you to a dermatologist, a skin specialist. It's the same sort of thing. I just want to make sure we're giving you the best possible care. However, you will still see me and I'll know what's going on with everything. Another pair of eyes won't hurt."

"I read about this, Sabrena. Dr. Scott is your primary, but you should also see an HIV specialist," Rach chimed in, suddenly sounding like an eager med student.

"Will everyone know I've HIV if I go to his office?" Sabrena asked the question before she even thought about it.

"No, Ms. Collins. Dr. Grier sees lots of patients with lots of different types of infectious diseases. He does treat many people with HIV, but, certainly, not all his patients have HIV. You don't have to worry about confidentiality. I understand and so does his staff," Dr. Scott assured her.

"How soon do I have to see him?"

"I would like for you to see him as soon possible, especially since we are starting medicines. I also need for you to see an eye doctor for a baseline evaluation. " Dr. Scott continued to talk to Sabrena as she handed her the referrals to Dr. Grier and an eye doctor.

"Dr. Scott, this is really overwhelming. What am I supposed to say or do with these doctors? How can I keep all of this straight? Sabrena began to feel panicky and Rachel patted her on her back.

"Ms. Collins, I can only imagine the range of emotions that you are going through. Also I know that doctors, including myself, are not your favorite people. However, once we get through these initial referrals you may be able to take a breather. There is one more specialist I would advise that you see—a psychologist." Dr. Scott knew that Sabrena would have some resistance to seeing a mental health specialist, but this was going to be vital to her total health.

"Dr. Scott, I respect you and all of that but I don't need to see a shrink. I am fine and with the support of Rach and prayer I will be fine." Sabrena was a bit irritated by even the suggestion of seeing a psychologist. She had acted crazy when she first found out and was sad now, but that had to be normal. There was no way that she was going to let anyone mess up her head.

"I am going to give you the referral and you will have to make the decision. However, I can tell you that it is natural for you to experience some depression and adjustment issues with a diagnosis that is this serious. I know that your friends and family will be there for you, but often you need someone who can be objective, a professional. I'm a person of faith as well. However, I believe that God gives people all kinds of tools to help them be well. We don't have to decide right now, but I need for you to at least keep an open mind." Dr. Scott had heard the objections to a referral to a psychologist or psychiatrist many times. This happened more frequently with her African-American patients than with her white patients. There was so much stigma associated with getting mental health help. She could only try to break down the barriers and, hopefully, this would change.

Sabrena had no intention of ever seeing a shrink, but she didn't want to hurt Dr. Scott's feelings.

"Okay, Dr. Scott, I'll take the information."

"On the issue of figuring out this whole health system and what you should get out of your visits to specialists, I want you to read this brochure. I was glad to see that you wrote down questions today and that you are involved in the discussion of your treatment. I know that you are comfortable with me, but sometimes doctors can make you feel scared. If you make sure that after each visit you walk out with the three questions on the brochure answered, you will be armed with the information you need." Dr. Scott liked patients to ask questions and take an active part in their health care. She gave most patients a health brochure that told them to ask or know the answers to three simple questions before they left the office.

Sabrena read the questions aloud, "1. What is My Main Problem? 2. Why is it Important to Me? And 3. What do I need to do about it?"

"You know, Dr. Scott, you're cool, but a lot of doctors don't want patients asking questions," Rach chimed in. She took one of the brochures off the wall for herself.

"I know, but you still have the right to ask the questions, and if a doctor doesn't want to talk to you, then you need to find a new one. For today's visit, make sure you understand everything and make sure I have answered the questions." Dr. Scott knew that patients often had issues with asking questions and didn't understand the medical mumbo jumbo. She tried to make sure she communicated in a frank, easy-to-understand manner, but even for her it was hard. This was especially true when explaining medications and how to take them.

"Ms. Collins, I know that this is a lot of information right now. We're in the final stretch. I am starting you on several medications that have a different role in treating your HIV/AIDS. The biggest threat with AIDS is that your immune system can't effectively fight off infection. The goal is to decrease the amount of the virus in your blood stream. I'll need for you to come back for repeat blood work every few weeks at first, and then every three months, to see if the medication is working." Dr. Scott handed her the prescriptions one at a time, explained the potential side effects, and what she could expect. After listening to her doctor and hearing all the possible side effects, Sabrena became nervous about taking the medications.

"What if I don't take the medications? What will happen if I eat right, exercise, and take my vitamins?" Sabrena asked, feeling overwhelmed. "I feel okay now, and it sounds like the pills are gonna make me feel worse."

"Well, that's certainly your choice. However, given the fact that you meet the criteria for AIDS and your immune system is not up to par, you would probably see a faster decline in your health. Ms. Collins, no one can predict what will happen. Usually it takes about ten years before a person develops AIDS. In your case, given the previous HIV test and just listening to your symptoms and time frame, I doubt that it has been ten years since you were infected. If you want to wait to start medications, I'll stand by you on that, but only if you make an appointment to see Dr. Grier in the next week or so." Dr. Scott could see how powerless Sabrena was feeling, so she put the decision to take the medication into her patient's hands.

"Whatever you think I should do, Dr. Scott, that's what I'll do. I trust you."

"Dr. Scott, are you giving her the stuff that Magic Johnson's on?" Rachel asked. "He looks good and has had HIV for over ten years. He must be on something good. Sabrena has good insurance, not an HMO. I'm sure they'd cover the best medication."

Dr. Scott chuckled at Rach. "I don't know about Magic, but the medications I'm recommending are generally supported as the best treatment option, though there are several choices now. I want to see how she does and, if we need to adjust in a few weeks, we will do that. Beyond medications, Ms. Collins, do just what you said—eat right, exercise, and take your vitamins. All of that I believe will help."

Dr. Scott continued to talk about the medications and something to treat what she called "thrush," which was yeast growing in her mouth. Sabrena had a bit of a sore throat but nothing major—the medication was supposed to get rid of it.

At the end of the visit, the nurse came in to give her the shots. Sabrena felt like a kid again and jumped when she got the one with the big needle. She felt a bit nauseated so she put her head down until the wave passed. While she rested, Rach walked out after Dr. Scott. Sabrena assumed she was going to make her appointment.

"Dr. Scott, could I speak with you for a second privately?" Rach whispered as she walked down the hall after her.

"Sure, Ms. Washington, step into this exam room." Dr. Scott took Rach into a room further down the hall.

"Sabrena is like, well—she's my sister—we couldn't be any closer. She's had a rough time but she's a great person and I just want her to be okay." Rach couldn't stop the tears. "What can I do? What do

I say, how do I help? I've always been there for her. She's always been there for me. I just don't know what to do." Dr. Scott reached out and hugged her. Rach felt comforted in her arms.

"All you need to do, Ms. Washington, is to continue being her friend, her family. That's all, just love her." Dr. Scott felt her eyes water as she felt the strength of their friendship.

The rest of the day passed quickly. Sabrena and Rachel stopped for a quick meal after the appointment and then picked up the girls. They played dress-up, made dinner, and read stories before Sabrena put them to bed. Sabrena was feeling wiped out after the busy day and when she looked at the bag of medications from the pharmacy, she mostly felt overwhelmed. Although Dr. Scott had gone over each prescription with Sabrena, she still felt confused and wondered what the medicine was going to do to her. Rach had called and made the appointment for her with Dr. Grier and she would see him on Tuesday. So many appointments, so much to think about. Sabrena had made an appointment for the girls on Saturday morning to get them tested. She knew that it was probably too much, but she had to be sure about her girls before she even thought about herself. She decided to spend the day with them and take them to a matinee after the office visit. She wanted to laugh through the movie with them, but her mind kept drifting back to their tests. She worried throughout the day into the night about the results to come.

Just as she was about to get into bed, Sabrena remembered that she needed to start taking her meds; Dr. Scott had told her to take one of them at night. She also had to gargle with some medication five times a day for the yeast in her mouth. Sabrena brushed her teeth, flossed, then gargled with the medication, which tasted horrible. She quickly spat it out.

"Whew, this is going to take some getting used to," Sabrena mumbled as she reached for the Pepsi™ she had brought with her to bed. She didn't know if she should take the medication with water or if the Pepsi™ would be fine. She just swallowed the pill dry and got into bed. Dr. Scott had written down all of the medications and their uses: some were to decrease the amount of HIV in her body and to treat the disease; others were to prevent her from getting pneumonia and something else she couldn't remember. All she knew was that it was a bunch of pills. She also had her vitamins and had committed to drinking more water. She would start exercising on the weekends. Tears flowed as she thought about the state of her life and she rolled out of bed and got on her knees.

> *"Dear God,*
> *Forgive me for all of my sins. I don't know if you're pun-*
> *ishing me for something horrible that I did, but I ask that*
> *you forgive me. Lord, I want to be healthy and I want to*
> *see my daughters grow up. I need your help to do all that I*
> *need to do. I'm tired and so afraid, but if you help me I can*
> *make it, even through this. I feel so scared, so all alone—*
> *please help me. Don't let my babies have HIV, they don't*
> *deserve it, and it would be too much to bear. Let it just be*
> *me. I freely give up my life, my health, anything that is nec-*
> *essary. Please God, don't let them have this, too. Amen."*

Sabrena continued to weep and pray. She eventually climbed back into bed and she felt Boxer rub against her feet. She felt better and more at ease after her prayer. She would have to go to church on Sunday. Just as she turned of the light, her phone rang.

"Hello?"

"Hey, did you take the medications?" Rach whispered.

"Yes, Dr. Rach, I just took the tablet for nighttime and the stuff you gargle. Is that all right?"

"Good, that's fine. Did you write in the journal we got? You have to write down when you start the medicines and if you have any problems," Rach whispered.

"Why are you whispering, is somebody there? Is it Barry?" Sabrena asked, thinking of Rach's on again, off again boyfriend.

"Yeah, he's here. I actually called him. Woman cannot live by vibrator alone." Rach said as she laughed aloud.

"You're crazy. I know he ran over there like a little lap dog. I don't know which one of you two is more pathetic. Don't talk about me ever again," Sabrena said. She reflected on their four-year relationship. Barry really loved Rach, but something in Rach always held back when it came to men. She didn't trust them, and when there was the slightest little problem, she usually broke up with them.

"Goodnight, I have to handle my business."

"Goodnight, Rach, don't hurt him." Sabrena gently put the phone in the cradle.

Sabrena thought of Steve and his late-night call. She would call him tomorrow, just as a friend, to see if he was okay. She looked at the picture on her nightstand of him, her, and the girls. She felt a sense of loss. Although she still felt right about breaking up with him, she couldn't bring herself to take down their pictures. As much as she hated to admit it, she still loved him.

Sabrena awoke early and began her day as usual, but with a major exception. She gargled again with the nasty medicine, weighed herself, and wrote down the information from last night and this morning in her journal. She took two different pills and her vitamins with her breakfast. She usually just ate some fruit, but she was going to have to eat more while she was taking these medications, so she made an omelet with toast. The girls were full of energy and happy that it was Friday. They were looking forward to a slumber party at their friend Tiffany's tonight, so they packed their sleeping bags in the car.

Sabrena felt pretty good for most of the morning, but by after-noon was feeling a little strange. She'd never liked medications and wondered if they were making her feel this way. She went to the bathroom at lunch and gargled again and made a mental note to get some peppermint to get the taste out of her mouth. Although she really had no appetite, she joined Vivian for a salad during lunch. Before she'd eaten three bites, she became very nauseated.

"Sabrena, are you all right?" Vivian asked. "You look funny."

"Yeah, I think its some medication that my doctor gave me that's making me a little queasy. I'll be okay," Sabrena responded, trying to perk up.

"What exactly did she say was the problem?" Vivian was con-cerned, but didn't want to pry too much. She had seen Sabrena totally withdraw when she got too close. But something told her that Sabrena wasn't doing well. She was worried, and didn't know how to help.

"Just a little bug, that's all, and I need to get more rest." Sabrena began eating her salad again so she wouldn't have to talk. She was barely used to the idea of her diagnosis and was certainly not ready to talk with her boss about it. She did remember that she needed to go by Human Resources to check on her amount of leave and other benefits, and to see if she could increase her life insurance without having another physical.

CHAPTER TWENTY-ONE

Sabrena picked up the girls a few minutes late, and their after-school day care teacher wasn't happy.

"Ms. Collins, I have children, too. When parents are late, I'm late picking up mine. This is the third time this month. Tell your friend Rachel to be on time when she picks them up, as well. I don't have the time or interest in just sitting here waiting for parents whose children are not a priority." The nasty teacher spoke loudly, as Sabrena hugged her daughters.

"I'm only eleven minutes late, count them—*eleven* minutes, and I'm usually *early*! Stop whining and tell it to someone else," Sabrena answered smartly, and walked the girls to the car. She really didn't like that woman talking to her in that tone in front of the girls. When the girls were buckled up, Sabrena turned to the woman and said sternly, "One more thing, don't you ever use that tone with me in front of my daughters. I don't care how late I am. It's not called for and if you can't be nicer, you need to find a new job. I hope that you're not treated this poorly when you pick up your kids." Sabrena stormed off and decided to call the school on Monday. The nerve of that hussy, talking about her for being eleven minutes late. Funny that she didn't say anything when she picked them up early.

Her cell phone was ringing. "Hello, Sabrena here," she said.

"Hi Sabrena, this is Steve. How're you and the girls?"

"We're fine. I just picked them up and had to tell off the after-school teacher, but we're fine." Sabrena hated it, but she was glad to hear Steve's voice.

"Can I speak to them for a second?" Steve asked sheepishly. Sabrena pressed the speaker button and gave the phone to Deena and Renee.

"Hi, Girls, it's Uncle Steve." Steve seemed warm.

"Hi, Uncle Steve," the girls said in unison. "We miss you. When are you coming to get us?" Deena, as usual, took charge of the conversation. " We want to go on the ponies again. You promised."

"We will, but I need to set it up with your mommy. I'll make a date with my girls. Can I have a date?"

"Yes, if you promise that we can get ice cream, too," Renee said. She beamed, as if Steve could see her through the phone. After more chatter and filling Steve in on their slumber party plans, they handed the phone back to Sabrena.

"Okay Steve, have a good day," she said, and quickly hung up the phone.

Although the girls were supposed to go over to Tiffany's house right after school, Sabrena needed to spend some more time with them. She wanted them to be well balanced and to have friends, but she really didn't like it when they weren't under their own roof at night. She took them for a quick slice of pizza and marveled at how quickly they were growing up. She felt a sharp pain in her chest as she thought of the possibility that they could have HIV. But she would get them tested. She would pick them up at about 11:00 A.M. and get to the noon appointment in plenty of time. She hadn't told them that they were going to the doctor yet. . . . Just like their mom, they hated going to the doctor, so she would wait until the last possible moment to tell them. She took the girls to the bathroom with her and quickly gargled again with the medication. This five-times-a-day was hard to do!

"Mommy, what's that?" Deena asked, always the curious one.

"Can I have some?" Renee stood next to her.

"No, it's some medication for Mommy's throat. This is for grownups, so you can't have any, Renee. Plus it tastes nasty, you wouldn't like it." Sabrena quickly rinsed her mouth and took the girls to the car.

Sabrena drove the girls to Tiffany's house. She stayed awhile with Tiffany's mom, Valerie, to talk over tea. Valerie was nice, but she talked too much.

"How're things with you?" Valerie asked as they sipped the jasmine tea.

"Oh, they're fine. The girls keep me busy."

"I don't know how you do it by yourself. Are you still seeing that fine specimen, Steve?" Valerie asked, always the nosy one. Sabrena should have asked if her husband was still seeing Keith, his boyfriend, but she didn't.

"No, we're not together anymore," she answered. Simple, to the point, that's all Sabrena needed to say.

"Really? You know the last birthday party he came to with you and the girls? You all seemed like the perfect family. What happened?"

"Just didn't work out. How're you and your husband?" Sabrena asked, trying to change the subject. She was getting more irritated by minute.

"Oh, we're great. He still travels a lot, but that's the price he pays to give us the life we deserve. He's the best. Tiffany and Kenyon love their daddy, and their daddy loves them. He just bought me a new car, a convertible, for the summer. We had it customized, and it will be delivered next week. Can you believe it?" Valerie was always one to brag and put too much stock in material things. *I wonder what he bought his boyfriend*, Sabrena thought.

"Oh, look at the time," she said. "I've got to go; I'm meeting someone for dinner. I'll be back around eleven in the morning to pick up the girls. Call me with any problems with the girls, and I'll call them before bedtime. Thanks, and ya'll have fun." Sabrena went to kiss Renee and Deena good-bye and rushed out of the house.

CHAPTER TWENTY-TWO

Sabrena went home to meet her dinner partner, Boxer. She fed him and looked through the paper for movie show times. She needed to escape her reality for just a few hours, so maybe she would go to a movie by herself. She had talked to Rach, but Barry was coming back over and they were going out. She didn't know why Rach pretended that it was only sex. She liked that man and he certainly loved her. Just as Sabrena had finished with another gargle of the medicine, her doorbell rang. She wasn't expecting anyone. She looked out the door and saw Steve standing there with flowers.

With the door half opened, Sabrena asked, "Steve, what are you doing here?"

"I came by to see you. I figured if I called you'd tell me no, so I took a chance." Steve looked apologetic, a look he'd mastered. Sabrena opened the door so the neighbors wouldn't be in her business.

"Steve, the girls aren't here, which you know, because I heard them tell you about the slumber party. I really need you to leave. I'm on my way out to a movie that starts in half an hour. Thanks for the flowers—they are lovely, but not necessary." Sabrena picked up her purse. She was determined not to sit in the house tonight.

"I don't want to bother you, but I did just want to see you. Sabrena, I love you and I know that you said it's over, but I really can't get you out of my heart. No games, no lines, just straight from my lips to your ears. That's all, I love you. I messed up big time, but that doesn't change how I feel." It sounded like Steve had practiced his words, but despite the fact that it was obviously rehearsed, it also sounded sincere.

"Steve, I really am on my way out. Thank you for the nice words, but that's all they are. Just words." She walked out the door and waited for Steve to come out as well.

"Can't we be friends? Can I go with you to the movies? I'll see whatever you want." Sabrena was confident she knew Steve's game, yet something seemed different. It couldn't hurt, she thought. At least she wouldn't be sitting alone on a Friday night in a movie theatre.

"Okay, Steve, since I don't have time to argue, you can come. We'll drive separate cars, so you can go straight home afterwards." Sabrena drove to the movie theatre a few blocks from her house. On the ride over, she couldn't fight the urge to call Rach.

"Rach, what's up?"

"Oh, nothing much. Barry is making dinner. What're you doing? Wanna come over?"

"I'm sure Barry would love cooking for three! Thanks, but I'm going to the movies."

"Really, by yourself?" Rach asked, knowing the girls were at a slumber party. A few hours earlier, Sabrena had told her that she was just going to stay home.

"Well, that's why I'm calling. I was headed out the door and then Steve popped up. He asked if he could join me, so he's following me there now." Sabrena waited for the wrath of Rachel Washington.

"You're *crazy*! Why are you even talking to that fool? I mean, he got some brownie points by giving you the cash for the girls, but I hope that you're not trying to see him again. Especially now, are you gonna tell him? What are you doing? What are you thinking, Bre?" Rach was obviously upset, but Sabrena was her friend, not her child.

"I'm almost at the theatre and I'm not thinking anything. I'm just going to sit in a movie with him. Give me some credit, but then again, why would you? You have a nice dinner with Barry, the man you break up with every three months." Sabrena hung up the phone and turned into the parking lot. A few seconds later, Rach was calling her back.

"Bre, I know you didn't hang up the phone on me. I know that you hit a bad spot and the phone disconnected. I'm not even going to ask you about it. But I'd have the decency to tell my friend good-bye, like a civilized person. Sabrena, darling, good-bye, and have a lovely evening." Rach's voice was dripping with sarcasm.

"Bye, Rach. You have a lovely evening as well." Just as she was about to hang up, she heard Rach clear her throat and mumble something.

"What was that, Rach, what did you say?"

"I *said* if you screw him, I'll kill you. Bye." Rach hung up the phone and Sabrena smiled. That was the Rach she knew.

Sabrena picked a romantic comedy. The same old story; boy meets girl, boy loses girl, boy gets girl back and they live happily ever after. Steve had put his arm around her and she didn't mind, but she knew she wouldn't let anything else happen. After all, it had been nearly a month, and besides a few phone calls, she hadn't heard from him. However, her life had turned upside down and she had no room or time for anything else. She wondered if they had contacted him so quickly. Was that why he came to her house? Was he going to tell her? Was he infected? Had he been during their relationship? So many questions, she needed too much time to look them up. She actually liked the company of a male. Funny they hadn't been to a movie together in over a year.

After the movie, Steve walked Sabrena to her car.

"Sabrena, can I come to your house so we can talk?" Steve asked as he opened her door.

"No, you cannot. I thought that I made myself clear." Sabrena was firm in her resolve. A movie was one thing, but she did not want him in her home.

"Okay, I'll follow you and make sure you get there safe. It's late, and I won't come in," Steve said. He closed her door and walked to his car before she could answer.

Sabrena saw Steve in her rearview mirror. What a difference a few weeks make. Now Steve wanted to protect her. Why the sudden renewed interest? Was he feeling guilty? She pulled into her drive-way, with Steve close behind.

"Steve, I'm really not letting you into the house, so that's that," Sabrena said as she fumbled for her keys.

"Can we sit in the car and talk for a few minutes? Please, Sabrena just ten minutes, that's all." Steve really didn't want the night to end and Sabrena was kind of enjoying watching Steve squirm a little.

"Five minutes, Steve, and in my car—but that's it." Sabrena sat back on the driver's side and watched Steve get into the car. He was still good-looking Steve, but he looked sadder than Sabrena could remember. "Sabrena, do you miss me at all—or is your heart just cold to me now?" He jumped right in, like a man on the clock.

"Of course I miss you Steve, but I don't miss the lies, the cheating, the disrespect, the mess that comes with you. I have to take care of my girls and me, and not chase down and wait on a grown man." Sabrena was surprised that Steve had opened the conversation in this way, but she was going to be honest with him. She did miss him, but the more she thought about it, the more she realized she missed a male figure, *any* male figure, in her life. She definitely missed sex, and even though he wasn't consistent, she missed hearing him breathe in bed next to her. She knew that she would never hear a male voice in her bedroom again.

"Sabrena, I'm sorry for everything. I know that we've been down this road before, but I want to be friends and I want to still be in your life. I definitely want to be in the girls' lives, but I want to be able to talk to you, to have dinner sometime, or just hang out. You don't have to say anything, just know that the games are over. Know that I miss you and love you."

With all sincerity, Sabrena said, "Steve, I hope I can be your friend, eventually, but this is all too fresh. I need to work some things out with me first and see what I want to do."

"Brena, are you already seeing someone else? Is there someone else?" Sabrena was a beautiful woman and Steve's friends had often told her how lucky he was to have made a catch like her.

"Steve, what difference does that make? I don't think you heard me. Anyway, your time is up and I've to go in. Good night." Sabrena got out of the car and Steve walked her to the door. He leaned over and kissed her on the mouth. Sabrena felt his tongue on her lips and she quickly pulled away.

"Good night, Steve." She went inside, filled with mixed emotions. The kiss felt good and her body wanted Steve in her bed, but her head and heart told her no, for several reasons.

Steve went to his car and sat outside Sabrena's house for another half hour. He couldn't believe that she wouldn't even let him in. Maybe he was stupid for trying to kiss her. She had backed away like he was a snake. He would have to work harder to win her trust, but he would have to make sure that this is what he really wanted. Just one woman, Sabrena. Was he ready for that? His cell phone rang, Trudy was calling at eleven at night and there was only one thing that she could want. He didn't answer, but instead drove toward his house. If he couldn't be with Sabrena tonight, he'd just be alone.

Sabrena peeked outside and saw Steve's car pull out of her drive. She undressed for bed, too tired for a bath. Then she remembered her final gargle of the day and that she had to take a pill. This was a routine that she was going to have to get used to. Earlier, she had felt a little queasy, but overall it had been a good day. As she curled up in bed, she began to think of Steve. Could he be for real this time? What would he do if he knew? Did he give it to her? Had he known that he was infected and intentionally infected her? She didn't need a man in her life right now. She needed to get herself straight and sort this out. It was too late to call the girls and she reminded herself to call first thing in the morning. She hoped they were having a good time. She laughed to herself thinking that, for the first time since receiving the bad news, she had enjoyed an evening.

CHAPTER TWENTY-THREE

The weekend was a blur of doctors appointments, piano lessons, cleaning the house, and church on Sunday. There was never enough time to do anything, and, before Sabrena knew it, Monday morning was here and it was time to start the week again. She felt sleepier than usual this morning, although she'd gone to bed early.

A few hours after going to sleep, she'd awakened in a cold sweat. She had a nightmare that seemed so real to her; something about a man with missing teeth who was chasing her. She tried to shake it off, but she couldn't get back to sleep and would need an extra cup of coffee to make it through the day. Sabrena was still feeling queasy, but couldn't afford to take time off from work, so she dragged herself to the car and headed to the store. Driving to work, she realized that she had taken the pills for the morning but had forgotten to gargle with the medication. Now she had to figure out exactly how to get them all in. As soon as she got to work, she would go to the bathroom and make up for the morning's missed gargle.

Sabrena was met by Vivian and Leigh, the manager of shoes, as she walked into the store. They were talking about the upcoming private sale and how to make sure that the floors were properly covered. Sabrena joined in and the three sat down in the break room for tea.

"Sabrena, I heard you were sick last week. How're you feeling, are you better now?" Leigh asked.

"Oh yeah, I'm fine. Just a bug." Sabrena was getting sick of everyone asking her about being out of work for a few days. She did not really know Leigh and wondered what would make her think she wanted to talk to her about personal things.

"There's something going around. I felt bad over the weekend, but that could've just been 48 hours with my husband. Men are such babies," Leigh said, and they continued to talk about work with the occasional bit of idle gossip. Sabrena noticed how uncomfortable Vivian got when Leigh started gossiping about someone having an affair with the store manager. A few minutes later, Vivian looked at her watch and said she had to go back to her department for a delivery. Sabrena took the hint and got up as well. It certainly wasn't a smooth exit, but she hoped Leigh got the point that her gossiping wasn't very professional. If she'd talk about the store manager, she'd certainly talk about her.

Vivian walked briskly to the department, obviously irritated.

"Vivian, are you okay? I know Leigh got on your nerves, but what else is it?" Sabrena asked.

"Oh nothing, Leigh just talks too darned much. She waits to see how you'll respond to her mess, and then adds it into the gossip. That's why I had to leave. I can't stand to be around her when she starts up. I don't want to be associated with that."

"I know, she gets on my nerves, too." Sabrena added, "I was glad to follow your lead." Sabrena and Vivian went to work in the department and the day passed quickly.

Sabrena had a two o'clock appointment with Human Resources and was glad to see Ms. Bernadette in the office waiting for her. She was an African-American woman in her sixties, who had interviewed Sabrena for her job years ago. She was a motherly type who had taken an early shine to Sabrena.

"Good afternoon, Ms. Bernadette. I'm so glad it's you that I get to speak with," Sabrena said. She sat down at her desk.

"Me too. When I saw the request, I told Sanford that I'd handle it. How're you—how 'bout those girls?" Ms. Bernadette asked. They spent a few minutes catching up. Sabrena always felt warmed when she talked to Ms. Bernadette. There was something different and comforting about her.

"The girls are fine, growing like weeds." Sabrena laughed.

"Good, that's real good. Well, you wanted to review your benefits and talk about your leave status." Ms. Bernadette, always the professional, went through Sabrena's benefits. Sabrena was able to increase her life insurance by another $25,000 and, because of her age, would not have to get another physical. She asked about any restrictions on her insurance policy and Ms. Bernadette gave her a copy of the information for her to read at home. Sabrena was surprised she had so many vacation and sick days left, many of which had carried over from last year. She took notes and asked a lot of questions. Ms. Bernadette also reminded her that she had a disability policy, for which she paid $2.12 per paycheck. Sabrena had forgotten about this policy, which also paid for doctors' appointments when she was out of work.

"Ms. Bernadette, I was out a few days last pay period. I used my sick leave, but can I also get a check from the disability company? I forgot about that coverage. I also had to leave early a couple of days for doctor's appointments," Sabrena explained.

"Well yes, you do have the coverage. Fill this out, call them, and you should get a check for the days you missed. If there is any problem, call me. I'm glad you came in. Most folks forget what they have after a few years." Ms. Bernadette smiled warmly, but she seemed to be waiting for Sabrena to say more about her sudden curiosity about her life and disability policies. She remembered when Sabrena was hired—she was a strong young girl who was a good employee and Ms. Bernadette liked her. Sabrena had received the employee-of-the-month award five or six times and even won employee-of-the-year for the region. Customers were always writing in about her and that made Ms. Bernadette proud.

"Sabrena, are you okay?" Ms. Bernadette asked as she got up to close the door. "Is there something that you want to talk about? Are you having health problems? Are you sick?"

Sabrena was taken off guard, but she was quickly able to get back on course.

"No, I'm fine, but being sick a few days kinda of made me want to make sure that I could take care of the girls no matter what. It was just a bug, but it was also a wake-up call. I'm all the girls have and I need to be sure that they're okay." Sabrena looked down at her hands. She wasn't a good liar.

Ms. Bernadette sat next to her and grabbed her hands. "I'm never one to pry and you know that I don't gossip. I just have this feeling that something isn't quite right. I'm not going to push, but know that you can come to me at any time for anything." Ms. Bernadette continued, "You know there's more to me than this job here at Bloomie's. My faith in the Lord is strong and He seems to let me know when people need a little help. Right now, I feel the need to pray with you. Is that okay?" She squeezed Sabrena's hands. Sabrena felt tears welling up in her eyes and nodded silently.

"Father God, we come in the Name of our Lord and Savior Jesus Christ. Lord, we come together—your children grateful that you have given us this opportunity. God, we thank you that your Word says that you hear us and that we can ask anything according to your will and that it shall be given. Father, we ask your blessing on Sabrena. Lord, I don't know, but you know. You can do anything but fail— so I commit her into your hands. Lord, whatever she faces, let her know that she isn't alone and that you're with her. Surround her and her children with ministering angels, protect them and keep them. Lord, give them the desires of their hearts, keep them healthy, and let them prosper in all ways. Father, I thank you, because we feel your presence in the room right now. God bless, deliver, and set free. Amen."

Ms. Bernadette finished the prayer with several amens and hallelujahs. Sabrena knew that she was a first lady at her husband's church, but she had never prayed with her before. She felt a sudden calm in the room and in her spirit.

"Thank you Ms. Bernadette, you don't know how much that meant to me. Thank you so much." Sabrena hugged the older lady and gathered her paperwork.

"Thank you for allowing me to do as the Lord led me. Please know that I'm here and we don't have to talk about anything. I'll continue to pray for you and you pray for me, too. We all have burdens that get too heavy for us to carry alone." Ms. Bernadette opened the door for Sabrena and said a silent prayer. She also made a note to request a salary increase for Sabrena. She would send a copy to her boss but she felt confident that it would be approved. The increase would more than cover the additional insurance premium and put a little more in her pocket. Ms. Bernadette was sure Sabrena needed it with those two girls.

Sabrena felt so good after being with Ms. Bernadette. She really needed the prayer and would send her a thank-you note. Sabrena ran into the bathroom prior to going back to the department to do a quick gargle. She wiped her face and went back to her desk to clean it up before leaving. She walked through the department and helped a few customers, which was always fulfilling. Women did love their fashion and Sabrena always found it interesting to see what women picked out. If she could help, that always made her feel good. Before she knew it, her workday was over and she went to find Vivian to say good-bye. As she turned the corner to Vivian's office, she heard Vivian yelling:

"What do you mean, you're tired of it all? What does that mean? You can't just give up. You have to fight, or this will get you, so I don't want to hear it!" Vivian's face was red and she had been crying. It was too late for Sabrena to walk away. When Vivian saw her, she quickly ended the conversation and hung up the phone.

"Vivian, are you all right?" Sabrena asked as she put her arm around her shoulder.

"Yes, I'm fine. Don't mind me, kids," Vivian said, as if that summed everything up. Sabrena knew that was as much as Vivian was going to say, so she said a quick good-bye and left to pick up the girls. Since she was a little early today, she decided to go inside. She hoped that the nasty after-school teacher was there. Sabrena didn't see the teacher, and the girls ran to her when she walked into the gym. On the ride home, they talked nonstop. When they got home, Sabrena was too tired to make dinner, so she called for pizza and went to her room to take a nap. The evening was a blur of activity. She finally got the girls to bed. Sabrena pulled out her journal and realized that she had only gargled with the medication three times and wondered if she could just skip the rest. She took her other medications and prepared for bed. She thought about a long bath, but was too tired to go through all of the preparation. She called Rach and after a few minutes of chitchat, Sabrena fell quickly to sleep.

CHAPTER TWENTY-FOUR

Finally, after two long weeks, Sabrena received the girls' test results—and she was grateful and relieved that they were negative. Sabrena was so anxious about the results that she just stopped by the pediatrician's office instead of waiting for them to call her. She asked for a written copy, amazing even herself at what an organized person she was becoming throughout this ordeal. However, she missed her scheduled appointment with Dr. Grier and rescheduled for a Thursday evening. She still was not comfortable going to see an HIV specialist.

Dr. Scott called her to see how she was feeling and reminded her that she needed to see Dr. Grier as soon as possible. Sabrena had been doing okay, but she just felt sick to her stomach a lot and had a few episodes of vomiting. One of the biggest problems she faced was a social nightmare: she was passing gas like crazy. She didn't know if it was from the medication or not, but she had bought some over-the-counter stuff that wasn't doing a thing. She also felt really tired, but she knew that was because of all of the weird dreams she'd been having. She must have been really stressed out, because every night she woke up from a nightmare. She didn't want to tell Dr. Scott, because she was afraid Dr. Scott would make her go see a shrink and that wasn't happening. Sabrena would just deal with it.

She knew that she was depressed, but who wouldn't in her situation? She was still crying a lot, even at the littlest things. It seemed like every night she stood outside the girls' door gazing at them—which inevitably brought tears to her eyes. She was irritable and was snapping at the department clerks. It seemed like her patience was just gone. She continued to lose weight, but that was a combination of having no appetite, always feeling nauseous, and just not having any interest in food. Sabrena really had no interest or pleasure from doing anything except for being with the girls.

The girls were both busy getting ready for their upcoming spring piano recital and their spring break. Sabrena felt overwhelmed, scared, tired, and so alone; she still hadn't talked to anyone except Rach. That was going to change, because Gerald was coming and she would talk with him.

Sabrena had been on the medications for over three weeks and needed to go into Dr. Scott's office for blood work before her next appointment. She drove over to the office and saw Denise, Dr. Scott's nurse, and was glad that there were no other patients in the office. It was quick and relatively painless. She would get the results when she saw Dr. Scott in a week. She was glad that Rach was going to pick up the girls. This would give her time to stop at the grocery store to pick up some things for dinner on her way home.

Sabrena had been avoiding Steve's store, but she didn't feel like going out of her way today. She couldn't avoid him forever. He had called once or twice a week over the last few weeks and talked to the girls, but Sabrena was sure that he also enjoyed the few minutes they chatted before she passed the phone along. Last Saturday, he had brought over the latest *Little Mermaid* DVD and watched it with them while she went shopping for a few hours. Sabrena felt good about the relationship Steve and the girls had and she didn't want to deprive them of this father figure, because they simply adored him. He was a big kid with them and although he was a man in his mid-forties, he felt no shame in having tea parties with her daughters. Since the night at the movies, he hadn't tried to ask for a date, and Sabrena was feeling more comfortable by the day with this new kind of relationship. She still was intent on finding out if he gave her HIV, but she didn't know how to get this information, and she wasn't strong enough to tell him about her diagnosis.

Sabrena tried to pick up her items as quickly as possible to avoid running into Steve. She saw him as she entered the store and looked the other way. While she was in the produce section, a very nice-looking man approached her.

"Hello, Miss. I hope that it is Miss. Can you help me pick out some peaches?"

"Ummm, okay. I always look at the skin and make sure there is no bruising and that it's nice and firm." Sabrena could have sworn that he was flirting, but she helped him anyway.

"I think that's how I like them, too. Nice, smooth skin, firm, and pretty."

"Well, enjoy your peaches," Sabrena said and began to walk away.

"Miss, it would be a shame if I could remember such a beautiful lady only by the word 'Miss.' Could I please know your name? I'm Darrell Cannon."

"Hi, Darrell, I'm Sabrena."

"Do you have a last name, Sabrena?" he said with a wink. He pulled his card out of his wallet.

"Yes, I do, but for now Sabrena is fine."

"You most certainly are. Here's my card with all my numbers on it. I hope that you could think of giving me a call, email, fax, or any-thing—just say my name and that would make me happy." Sabrena laughed at the weak lines of her newfound peach friend, Darrell.

"Thank you, Darrell, but no promises."

"Can you do me the honor, the great honor of giving me your number or some way of contacting you in case I need help picking out more produce?"

"Darrell, I hope that you enjoy your peaches. I tell you what, if we see each other again, I'll give you my number. Let's leave it to chance." Sabrena smiled at the player and was sure that she would not be the only victim of his corny lines today. However, it helped with her very fragile ego. She laughed as he closed his eyes and dra-matically opened them again.

"Okay, well, I see you again—now can I get the digits?" She had to give him a few points for originality and they laughed together. Steve abruptly interrupted the exchange.

"May I help either of you?" he asked.

"No, Bro, I'm fine. This little peach taught me how to pick a peach," Darrell said as he turned to walk away. "Miss Sabrena, please consider doing me the honor of granting me just one phone call. Seriously, I'd love to spend a few more minutes with you."

Steve looked angry and stood next to her with his arms folded. "Sabrena, you come into the store to pick up men in front of my face. That's how we roll now?"

"Steve, give me a break. He needed help, that's all." Sabrena smiled at the jealous Steve. *Serves him right.* She thought she did look rather cute today in her mauve suit with brown pumps. The suit was a size smaller than she usually wore and it hit her hips at just the right places.

"I'll see you around. I need to finish picking up some things," Sabrena said nonchalantly as she strolled down the aisle, making sure to put an extra twist in her hips. She glanced back and Steve was looking at her, still angry. Sabrena felt the urge to run back to him, but she resisted. She finished her shopping and, as she went to her car, she wished she would have said something else to Steve. She looked around for him but he wasn't in sight. Maybe that was a sign.

"Hey, Brena," Steve called from behind her as she was opening the car door.

"Steve! You scared me!" Sabrena squeaked, getting into the car, uncomfortable with him so close to her.

Steve leaned down to the window and said, "Sorry about that. I just wanted to apologize for how I acted. You're right, we're not together. I'm sure that you're dating and I have no right to expect anything from you. I just wanted to apologize, that's all."

Sabrena saw his honesty and she couldn't put her finger on how, but he was different. She was used to the game of him trying to woo her back when they had broken up, but this was different. "That's okay, Steve, it's only been a few months. I understand." Sabrena turned on the car in an effort to cut the conversation.

"Ummm, Sabrena, can I come to the girls' piano recital? I've never missed one and Deena asked me to come when I was over last week," Steve asked nervously, unsure of himself around this new Sabrena.

"Yes. I think the girls would love it. I'll call you with the details."

"Can I also take you all out afterwards, just as friends, of course?" Steve pushed even harder.

"We'll talk about it, okay? Good-bye Steve," Sabrena said as she put the car in gear. She pulled out of the parking lot and headed home. She was confused and needed to stay as far away from Steve as possible. She was so lonely these days that the slightest kindness from him had the potential to make her go back to a bad situation. Then she caught herself and wondered what she was even thinking; the minute she told him she was HIV-positive, she was sure he would run the other way—unless he was positive, too. Sabrena continued to wonder about him. He didn't look any different, but then again, neither did she.

Sabrena laughed aloud as she thought of how "HIV/AIDS" looked. How many times had she and her friends talked about someone looking like they had HIV? She remembered her cousin Edward who had died of AIDS. He'd lost a lot of weight, his hair became very thin like a baby's, and he had these black marks on his legs. He looked sick in the last year or so, but he also had friends who came over who were positive and looked fine—some of them *real* fine. They looked so good and healthy Sabrena hadn't believed it when he'd tell they were positive. She wondered what people would say about her. How could she tell anyone? She couldn't do that to herself or her girls.

Rach was just driving up as Sabrena pulled into the driveway. She should have known, Rach was always late. "Tell me you weren't late picking up my daughters," Sabrena said as she greeted Rachel.

"Yes, I was about twenty minutes late. Traffic was bad. Be glad that I got there," Rach said with an attitude, as the girls giggled away in the backseat.

"Mommy, Auntie Rach said a bad word to the teacher," Deena declared with her hands on her hips. She was always the reporter.

"Rach, you didn't cuss at a teacher. The girls have to go back there, you know." Sabrena knew before asking just who she had told off, and that nasty wench probably deserved it.

"I most certainly did, with this heifer telling me that she had children and couldn't be waiting on me or their mother every day. She was nasty. I was late and in traffic, its tax time, I'd had a bad day, and she just talked too much." Rach talked and rolled her neck— always a bad sign. "She'd better be glad my nieces were looking at me, otherwise I would have slapped the taste out of her mouth, talking 'bout she told their mother not to be late again. She guessed she would have to call and remind you that your children were *your* responsibility and not hers." Rach was getting more animated as she told the story.

Renee chimed in, "Mommy, Auntie Rach told her to go to where the devil lives." Sabrena took the girls into the house, where they sat waiting for their aunt to recount the story.

"Bre, you know that I'm stressed out at work; the last thing I need when I get there is dealing with that woman. It's not like the girls were the last ones there. There were still two little white boys left acting a fool. I bet she wasn't going to tell *their* parents about *their* responsibility. I wasn't having it. She won't be opening her mouth again, I guarantee. By the way, her name is Tina Long." Rach laughed.

"Rach, what did you do to the woman?" Sabrena asked, inwardly happy that someone had set the teacher straight.

"I told her that she could go to hell, I told her she better not *ever* speak to me in that tone and that she had better not say anything to the girls. I then asked her the names of her children. She stuttered and then I looked at her hands and didn't see a ring, so I just went there. I asked her again for the name of her kids. She couldn't think of a lie. She ain't got any kids—you know I just had a field day! I told her that if she would fix her attitude, she might get a man and one day might have a child. I also told her that if I heard one word from the girls or their mother about her being mean to them I would be back and it wouldn't be pretty." Rach was laughing hard at this point and Sabrena stood with her mouth open. What kind of teacher makes people feel guilty about imaginary kids?

"Rach, it doesn't matter. We should be on time to pick them up. Why you gotta go tell the girl about her attitude and getting a man? She could be happy in a relationship, how do you know? You probably sent the girl to therapy." Sabrena was giggling herself, all the while feeling sorry for the teacher. She had just picked a fight with the most dangerous woman of all: Rachel Washington, mad accountant during tax season.

"Oh, no, we're fine. By the way, she's a teacher's aide. She just won't be running her mouth anymore, and I'll be a little quicker to pick them up. Girl, every once in a while, with my college education, good job, good looks, and in my new 7 series BMW, I've got to get *ghetto*—that's universal language from grade school to the boardroom. You gotta go there, so I did," Rach said definitively.

Sabrena laughed at Rach, but decided to call the school and make an appointment to talk with someone about the episodes. She didn't want her girls to be treated poorly because their rides were late a few times and would work on that. However, she also didn't think that teacher was appropriate—so she would just go talk to someone.

She was too tired to cook and the smell of food had been making her nauseous over the last few days. She ordered some Chinese and helped the girls clean up their room. Sabrena noticed that when she bent down, she was getting dizzy—this had happened before and she just thought it was because she was tired. However, today the room was really spinning and she had to sit on the floor.

"Mommy, are you okay?" Deena asked, seeing her mommy on the floor.

"Yeah, baby, just a little tired, that's all."

"I'm gonna get Auntie Rach," Deena said. She was frightened and ran out of the room. Renee looked at her mother and walked over and handed her a Barbie and a comb. Sabrena began combing the doll's hair and playing with Renee. The dizziness passed as quickly as it came, and by the time Rach came into the room, she was feeling better.

A few minutes later, the food came, and after getting the girls settled, Rach and Sabrena had time to talk.

"How's it going? I know you told me okay before, but really how are you?" Rach asked, concerned about her friend.

"I'm okay. My stomach feels funny most of the time and I have been itching a lot the last few days. I don't know what that's from," Sabrena shrugged, failing to bring up the horrific gas.

"Have you called Dr. Scott?"

"No, I'll see her next week and I'll see Dr. Grier on Thursday. I'll bring it up then," Sabrena said. She was hoping to change the subject, but Rach wasn't having it.

"Where is your medication journal? How is that going?" she asked.

"Rach, it's hard. I'm not used to all of these pills and thinking about my health every single waking moment. Okay, I have missed a few doses, but I'm getting into a routine. I can't sleep well at night. Between sweating and dreaming that someone is chasing me . . . I just can't sleep," Sabrena confessed.

"Have you taken Tylenol PM® or something?" Rach asked, making a mental note to call Dr. Scott in the morning. Sabrena didn't want to be a bother, but she didn't care.

"It's bad enough that I take all these horse pills. I don't need to add any more," Sabrena said, starting to get irritated. Sabrena felt 100 years old and just wanted to forget everything; she wanted to have her life back. "I really don't want to talk about this right now. Can we just talk about something else for *once*?" Then she told Rachel about bumping into Steve.

Rach was predictable, negative and unsympathetic, towards him. "Good," she said, "the old dog needs to be sorry and pitiful, good for him. You need to just stay tough."

They talked and played with the girls, who never seemed to run out of energy. Sabrena cleaned up the kitchen and put the girls in bed. Rach decided to stay over and, after her second serving of ice cream, went to bed. Sabrena ate some jello, one of the few things that didn't upset her stomach, and went through her new ritual of taking medications. She forgot that she had to take the one pill on an empty stomach but figured the jello wouldn't hurt. She decided to take a cool shower before bed, hoping maybe she wouldn't sweat so much. Maybe some baby oil would help with this itching. She prayed for a peaceful night of sleep.

CHAPTER TWENTY-FIVE

Sabrena awoke feeling refreshed. She was glad it was Friday. She felt better this morning; she'd slept better last night and took a few extra minutes in her morning shower. Sabrena noticed scratches on her chest; she assumed that she had scratched it in her sleep. She also noted more red bumps on her body. She would wait to see what happened.

She quickly got the girls and Rach out of the house and ended up being early to work. She even had time to stop by Starbucks. Sabrena called Steve while she sat in Starbucks reading the paper. She called his house so she could just leave a voice mail message, told him the recital time on Sunday, and accepted the dinner invitation. The girls loved him and it would be good for them to get out. If Rach came, that would be like two bulls in a china shop, but they would handle it. Steve was the one who had started the girls with piano lessons and had personally paid for each one. In the past, he had taken them to practice and waited patiently for them. Their teacher thought he was their father and commented on how proud he was of their progress.

Her moment of luxury soon vanished, as she realized she had to get to Bloomingdale's. The morning coffee helped give her the artificial boost of energy she needed. She had gargled this morning with the medication for the yeast in her mouth and noticed less of the white patches that Dr. Scott had pointed out to her. She cancelled her appointment with Dr. Grier—she didn't want to go to that office. As she put her purse up and cleared her desk, she wrote, CALL G on her calendar. Sabrena knew that, although she was procrastinating, eventually she needed to just bite the bullet and take care of this.

Sabrena usually enjoyed work, but today she was preoccupied by the constant itching. It was hard to be pleasant when she felt like a thousand ants were crawling all over her. She ran to the pharmacy and bought some more anti-itch cream but that wasn't helping and she was beginning to see little red bumps on her arms. Sabrena left the sales floor and stepped into the dressing room. She got some relief from scratching, but she just couldn't reach all the places. She wondered if Boxer had given her scabies or something. She had never felt like this. Sabrena called and left a message for Dr. Scott and then called Rach at work, something she very rarely did.

"Kearney and Associates, Ms. Washington's office," Rach's secretary answered the phone in a flat, monotone voice.

"Hello, this is Sabrena Collins. May I speak with Ms. Washington?"

"Hold on, I'll see if she will want to be in," the secretary mumbled. Sabrena laughed to herself, thinking this casual tone marked either a temp or a permanent hire that wouldn't be around very long. Rach was a trip the second she left work, but, at the office, she was an utter perfectionist. She was senior vice president at her accounting firm and ran through assistants on a monthly basis.

"Bre, what's wrong?" Rach immediately assumed something was wrong, because Sabrena never called her at work.

"I'm itching even worse and I'm breaking out in bumps. I called Dr. Scott," Sabrena told her friend. She tried to scratch her back.

"Do I need to come and take you to the emergency room?" Rach asked as she began to look for her keys and purse.

"No, I'll just wait until Dr. Scott calls me. I shouldn't have bothered you," Sabrena said, trying to sound convincing, but the itching was driving her crazy. "You know, Rach, I'm going to call Dr. Scott back now, and I'll let you know what she says."

"Okay Bre, I'll be waiting for your call." Rach hung up the phone and contemplated getting back to work while she waited for her friend to call back. But she had known Sabrena for a long time: if she called her at work, this was a major problem.

Rach pressed the intercom for the temp Human Resources had sent her. "Shaquita, please bring my schedule for the day," she said. Shaquita certainly wasn't the sharpest pencil in the box. Rach had tried to give the sister a break, but, after two weeks, her patience was running thin.

"I'll be with you in a second!" Shaquita yelled back to Rachel—no intercom, no nothing, like she was in the backwoods of West Virginia. That was it, Rach would have to handle this irritant now.

"Shaquita, come into my office now," Rachel said over the intercom, without waiting for a reply. The girl walked into her office, lips upturned and pulling at her burgundy extensions with her long acrylic nails. Rachel just looked at this girl, who couldn't have been more than 24 years old. Rach needed to start a class on what to wear and what not to wear to the office. Under all the heavy foundation and makeup, the girl was almost pretty. However, her ridiculous makeup, hair color, and garish nails were hiding any possible hint of beauty. Not to mention the short skirt and form fitting shirt—Rach could swear she saw the girl's nipples. How could she let this person be the interface between her and the world? She would call Human Resources from the car and demand a replacement by Monday. She had tried to talk to Shaquita and help her, but all her advice had fallen on deaf ears. She had talked to her about phone etiquette, excessive personal calls, and her boyfriend "stopping by the office." She had asked Shaquita to schedule her appointments and put a schedule on her desk every morning. Rachel had reminded her that she was her boss, not her friend. She wasn't a tyrant, but she expected to be addressed as Ms. Washington by her secretary. Rach just didn't get it. Why was it so hard to find decent help?

"Shaquita, did you bring my schedule?" Rach asked impatiently.

"No, *you* told me to come in *right now*, so I came in *right now*," Shaquita replied, clearly with an attitude and perturbed.

"What! First of all, if you actually listened and acted on what I told you, this wouldn't be an issue. On your *first* day, I told you that you should be in the office at 8:30 A.M. and should put my schedule on my desk before I get here. I do not see a schedule, and you've been late every day since your first day in this office. Get my schedule *right now*," Rach said with all the professionalism she could muster. She was tired of the second, third, fourth, fifth chances for this girl. This would be her last day in her office. Shaquita mumbled, printed the schedule, and handed it to Rach.

"What else do you need, Rachel, or do you just want me to stand at your beck and call?" Shaquita said bluntly.

"Oh, I don't need anything else, Shaquita, and thank you so much for bringing my schedule. The other things I was going to talk to you about, I see, are no longer an issue. Please close the door on your way out, and again thank you so much." Rach smiled as the door closed and she quickly picked up the phone. This was not the day and she was not the one to mess with; she wouldn't wait until she got into the car.

"Hi, Jerry, this is Ms. Washington."

"Hello, how're you?" Jerry worked in Human Resources and became tense when she heard Rachel Washington's voice. She only called when there was a problem. She knew that it had to be the temp.

"Not good at all. If you don't get this temp gone wild out of my office in fifteen minutes or less, I am going to throw her out the window." Rachel was fuming but had other issues she had to deal with besides the temp.

"All righty now, I'll be down and bring security. I'll call the agency for a replacement." Jerry quickly began to pull the files and knew that she would have to rush downstairs to handle this personally.

"I want to interview any new temp before she starts work. I can't leave that up to you all any more. I don't know what is happening with the applicant pool, but I just can't handle the attitudes and the unprofessionalism. Thank you." Rach hung up the phone and began canceling her appointments. This was not a good time, but when all is said and done, there was never a good time, and Sabrena needed her. She had trained her team well and her team leader, Randall, was able to handle things in a crunch. She shot him a quick email and would call him from the car.

After Rach cancelled her appointments, she called her boss's voice mail to let him know she had a family emergency and would be available by phone and Blackberry®. No one was watching over her shoulder at this stage in her career, but she had gotten where she was by keeping her colleagues in the loop. She was the consummate professional. She had a problem with early morning, so she didn't schedule appointments before ten in the morning if she could help it. She kept her clients happy and, more importantly, informed and up-to-date on their requirements. Rach worked hard, often stayed late, came in on holidays, and had only been out sick two days in the six years she'd been with the firm. She got up to lock the lateral file cabinets and she smiled to herself as she glanced at the vacant desk next to her office; she knew that security had "helped" Shaquita to her car.

CHAPTER TWENTY-SIX

Sabrena called Dr. Scott's office again, but wasn't having any luck.

"Dr. Scott isn't available, but I'll give her your message. If this is an emergency, you should go to the Emergency Department and tell them to call us." The receptionist was nice, but Sabrena didn't want to be bothered with an ER. She wanted to see Dr. Scott.

"Does she have any appointments open for this afternoon? I really need to see her and I don't want to go to an emergency room." Sabrena was beginning to feel a little frantic.

"Let me talk to Dr. Scott and see what she wants us to do. Can I have a number where I can call you back?"

"Yes, call me on my cell. I am going home and will wait for Dr. Scott's call." Sabrena hung up the phone and looked for Vivian to tell her that she would have to leave soon. She didn't think that she could make another four hours at work. She would go home and take a cool shower and put the itch cream all over her body. In the meantime, maybe she'd hear from Dr. Scott.

"Hey, Vivian, I'm going to have to leave in a few minutes. I'm really itching and have broken out in some red bumps," Sabrena told her boss.

"Oh, my God, Sabrena! Your face is all broken out and your eyes look like they're swelling!" Vivian shrieked as she looked up at Sabrena. "You need to see a doctor. I can take you to an urgent care center or an emergency room, but you need to see someone."

"It's okay. I already called my doctor and I know she'll be calling me back. I'm going home to take a shower and by then she'll call. Thanks for the offer," Sabrena said. She wasn't about to let Vivian take her to any ER. She quickly walked out to get her purse. As she walked back towards the employee exit, she heard her name on the

PA system, being called back to her department. Sabrena was feeling sick now and really wanted to bolt out the door, but she decided to call the extension. The part-time associate, Grace, answered the phone and told her that a Rachel Washington was waiting for her. Sabrena smiled and quickly walked back.

"Rach, I thought I told you I was all right. You didn't have to come down here. What about work?" Sabrena said, relieved to see her best friend.

"Girl, when you call me at work—it's serious. Anyway, I had a light day and needed to get out. Bre, we gotta go. You really have to see Dr. Scott." Rach looked at her friend, trying to hide the shock on her face. She was going to take her friend right over to Dr. Scott's office and if she couldn't see her, to the emergency room. She quickly got Sabrena out of the store and to Dr. Scott's office.

They reached the office right before they were closing for lunch. Denise, the nurse Sabrena was most comfortable with, saw them in the lobby and brought them immediately into an exam room. Sabrena heard her cell phone ringing, but ignored it while Denise took her temperature and blood pressure. She also gave her a gown and asked her to get undressed, so that Dr. Scott could examine her skin.

"That's what I'm talking about. That's service," Rachel said, marveling at how quickly they had been taken into the exam room.

"I know, I like it here—for a doctor's office," Sabrena replied, still scratching.

"Well, hello, Ms. Collins, Ms. Washington. I didn't know you were here until Denise came and got me. I just called your cell phone, that's funny," Dr. Scott said, as she walked into the room. "When did this start?" Sabrena answered all of her questions and the doctor began to examine her. Dr. Scott quickly asked her to get dressed while she went to her office. Within a few minutes, she had returned with a prescription and some written instructions.

"Ms. Collins, this is an allergic reaction to one of the medications. I didn't see in your chart that you had an allergy to Sulfa drugs, but that's what this is, given the date the symptoms began and how things look today. You need to get this medication filled today and start taking it. It shouldn't be long at all before you start to feel better. Most importantly, stop the Bactrim and I'll note the allergy on your chart. If you ever have to go to an emergency room, make sure you tell them that you're allergic to Sulfa drugs." Dr. Scott was certain of the problem and made a note to call Dr. Grier and tell him about the severity of the reaction. She gave Sabrena a few more instructions and told her to call her at the first sign of any problem.

"Have you seen Dr. Grier?" Dr. Scott inquired.

"No, not yet. I had to reschedule, but I'll call again today."

"Why don't I get Denise to call while you're here? I really want you to get in to see him and it's been weeks now since I gave you the referral."

"No, Dr. Scott, I promise that I'll call him when I get home."

"Okay, but call today. He will more than likely give you a replacement medication to help prevent pneumonia. Don't take the pills anymore." Dr. Scott was insistent on their plan of action and elicited the help of Rachel in getting it done.

Rach asked a few questions, thanked her, gave kudos to Denise, and left, mindful that this hadn't been a scheduled appointment. They wanted Dr. Scott to have her lunch.

"Thanks again, Dr. Scott. I will make sure that she makes the appointment with Dr. Grier and that she gets the medication."

Sabrena felt so much better after her long, cool shower. Rach dropped her at home and went to get the medication. Sabrena stayed in the shower for over an hour and just let the water drip over her itching body. It soothed her. The reality of this disease was slowly settling in. She wondered how many more episodes and unexpected twists lay ahead for her. She was grateful for her sister, her best friend, Rach. Not many women would go out on a limb over and over for a friend. She lay on her bed to let her body air dry as the roughness of the towel would only start her itching again. Sabrena put a generous amount of the anti-itch cream all over—sparing only the areas that she couldn't reach. Just as she struggled to reach the middle of her back, she heard Rach opening the door.

"Hey Rach, I'm in my room," Sabrena called to her friend, trying to pull the robe around her.

"Hey, how was the shower?" Rach asked as she took the jar of cream from Sabrena, and without any exchange of words began to smear it on her back.

"Great, the cool water works well," Sabrena answered with a laugh. "Who woulda thought that at thirty-eight I'd still be taking cold showers?"

The friends shared some old pizza and Sabrena took a handful of pills that Dr. Scott had prescribed. Rach left to pick up the girls and told Sabrena to go to sleep. She was taking the girls to Chuck E. Cheese for dinner.

Sabrena quickly fell asleep. Before she knew it, her bedside clock read 9:50 P.M. She got up, stretched, and went into the living room, where she found Rach working on her laptop.

"Rach, why'd you let me sleep so late? Are the girls in bed ? Did you make them wash up?" Sabrena asked.

"Don't ask me about those girls. You know that I have my own routine. That's why they love me." Rach didn't look up from her laptop. She needed to respond to the numerous e-mails from the day and wanted to make sure they went out before Monday.

Sabrena looked in on the girls, who were fast asleep. She got something to drink and took her evening meds. She had no appetite and was feeling a bit dizzy, so she sat down on the couch. Rach continued to work until she was interrupted by her cell phone. Rach recognized her "friend's" number and decided to answer the call. "Hello, Barry, what's up?" she said.

"Hey, baby, you standing me up? I'm at Tuscany's and have been waiting for over an hour." Barry sounded irritated. Rach had forgotten all about her dinner date.

"First of all," Rach started in with immediate attitude. "Who's a baby? I'm a grown woman. I've told you about calling me that. Anyway—I'm sorry. I totally forgot. Sabrena got sick and I took her to the doctor and got things together with the girls. I didn't mean to leave you hanging, I really just forgot. I also got rid of my temp today—drama everywhere. Can you forgive me?" Rach ended with the sexiest voice that she could muster after such a long day.

Sabrena knew Barry was asking about her, because Rach answered, "No, she's okay. No, you don't need to bring anything over. Tell you what, have dinner, and call me when you're about to leave. If everything is okay here, I'll meet you at your house for a nightcap. That is, if you still want to see me." Rach and Barry talked for a while longer. Sabrena went to her room to lie down, and quickly went back to sleep. She prayed that she would not have another nightmare.

When Rach hung up, she went to look in on her best friend, who was quietly scratching in her sleep. She smiled as she saw Boxer curled up against Sabrena's feet on the bed—it was his favorite place to sleep. Rach thought of all the nights they had stayed up talking, crying together, laughing, and even partying. They'd always been a pair. She remembered when Deena was born. That stupid Carlton refused to be in the delivery room with Sabrena, so she'd been there, even though she always got sick at the sight of blood. Rach smiled as she remembered feeling faint, but toughing up as she heard Sabrena scream in pain. She'd been glad she'd a rum and Coke® before the delivery. Otherwise, she'd have been in the hospital herself, probably passed out. The scene replayed itself when Renee was born, but this time Rach was a pro and only needed two glasses of Chardonnay.

Rach couldn't bear to think of Sabrena not being well and, worse yet, dying. She had to help her. She'd already read several brochures and started reading a book on HIV/AIDS. She'd secretly called Dr. Scott after the first visit and they'd talked for a long while. She could never tell Sabrena that she had asked Dr. Scott for something to help her sleep in the first week or so. Rach had to be strong for her, but, looking at her friend, who was in obvious discomfort and had fear in her beautiful eyes, Rach felt helpless. She knew that this was taking a toll on her. Even Barry continually asked Rach what was wrong with her.

Barry, her sort of man, she thought. He was a good guy, but Rach couldn't get caught up with anyone. She cared for him, but her uncle had always told her to make sure the man in her life loved her more than she loved him. That way she wouldn't get hurt. Rach had tried to stick to that rule, and, with the exception of her first college boyfriend, she'd done pretty well.

Rachel walked back into the kitchen and poured a glass of wine. At thirty-eight, she'd never been married, although she had rejected two proposals. Rachel's thoughts returned to Barry. They had been dating on and off for close to four years. Whenever Rach got too close, too comfortable, and he started asking for more of her, she broke it off. Rachel laughed to herself as she thought of some of the foolish excuses she had made to break up with him over the years. One night, he told her her skirt was too tight. She broke up with him, telling him that obviously she wasn't skinny enough for him. He kept apologizing for months. Little did he know that it was just a front. The truth was that she couldn't allow anyone to get close enough to hurt her again.

Barry was good and handy, too. He took excellent care of her BMW and she saved a fortune on tune-ups. Rach hated to admit it, but she loved him, and, right now, she needed him. She was so afraid of ever uttering those words and, more importantly, of knowing in her heart that they were true. She looked in on the girls, who were peacefully sleeping, and decided to go home. She would stop at Barry's if he called from the restaurant before she got home. Otherwise, she would curl up in her bed alone.

Sabrena heard herself screaming and sat straight up in bed, wet with her own sweat.

"Mommy, Mommy, wake up!" Deena screamed, as she pulled at Sabrena's arm. "Mommy, what's wrong?"

"Ahhhh, nothing's wrong, baby. Mommy just had a bad dream." Sabrena took Deena in her arms and rocked her. She felt her little body trembling against her breast. "Shhhh, honey. I'm fine, just a bad dream."

Deena pulled away from Sabrena and rubbed her sleepy eyes, "Mommy you're wet and sticky," she said.

"So you don't want to hug me?" Sabrena tickled Deena and took her back into her own room, where Renee was sound asleep. She tucked Deena back in and rubbed her back until she, too, was in a deep sleep.

Although it was now the middle of the night, Sabrena was wide awake. She flipped through the channels on TV, but found nothing of interest. She decided to take a long bath and try to read a book. She went to the kitchen to get some water and took another medication for itching. She stopped by the girl's room and listened to their soft breathing. They were so innocent, so peaceful and helpless. Sabrena stood at the door wondering what lay before them. She wanted to protect them and make sure that they were able to rest in their own beds, in the home she'd made for them. She was going to fight this thing, for herself, and for her daughters. She couldn't resist the urge to kiss their chubby cheeks before going back to her room. The girls would have a million things for her to do in the morning and she needed to be ready. Sabrena once again welcomed the sight of her bed, but she was also afraid of the creatures that she might meet in her dreams.

CHAPTER TWENTY-SEVEN

Steve went into the store early Saturday morning to finish some paperwork that should only take an hour or two. He found himself feeling happier than he'd been in weeks. He knew that it was because he was seeing Sabrena and the girls tomorrow. It was important for him to still have them in his life and more than ever he knew that Sabrena was the one for him. Steve didn't know if he had totally messed it up with her. The last few weeks had been filled with a few mindless dates with bimbos he didn't care about. Sabrena was special and he had been a fool. He loved the girls and wanted to give them the world, but he also knew that he loved Sabrena. Why it had taken this long to realize it, he didn't know, but he would win her back.

"Hey, Boss man," Chester said. Steve liked Chester, he was dependable, friendly, and always available in a crunch.

"Hey, man. How you doin'?" Steve grabbed Chester's hand, ready to chat.

"Oh, fine, glad to be alive."

"That's all right—nice day out, huh?"

"Yep, I'm ready for the summer. I'm gonna take my grandkids to Disney World. My oldest grandson, named after me, keeps talking about it, and I'm gonna take him."

"Good for you. That should be fun. You know I'm thinking about taking my girls this summer. You have to let me know how the plans go." Steve would have to talk with Sabrena. He had always said that he would be the first one to take them to Disney, and maybe this summer would be the right time. He smiled as he thought of little Renee seeing Minnie Mouse. He had bought her a Minnie Mouse phone for her room and she'd slept with it on the first night. He smiled, but reminded himself to focus, or he wouldn't get all his work done in time. He still had to get a shave and haircut and pick up his suit before the cleaners closed. He felt like a kid, all over a piano recital and dinner.

Sabrena didn't have the strength to wrestle with the girls' hair today, or even her own, for that matter. She was glad that she had called Paula, their hairdresser, and made afternoon appointments. After getting the girls dressed and fed, she went to pick up their dresses from the store. This was one time that her discount came in handy. She bought them matching purses and shoes, and even though Sabrena was always watching their budget, it felt really good to splurge once in awhile. Sabrena would pull out her old faithful brown suit and spruce it up with a bright blue blouse. The piano recital was small and to anyone else not a big deal. However, for Deena and Renee, they might as well be playing at the Kennedy Center. They were giddy and nervous, which reminded Sabrena of their last recital. Renee had gotten stage fright and ran from the piano directly into Steve's arms. He had grabbed her and wiped her eyes, told her to be strong and walked her back to the piano. It was an odd sight, but he stood beside her during her entire performance. They were both proud when she took her bow at the end.

Steve would be there tomorrow. Sabrena missed him, but knew that she didn't need him in her life. Dr. Scott had told her that she could have contracted HIV anytime over the last ten years or so, and Steve was certainly a suspect. Steve was a dog, always had been, and always would be; no need in her missing him. She had too much drama going on; she needed to settle into her own routine and figure out her next steps. However, she couldn't deprive her girls of his love. Last week she had come home to find a card taped to the door with $300 and a note telling her that this was to help get their outfits for the recital and whatever else they needed. She knew that Steve cared, even more than their stupid father, who hadn't seen them in years. Sabrena appreciated Steve's love for them, and they were crazy about him, so she would have to find a way to make this work.

"Sabrena, you need a perm. Do you have time today?" Paula asked.

"Yeah, if we can blow it dry. How long will it take to press and comb the girls?" Sabrena knew that Renee wasn't going to be happy. She hated getting her hair done—she was too tender-headed.

"Not too long, I should have ya'll finished in about three hours."

Paula laughed. She knew she wouldn't get all of their heads done in that time, but it sounded good.

"Okay, straighten me out," Sabrena responded, preparing herself for the next five or six hours. Paula was such a bad liar, but a good beautician.

Despite being held hostage at the hair salon for most of the morning, the day flew by, and, in no time, Sabrena was trying to get the girls settled down early for the night. After all, between church in the morning and their four o'clock recital, followed by dinner, they would be worn out. By the time she had them bathed and their curly locks pinned up for the night, they were zonked.

"Mommy, what's that on your arm?" Renee asked, touching her bumps. "Did you get a boo boo?"

"Yes, honey, but it's fine." Sabrena forgot to keep her arms covered so that the girls wouldn't see her rash. She didn't want them to be worried or ask questions that she couldn't answer. She didn't want to lie to them.

"Is that why you've been so sleepy?" Deena asked as she rubbed her mother's arm.

"Yes, a little, but I've just been working hard. I feel good; you don't need to worry about Mommy. Let's say our prayers and get you two in the bed, you have a big day tomorrow."

"I know. What time is Uncle Steve picking us up? Where are we eating at afterwards? Is Auntie Rach coming?" Deena's mind was racing and she was getting revved up again.

"We'll talk about all that in the morning. Whose turn is it to pray? Renee, why don't you lead tonight." Sabrena knelt with the girls by Renee's bed and listened to her baby recite her prayers.

"Now I lay me down to sleep, I pray the Lord my soul to keep. If I should die before I wake, I pray the Lord my soul to take. God Bless Mommy, Uncle Steve, Auntie Rachel, Deena, Boxer, Uncle Gerald, Grandmamma and our whole family. God help me and Deena do good tomorrow and don't let us miss a note. Amen."

Sabrena tucked them into bed and kissed them goodnight. She stood outside the door and took a deep breath, saying a prayer for her babies and herself.

It had been a good day, a day unlike most recently, and Sabrena didn't think a lot about her diagnosis. She did get sick to her stomach in the morning after taking her meds and had to take the gargle medication, but beyond that, she had only good things on her mind. She knew not every day would be this good, so she cherished it.

It didn't hurt that she had a full-time doctor available whenever she needed her—Rach. Her friend had become her surrogate doctor, always giving her new information. She would also see Dr. Scott in a few days and find out how the medications were working. She thought of the upcoming week's appointment with Dr. Grier and about seeing her brother. How could she tell Gerald? Funny, how quickly her emotions seemed to swing these days. But just as fresh tears began to well, she was startled by the phone.

"Hello?" she answered, with a groggy voice.

"Hi Sabrena," Steve said shyly. "I didn't realize that it was too late to call. You sound like you're asleep." Steve sounded surprised that Sabrena, usually the night owl, was asleep before 9:30.

"Oh, I'm okay. I just dozed off." Sabrena tried to compose herself and went to wash her face. "What's up, Steve? How're you?" she asked, splashing cool water on her face.

"I'm good. Anticipating seeing the girls and you tomorrow." Steve felt like a school boy before a first date. "I got your message and wondered if I could just stop by and pick you all up so that we wouldn't have two cars."

"Oh, that's okay. Rach is going to be with us and she'll drive us to the recital and we'll ride to dinner and home with you." When Sabrena told the girls that Steve would be at the recital, they were out of control. They could hardly contain their squeals of excitement. Sabrena had to admit that she was looking forward to seeing him in some ways, but wondered if it was just loneliness or real feelings. She continued to wonder if Steve had been contacted by the health department about getting tested for HIV. Then again, she still wondered if he was the one who had given her HIV. She would have to confront him, but she couldn't imagine finding the right moment for that. She quickly got off the phone, took her medicines, and went to back to sleep.

CHAPTER TWENTY-EIGHT

The girls awoke with a nervous energy that couldn't be contained. This didn't help Sabrena, tired from a restless sleep filled with recurring nightmares and itching. She had awakened at 4 A.M. in a cold sweat, with her heart racing. These dreams were so vivid, worse than a horror movie. She prepared a heavy breakfast and tried to calm the girls down on the way to Sunday school. She knew that staying for the full church service would be cutting it too tight, so she planned to sit with them in their Sunday school class and volunteer as a helper. Sabrena would miss going to service today. She had tried to be consistent over the last few months. She definitely was praying more and trying to come to terms with her life. Part of Sabrena was mad at God, although she was too afraid to really say it. She was nearly forty, with two failed marriages, a recent failed relationship, and now HIV.

On some days, she felt that it was all her fault and that she deserved her current mess, but on other days she was mad as hell. Why was this happening to her, did she deserve this? Did her girls? These thoughts plagued Sabrena as she got the girls and herself together and drove to church. There had been many days when she had contemplated suicide, just to end it all. She tried to figure out how she could make it look like an accident. She had a will and everything in place to take care of the girls if she died. It would be easier for them to know that their Mom died in a car accident rather than from AIDS or even suicide. Sabrena shook her head, trying to erase the thoughts. As she glanced at her daughters, she knew that wasn't the answer.

As she pulled into the parking lot, she spotted Valerie parking her new champagne-colored Mercedes. Valerie made sure that

Sabrena saw her by waving like she was in a parade, and, with Tiffany in tow, she bolted across the lot to Sabrena and the girls.

"Good morning, ya'll," Valerie said. She was a true Southern belle with her North Carolina accent dripping down the front of her expensive navy suit and her face shaded by a wide-brimmed church lady hat. Tiffany had on a miniature version of her mother's suit and looked like a little old lady. Valerie had probably spent a fortune on the outfits.

"Good morning, Valerie," Sabrena mumbled, making sure that she straightened her girls' dresses. Sabrena had to admit that her daughters were absolutely beautiful, not that she was biased. They didn't have the matching dress and little gloves like Tiffany, but there was no comparison between her and Deena's and Renee's natural beauty.

"Good morning, Ms. Valerie and Tiffany," the girls said in unison. Tiffany hadn't even parted her lips yet to speak. Sabrena would invite that little girl over for a slumber party so she could help teach her some manners. It wasn't her fault her mother was stuck up.

"Where is your husband and Kenyon?" Sabrena asked as they began walking towards the church.

"Oh, uhh, Marcus is tired and wanted to sleep late. He's going to work out later and Kenyon is just hanging out with his daddy," Valerie said, smiling as she dramatically locked the new car. "I can't figure out these new-fangled cars," she said, beaming at her convertible.

"That's a nice car, Valerie—looks like it just came off the showroom floor," Sabrena remarked. She knew Valerie would continue the wild gestures until she complimented her. Sabrena was too tired to go through the whole routine, and decided to give her a break.

"Oh, thank you. God is good. Marcus bought it for me for my birthday. He really shouldn't be so extravagant, but he loves me and likes to show it," Valerie said, beaming from ear to ear. She took off her Chanel sunglasses. Who in the world needed sunglasses when the sky was overcast at 9 A.M. on Sunday morning? That was Valerie; she always had to flaunt her stuff. Sabrena bet that Marcus was working out, all right, just not at the gym.

"Good morning, ladies," Deacon Cliff Johnson called. He ran to open the door for them. "Ms. Collins, you're certainly looking beautiful this morning."

"Good morning, Deacon Johnson. Thank you very much." Sabrena made sure she didn't linger in the vestibule. The girls were late for Sunday school and she certainly didn't feel like making up another lie for why she couldn't have lunch, dinner, and a movie, or walk in the park with Deacon Johnson. He was nice, but he really wasn't Sabrena's type. Right now, she didn't have the time to even think about dating. Without any encouragement from her, he never failed to call her at least once a month to ask her out. Sabrena had run out of excuses and now relied on the answering machine or just flat out said no. She could end the calls now by telling him about her disease: a sure-fire man repellant.

She scooted the girls into their class and whispered to the teacher that she was available to help. The Sunday school class was actually fun, and it was good to see Renee and Deena interact with the other kids. Deena was very protective of Renee, getting juice for her and helping her with her craft project. Sabrena hoped they could always stay like that, just like it was with her and Gerald. She hoped they'll learn the lesson about God's mercy and love for his children. Once, Renee had brought tears to Sabrena's eyes when she asked, "So God is my daddy?" when the teacher talked about Him being our heavenly Father. Sabrena wondered if she would ever experience God's mercy or feel His love again.

Rach got to the house before Sabrena and the girls got home from church, and let herself in. She surprised herself by being early, but knew that it would be a busy day and that Sabrena would need her help. She also knew she needed to prepare herself to see that dog, Steve. Rach began to clean the morning dishes and made some coffee for herself. She could go to church every so often, but Sunday school was totally out of the question. Who in their right mind would get up early on Sunday morning? She and Barry had enjoyed a quiet evening at her house, with Barry cooking an extravagant dinner. Rach knew she would soon have to take a break from him—he was getting too close and she liked it too much. A man who was a mechanic, could cook, and was a wonderful lover was a dream too good to be true. Rach had waited to see the flaw in Barry. She had tested him to no end, but he was tried and true. She still didn't fully trust him, because she knew that the minute she really let him in, he would hurt her. They all did that sooner or later.

"Not gonna happen," Rach said aloud, but she smiled as she continued to think of him. She didn't care about the difference in their education. She used to think that she made a lot more money than he did until she did his taxes last year. She had to give it up for the blue collar brother, who, with overtime, was making some cash. His savings account was double the size of hers and he had no debt except for his mortgages.

At a cookout once, a friend of Sabrena's made a snide comment about Rach dating a mechanic. Rach smiled as she thought of that wench—Valerie, her name was. Valerie had asked about everyone's jobs, and after Barry walked away, said loudly that she could never settle for a noncollege graduate. Sabrena hadn't heard the comment, but Rach confronted Valerie.

"What did you say? What do you mean, you could never settle?" Rach went straight for the jugular.

"Oh, nothing. I just meant, what would you have in common?" Valerie stuttered, obviously surprised by the confrontation.

"What do you have in common with your husband? Oh, yeah, you both like to get it on with. . . ." Sabrena pulled her away just before she spilled the beans that everyone but Valerie seemed to know. Rach thought sometimes Sabrena was far too nice to people who would never return the favor.

Rach turned on the radio and listened to gospel music; that was as close to church as she'd get today. She decided to finish cleaning up the kitchen, a true testament to her love for Sabrena. She was singing aloud with the music when she heard Sabrena's keys in the door and went to greet them.

"Hey! How was Sunday school?" Rach asked Deena and Renee as they came bounding into the living room.

"Hi, Auntie Rach! It was fun," Deena answered as Renee showed Rach her craft project from Sunday school.

Sabrena said, "Girls, go put on your play clothes and come eat lunch." She was going to have to try to contain their excitement about their recital.

Sabrena looked around the kitchen in amazement. She backed away slowly. She asked, "Who are you and what have you done with my friend?"

"I can handle myself in the kitchen. I'm *every* woman and don't forget it." Rach smiled, playfully hitting Sabrena with the dish rag. "You look better. There's no swelling and the rash is almost gone. How're you feeling?"

"I'm just so tired. I'm sleepy all the time and I think that's making me irritable. I'm snapping at work, and at the girls. I just don't feel like myself, but I'm okay," Sabrena said with a forced smile. "The good thing is that I'm not itching as much anymore, since I stopped that medication and took those steroids and the hydroxyzine for the itching Dr. Scott prescribed. If I could just give my brain a break, I'd be great. But I'm having bad dreams and feeling anxious all the time."

"When is your next appointment? I know you keep putting off seeing the specialist," Rach scolded. "I'll go with you if you need me to, but you have to go."

"I'll see him on Thursday. I meant to ask if you could pick up the girls, or I'll see if Vanessa is available."

Sabrena made a mental note to call Vanessa, her younger friend and neighbor who often watched the girls for her. She liked Vanessa and admired her for being determined to finish her college degree. She was enrolled part-time and took care of her three-year-old son with no help from anyone except her mom who lived with her. Sabrena made sure that she gave her a few dollars every time she babysat for her. She knew it could be rough as a single mom, especially at such a young age.

Sabrena herself was watching every penny these days, but she also knew how important it was to help her friends who were always helping her. Sabrena sensed she'd be relying on them even more in the coming days. The co-pay for the doctor and her medications were costing her a lot and eating away at her monthly extras. Thank God she had insurance, but even then the costs were getting to her. The co-pay on each of her prescriptions was $25 dollars; each time she got a new one, she cringed.

Sabrena shook her head. So much to worry about! She thanked God for a friend like Rach.

"I've a senior management meeting at three, but I can pick them up from Vanessa if you need me to," Rach said, proving once again what a good friend she was. "Let me know what I need to do." Rach knew that it would be nearly impossible to get out of her quarterly meeting, but if she had to, she would.

"Thank you for everything, Rach. I don't say it enough, but I really do appreciate all you do for us. Please get me up in an hour." Sabrena went to lie down. Before crawling into bed, she made sure that she gargled with the nasty medicine.

"Shoot! I forgot to take the rest of that darn medicine this morning!" Sabrena picked up the bottles and threw them against the wall. She was sick of feeling tired and taking all these pills. "I'm just going to *live*! I'm not taking any more of these damned pills," Sabrena hissed as she looked at herself in the mirror. Her skin still had a few spots from the rash and she was looking thinner every day. More than the pain or nausea, it tore at her insides that she couldn't just enjoy this day with her daughters without feeling sick and old.

The melancholy overtook her and she threw herself on her bed, praying that she wouldn't have another nightmare, which sometimes struck her even during brief naps. As she closed her eyes, she felt Boxer at her feet. Maybe she imagined it, but she thought she felt Boxer slide under her feet, as if he were urging her up. Looking at the picture of Deena and Renee on the nightstand, she nodded and got out of bed to take her morning medications. Though the bottles lay on the floor, the child safety caps ensured that the pills had not fallen out. Sabrena laughed. "God help me!"

CHAPTER TWENTY-NINE

The recital wasn't until four, but the girls had to be there by 3:30. Rach did some quick calculations and decided that she would get the girls dressed and ready by three so they would have plenty of time. Sabrena said to wake her in an hour, but if Rach got the girls dressed, she could let her sleep longer. She was worried about Sabrena: she looked tired and had lost more weight. Rach's eyes filled with water as she thought about what would happen, what could happen, and when. She wiped her eyes and went in to play with her nieces, who were bouncing off the walls with excitement.

Steve dressed carefully in his gray suit. He had bought a new shirt and tie to spice it up for the recital. He would arrive early to wish the girls luck and to make sure that he sat next to Sabrena. Steve wasn't looking forward to seeing Rach, however. It was Sunday, so he stopped himself from thinking too horribly about her. They had never hit it off and he was sure they weren't going to now. As he picked up his keys, he looked at the letter he had received from the health department, but tossed it aside as he headed out the door. Today was a day for his family—even if not by blood.

Deena was the first to perform and she looked adorable. Sabrena beamed as she played her solo, so polished and intense. She looked like a little woman, not a seven-year-old. After she finished, she took her grand curtsy. They jumped to their feet applauding.

"That's my baby," Sabrena whispered as she watched Deena leave the stage. She silently wiped away the tears that were rolling down her cheeks. She was both proud and petrified. Could this be the last recital she would attend? Sabrena excused herself quickly and ran to the ladies room. She felt the walls caving in around her and began breathing fast. She sat in the stall and tears dampened her face. She whimpered like a wounded animal. How could she have been so stupid? How could she have put her girls' lives at stake just for a man, for some sex?

"I gotta pull it together," Sabrena said aloud as she frantically wiped her face. "I gotta pull it together. Renee will be on in a few minutes." Sabrena took some deep breaths and whispered a prayer.

"Bre, are you okay?" Rach was standing outside her stall.

"Yeah, I'm fine. Go back in. Renee will be playing in a few minutes," Sabrena said.

"Bre, I'm not leaving without you. Are you okay?"

"*Leave me alone*! Dammit, Rach, I just lost my breath for a minute," Sabrena said curtly. This hovering mother hen Rachel was beginning to get next to her. She needed some space. She couldn't talk about *everything*. She just needed to breathe.

"You've lost your mind! Don't talk to me like that! Go on, pass out, I'll leave you here on this dirty floor," Rach said as she left the bathroom in a huff. When Sabrena thought about it, she realized Rach was just trying to help, but, lately, she was having a hard time holding in her frustration. How could anyone understand everything she was going through? Even Rach, how could she possibly understand? It was her life, her children, her body, her mess that she faced every single day. She pulled herself together and headed back into the auditorium, where she saw Steve looking around for her.

"Where's Sabrena?" Steve asked, puzzled by her abrupt flight.

"In the bathroom," Rach said tartly.

"Is she okay? Steve inquired, gazing around the room. "She looked funny."

"Are *you* okay, Steve? Is there something *you* need to share?" Rach turned up her lips and faced Steve. He didn't need to pretend to be so concerned, she thought. She bet it was because of him that Sabrena was in this mess.

"What are you talking about?" Steve hissed. "You're still crazy! What are you talking about? You don't know me like that!" Steve had never liked Rachel. She was mean and always in his and Sabrena's business. He bet that she was the one who told Sabrena to break up with him.

"Shhhh, listen to this child," Rach said. She tried to regain her composure, but all the while wanted to beat Steve down. She swore that if she found out that Steve had given Sabrena HIV, she would make sure that he was sorry—painfully sorry.

Sabrena slipped back into the row, looking sweaty. "Rach, you know I'm sorry," she whispered as she grabbed her best friend's hand. "Renee is next."

Rach patted Sabrena's hand and that made all the difference.

All the hard work and practice had paid off for Renee and Deena. The recital was a hit and they talked nonstop with Steve at dinner. They were excited about being in a "grown-up" restaurant. Sabrena watched Steve and marveled at how he gave the girls his undivided attention. Her mind flickered from how this man could be the one to have changed her life (for the worse) to how wonderful a father he would make. She was abruptly brought back to reality when she heard Renee squeal.

"Mommy, can we go? Can we please go with Uncle Steve?" Renee tugged at Sabrena's arm.

"Calm down. Go where? What are you talking about?" Sabrena asked, puzzled.

"Uncle Steve wants to take us to Disney World. He wants to take us, all of us," Deena answered for her sister, her big eyes filled with excitement. "Can we go?"

"Please Mommy, pleeeeeze," the girls said in unison.

"What? Steve, what are they talking about?" Sabrena was confused by the sudden change in the conversation.

CHAPTER THIRTY

Rach was happy to be done with Steve for the day and to see Barry at her house preparing dinner. However, her thoughts kept going back to Sabrena. She was too preoccupied to eat.

"Baby, what's wrong? You haven't touched your food," Barry said as he touched her hair.

"I just have stuff on my mind, that's all. More importantly, I keep telling you that I'm not a baby. My name is R-A-C-H-E-L. Can you get that—repeat after me, *Rachel*!" Rach jerked her head from his touch and regretted the words as soon as they came out of her mouth.

"You know what, Ms. Rachel, I'm gonna let you keep all the stuff on your mind and deal with it by yourself. I'm getting tired of being treated like a nuisance. I'm a *man*, Rachel, not a boy, not your lap dog, but a *MAN*! It seems to me that you don't want a man— you want something else! Well, I'm finished trying to see the good in you and take care of you. You think you're so hard and so emotionally unattached, but deep down I see a scared little girl who doesn't want to get hurt. So yeah, I call you baby, because to me in a lot of ways you are a baby—someone I need to hold, protect, and take care of. Maybe you don't want that, maybe you think that you can do it all by yourself, but you're not fooling me, *Rachel*!! I know you're scared out of your mind that you could love someone. I don't know what, who, or when someone ripped your heart out, but I'm not going to take responsibility for something I never did. I love you, God knows I love you, despite *YOU* and I want to spend the rest of my life with you. But only if you let me in. I don't want to be the engine and the gas for this relationship. I need to be loved and wanted, too. When you feel like you can handle me and what I have to give you, call me. But not until you can handle it all. You better pray that I'm still around waiting on you, because I'm one of the few good men left and one of the few who will put up with your bullcrap." Barry stormed out the door.

Rach was sitting on the couch with her mouth wide open. She had never seen him react so emotionally or yell so loudly. Or yell at all, now that she thought about it. Her first reaction wasn't to miss him or forgive him or even think about what he'd said. Instead, she slammed the door behind him and yelled, "Fine! Go ahead and leave! Leave! You all do! I don't need you, I don't need anybody." She slammed the door one more time for good measure and screamed.

She couldn't believe that Barry had dumped her! That was her department, but she knew that he would come running back. She prayed that he would. They had broken up several times before, all on her terms. However, this time was different, and while she was mad at him for going off on her, part of her smiled because he stood up to her mess. Maybe it was time to cool it again. The last thing that Rach ever worried about was a man. She always had a "spare." She should call Garfield just to say hello and get back at Barry. Somehow, that didn't appeal to her today. Maybe she'd let the best thing that ever happened to her walk out the door.

"I always have my Häagen Dazs®," Rach said aloud. She opened the freezer and found comfort in chocolate ice cream.

CHAPTER THIRTY-ONE

Sabrena got the girls into bed and allowed Steve to read them a bedtime story while she made a pot of coffee. What was he trying to pull? Disney World? They had talked about it over a year ago, but never made any plans. Why now?

"The girls are knocked out," Steve said as he sat at the counter. "The day was just too much for them."

"Yeah, they were really excited. They've worn me out." Sabrena took a sip of her coffee and said, "Steve, we have to talk about Disney World. I appreciate all you do for the girls and always have. You're the only man who has really been a consistent male figure in their lives. There's no way I could afford to keep them in piano lessons and summer camps without your help. But we're not together now and they're not your responsibility. I work hard to make sure they have what they need. I've never asked you to take care of them—or me, for that matter!" Sabrena wanted to just clear the air and move forward with Steve. "I want them to experience everything that little girls dream of, but Disney World is too much to allow you to do for them. Furthermore, you should have talked to *me* about this before bringing it up with them. If I say no, I'll be the Wicked Witch of the West."

"Sabrena, I've told you over and over that these girls are *my* girls. I love them like they were my biological daughters. Don't take this away from me, please. I know that I'm a horrible boyfriend, but let me try to be a good uncle and a good dad to these girls. It's just as much for me as it is for them. You don't know how proud I was to see them on stage and playing so well. I have to admit that it also felt good to feel how much they love me. Their hugs and smiles were enough. Now, I know you don't want to be with me and I can only hope that will change, but I still love the girls and want to be in their lives. I've always promised them that I would take them to Disney, so why can't I? It would be a good break when school first gets out and we can stay for four or five days and come back." Steve's eyes pleaded with Sabrena and she didn't quite know what to make of it.

"Steve, if you loved them so much—why did you . . ." Sabrena looked away, refusing to get into a discussion about their relationship or to bring up the HIV/AIDS. "You know what, I'll think about it and let you know."

"Okay, that's fine. It's up to you, but I'd like to settle the plans in the next few days so that we can get the time off and stuff. I gotta get some credit. I sat next to Rachel for two hours," Steve said with a chuckle, noticing Sabrena's body without her jacket on. She had lost some weight. She looked good, but something was bothering her. She had barely touched her food in the restaurant. Although it was her favorite, she just moved the food around on her plate.

"Sabrena, are you feeling okay? What are those red marks on your arms?"

"I'm fine. I had a reaction to something and got a rash, but I'm okay." Sabrena was uneasy and she was ready for him to leave the house. This wasn't how Steve wanted the night to end. He needed to make some headway in winning her back.

"Sabrena, can we listen to some music? I need to just wind down a bit before driving home," Steve said as he went to the music center. He found his Grover Washington CD and put it on. He was glad she hadn't given it back to him.

"Steve, it's getting late and we both have to go to work tomorrow," Sabrena said, remembering that she had to do two more gargles before the night ended and take more pills. She was feeling queasy, sleepy, and her head was beginning to ache. Sabrena had the urge to scratch in a few places that were not socially acceptable.

"Okay, let's just listen to this and relax for a minute. Sit down; I'll get a glass of wine for us." Steve walked into the kitchen, thinking how much he missed being here. But he'd be back soon, for good. This was his home.

"All right, excuse me. I'll be right back." Sabrena went into her bathroom and gargled with her medication. She took a deep breath and tried to keep her head clear. She knew Steve's old tricks and he was pulling out all stops. Not too aggressive, but trying nonetheless.

Even though she was damaged goods and no man would ever want her again, she wasn't anxious to start up with Steve. He couldn't be trusted, so she'd let him visit for awhile and promptly put him out. Sabrena had looked, listened, and tried to observe any hint about Steve's HIV status, but she was coming up empty-handed.

When she returned, Steve was sitting on the couch with his head back listening to the music. He was handsome and looked so innocent in her living room. Sabrena was too wise to go down this road again. She'd have a glass of wine, which she would only put up to her lips, but not swallow. She would say good night to him and get in her bed.

"This is nice. You have to admit it's like old times, Sabrena," Steve said. He didn't speak nearly as smoothly as Sabrena had imagined he would. He actually seemed sincere.

"No, not really, Steve. The old times I remember are of me waiting on you to come, and then of you coming up with some wild lie as to where you were," Sabrena said. She felt stronger by the moment. "Yeah, the times I remember are of waiting, worrying, getting mad, and then crying myself to sleep, wondering why I was still with you."

"I know that I've been bad in the past, but Sabrena—you don't have to believe me, I'll show you. You've made me a better man and I'm ready to be with you and you only. Sabrena, these last few months have showed me what a damned fool I've been. I want you and only you. I love you and love who I am when I'm with you." Steve hadn't planned to spill his heart like that, but he couldn't stop himself from telling her how he felt. He reached for her and hugged her. She felt good in his arms and she didn't pull away. "I love you so much, Sabrena. I really do," Steve whispered in her ear and began to softly kiss her neck and slowly touch her breasts.

Sabrena felt her strong will melting as she felt his arms around her body. She couldn't deny that all her feelings weren't gone for Steve, but right now it wasn't about him, it was about someone touching her and holding her. She needed the strong arms to make her feel like a woman, not a leper. His lips felt good on her neck. Feelings she hadn't had in months rose in her very core. As Steve began to open her blouse, she felt herself leaning back on the couch and getting lost in his touch. She shivered as his hand massaged her bare breast. He began to kiss her passionately, and she felt her body respond as he began to rub himself against her. She willed her body not to betray her, but she couldn't stop herself from responding. It was as if she were putting on a favorite pair of jeans; they just fit in all the right places. Steve knew how to turn her on and please her. He lifted her from the couch and before she realized it they were on her bed. Steve began to undress her with his mouth and she felt him touching her. She felt her body pulsating.

"Steve, *no*! Stop, this can't happen," she cried. Sabrena pushed him off and pulled her blouse together. "You've got to go. I'm sorry, but this isn't going to happen," Sabrena said sternly. She pushed his hands away.

"Honey, you've got to be kidding. You know you want me. We're meant to be together. Your body doesn't lie," Steve said, bewildered at Sabrena's abrupt behavior.

"Steve, please leave. I'm sorry. I didn't mean to lead you on. Yes, my body may want you, but my mind knows that this isn't good. Please show yourself out." Sabrena opened her bedroom door. Steve was obviously aroused and appeared confused, but that wasn't Sabrena's problem. She shut the door before her tears began falling. Once again she'd been stupid. How could she even think about sex, especially with Steve. She would never be held or loved again. She was tainted and dangerous.

CHAPTER THIRTY-TWO

Sabrena's morning was hectic. She overslept and the girls were dragging. She finally got them to school, ran a few errands, and went to work. She forgot to take her medications again and planned on catching up at lunchtime. Her desk was full of notes and things she needed to get done, so her morning flew by. The only reason she even took time for lunch was that she and Vivian had scheduled a meeting at noon.

Sabrena got a bottle of water and took her morning medications after she gargled in the ladies room. Just as she was spitting in the sink, Vivian walked in.

"Hey Sabrena, are you ready for our meeting?" Vivian asked. Sabrena quickly put the bottle back in her purse and rinsed out the sink.

"Oh! Vivian, you scared me. Yeah, I'll be right there." Sabrena wondered what Vivian had seen and hoped she wouldn't ask her about anything. She couldn't talk to Vivian about this. After all, no matter how nice she was, Vivian was still her boss and Sabrena needed her job. They met for lunch and talked about hiring for the summer months and coverage for vacations. Vivian told her she was going to take a few weeks off for personal reasons and she would need her to make sure things kept going.

Sabrena noticed that Vivian looked teary as she spoke about needing time off, and she was concerned. "Vivian, I'm not trying to get in your business, but I know that there is something wrong. If you ever feel like talking about it, I'm here," Sabrena said as she grabbed her friend's hand.

"Thank you, Sabrena. I can't really talk about it now, but I know that it will be all right. It's just hard. My number one job is to be a wife and mother and I need time just to take care of that part of my life," Vivian said. Tears streamed down her cheeks.

"Whatever it is, just know that you're cared for and that I'll be praying for you," Sabrena said, wiping back her own tears. Vivian was her friend and she hated seeing her in pain. It really wasn't any of her business, but she knew it had to be hard. She had never seen Vivian like this before. "Well, aren't we a sight," Sabrena said as she looked at their tear-stained faces in the mirror. "Let's get our faces together and get back to work." Sabrena laughed and handed Vivian a tissue.

"Sabrena, can we just keep this between you and me? I don't want to be the subject of the rumor mill. I just need some time."

"No problem, Vivian. I wouldn't have it any other way. Please feel free to talk to me about anything. I'll be here for you." Sabrena knew that no matter what she was going through, she also needed to help Vivian.

CHAPTER THIRTY-THREE

The rest of the week passed quickly and before Sabrena knew it she was sitting in the parking lot of Dr. Grier's office. She panicked before going into the office, so she sat in the parking lot and watched people come and go for some time. The office building was large and no one would know she was going in specifically to see Dr. Grier. Sabrena knew that she was being paranoid, but she couldn't risk people finding out about her diagnosis. She sat in the car until exactly four minutes before her appointment time, and quickly walked into the building with her sunglasses on. She was grateful that there were several offices on the fifth floor. The floor was already pushed when she got into the crowded elevator. Sabrena was the last one to get off the elevator and as she looked for the suite number, she saw a very handsome man walking out of the office. He held the door open for her, but she looked down, careful not to meet his eyes. She wondered if this man had HIV. She was living proof that you can't tell by looking.

"Hello, I have a 3:45 appointment with Dr. Grier," Sabrena said in almost a whisper, looking over her shoulder at the other person in the lobby.

"Oh, you must be Ms. Collins. Please fill out these papers and we'll be right with you," the receptionist said. She handed Sabrena the clipboard.

"Uh, can I go into a room to fill this out? I really don't want to . . . ," Sabrena said, looking around the waiting room.

"Sure, let me take you into your exam room." The receptionist was nice and seemed to understand. Sabrena felt a wave of relief as she sat alone in the exam room. A few minutes later the receptionist came in to get her co-pay and the forms. "Dr. Grier will be right with you."

A nurse came out to the waiting room to get her. "Hi, I'm Karen, Dr. Grier's nurse. Let me take your blood pressure and get your weight and other vitals. How're you feeling, Ms. Collins?"

"I'm fine, thanks." Sabrena knew the routine. The nurse was nice, but Sabrena was glad when she finished up and closed the door, adding, "The doctor will be right with you."

Sabrena sighed. Once again, she was left in a doctor's exam room. She looked at some of the posters on the wall and picked up information. She was curious about the living will instruction sheet and form the nurse had given her but quickly stuffed them into her bag. Thinking about a living will meant thinking about death and she wasn't ready for that yet. There was a soft knock on the door and a man in his late fifties entered, extending his hand warmly toward her.

"Hello, Ms. Collins. I'm Dr. Jonathan Grier."

"Hi, Dr. Grier, nice to meet you." Sabrena nervously shook his hand.

"I have gone over the paperwork that Dr. Scott sent over and the forms you completed. I know it's a lot of work, but I like to get a fresh start with all my new patients. I need to ask you some questions and then we'll do a full physical examination." Dr. Grier went over the papers with her and asked her what seemed like thousands of questions, most routine, but some very intimate. Sabrena felt comfortable with him, even though she did prefer female doctors. He did a very thorough examination and, although Sabrena felt a little shy being naked while he examined her skin, his nurse made every effort to keep her as covered as possible.

After the examination, Sabrena breathed a sigh of relief and pulled out the pad that she had written her questions on. She hoped that she could ask him questions. Although Dr. Scott was Sabrena's favorite, she did like Dr. Grier and how he had explained everything to her again.

"Ms. Collins, it's up to you as to how you deal with the treatment of your disease. You know that there is no cure for AIDS, but we've good success in helping people live longer and lead more normal lives. But I'm a very busy doctor and I have a tight schedule. I like to spend extra time with my patients so that I can accommodate their needs and give them the best possible care. When a patient misses appointments or continually reschedules, it limits what I can do for the other people who need to come into the office. I depend on people keeping their appointments and telling me what's going on. I'll work with you as long as you work with me, but not keeping appointments, stopping medications, and forming bad habits all lead down a path that isn't good for you or your family." Dr. Grier spoke as he gave her a sheet with all her medications, how to take them, and a pillbox to put them in.

"Okay, Dr. Grier, I'll do better. I was just scared to see you, but I'll keep my appointments with you and Dr. Scott. I'll do what you say and try to stay on track," Sabrena said confidently.

"Ms. Collins, did I bite? Hahaha. I understand your fears, but believe me, your information is confidential. My staff is very professional and if you have any questions or concerns, call my administrator, Tanyel."

Dr. Grier had told her that, according to the latest blood tests Dr. Scott had sent, the amount of the HIV virus in her body—they called it her viral load, had gone down significantly and her CD4 count had gone up by several points, which indicated that the medication was working. He also told her that she could stop the medication for thrush, because she no longer had it and only needed to start the gargle again if the white spots came back.

"See, if you'd kept your appointment," Dr. Grier said with a wink, "you wouldn't have been still gargling five times a day."

"Okay, okay, I got it. What else do I need to do? Can I stop any more medications?" Sabrena asked. She felt better about seeing him.

"Well, not right now. As a matter of fact, I'm going to replace the medication that Dr. Scott stopped when you had the rash. You had a reaction to one of the medications that helps keep you from getting a type of pneumonia called PCP, which stands Pneumocystis Carinii Pneumonia. That's the most common type of pneumonia people with AIDS get. Because your CD4 count is low, which remember is how your body fights infection, you're at risk for PCP. So we need to start another medication for prevention. You'll need to take this medication once a day."

"Dr. Grier, I'm sorry, but I don't understand. Do I have pneumonia or not? Isn't PCP a drug? If I don't, why do I have to take a medicine every day?" Sabrena was confused.

"No need to apologize, I want us both to be on the same page. No, you don't have pneumonia, but we want to keep you from getting this type of pneumonia as much as we can. Think of it like your children and vaccinations—they don't have the disease, but they get a vaccination to prevent them from getting it. PCP are the initials we use for both the street drug and this type of pneumonia." Dr. Grier handed Sabrena another brochure for her to read. She felt like she was in class, HIV 101.

"Okay, I sort of understand, since you put it like that."

"Good, I'll see you in about three weeks," he continued. "Stop by either my office or Dr. Scott's office to get blood work two weeks before your appointment. I'll fax over a note to her. I notice that you have not had a test for something called Toxoplasmosis. We call it Toxo for short. We'll do this test with your next set of labs, but, in the meantime, don't change your cat's litter box without gloves. Or better yet, get your girls to change it every day." Dr. Grier handed her an instruction sheet with the information and how to take the medications.

"What does the cat's litter box have to do with this? Do I need to get rid of Boxer, my cat?" Sabrena was confused.

"No, but you do need to protect yourself from the fungus which cats can carry. They can give it to you in their litter. Did you buy him at a pet store or was he a stray?" Dr. Grier asked.

"He was a stray neighborhood cat. He's been with us for over a year." Sabrena immediately thought about how she would tell the girls that Boxer would have to go. That would be hard.

"Well, right now we don't have to do anything but make sure you don't come in contact with the litter box without thoroughly washing your hands, and make sure that it gets changed every day. Also, don't eat raw or undercooked meat or seafood. Read the pamphlet I gave you on what to eat and how to gain some of your weight back. It's important for you to follow a healthy diet and to eat, even when you sometimes don't feel like it. Avoid alcohol and I'm glad to see that you don't smoke. Your food may start to taste funny, like a medicine, or have a metal-type taste. I recommend that you suck some lemons or limes and gargle to help with that, but try to continue to eat." Dr. Grier didn't want to overwhelm Sabrena, so he would tell Karen to schedule her next visit on a day when the nutritionist was at his office.

"The raw meat thing is not an issue; I don't like sushi or rare meat. I don't really have an appetite, but I don't want to lose any more weight." Sabrena had read that she should buy some nutritional bars or drinks to help with the calories.

"I'll be watching your weight. I also have a few other tests that you need to schedule. I want a bone test, which is also called a DEXA scan." He closed her chart and extended his hand again. "It was a pleasure meeting you, Ms. Collins. Call me if you have any questions or problems at all, and remember our deal." Dr. Grier got up from his chair, but Sabrena touched his arm and he sat back down.

Sabrena felt a huge lump in her throat. She swallowed before speaking. "Dr. Grier, how long do I have to live? I have two young daughters and I'm really all they have. I need to be around for them. Who else can be their Mommy? That's my job. I can't leave them." Sabrena began to weep. She felt Dr. Grier's hand on her back, and she tried to regain her composure.

"Ms. Collins, I wish I could answer you, but I can't. What I can tell you is that I treat many people who've been diagnosed with AIDS and they're still living happy, full lives. There are also many people with AIDS who started the medications, began a healthier lifestyle, and now no longer have AIDS but remain HIV-positive. AIDS is now really a chronic disease that we can treat. There is no cure and we certainly want to prevent people from getting this disease. It's not a "pretty" or predictable disease and it will take work to stay healthy. It'll take a commitment to your health, your family, and to yourself to do everything possible to get the best treatment. As I told you before, you're on what we call the HAART regimen. This stands for Highly Active Antiretroviral Therapy, and this has really changed how we think of HIV/AIDS. Already, we have seen the amount of the virus drop in your blood system. Your immune system is improving, which we measure by your T-cells and CD4 counts. We just need to continue to work on getting you the best treatment." Dr. Grier gave her a tissue to wipe her eyes.

"Okay, Dr. Grier, I'll do all I can. How long do you think I've had HIV?" Sabrena asked, still trying to figure out who infected her.

"That's a very difficult question in your case. Your history and your counts don't directly point to the time of infection. I would guess that you were infected between as few as two to four years ago, which would be possible but unusual, and as much as five to seven years ago. We just can't be one hundred percent sure." Dr. Grier went on to address Sabrena's real question. "You want to know who infected you, which is a natural response. Unfortunately, African-American women are getting HIV/AIDS at twenty-five times the rate of white women. Eighty-three percent of all AIDS diagnoses in women are in African-American and Hispanic women. In fact, anyone you've slept with during the last ten to, even in very rare cases, fifteen years can be a possible source of the infection. But who gave it to you is far less important now than how to get you as healthy as we can. I know you gave names to Dr. Scott, which were sent to the health department, and that's a good move to try to stop the continued spread. If you're sexually active, or planning on being sexually active, you should tell your partner about your status and of course use condoms."

"No, Dr. Grier, I don't think that sex will be an issue for me anymore," Sabrena said as she looked down at the floor. "Who would want a woman with AIDS?"

"Don't ever rule out the possible. There are many patients with HIV/AIDS in healthy relationships who are still sexual. You're still a woman with desires. I can't sugarcoat this diagnosis for you, but you still have a life to live. Don't shut down your emotions, but be responsible," Dr. Grier said, reaching for yet another pamphlet. "I want you to consider joining a support group. There's a support group that is primarily for African-American women with HIV/AIDS. Here's the number. Ms. Collins, I need to tell you—this is not your fault. You have nothing to be ashamed of, just as people with high blood pressure, diabetes, breast cancer, or any other medical condition have no reason to be ashamed. I can imagine what's going through your head, but in time this will get better. Trust me."

"Thank you, Dr. Grier. I'll see you in a few weeks. I'm not ready for a support group. I can't talk to anyone but my best friend about this right now." Sabrena reached for the door, aware of the time she had taken with the nice doctor. She made her appointment at the desk and went to get the prescriptions filled.

CHAPTER THIRTY-FOUR

Sabrena drove to the pharmacy, which was a bit of a distance from her house in a predominately white neighborhood. She wanted to avoid seeing anyone she knew if at all possible.

"Hi, how long will it take to get these filled?" Sabrena asked the kind-looking clerk behind the counter.

"Oh, not too long—let's see what you have here." The clerk, an older woman, took the prescriptions; Sabrena swore that she saw her take a step away from her and immediately become tense. Her smile disappeared.

"Uhh, I'll, ummm, give these to the pharmacist right away. I don't know how long it'll take. Maybe you should come back later." The woman's face was turning red and Sabrena knew that her secret was out; she felt embarrassed and wanted to run out of the pharmacy. However, she needed the meds—she'd her girls to think about. Thinking of them, she became angry at the reaction of the clerk, who was suppposed to be a professional.

"Excuse me, but I'll just sit right here and wait," Sabrena said curtly as she stared down the pharmacy clerk.

Sabrena read a magazine as she waited for the prescriptions to be filled. She saw the clerk stealing glances at her and whispering something to the pharmacist. Sabrena didn't know how she would endure this and all of the other bad situations that she could be placed in because of this disease. She couldn't let her daughters be treated differently—she would have to find a way to keep her diagnosis from anyone that could be connected to her daughters and her family.

When the medicines were ready, she was shocked to find that they cost over $180 for a month's supply. She was too embarrassed to question the clerk on the costs and she wanted to get out of the pharmacy. She now felt like all the staff was looking at her funny. She would call her insurance company in the morning and find out why they cost so much. In the meantime, she would have to dip into her savings account to cover groceries and after-school care costs. The raise she'd received had been a nice surprise, but her medical costs were eating up all her extra money.

Sabrena picked up the girls from Vanessa and took them to the park for a few minutes, while there was still some daylight left. She loved seeing them run around with their ponytails bouncing. This was the time of year Sabrena loved: springtime, with summer just around the corner. The flowers were blooming and the weather was warm enough to go out with a light sweater. She took a deep breath and in the midst of it all gave thanks for life. She didn't know what lay ahead, but she was here and going to do everything she could to stay alive. Sabrena mustered up the energy to run over to her girls and join them on the swing set. Their laughter provided the fuel she needed to keep going. The discomfort she felt at the pharmacy soon faded, drowned by the joy of her daughters.

When the sun dipped out of sight and the night breeze started to blow, Sabrena got the girls settled in the car and stopped by McDonald's for dinner, happy to avoid cooking. She was tired and had so much to think about. She put them in the tub and read to them until they fell asleep. Sabrena listened to her voice mail while she ran a bath, and was a bit relieved that Gerald called to say his trip had been postponed. She wanted to see him, but now wasn't a good time. Rach called and she decided to call her back. They hadn't talked since the recital. Steve had also called almost every day, but she wasn't ready to face him yet.

"Hey, Rach, what's up?" Sabrena asked.

"Oh, nothing. What's up with you? Did you go to the doctor today?" Rach asked. She wiped her eyes. She'd been feeling sorry for herself and missing Barry.

"Yeah, but I don't want to talk about me for once. That's all we've been doing for weeks. What's wrong?" Sabrena knew Rach and knew the inflections of her voice.

"Nothing, tell me what Dr. Grier said." Rach really wasn't in the mood to talk about her life. When she hung up with Sabrena, she planned on drinking some wine and going to bed. Sabrena and Rach caught up and made a brunch date for Sunday, when the girls would be at a birthday party.

"It was a good visit, better than I thought, but I don't want to talk about it right now. I'm exhausted. Is Barry there?" Sabrena asked tentatively.

"Nope, and it's over for real," Rach answered, with fresh tears forming in her eyes. She felt so stupid.

"You kicked him to the curb—*again*? You know that all you have to do is apologize and he'll be there." Sabrena was used to her friend's on and off relationship: just as she got closer to him, she would find an excuse to break up with him. Sabrena knew what Barry and all Rach's other ex's didn't: when Rach's father left them, she had put on a brave face, but it had gutted her so deeply that she'd never completely healed. Then her college boyfriend inflicted yet another wound. Every man she'd met since was paying for their betrayals.

"I didn't break up with him, Sabrena, he left me. Said he was tired of my BS and left. I've never seen him so mad. I gotta go. . . ." Rach needed to control herself. No one was worthy of her tears.

"Girl, call me in the morning," Sabrena said. "Do you need me to come over, or do you want to come over here for tonight?"

"No, I need to be by myself. I'll call you in the morning." Rach hung up the phone and pulled out a bottle of wine. She immediately put away when she read the label and realized it was from Barry. She decided to go to bed, alone again with an aching heart.

CHAPTER THIRTY-FIVE

Sabrena went into work earlier than usual to see Ms. Bernadette in Human Resources about her insurance plan and to thank her for the raise she'd received a few weeks ago. Sabrena was sure she was behind it. Sabrena had called her insurance carrier before leaving the house and they'd told her that two of her medications required higher co-pays because they weren't on their preferred list. It had been two weeks since her visit with Dr. Grier and soon she would have to get refills. The insurance company also told her that as of July first, all of her co-pays would be going up for her medications and doctor visits. The only good thing was that the person on the phone gave her information on how to get her medications through the mail for three months at a time for the same price she paid in the pharmacy for one month. This would be good in two ways; she didn't have to worry about being seen at the pharmacy and the costs would be less. Dr. Grier had told her that if she responded well to the medications, she might be able to come off them in a few months. Sabrena was committed to following his instructions and taking whatever he prescribed, but she also needed to be as smart as possible about her finances.

"Good morning, Sabrena," Ms. Bernadette greeted her warmly and invited her into her office.

"Good morning, do you have a couple minutes for me?" Sabrena asked, aware that she hadn't call ahead.

"Of course, it's early yet." Ms. Bernadette winked. She really liked Sabrena and had made it a point to put her on her prayer list. She just felt that Sabrena was going through a battle and she wanted to keep her covered with prayer.

"First, let me thank you for the raise. I know that you had something to do with it. It really came in handy, and I appreciate it, as well as the forms to get reimbursed for my time off at the doctors' and when I wasn't feeling well."

"Oh you're welcome, you deserve it. I was just doing my job."

"Well, I know that it was more than you trying to do your job, so thank you," Sabrena said. She looked at the motherly woman. Why wasn't her mother so warm and kind?

"Ms. Bernadette, I need to know what the other options are for my health insurance. I was prescribed some medication and was told that the co-pay was higher for it. Also, the insurance company said that as of July first, my co-pays will be higher for everything." Sabrena was careful with her words, so that she wouldn't give out too much of her business.

"You actually should be getting a letter in the mail with the information. It's true that they're changing the co-pays and the monthly premium is actually going up by a few dollars, but the company is going to pay that. We could put you in an HMO plan that would reduce your co-pays by a few dollars, but there are some restrictions on what doctors you could see, and if the medications aren't on their preferred list, you would pay more, as well. Let's look at these." Ms. Bernadette pulled out the folders with all the insurance options and discussed them at length with Sabrena. She also gave her things to take home to read. Fortunately, open enrollment was coming up and Sabrena would be able to change her plan if she decided to. However, there were a lot of things to consider, including hospital coverage. She appreciated how patient Ms. Bernadette was with her and she felt comfortable in her office.

"Okay, I'll read this and figure out what I need. Can I call you if I have a question?" Sabrena was a bit overwhelmed by all of the information and was going to call both Dr. Scott's and Dr. Grier's office to see if they took the HMO plan.

"Sure, call me anytime, and Sabrena, here's my home number. Call me if you just want to talk about anything." Ms. Bernadette was convinced that this young lady was facing some health challenges. Although she didn't like mixing her business with her personal life, she knew that God was putting Sabrena in her path.

"One more thing, Ms. Bernadette, I need to increase the money I'm putting into my 401K, but need to balance that with keeping some of the extra dollars from my raise in my paycheck. What do you suggest?" Sabrena wanted to increase her savings and take advantage of company matching, but still faced the reality of needing to pay all of her bills.

"Let me give you the forms to fill out. I can do the calculations and let you know what your take-home pay would be." Ms. Bernadette showed her how to save more and actually take home about the same amount because of the money being taken out before taxes. "Another bonus is that Bloomingdale's will increase the amount they match because of the increase in your contribution."

"Are there any other recommendations that you can give me?"

"Well, I think between the things we did last time and the changes we made today, you're in good shape. You already have a significant amount in your 401k and I think that this will help increase your nest egg. "

"Thank you so much. I'll get these forms back to you next week. I have to run, but I hope you have a great day." Sabrena left the office feeling more in control of her finances than she had in a while. She'd get a second opinion from Rach, but she felt like she was in good shape.

As she walked into her department, she sensed that something was not right. Vivian was waiting at Sabrena's desk with her sweater and purse in her hands. She'd obviously been crying.

"Hey, Sabrena, glad to see you. I need to leave and will call you over the weekend to let you know if I'll be in early next week." Vivian handed her a list of unfinished items that needed to be handled. Her face was red and she looked so fragile.

"Vivian, are you all right? How's your family?" Sabrena asked. She reached out to hug her boss. Vivian began to cry on her shoulder and her body went limp. Sabrena shut the door and pulled up a chair.

"Vivian, it's okay. Whatever it is, it will work out." Sabrena had never seen her boss like this and was worried.

"Sabrena, my Vance is dying, he's dying. It's not supposed to happen like this. He's just given up and now he's dying. I'm his mother; I'm supposed to die first. I don't know how to do this, I don't know how to watch my son die." Vivian sobbed and put her head on Sabrena's shoulder. Sabrena's eyes were filled with tears as she tried to comfort her boss, her friend. She felt the pain of a mother and couldn't imagine how hard it was for Vivian. She let her cry until she regained her composure and wiped her eyes.

"I'm sorry for dumping this on you, Sabrena. I just can't take it today. The hospital called me and told us to get there as soon as possible. My husband refuses to go, says that Vance is reaping what he's sown. But this is my baby, and I have to be there for him."

Vivian looked embarrassed by her outburst and quickly tried to pull herself together. Sabrena just stood as a comfort to her friend.

"Vivian, I'll take care of these things. You go and take care of your son. Let me know if there is anything that I can do. What hospital is he in?"

"Mercy Hospital, in Intensive Care, but please keep this between us." Vivian said as she gave Sabrena a final hug and swiftly walked out the door.

Sabrena had met Vance once or twice when he had come to take his mother to lunch. He was a very handsome guy who clearly loved his mother. They seemed so close. She wondered why he was now in Intensive Care and if this was what had been bothering Vivian for the last few weeks. She whispered a prayer for him and for her boss and began to work on the outstanding issues that Vivian had pointed out.

Sabrena spent a few hours out on the floor with the sales associates and gave some pointers to the design team on how to put out the summer display. She was tired and had a nagging headache all day, but she had to keep pushing. Her appetite was still gone, but she drank a milkshake at lunch and forced herself to eat a chicken salad. Unfortunately, she had another vomiting episode and everything came back up. She would have to speak with Dr. Scott or Dr. Grier about the vomiting. She was used to the nausea, but she needed to keep her food down. After spending a few minutes with her head on her desk, she felt better and got back to work. She liked being busy, and although the day breezed by, she continued to worry about Vivian and Vance.

CHAPTER THIRTY-SIX

Sabrena couldn't imagine Deena or Renee being near death in a hospital, and her heart grieved for Vivian. She couldn't help but think about her own situation. What would it be like when her time came? Despite her own challenges, she needed to be a friend to Vivian. Before she left for the day, she called Vanessa.

"Hey Vanessa, how're you?"

"Oh, I'm fine. What's up with you?"

"I have a friend whose son is in the hospital and I wanted to stop by for a few minutes. Are you able to pick up the girls from school?" Sabrena asked.

"Not a problem. I'm just studying. I'll take a break to go pick them up. Take your time. My cousins are here and they'll have fun with Deena and Renee." Vanessa loved the girls. They were well-mannered and no trouble at all.

Sabrena left the department after she had cleared her desk and made sure the evening associates were settled. She would have to come in early in the morning to make sure that all the sale signs were put up and there was enough floor coverage. She would bring in the girls, then run errands and go out to lunch. Sabrena's thoughts went back to Vivian. As she drove to the hospital, which was in a neighboring town, she could only imagine Vivian's pain. She stopped at a drive-through and picked up some food for herself and her boss.

Sabrena hated hospitals. As she entered Mercy, she was filled with dread. She felt selfish as she thought about her own health and the reality that she would probably be in the hospital some time in the future. She prayed that she could stay healthy and beat all the odds. She was definitely going to do her part.

The receptionist gave her directions to the ICU waiting room and the volunteer called to tell Vivian she had a guest. Sabrena didn't know if she really should've come. She and Vivian were friends, but sometimes people needed their privacy. She certainly did.

"Sabrena, oh my goodness, thanks for coming," Vivian said. Vivian looked as if she had aged in the few hours since Sabrena had seen her. Her entire face was red, her hair was disheveled, and she had a face mask around her neck.

"Hey Vivian, I was worried about you and wanted to make sure you had something to eat. I also thought you might need some company for awhile." Sabrena felt a bit awkward and didn't quite know what to do with her hands. As they sat down she just folded them in her lap.

"Are any of your family members here?" Sabrena asked, hoping Vivian wasn't alone.

"Yes. Becky and Vance's friend is here," Vivian said. She looked around the room. "Let's go outside for some air."

The two exchanged awkward pleasantries and idle chatter about the store, but Sabrena knew that Vivian's heart was with her son, who was fighting for his life.

In the middle of Sabrena's discription of the new displays, Vivian said, "Vance has pneumonia in both lungs and they don't expect him to live. He's tired. I think he gave up awhile ago on life. He just doesn't want to live."

"I'm sorry, Vivian, but anything is possible. This is a good hospital and he could turn the corner. We still have to have hope and pray."

"I know, but I also don't want to see my son struggle so much. He's on a respirator and looks so scared when he's awake. Other times, he's so sedated that he doesn't look like my boy. I try to keep an upbeat attitude, but the last few days have been rough. Hell, the last few years have been rough." Vivian stood and looked out into the distance, not really focusing on anything. "He was diagnosed with AIDS six years ago and told me and his father last year. We knew he was gay; he told us that about ten years ago. His father didn't take it too well and told him that no son of his would be a sissy. It broke his father's heart. But I knew all along, ever since he was a young boy. I never said anything, and when he went to college and dated a few girls, I was always able to see through the façade. There are some things that a mother knows.

"Vance and his dad were always close, but they've not really spoken since he told his father about his sexuality. They've said a few words to be cordial, but when Vance told us he had AIDS, I knew that it would kill his father and any chance of their reconciliation. Joseph is a stubborn man, set in his ways, but a good man nonetheless. He has two boys, and for the oldest to be gay and now have AIDS is just too much for him to handle. Joseph told Vance that this was his punishment from God and that he was going to rot on earth and in hell. They have not spoken since, and I've been stuck in the middle for years. But *nobody* will make me turn my back on my son. Not even my husband. I know it's hard for everybody, but I've got to be here for him. I was here when he came into the world and I'll be here when he leaves," Vivian said, tears flowing freely down her face.

Sabrena didn't know if Vivian was really talking to her or to herself. She felt hot tears running down her own cheeks and so many emotions. She wiped them away quickly. She could only put her arms around her friend and stand in silence. After a few minutes, Vivian straightened herself up and turned to go back into the hospital. Sabrena knew without asking that Vivian didn't want Sabrena to follow her in.

On her way out the door, Sabrena stopped in the hospital chapel and said a prayer.

"Dear God,
I don't have a lot of words to say, but you know my heart.
For the last few months, I've really only prayed for me, but
now someone else needs even more prayer than I. Lord,
please help Vivian and her family. I know that you can do
anything. I ask that you heal Vance and allow his mother
some peace. But Lord, I also ask that you heal this family
and bring them back together. Amen."

Sabrena didn't turn on the radio in her car for the drive back. She needed to just hear nothing, to clear her thoughts and pull herself together. She needed to be fresh for the girls. Sabrena hated picking up the girls late, no matter what the circumstances. They needed some Mommy time and she needed to hear about their day. By the time she got to Vanessa's, they had eaten dinner and Renee was too sleepy to walk to the car. She put them to bed quickly and was grateful that it was Friday. She poured a glass of wine, and although one of her medication packages told her to avoid alcohol, after the evening she'd had, she needed something to calm her. Maybe just a small glass wouldn't hurt.

She decided to take a warm shower after drinking the Chardonnay. Her thoughts returned to Vivian and Vance. She'd seen Vance through the glass before Vivian met her outside his room, and he really was just a skeleton of the man he'd once been. He looked so pale, so frail—he looked like death. Sabrena wondered if it would be the same for her in a few years or even months. She couldn't hold in the tears as she thought of the possibilities, and felt an overwhelming surge of anger. Sabrena's lips curled and her fists clenched as she thought of the road ahead.

She needed to know. Who did this to her and why? Who was the bastard? Was it Steve, Carlton, or Francis? She was going to find out. The doctors said it didn't matter, but to her it did. She wanted to know who had put her life in jeopardy, and God help him when she found him.

CHAPTER THIRTY-SEVEN

Sabrena struggled to get herself and the girls going early on Saturday morning. She ran into Bloomingdale's and checked the department signs put up by an associate after closing. Fortunately, she made it in before the doors opened for the Saturday bargain hunters, because several signs were in the wrong place. It would've been a hassle to make the adjustments while sales were going on. While she worked, she sat the girls at her desk and logged them into the computer to play games.

The part-time associate had put the new shipment of Ellen Tracey on the floor and attached a sign for thirty percent off on the rack. This could truly have been a disaster. Sabrena had to move the merchandise to the stock room and fill in the rack with other clothing. Sabrena had twenty minutes to replace the new items with the clothing set aside for the sale. She couldn't find anyone to help her, because all the Saturday staff was running around preparing for the sale. Fortunately, she found a box cutter and went to work on opening the wardrobe box. Sabrena prided herself on getting things done and making no excuses. Today, especially, she needed to be on point, because Vivian wasn't available. Her mind drifted to Vivian. She would call her later.

Sabrena laid the box cutter on the top of the shelf and tried to finish opening the wardrobe box, but a corner was hung up. She reached for the box cutter and pulled the corner as she tried to slice it open.

"Aggghhhh!" Sabrena screamed as she felt the box cutter slice into her palm. She saw fresh blood oozing out of her hand; she quickly picked up a paper towel and tried to apply pressure to stop the bleeding. Sabrena heard Leigh in the corridor calling her name.

"Sabrena, Sabrena is that you?" her noisy co-worker called out.

"Yes, I'm in the back. I'm okay." Sabrena frantically looked for another towel or something more substantial to cover her hand and to apply pressure. Leigh was the last person she needed to see right now.

"Oh, my goodness! You're bleeding. Let's get over to the sink. I'll get the first aid kit." Leigh was nice enough, but she was just too nosy, and now Sabrena would never hear the end of it. While she ran to get the first aid kit, Sabrena looked at her palm and saw a deep gash that continued to ooze blood. She needed to stop the bleeding and to get the blood off the floor before Leigh came back.

"Mommy, Mommy, we're hungry," Deena and Renee called out in unison. They walked hand in hand into the stockroom.

"Deena, Renee—*don't come in here*!" Sabrena yelled, eyeing drops of blood on the floor and the bloody paper towels on the sink. She couldn't have the girls touching them. She tried to calm her voice before she said, "Mommy will be right there. Just wait for me outside, okay?" Sabrena's voice startled the girls and Renee began to cry. Fortunately, Sabrena was able to slow the bleeding down and wrapped a stray T-shirt tightly around her hand.

"Here's the first aid kit. there should be a bandage in here," Leigh said. She began rummaging through the kit. "Let me see," she said, as she reached for Sabrena's left hand. Sabrena quickly turned her back to Leigh.

"*No*! I got it, Leigh, its better now. I got the blood to stop. Why don't you go back to your department while I clean this up? Customers will be coming in soon and Carla should be here to open up any moment." Sabrena spoke fast and with a stern voice. She did not want any extra attention, but, more importantly, she didn't want anyone touching her blood. Leigh was taken aback by Sabrena's tone.

"Sabrena, don't be silly. Let's see. We'll put some Neosporin on it and wrap it in a bandage." Leigh pulled on Sabrena's forearm, but Sabrena abruptly jerked away.

"Leigh, *no*, I'm okay. Please just go to your department. I'm fine!" Sabrena moved away from Leigh.

"Whatever, I was just trying to help. Screw it." Leigh turned on her heel and stormed out of the stockroom.

Sabrena quickly rinsed her hand again and put a 4x4 bandage on the cut and wrapped the Ace bandage around her palm to apply pressure. Then, she frantically cleaned up the blood on the floor and discarded the box. She would get some bleach and put it on the floor to get up any traces of her tainted blood. Sabrena put the blood soaked paper towels and T-shirt in a shopping bag, which she would take home and burn. By the time she finished, she was sweating profusely and breathing heavily. As she walked out the stockroom, she saw Deena hovering over Renee, who was still whimpering.

"Baby, Mommy didn't mean to yell. I just didn't want you all to see my little accident." Sabrena sat down the bag and went to hug her little Renee. "I'm not mad, don't cry, Renee. It's okay." She kissed Renee all over her face and tickled her belly, something that had always made her giggle, ever since she was a baby. Sabrena saw Carla at the register and security coming around to open the doors for the waiting shoppers. Deena, always the helper, picked up the shopping bag as they began to walk toward the register.

"No, Deena, Mommy will take the bag. You hold onto Renee." Sabrena picked up the bag from her daughter and made one last sweep of the department. She was a bit shaken up and nervous about her mishap. When she got to the car, she took several deep breaths.

Once she had calmed herself, she called Dr. Scott's office. "Good morning, answering for Drs. Clunie, Holloway, and Scott." Sabrena was anxious to speak with Dr. Scott to see if she needed to go to an urgent care center.

"Hello, this is Sabrena Collins, a patient of Dr. Scott's. I just cut my hand and wanted to speak with her if possible."

"Hold please. Dr. Clunie is on call this weekend for Dr. Scott. Would you like him paged?"

"No, I really need to speak with Dr. Scott. Could you let her know that it is Sabrena Collins? She knows me well." Sabrena hoped that she wouldn't have to push to speak with her doctor and she certainly wasn't going to talk to anyone else. The girls were getting restless in the back seat, even with their DVD player blaring.

"Hold please." Sabrena waited for what seemed like an hour, until the receptionist said she'd put her right through. While she waited to be connected, she watched blood seep through her bandage. She elevated her hand to slow the bleeding.

"Ms. Collins? Are you all right? My answering service says you had an accident." Sabrena was relieved to hear Dr. Scott's voice. She explained her situation and waited for directions.

"When was your last tetanus booster?" Dr. Scott asked as she motioned to her husband to wait before ordering breakfast. She and Darren needed time away and had flown to Hilton Head, South Carolina, for the weekend. She knew he was getting perturbed that she had taken the call, but she couldn't help it. She'd make it up to him later.

"Uh, I don't know—probably not since I was a kid," Sabrena mumbled. She had no idea what tetanus was, but didn't want to appear stupid.

"Okay. I'm not in my office, so I can't check your chart. I suggest you go to the Urgent Care down the street from my building just to get them to look at your hand and decide if you need stitches or a tetanus vaccination. Denise may be in the office filing. If so, I'll get her to pull your chart." Dr. Scott tried to hurry off the phone as she looked at the growing scowl on Darren's face.

"Okay, Dr. Scott. I'll go now. Uh, do they need to know about . . . you know?" Sabrena hoped that she would pick up what she was saying.

"Well, I'll talk with the physician and answer any questions about your health status. I hope you know that all of your health information is confidential, whether it's in my office or any other office. However, I do understand your concerns. We need to get the cut taken care of." Dr. Scott was sensitive to Sabrena's need for privacy.

Sabrena was only a few minutes from the urgent care and needed to occupy the girls' time while she waited to be seen. Fortunately there weren't a lot of cars in the parking lot, so hopefully she could get in and out quickly.

"Hey girls, Mommy needs to go see the doctor about her hand. I need for you to be good, like you always are, but very good while I see the doctor."

"Okay, Mommy, I'll watch Renee," Deena said, as she grabbed Renee's hand.

"Thank you, Deena, I'll give you a special treat if you two behave." Sabrena pulled out books for the girls.

"Mommy, we don't need a treat. We'll be good," Renee said, as she walked through the door like a little woman, holding her sister's hand.

Sabrena signed in, showed her insurance card, and paid her co-pay. Her co-pays were really adding up. She was taken to the exam room rather quickly. The girls were glued to the TV in the kid's room. One of the receptionists said that she would keep an eye on them.

"Hi, Ms. Collins, I need to take your temperature and blood pressure. Do you have any allergies?" The nurse asked as she began to prepare her to see the doctor.

"Hi, yes, I am allergic to Bactrim® and antibiotics like that," Sabrena answered, trying to remain calm. The nurse took her vitals and told her that the doctor would be in shortly.

"Hi, Ms. Collins, I'm Dr. Harris. Let me take a look at this hand." The doctor was young and quite handsome.

"I thought I had patched it up pretty good, but it keeps bleeding," Sabrena said. She watched him take off her bandage. He examined her hand and she became light-headed as she looked at the gash.

"I'm going to put in a few stitches to help this heal and stop some of this oozing with some silver nitrate. Let me numb it up and you'll be on your way." Dr. Harris was gentle, but Sabrena still hated needles and she almost passed out when she saw the long needle with string attached. Dr. Harris called for a nurse and Sabrena took the time to lie back while they quickly worked on her hand.

"Dr. Scott's nurse called and faxed over some of your records. The nurse said you actually had a tetanus booster a few months ago in her office." Sabrena didn't know if it was her imagination but she thought she saw the nurse put on two pairs of gloves. She noticed she was standing back a bit further than she should have, and Sabrena suddenly became more uncomfortable and self-conscious.

"Oh, I didn't know. Thanks for checking," Sabrena replied, still unaware as to when she had the tetanus booster or really what it was. She would call the office on Monday and speak with Denise.

"That's it, all done," said Dr. Harris. These will dissolve on their own. Try to keep your hands as dry and clean as possible for the next few days. Follow up with Dr. Scott at the end of next week. Call us if you have any fever, oozing, or pus draining out, but you should be just fine." Dr. Harris prepared to leave the room and the nurse wrapped Sabrena's hand in a neat bandage. Sabrena felt funny with the nurse; she sensed that she was being distant and overly cautious, but neither said anything except for the usual pleasantries. Her feelings were confirmed when the receptionist handed her the paperwork and quickly placed it on the counter, making every effort not to touch her. Sabrena left, feeling dirty and ashamed and wondering if this was how it was going to be for the rest of her life.

Despite feeling like she'd lived through a whole week since the morning, Sabrena still needed to run a few errands. She decided to do them when the girls had their piano lessons. They went to Chuck E. Cheese for an early lunch and then she dropped them off at their teacher's studio for their hour session. Sabrena needed to run to the grocery store, and hoped that Steve wouldn't be working today. She hadn't returned any of his calls and was embarrassed and confused by her actions. Luckily, she was able to run in and out without seeing him. She couldn't hide from him forever. She still had to make a decision about Disney.

Just as Sabrena had finished packing the trunk with groceries, her cell phone rang. "Hey girl, where are you?" Rach tried to sound upbeat, but had been off-center all week.

"I'm going to pick up the girls from their piano lessons. What are you doing?" Sabrena was glad to speak with her friend, but didn't like how she sounded. She knew Rach was hurting over Barry, though it would be hard for her to admit.

"I need to go to get some black pumps for work and run a few errands. I hear Bloomie's is having a sale. Did you see anything good?"

"Yeah, a few things. If you go by, just tell them to hold it under my name. I was there this morning." Sabrena didn't want to alarm her friend by going into the details of her cut, as Rach was already on edge. "Rach, I'm going to cook this afternoon. Why don't you rent some movies and come by so we can hang out?"

"Sounds perfect, I'll be over in a few hours. Call me if you want me to bring something else."

Sabrena picked up the girls and spent the rest of the day cleaning and cooking with them. She looked at them as they "dusted" the living room. They were so cute. Deena, always the prissy one, put a scarf over her head and was very meticulous. Renee wasn't the least bit concerned with how she looked while cleaning. She just wanted to please Mommy. Sabrena turned up the radio and began to sing and dance with them. They all ended up in a heap on the floor, laughing at each other.

The day flew by and Sabrena began ironing their clothes for church. Renee ran to answer the doorbell.

"Auntie Rach!" Sabrena heard Renee greet her friend, followed by squeals of delight with the movies she'd brought for them to watch.

"Hey girl, dinner's ready. Let me finish ironing and we'll eat. Deena, will you and Renee please set the table?"

"What happened to your hand?" Rach asked.

"Long story, it looks worse than it is." The girls continued to help their mother and Rach prepared the plates for everyone, while Sabrena finished ironing. The setting was so familiar to each of them. They were family. Sabrena was nauseous and had a funny taste in her mouth, something that had become common. She drank the lemonade she'd made for them and forced herself to eat. She was determined to put on some weight.

Sabrena and Rach sat down with their favorite, chamomile tea, lit candles, and put on some jazz. The girls were watching their movies and snacking on dried fruit. Sabrena would put them to bed after the movies so they would be fresh for church tomorrow. She was glad that Rach had brought an overnight bag and she hoped that they could all go to church together.

"So now, friend, tell me what's up?" Sabrena began, knowing Rach had a lot to get off her chest.

"Nothing, just work and life. This was a rough week," Rach replied. She looked at her friend and tried to keep a stiff upper lip.

"Blah blah blah. Obviously, you think I'm someone else. What's really up? It's me talking."

"Nothing, you have too much to worry about. Let's talk about you," Rach pressed. She had intentionally not talked about Barry with Bre since their breakup. With all that she was facing, her breakup was low on the totem pole.

"Rach, don't do that to me or our friendship. This never has been, nor will it ever be, a one-sided relationship. I know you're hurting, so let's do what we always do—just talk. I really want to help." She spoke with total sincerity, and then produced an evil grin. She said, "But more importantly, I want to know what happened and how Barry got the balls to tell you off." Sabrena threw a pillow at Rach, who then began to talk about the breakup. Sabrena could have sworn that she saw tears form in Rach's eyes. She hadn't seen Rach this upset over a man in decades.

"Barry is a good man, Rach," Sabrena said. "Why're you still trippin'? You've been stringing him along for years, all on your terms. I'm actually glad that he stood up for himself." Sabrena knew that Rach wasn't going to like what she was saying, but it didn't matter. "Rach, do you love him? Do you love him enough to swallow your pride and forget your past?"

"I do care about him a lot, I'm not gonna lie. But I can't give him what he needs or what he deserves. I'm just not made like that. I guess it's all for the best." Rach couldn't even tell Sabrena how her heart ached for Barry and how she secretly feared he was truly gone.

"All for the best? Are you crazy? Rach, I know that when you open yourself up, you risk pain and that sucks. But you're also missing out on the joy of being with someone as special as Barry. I'm not the poster child for good relationships, but I can tell you that when I've loved, I've loved completely, with all my heart and soul. The feeling of being held by the one you love and connecting on that level is better than any drink, any new pair of shoes on sale, or strawberries dipped in chocolate. I want you to really open your heart to that kind of love. You love Barry and you should be free to just let your love blossom without always trying to control it. You're gonna really miss out if you let him go." Sabrena looked at her friend and could feel her pain.

Rach shook her head and said, "I did love like that once, and look where it got me. I'm not a silly college girl anymore. I can't put myself out there to be dogged again. Anyway, enough about me." Rach tried to keep the conversation moving away from her, unaware that tears had trickled down her cheeks.

"I won't press, but I'll pray and pray again. Rach, you have so much love to give, and I think Barry is worth the risk. After all the mess that I've been through, I still want to believe that there can be a love that is deep and sincere."

"I know, Bre, but it's hard. I just don't want to be hurt, don't want to be so dependent on someone else to make me happy."

"Well, think about it—how do you feel now? Is this strong, independent, self-sufficient, 'I don't need a man' woman happy?"

"You know what, you are a smart tail! *No*, I'm not happy, but I'm not miserable. Then again, I am!" Rach laughed and fell onto Sabrena's lap.

"Rach, sometimes it takes more courage to love than not to. I've watched you over the years and I know where this comes from, but everyone is not your dad or Everett. Barry is tried and true, and, my dear friend, you are *sprung*!"

"I know, but I don't want to be. Bre—if I tell you something, will you not throw it back in my face?"

"Of course I won't."

"I love him, Bre, I really love him and I'm scared that I killed any feelings he had for me." Fresh tears flowed freely from Rach's eyes.

"What! Fool, I know you love him. I thought you were gonna tell me something. Please, you've loved him for a while—we all know that, even little Renee. I was ready for some juicy info." Sabrena laughed hysterically and soon Rach joined in. They continued to talk. Sabrena looked in on the girls, who were fast asleep. She put them in bed and tried to roll her hair for church, but her hand was throbbing.

"Girl, this is gonna be a mess. Let me do that for you." Rach came to the rescue.

"Rach, you're gonna have to call Barry. He probably is exercising his option of being the man in this relationship. I ain't sayin' nothing else about it, but if you love him and want him—dig deep and find it in your heart to take the chance."

Before falling asleep, Sabrena called the hospital and asked for the ICU. She wasn't surprised to find Vivian there. They chatted for a few minutes and she was glad to know that Vance seemed to be stable. Vivian sounded tired and old. Sabrena would try to see her tomorrow. Sabrena remembered to take her medications and quickly fell asleep. But her sound sleep was interrupted, as usual, by vivid nightmares. There was always someone chasing her and she awoke right before they caught her. Maybe the doctors were right. Maybe she needed to see a psychologist.

CHAPTER THIRTY-EIGHT

Sunday raced by with church and an early lunch, with Rach and the girls taking up most of the morning. In the afternoon, Sabrena agreed to let the girls go over to Tiffany's for a few hours. She was glad that Valerie came to pick them up, because she needed a nap. Rach went to the mall and Sabrena was able to get some much needed quiet time.

She woke up a bit refreshed and thankful that she'd had a peaceful nap. Sabrena put some food together and drove to the hospital for a quick visit with Vivian. Her hand was throbbing, so she popped two Tylenol®, which had become a regular thing with her headaches and now this pain in her hand. She was glad to see her friend and pleasantly surprised to see Vance without the breathing tube in, although he still had on a face mask. Sabrena, like everyone else, wore a face mask in the room and tried to be upbeat. She really didn't know Vance that well, and it was hard to ignore his labored breathing and the alarms that kept going off. Vivian introduced her to Paul, his partner, who hovered over Vance's every move. Sabrena felt like an intruder on a very private setting and quickly excused herself. Vivian came out after her and they sat to chat.

"How's it going, Vivian? He looks better," Sabrena said, aware of her racing heart.

"He is better today, but it's still just a matter of time now. His T-cells are very low and the doctor says that his viral load is higher than it's ever been. Hmmm, I sound like a doctor, with all of that mumbo jumbo. I know you don't know all that stuff, but, anyway, I've learned the lingo. He's still sick and is going to die," Vivian said matter-of-factly. Sabrena couldn't bring herself to tell her that she knew exactly what a T-cell or CD4 count was, probably better than Vivian did.

"What happened that made him get this sick?" Sabrena asked.

"He just kinda got tired of it all and stopped his medication. This has been a long struggle for him and he says he's ready to go." Vivian wiped her tears and looked at the floor.

Sabrena squeezed Vivian's hand and tried to change the subject. "Any change with your husband?"

"Nope, he won't even talk about it. But I know he's hurting."

Sabrena stayed with Vivian and tried to make light conversation for awhile. Then, surprising even herself, she asked Vivian if she could pray with her.

> *"Dear God,*
> *We come together as friends seeking your face. Father, we lift up Vance, his life, and his health, and we ask that you send angels to minister to him. Lord, give Vivian the strength she needs to stand by her son, and bless her entire family. God, we know that you're able to do anything, so we come together asking for a miracle with Vance. Lord, make him stronger and heal his mind, body, and soul. We will give you the glory and the honor. Amen."*

Sabrena hugged Vivian, but declined to go back into Vance's room.

She would need to call Dr. Scott or Dr. Grier and ask them what she needed to do to protect herself. Images of Vance continued to flash in Sabrena's mind as she drove home. She felt a surge of tears and had to pull the car over. Her emotions were raging and she needed to just breathe. She remembered the words of her pastor's sermon: "God has the master plan and the purpose for your life. No matter what you're going through, there isn't *anything* too hard for God."

In church, Sabrena had gone to the altar for prayer. She knew she needed to get closer to God and was trying to sort out her life. She knew that she was weak and had issues that only God could handle. Part of her felt dirty and ashamed, like God was punishing her. She also felt a warm presence that engulfed her as she knelt at the altar and asked God to take over her life. When she opened her eyes, she was surprised to see Rach kneeling next to her and crying openly. Deacon Johnson stood behind her with his hand on her shoulders, in prayer as well. She felt such a warmth flow through her body and she felt stronger.

"There isn't *anything* too hard for God" Sabrena said aloud as she wiped her tears. "There isn't *anything* too hard for God." She drove toward her house.

The next week was a blur, as Sabrena took on the extra responsibilities at work and kept two important appointments.

She saw the eye doctor on Tuesday morning before going into work; she frowned as she thought about her experience. She had been greeted by Dr. Hart's receptionist and had handed her the referral that Dr. Scott's office had given her. The receptionist had been nice and her wait to be taken into the examination room was short.

Dr. Hart was a middle-aged man with a burly build. He seemed to be in a hurry. "Hello, Ms. Collins, welcome to the office," he said as he entered the room without knocking. I see that Dr. Scott referred you for a full eye examination and field vision test. Are you having any problems with your vision?"

"No, I just need to get a test done because of a new illness or whatever. My doctor told me to come for an exam, a baseline exam." Sabrena was feeling uncomfortable and knew that she would have to say the diagnosis out loud.

"What kind of diagnosis?" Dr. Hart asked as he began to set up the machine and write on his clipboard. When Sabrena didn't answer right away, he impatiently repeated his question, "What's the diagnosis?"

"HIV, uhh . . . AIDS." Sabrena looked down at the floor and felt a huge lump in her throat.

"Oh, oh. I'm sorry to hear that. Let's get this eye exam done. Did you bring a list of your medications?" Dr. Hart asked. Usually you'll get a full eye exam to make sure that your vision is fine, but more importantly, it's possible that some of the medications can cause eye problems."

Dr. Hart went to a drawer and pulled out a pair of gloves and began to examine Sabrena it was an odd thing—he never touched her.

"Everything seems to be all right. You'll need to see an eye doctor once or twice a year, more, depending upon any new medications." Dr. Hart paused for a moment and then said, "I don't see a lot of patients with AIDS. You may feel more comfortable with someone who takes care of more patients like you. Best of luck."

Dr. Hart opened the door and walked her to the front, giving her chart to the receptionist.

"Do you need to make a follow-up appointment?" the receptionist asked as she looked at Dr. Hart's diagnosis sheet. Her mouth flew open and, before she could catch herself, she quickly looked up at Sabrena in shock.

"Close your mouth, honey! No, I won't be back, but thank you anyway," Sabrena said as she left the office in a huff. She felt warm tears stinging her cheeks; she felt humiliated and dirty.

Sabrena had no choice but to keep moving. Despite the hurdles and mess that she seemed to continually deal with, she needed to get her life together. Sabrena took an extra hour for lunch on Friday for an appointment with attorney Octavia Roberts, the same attorney who had handled her divorce. She was glad she was still in the same location and had knowledge about changing wills. Sabrena went with an open mind and the information that Dr. Grier had given her.

"Hello, Ms. Collins. Good to see you again," Attorney Roberts said. She was a stylish middle-aged woman who looked about 45. Sabrena noted the perfectly fitted St. John suit on her thick frame and the Louis Vuitton briefcase sitting next to her desk. Her office looked like it was out of one of those fancy designer books, but it remained warm and inviting. Her face was round and she had the smoothest skin Sabrena had ever seen, a nice mocha complexion that was flawless. Her nails were perfectly groomed and she wore very tasteful makeup, which accentuated her striking features. She had gained some weight since Sabrena saw her, but she was still beautiful.

"Good to see you, well, not under these circumstances, but . . ." Sabrena said, suddenly feeling awkward. Besides Rach and her doctors and their staff, no one knew of her HIV status. This was going to be difficult.

"How can I help you? My assistant told me that you needed to revise your will and other documents." Attorney Roberts was a kind woman and Sabrena liked that she had always seemed to take time to listen. In the very difficult period of her life when she left Carlton, her lawyer had been the voice of reassurance and calm, helping her navigate the separation and divorce.

"Yes, I do. But I need to make sure that everything I talk with you about is going to be confidential. I know about the whole attor-

194

ney/client thing, but I just need to say it." Sabrena began to shift in her seat.

"Certainly, Ms. Collins. I cannot and will not divulge anything you tell me. I hope that you remember our previous working relationship. I'm here for you and your interests alone." Attorney Roberts shifted in her seat as she felt that nagging twinge in her chest; it must be indigestion from eating lunch too quickly. She was sure that Ms. Collins couldn't tell her anything that could shock her. She smiled inwardly, remembering how cunning Sabrena had been when she left her husband. She was a smart lady who was ferociously protective of her children. "How can I help you?"

"I need a new will, because I've been diagnosed with a disease that can't be cured. I also need a living will to give to my doctor and to keep in my files." Sabrena didn't think that it was necessary, unless asked, to go into any details about her disease.

"I'm sorry to hear that, Ms. Collins, I really am. I'll do all I can to help." She tried not to show her emotions, but immediately reached to touch Sabrena's hand. Although she was a professional, she couldn't just put her emotions on a shelf. She was surprised that Sabrena was facing a major illness—she looked fine.

Sabrena talked to attorney Roberts for the remainder of the hour and had to answer some hard questions. However, she felt good about making decisions for her daughters and her life. Attorney Roberts recommended that she speak to a financial planner and gave her the name of an associate. She told her she would have the first drafts a week or two after Sabrena filled out the necessary paperwork. In the meantime, Sabrena needed to think about issues of guardianship and a list of other things that might affect her daughters. Sabrena was shaken to the core when her attorney brought up Carlton and the possibility that he would seek custody if something happened to her.

"I've not talked to him in years. He's never tried to contact me or the girls. Why would he be an issue?" Sabrena asked, feeling tightness in her chest.

"In the state of Pennsylvania, he's the biological father and does have parental rights. Yes, he did sign away some of those rights in the divorce, but if you die before the children turn 18, this could become an issue. I just don't want you to be blindsided, but we will try to work this out," attorney Roberts said reassuringly.

"Under no circumstances can my girls be raised by Carlton. He gave up his rights and he has not sent them one birthday card, Christmas card, or made one phone call. That's fine with me. My girls are well balanced and better off without him, and you know that I made that decision. Attorney Roberts, we have to be sure that he is never around them again and certainly not raising them." Sabrena ended her visit and went back to work with her mind racing.

Having gotten one part of her life at least on the road to being a little more organized, Sabrena felt it was time to do the same for another part of her life. Right before leaving for the day, she picked up the phone and a piece of paper with a number she'd been carrying around for weeks.

"Hello, may I speak with Francis?" Sabrena tentatively asked the voice on the other end of the telephone.

"Who is this and why are you calling here?" The woman's voice was fierce.

"I'm an old friend and was just trying to find Francis. A mutual friend, Ray Stevens, gave me this number and said I may find him here," Sabrena said, trying to sound upbeat.

"Well, he's not here and won't be here for another eleven years at least. He's back in prison. Don't call here again." The woman was curt and promptly slammed the phone down in Sabrena's ear.

"Well, that's a dead end if ever I heard one," Sabrena said aloud as she hung up the phone. She wondered what Francis had done to land himself in prison, but she wasn't in the mood to find out. She replayed the woman's words in her mind, *"Back in prison."* She wondered if he was incarcerated before he dated her—they never talked about it. She knew it was a very slim possibility that he had infected her, but she was going to investigate all possibilities. All who remained were Carlton and Steve. Now she would go back to her painful past. Sabrena shrugged her shoulders and tried to perk up. It was time to pick up her girls.

CHAPTER THIRTY-NINE

Rach was in a funk that she just couldn't get herself out of. She was working long hours and finishing up some audits, but even being tired didn't keep her mind off of Barry. She would never tell anyone, but she had called him. She dialed * 67, so her number wouldn't appear, and just held the phone. She did miss his voice, and she missed him. How could she have let herself fall in love again? What could she do now? She didn't have the energy to try to work things out. There were too many things going on in her life. Rach had to be there for Sabrena, for work, and she had to maintain herself. She felt her eyes burning again as fresh tears welled in her. She would have to forget him and just move on. Just as she'd wiped away the tears, her phone rang.

"Sabrena Collins for a Miss Rachel Washington," Sabrena said mockingly, laughing before she finished her artificial greeting.

"Ms. Collins, lovely to hear from you." Rach laughed at her friend. Sabrena's timing was perfect.

"Hey, Rach, the girls are going to a slumber party tonight. Do you want to come over for dinner?" Sabrena knew that Rach was hurting, and a little food and some German chocolate cake would help, at least for a moment.

"Okay, I'll stop by. I'll warn you, I'm not much fun. Work is getting on my nerves, I just fired another temp, and my plate is full. But I'll be over in a bit. I'll stop for ice cream, the good stuff."

Sabrena packed the girls' overnight bag and dropped them off at their friend Keisha's. Her head was throbbing, but she refused to let the girls see that she was in pain. Deena and Keisha had both made the cheerleading squad for the school's flag football team and had become fast friends. Deena and Renee were excited to be out for the night, but Sabrena always regretted the time that they weren't at home. She couldn't even count the nights she had just stood outside their door watching them sleep, so innocent, so beautiful—the joy of childhood.

"Hugs and kisses," Sabrena said to her girls as she rang the doorbell.

"Bye, Mommy. See you tomorrow." Deena kissed Sabrena on the cheek and quickly went in to find the other kids. Renee was always a bit shy and loved hanging onto her mother.

"'Bye, Mommy. Come early so I can sit with you at the game, okay?" She said, as she nuzzled Sabrena for another few moments.

"Okay, Renee, I'll be there early."

Renee squeezed Sabrena tightly and turned to watch her get in the car.

"Renee, I thought you wanted to come to the party. If you want to come home with me, its okay," Sabrena offered, sensing Renee's hesitation.

Keisha's mother, Heather, looked on and encouraged Renee to stay. The little girl ran inside, but Sabrena told Heather that if there were any problem, she would quickly come to pick her up.

Sabrena and Rach spent time eating and watching television. Sabrena knew when and if Rach wanted to talk she would open up. In the meantime, it was good to just sit, listen to music, and relax with her friend.

"Have you decided about Disney and Steve?" Rach asked as they dug into the cake.

"Yeah, I think that we're going to go, but only for four days right when the girls get out of school." Sabrena had finally called him back and made the decision after he understood that they would need two bedrooms and that this really was about the girls. He had begged her to let him take them, and although they weren't dating, they were cordial. In fact, they talked more on the phone now than in the last few months that they were together.

"That's good. I can't believe that I'm saying that, but it is. He does love them. As long as you don't start back up with him," Rach said, thinking about how Steve had looked at the girls and Sabrena at the recital. "Have you told him?"

"No, and I don't want to talk about it." Sabrena hadn't told her friend about her close call with him as she was still trying to sort it out herself. Rach decided to go home, so that she could get some work done for Monday morning. Sabrena spent the evening writing in her journal and reviewing the papers from the lawyer. She had some major decisions to make. Her thoughts were interrupted by her cell phone.

"Hello?"

"Hello, Sabrena. In case you don't remember, you do have a living mother!"

Sabrena cringed. "Hi, Mom, I actually called you earlier this week." She didn't mention that she'd called when she knew her mother would be at Bible study. Her headache was bound to get worse after talking to her mother. Sabrena reached for four Extra Strength Tylenol® and gulped them down.

"Did you call? I didn't get the message. I'm the mother, why am I always tracking you down?" Sabrena's mother was unstoppable when she got started, so Sabrena just let her get it out of her system.

"When do my granddaughters get out of school? I want to send for them for part of the summer."

"They get out in about a month. Mom, maybe I'll take a few days off and the three of us will come see you." Despite her upbeat tone, Sabrena immediately felt panicky. Eventually, she would have to tell her mother. It would be another example of how Sabrena had messed up her life, and Sabrena was sure her mother would be merciless. However, she had a short list of potential guardians for her girls, and although her mother was near the bottom of it, she was on that list. Sabrena had to admit that her mother was different with the girls. She was warm, loving, and always telling them how smart and pretty they were. The girls adored her as well.

Sabrena checked Boxer's litter box and regretted not asking Rach to change it before she left. The girls had been good about doing it, but in the excitement of the slumber party, they had forgotten. She put on two pairs of gloves, changed the box, and washed her hands thoroughly. Sabrena called Vivian and was glad to hear that Vance was doing much better. Miraculously, her husband had agreed that he could stay at their house after he got out of the hospital for a few weeks. Thinking about Vance reminded Sabrena to take her medications and write in her medication journal. The new medication had hiked her nausea up to a new level, but she was finding that if she ate some toast with it, she felt better.

Sabrena ran her bath and just as she was getting ready to get into the sudsy tub, she heard her phone ringing again. Miss Popularity, she thought to herself.

"Hello?"

"Hi, Mommy, can I come home? Come get me, I'm scared," Renee was sniffling with each word and breathing hard, and Sabrena knew that she had been crying. Before she'd even finished talking, Sabrena had pulled the plug in her tub and quickly put her jeans back on.

"Sure, baby. I'll be over in a few minutes. Let me speak to Keisha's mother, okay?"

"Hello, Sabrena, Renee wants to come home. I'm sorry, but she keeps saying that she wants her Mommy." Heather was very polite, but Sabrena knew that a crying child in the midst of other children could only be a problem.

"No problem, Heather, I'll be right over. If Deena wants to stay, that's fine; otherwise, pull her stuff together as well." Soon Sabrena was bringing Renee back into the house. They played dolls and snacked on Renee's favorite, chocolate chip cookies and milk. The milk tasted funny to Sabrena, but so did most food these days. She sucked on her tried and true lemons in an effort to rid her mouth of the taste.

As Sabrena brushed Renee's hair after her bath, Renee asked, "Mommy, can I sleep with you in your bed?"

"Sure. I was going to ask you if you were too much of a big girl to sleep with your mommy." Sabrena smiled as Renee's eyes lit up. She took a flying leap into Sabrena's bed and patted the space next to her. Sabrena burrowed under the covers and nipped Renee's toes until she squealed and demanded that she stop. Within minutes, Renee was blissfully asleep and Sabrena just watched until she couldn't keep her eyes open any longer. Tonight, she thought, as sleep overtook her, I'll sleep the sleep of angels.

CHAPTER FORTY

Sabrena had the much dreaded chore of going in to work for Bloomingdale's infamous Private Sale. The women would be out in droves, and, while that was good for business, Sabrena just didn't feel like all the hustle and bustle today. She still hadn't been sleeping well, the nightmares were constant, and she was feeling grouchy all the time. She felt like she was coming down with something. She was coughing—a dry cough, but very irritating—and last week she got another yeast infection, which Dr. Scott told her was probably from the antibiotics she had been given for a sinus infection. What wasn't wrong with her, she thought wryly.

She was so sick of the damned medications, schedules, doctors' appointments, and all the demands of just living with the disease. Sabrena wanted a break. At her last appointment with Dr. Grier, she had been told that she was on track and that he wouldn't have to see her for another three months. Her CD4 count was now 266 and her viral load was under 1,000. She had the repeat Pap with Dr. Scott and it was normal, so they would repeat that test in six months. So, she thought, what would be so bad about just taking a minute to breathe? No medicines, no doctors, just to live a few days without HIV being the first thing on her mind in the morning and the last thing at night. Even when Sabrena had a good day, taking the medications reminded her that she wasn't clean, that she was contaminated.

Sabrena was glad that the girls were getting out of school this week and she looked forward to going away for a long weekend. Steve called almost daily with updates and questions about their Disney trip, until she finally told him yes, they could go to Disney on her terms. He agreed and was more excited than she had seen him in years. Steve had come by the house to tell the girls himself. Sabrena was surprised when he also gave her an envelope with money to buy some clothes for them and the deposit for their summer camps. It was no use arguing with Steve; he remained committed to the girls, even though they weren't together. Steve was footing the bill for everything, but she was going to make sure that it remained innocent. Sabrena had to talk to him. She needed to know if he was the one. Was this guilt? Did he want her because he was infected, too?

As he walked into the travel agency, Steve was on cloud nine. He had taken money from his savings account to take his family to Disney and he couldn't wait until Friday. It would be the first time Deena or Renee had been on an airplane and he wanted the airline to give them the pin he saw other kids get on their first flight. He had planned everything with the travel agent, who was no doubt tired of all his questions by now. Steve didn't care, though; he wanted the long weekend to be perfect for all of them.

"Are you sure this is the best hotel for kids in the area?" Steve asked the agent.

"Yes, Mr. Addison, it is very nice, I've stayed there myself. They have pools, supervised activities, and it's actually inside the theme parks. Please sign here."

"Okay. What about the Sunday evening time? Did you arrange for child care?" Steve knew that he needed a window of opportunity to be alone with Sabrena, and had arranged for what they called Kid's Night Out for the girls. He would have to make use of the time wisely. In his heart, he knew that Sabrena was meant for him and that she still loved him. He just needed to have time with her. The phone calls over the last few weeks just let him know even more that she was supposed to be his wife. The phone calls, but also the scare with the health department, gave him cause to reassess his life and put an end to the gambles he was taking.

As Steve walked back to his car, he remembered the letter from the health department and the subsequent phone call. He couldn't believe that someone he'd been with was HIV-positive and had given his name to the health department. Steve was glad that he could go to his own doctor and not have to go down to the clinic for testing. He shuddered as he thought of his doctor's appointment and waiting for the results. He had never prayed so much in all his life. Steve vowed that he would be a new man, and he was determined to keep that vow. Since the results, he had no desire to sleep with anyone, but he'd been really feeling that way since he and Sabrena broke up over six months ago. He'd been with a few women, but his heart wasn't in it; the player had died, a man was born, and this man needed his family.

Sabrena was surprised to see Vance sitting out on the deck at Vivian's home. She wanted to make sure she saw him before she left for Florida. Over the last few weeks, Sabrena had tried to be there for Vivian, and after Vance was released from the hospital, had brought them some food and given them support around the house. At first it was awkward. Although she'd been invited on several occasions, she had never been to Vivian's house until Vance moved in. It was strange, but she felt connected to Vance, and although she hadn't shared her secret with either of them, she was drawn to the family.

"Hey, Vance, how're you doing today?" Sabrena reached over to hug the still frail man seated in an electric wheelchair with an oxygen tank by his side. He looked haggard and much older than his years.

"I'm good, how about you? I didn't know you were coming by this afternoon. Did my mother send you to spy on me?" Vance smiled as the home health aide said her good-byes.

"Nope, I left her at work. I did tell her that I was stopping by to bring you some of my world-famous lasagna." Sabrena smiled and soaked in the sun with Vance for a few minutes. The medicine she was taking had instructions to avoid direct sunlight for an extended amount of time but a few minutes should be fine. "Your mom tells me you're doing better each day. Is that really true or are you just trying to put on a good face for her?"

"No, I'm feeling better, but I never know what my days will hold. I'm not responding to the medications anymore. I'm resistant to them and the doctors want to put me on some experimental drugs. I haven't told Mom. I don't want her to worry and I don't want to be a burden to my parents. It's kinda weird, Dad never mentions my disease, but at least he's talking to me and he is cordial to Paul when he comes by, if he comes by." Sabrena sensed sadness in his voice when he talked about his partner.

"Vance, you know that your parents love you. Your Dad may show it differently, but he loves you. Vivian doesn't see you as a burden at all. She just wants her son to live and not give up." Sabrena felt her heart swell as she thought of her own mother and when someone would need to have this discussion with her.

"I know and I'm blessed to have them. It's hard with Dad, but I understand in a way. He doesn't accept my lifestyle and, even more so, he doesn't know a lot about AIDS. I think I see fear in his eyes when he has to help me, but he does it anyway, out of his love." Vance looked at Sabrena intently as she wiped some drool from his mouth.

"Sabrena, why are you here? I mean, you know that I like talking with you, but we really didn't know each other before I was in the hospital. Now, I talk to you more than I talk to many of my old friends, who have mysteriously disappeared and don't return my calls. I know that you and Mom work together and are friends, but I sense something else. Are you just an angel in disguise?"

Sabrena laughed. "I'm certainly no angel. I don't know, but I just feel like I need to, that's all. I had a cousin who had AIDS a long time ago, so I'm not scared, and know that it can get lonely. Plus, I never pass up a chance to talk to a fine man." Sabrena said with a wink. She was being as truthful as she could be at the moment, but she couldn't share her secret with Vance.

"Is your cousin dead?"

"Yes."

"Good, it's often better than living." Vance maneuvered his electric wheelchair into the kitchen where he took some pills and gulped them down with water. "I'm sorry, Sabrena, that wasn't called for. I'm just so tired and probably feeling sorry for myself. I should be grateful. My doctor didn't think that I'd make it out of the hospital, but I'm still here." Sabrena warmed some lasagna for Vance, and as she'd seen Vivian do on several occasions, she served him on a saucer. They laughed at *The People's Court* and before they knew it, two hours had passed. Sabrena needed to go pick up the girls and finish getting ready for their trip.

"Vance, I've got to go, but I'll come see you when I get back. Stay strong and don't give up. I need you not to give up." Sabrena hugged him again and made sure that everything was within his reach before leaving. She called Vivian's cell phone once she got in her car.

"Hey Vivian, are you on your way home?" Sabrena asked.

"Yes, I'm a few miles away," Vivian responded. She was glad to hear that Sabrena was just leaving; she didn't like leaving Vance alone for more than an hour or so. She was grateful for her friend, and marveled at how God put certain people in her life for the rough times.

CHAPTER FORTY-ONE

The girls were full of nervous energy as they boarded the plane. They had talked nonstop in the car, through security, and while they waited for boarding. Sabrena had to take an extra vitamin and Tylenol®; this was going to be a long day. She made sure that she put her medications in her purse in the pill box. She had promised Rach that she'd call her every day and that if anything happened she would call her doctors. As much as she hated to admit it, she was glad to go away for a few days and enjoy watching the girls' fantasy come true.

"Wow, Disney World!" Renee and Deena were out of their minds with squeals of excitement as they saw the famous resort from the car. Steve had booked a hotel right next to Disney World, with a train that ran right through the hotel and would carry them all the way to Disney. Everything looked so magical; the girls could barely contain themselves. Sabrena, however, was worn out and needed to take a nap.

"Mommy, we want to go to the pool, can we?" the girls asked as soon as they got into their suite.

"Not right now. We need to get some food and then we'll see about it." Sabrena looked around the suite, which was large and, as she had requested, had separate sleeping quarters. She and the girls would sleep in the bedroom with two queen-size beds and a daybed, and Steve would take the other bedroom. It was like an apartment with a sitting area in the middle and a kitchenette to one side. Sabrena plopped wearily on the couch and tried to relax while Steve got the luggage from the bellman. She had to admit, she was impressed, and a bit scared about the next few days.

"Uncle Steve, will you take us to the pool?" Renee asked. She was trying to find her swimsuit.

"After lunch, if it's okay with your Mom."

The squeals started again as the girls tried to contain their energy. Sabrena wished that she could bottle some of it up and open it up as needed. She had to pull herself together; this was the dream trip of any child and she wasn't going to spoil it for her girls. They walked downstairs to the hotel restaurant for a light lunch. Sabrena drank a milkshake and ordered a chicken platter. She'd learned how to get extra calories, even when she wasn't hungry. She also had some nutritional bars in her purse and she would eat one later.

Sabrena called Rach as soon as Steve and the girls went to the pool. She would join them later. "Hey Rach, what's up?"

"Glad you made it," said Rach. "How was the flight and how're you feeling?" Rach sounded worried. Sabrena knew Rach still wasn't too keen on her going away with Steve.

"I'm tired, but okay. I took my meds and I'm going to take a quick nap, Mommy Dearest. Anything else?" Sabrena laughed, but her sarcasm was based in a bit of truth.

"Did your sorry butt bring condoms?"

"No, I don't need them. I'm not going there."

"Just checking. You know your little confession after a glass of wine—you were close before. The snake is going to try to get in your pants." Rach knew Steve, and although she admired how he had hung in there with the girls for the last several months, she still doubted he was the changed man he declared to her.

"Don't worry about it. Believe me when I say, if anyone needs a good make-out session, it's me, but I have it under control," Sabrena told her friend, remembering the last time she and Steve had been alone. Sabrena and Rach chatted for awhile longer and they said their good-byes.

Although her doctors told her it was normal for her to have sexual desires, she wanted them to go away. Sabrena prayed for the strength to be celibate, not only because of having the disease, but especially since she wanted to live according to God's plans. After all, it was sex that had gotten her into this mess. If only she could convince her body that this was the new plan. Dr. Grier had advised her to make sure she used condoms, even if her partner was infected, and had encouraged to tell her partner, prior to being intimate, because it was the right thing to do. Sabrena and Dr. Grier had a frank discussion about kissing and possible transmission of the virus and he advised against open mouth kissing. Although the risk was low, it still was there. Sabrena's mind drifted back to the close call with Steve and had to know if he had given her HIV/AIDS. Had he been positive and just hadn't told her? Or had she infected him? Either way, she had to know, and either way, finding out would be painful.

Sabrena continued to take advantage of her quiet time. She called Vance, to whom she had grown increasingly close.

"Hey Vance, I'm in Disney! How are you?"

"Hello, Sabrena how is it? What was the girls' reaction?" Vance was touched that Sabrena called him during her little vacation. She'd become one of his closest friends. She was easy to talk to, and when they talked, he was able to forget some of his challenges.

"It's very nice. Steve went all out, and the girls couldn't be happier. How're you? I know that Vivian and your dad have a date tonight, so I just wanted to check on you. Plus, I needed to talk to my man." Sabrena and Vance chatted for a few more minutes and then said good-bye.

Sabrena looked over the spacious pool, with its real beach look, sand and all. She spotted Steve and the girls splashing around. The girls looked so cute with their life vests on and Steve was beaming. It was funny to see a grown man splashing in the kiddie pool, but you would've thought from his grin that he'd won the lottery.

After a moment, she looked up, at the clear blue sky, and took a long, deep breath. For just a moment, all was right with the world. As if summoned by God Almighty, Sabrena lifted her arms to the sky and whispered:

"Lord, thank you so much for this moment. Thank you for life and especially the blessings of my daughters and motherhood. I don't know what I ever did to deserve them but I thank you so much. Thank you for the love that Steve has for them and for allowing me to see him make one of their little dreams come true. I don't know what you have planned for me, but I thank you for the love in my heart that you are allowing me to feel right now. I don't want to ask you for anything, I just want to tell you that I am so grateful for this moment in time. Thank you God."

Sabrena wiped the fresh tears from her eyes and ran over to Steve and the girls. She couldn't help but smile as look into Steve's laughing eyes. Her heart betrayed her again as it gave way to the feelings of love that remained for him.

What would day two in the Magic Kingdom hold? Sabrena awoke to her daughters, who were fully dressed and standing over her bed.

Sabrena heard Deena whisper, "Be quiet, Renee; wait 'till Mommy wakes up."

"You be quiet, stop telling me what to do! I wanna go outside." Renee was searching for her independence.

"Shhhh, Mommy's tired, and we have to wait."

"Good morning, princesses, I must have overslept. Wow, you guys are already dressed. Did you take a bath and brush your teeth?" Sabrena sat up on the queen-sized bed and stretched. She had slept well, with no nightmares, so she was grateful. "Where's Uncle Steve?"

"He went runnin'. He said that when he came back he'd take us to the Magic Kingdom." Deena was always in the know and setting the agenda.

"Okay, well, we will wait for him. Let me take a shower and get dressed. You girls watch TV and we'll go get breakfast."

"Mommy, I'm not hungry. I wanna go on the train to the castle. I'm really not hungry." Renee was becoming impatient, but Sabrena would make sure that the girls had full bellies before they began the day.

On the surface they appeared to be one big, happy family. She had mandated that they have a good breakfast before hitting the theme park. It felt good to see them so happy and full of excitement. She didn't regret her decision and Steve looked happy. He was totally into the girls and taking them everywhere. They'd gone to the pool yesterday afternoon and then he took them all to the bumper cars and dinner. Sabrena had to admit that this break from her own worries was a positive one, and she enjoyed living in the fantasy, if only for a few days.

"Sabrena, Sabrena are you all right?" Steve asked as Sabrena grabbed the bench and slid onto the seat. She was sweaty and the earth was spinning.

"Yeah, yeah. I'm okay, just a little dizzy." Sabrena looked at Deena, who was holding Steve's hand as they walked toward the Tea Cup ride, her smile fading as she looked at her mom. Sabrena forced herself to smile and assured him, "I'm just a little hot, and these old legs can't keep up. Why don't you take them to the ride and I'll rest for a moment."

"Girls, sit next to your mommy. I'll go get something for her to drink." Steve walked to the concession stand and looked back at Sabrena. She was worried about the spells of dizziness and some-times she felt confused, like her brain wasn't working right. Sabrena knew it was all the excitement that was getting to her today, but that she wasn't going to spoil their vacation. She had decided not to take medication last night or this morning—she wanted to feel her best and sometimes the medicine made her feel sick. She would start back when she got home, but she did take her multivitamin, vitamin C, and some natural pills that Rach had given her for energy.

"Mommy, you don't look right," Renee said with tears in her eyes, sensing that her mother was not well.

"I'm fine, baby—it's just the excitement." Sabrena mustered a smile and took a deep breath; she wasn't going to spoil their fantasy.

"Here you go, Sabrena. Do you need to go back to the room?" Steve offered. "I'll take you and bring the girls back out later." He also put a damp napkin around her neck.

"No, thanks. I'm feeling better already. Let's go, girls! There's a teacup with my name on it!" Sabrena drank the Coke and willed her-self to keep going. This was the girl's dream and nothing was going to mess up it up. Renee held tightly onto her hand as they walked toward the ride.

The day flew by and the girls, despite not wanting to admit it, were dead tired after the day at the park. Sabrena put them in the shower and got them ready for bed, promising that tomorrow would be a whole new day at the parks. Sabrena and the girls changed into their matching PJs. She was grateful for the sleeveless top and shorts, which would keep her cool. The night sweats had eased up, but were still an issue for her, and she didn't know if it was menopause or her disease. She was thankful that the girls were tired. It would give her time to catch her breath and get to bed early. She got on her knees with them and listened as her little one said their prayers:

*"Now I lay me down to sleep, I pray the Lord my soul to
keep. If I should die before I wake, I pray the Lord my soul
to take. God Bless Mommy, Deena, Uncle Steve, Grandma,
Auntie Rach, and the whole world. Thank you for our trip
and thank you for Uncle Steve and Mommy bringing us
and us all being together again. God, please make Mommy
feel better. Amen."*

Sabrena quickly wiped the tears from her eyes and tucked in the
girls. They were asleep within minutes. She gently closed the door
and walked into the living room, where Steve was watching the
news.

"They're zonked out and I'm glad, 'cause I couldn't take another round of 'what are we gonna do next'." Sabrena pulled out a bag
of chips and plopped on the couch.

"You know, I'm older than you, and I can tell you that they've
really worn me out! I tried to put up a good front, but my feet are
hurting, back aching, and I'm still not right after that little roller
coaster," Steve said with a smile as he looked at Sabrena. What he
couldn't say was that he hadn't been this happy in a long time. He
had really messed up their relationship and gambled with losing the
best things in his life. He only hoped that he could pull it back
together. Actually, he was going to get his family back.

"Thank you, Steve. No man has ever cared for the girls like you
do, and certainly not their deadbeat sperm donor. Thank you for the
sacrifice in bringing us here and just for this part of you," Sabrena
said, her eyes misting over. She realized just then that she still loved
him for many reasons, one being who he was with her girls. It was-
n't about the money; it really was about the time and his commitment. It was about how he picked up Renee when she was tired and
didn't want to walk anymore. How he always made sure Deena
didn't feel left out and let her make some decisions. Sabrena saw
how he looked at the girls and how he called them "his girls." She
smiled as she thought of the grown man singing and recording the
Mickey Mouse theme song with the girls, with enthusiasm and without worrying about looking stupid. Steve had always been that way
with them and this trip was good for them all.

"Sabrena, I can't thank you enough for letting them come. You
don't know how much it means to me. They're my daughters and I'm

gonna always be there for them and you," Steve said, suddenly feeling as emotional as Sabrena looked. He wanted to say more, but it wasn't the time. They walked onto the balcony and relaxed together in silence. Sabrena feel asleep on the patio chair, and Steve lifted her and took her to her bed. Steve loved when she put her arms around him as he carried her. Even though he knew she was asleep—it still felt good. Was he ready for tomorrow? Was he really ready for what he had to say to Sabrena?

CHAPTER FORTY-TWO

Steve was nervous. The girls were set and he and Sabrena were going to spend some quiet time together. He'd thought about what he was going to say, how he was going to break the ice, and what he was willing to do. The day had flown by, with Magic Kingdom in the morning and the waterslides in the afternoon. Sabrena had come back to the suite and, at his suggestion, taken a nap. This worked out perfectly, as he set the stage for the evening. The girls were still bubbly and ready for the next adventure. The caregiver from Kids Night Out picked them up and Steve made sure that he gave her the key to the private door into their bedroom. He had arranged for room service to deliver a special meal, and the concierge had arranged for the CD player. Steve took a deep breath as he decided to put all the cards on the table and take the biggest gamble of his life. Steve quickly showered and put on her favorite cologne, Michael Kors for men. He took time to change into the new outfit that he bought especially for tonight. He hadn't been this nervous in years. Could he finally be totally honest with Sabrena? What would she say? Was there any way that she could forgive him?

Sabrena awoke in the quiet room and felt refreshed. She was getting good at making excuses for her naps. She had a nagging headache and hoped that the Tylenol would take it away. It was nearly time for dinner and she knew that the girls would want to do something. Sabrena quickly called Rach to touch base.

"Hi, Rach, what's going on?"

"Well, I'm miserable, how're you?" Sabrena didn't like how Rach sounded. "Are you doing anything tonight?" Sabrena asked.

"Nope, it's another night at home along." Rach told her she had gone to church that day, which was a rarity, especially when Sabrena wasn't there to drag her and the day had ended in a very un-Christian manner. Rach had a run-in with Valerie in the church parking lot. Valerie, who had heard that Rach and Barry had split up, told Rach she was better off, and that she needed to set her aims a little higher next time. Even though she wanted to out Valerie's husband, Rach just told her to spend less time watching other people and more time keeping an eye on her own relationship. Sabrena was surprised by her bit of restraint with Valerie.

"Girl, I'm so glad that you didn't totally go out there. Valerie couldn't take it if her world wasn't perfect. Did she show off the car again?"

"Yeah, she tried to, but I just ignored her. Guess who walked into church today? That crazy after-school teacher. I think her name is Tina."

"Really, I've never seen her there before. Did she recognize you?"

"I don't know, she wasn't studying me. She was broke down. She was crying and falling over at altar call. Deacon Johnson announced that she was coming to be saved and was going to join the church. He asked for us all to pray for her and her family. You never know what people are going through."

"You got that right, I'll pray for her. Maybe that's why she's so mean."

Sabrena and her friend chatted idly until finally she encouraged Rach to call Barry, just to talk.

"You know that you love him, Rach, and it's okay. You need to talk with him, before someone else gets your blessing."

"I can't, Bre, I just can't. I don't even know what to say." Rach wanted to find a way back to him but she remained guarded.

"What about: I love you; I L-O-V-E Y-O-U?" Sabrena said, exaggerating the words. "Yeah, what about that, and I'm a stupid fool, but you love me, so let's do this."

"You're a witch. I love you, but you make me crazy," Rach laughed.

Rach thought about the sermon that morning: *Courage to Face our Greatest Fears*. It felt like the preacher was having a one-on-one conversation with her. She actually shed a few tears during the service, but felt stronger as she left. Rach just didn't know if now was the time to change the formula; it had worked for years. Barry was different. She could trust him. Usually, he would start calling and coming around within a few weeks of her dismissing him. But this time he'd walked, and she knew that he was serious.

As Rach curled up on her couch she thought about her life. She had everything going for her. She had a career where she pretty much set her own rules and was appreciated, so much so that she was hearing rumors about them making her a partner. She had a beautiful home and a nice car. She was financially stable and she wasn't bad to look at—she was cute, really. But she still had a need that wasn't met. She needed to feel safe, safe enough to let her underbelly show, and not feel vulnerable. She didn't know if she could do it, but she knew that she was hurting now. Rach couldn't deny it. Despite her best efforts, she was head over heels in love.

Rach felt good in Barry's arms, as he hugged her. She'd called him and asked him to come over so they could talk. She'd even tried to cook some food, but ended up calling Boston Market for a delivery. That's as close to home cooking as she could get.

"Barry, I missed you and I wanted to tell you something." Rach was nervous, but happier than she'd been in weeks. Barry looked good, better than before, and he seemed taller.

Barry smiled. "I missed you, too, Rachel, but this has to be right, or it's not worth our time."

"Barry—well, I uhh, I think, I need to, humm, I . . ." Rach had always prided herself on the frankness of her words, but her tongue felt like a piece of lead. "Hell, Barry, I love you, I can't help it. I love you and that's it. I love you and want another chance."

"Good, I'm glad you finally figured it out—Whew! That was close." Barry was smiling ear to ear.

"What do you mean, 'that was close'? I just said that I love you, what do you mean?"

"Well, I'm tired of being a play thing for you, your yo-yo. When you want me, you pull me close, but when I get close, you push me away. I know that you're scared and that this is a big step for you, and I'm very grateful. But, Ms. Washington, we've only just begun. The love is the foundation on which we'll build the rest of our lives. You're the one, mean as a snake, but you're the one." Barry pulled Rach in his arms and kissed her. They both felt home, and, for the first time in years, Rachel felt complete.

Steve had pulled out all the stops. Dinner consisted of all Sabrena's favorites and the right music playing, as well as roses for her. The girls were with the caregiver, but Sabrena had still asked repeatedly about their safety.

"Steve, you really didn't have to do all of this," Sabrena said as she tried to keep herself from smiling.

"I know, but we need to spend some time together and just talk. I miss you and I want you to know that I do still love you," Steve said, feeling like a 16-year-old on his first date. He looked at Sabrena. While he saw the woman he loved, he sensed that she was different, that something was very different. He hoped she hadn't found any-one else and that she still loved him.

After dinner, they went out on the balcony and danced to the sound of Luther Vandross in the background. No one crooned like Luther; even now he was still the greatest. Steve had candles every-where and Sabrena's heart stirred as he touched her back. Steve leaned in to kiss her and she let him. She put her arms around his neck and wallowed in the comfort of his strength. She felt his tongue begin to probe her mouth and she heard Dr. Grier's words echo in her brain.

"Steve, we need to stop. Let's go back inside," Sabrena urged. She abruptly turned and sat on the couch. "I need to talk with you and now is as good a time as any."

"Brena, what is it? You know that I love you. I know that I've made mistakes, over and over again, but believe me, I'm a changed man. I love you more than anything and I love my girls. Please don't shut me out. I've learned more in the last few months than I've learned in all my life. I know who I am and I know that you've made me a better man." Steve knew that his moment of truth was now.

Sabrena was sitting on the couch and he reached in his pocket and pulled the box out. Steve knelt next to Sabrena and kissed her again, softly. "Brena, we've been through a lot over the years and I've been stupid. I've been unfaithful and full of lies. I'm ashamed of my life and who I've been, especially as it relates to our relationship. But, baby, that's who I was. I'm a different man now, a real man, and you've made all the difference. I love you. I love your smile, your eyes, and your body, but more than any physical stuff, I love you— the mother to the girls, the woman who's always told me I was going to make it, before I even knew it. I love how you brush your hand on my cheek, I love how you say my name when you're sleepy, I love how you take care of everybody and make them feel warm just being in your presence. I have a lot of junk in my past and a lot of demons that I have to deal with about relationships, but I'm willing to face them if you will stand with me. Brena, I love you and I want you to be my wife. No jokes, no procrastination. Just be my wife for the rest of our lives, just you and me. Sabrena Collins, will you marry me? Will you become Mrs. Sabrena Addison?"

Sabrena felt as though she was having an out-of-body experience. She had waited for over two years to hear these words from Steve's mouth. They'd talked about it before, but he'd never been really serious and certainly never bought a ring. She looked at him on his knees and the ring. She just took it in. She was in the Magical Kingdom, but she was no princess, and despite Steve's great words, he was no prince.

"Please get up, Steve. I need to talk to you and I need to do it right now." Sabrena stood and turned her back to him.

"What? What's wrong? Is there someone else? Don't you love me anymore? Am I not good enough for you? What is it? Whatever it is, we can work on it, as long as you still love me," Steve pleaded, surprising even himself with the desperation in his voice. He had nothing to lose, except for Sabrena and she was worth the begging.

"No, Steve, there's no one else. There hasn't been anyone else for me since I met you. Despite my best efforts, I do still have love for you. But my life is a mess right now and I can't think clearly." Sabrena searched for the words and continued, "What about you? Is there something that you haven't told me? Is there something I should know about you, your health, anything?" Sabrena searched Steve's face, which looked more puzzled than guilty.

"No, I'm fine. I went to the doctor a few weeks ago and my cholesterol needs to be lower, but I'm fine. Why, do I look bad?"

"No, Steve, but you can't always tell by looking," Sabrena said. She took a deep breath. "Steve, you admitted that you've been unfaithful. Did you get anything and not tell me?"

Steve's plan was crashing around him. This wasn't how he'd planned it. He may as well come clean with Sabrena; he couldn't let the moment pass.

CHAPTER FORTY-THREE

Steve began. He couldn't bear to look in Sabrena's eyes. But, as he continued to talk, he found the strength to do so.

"Sabrena, I have some issues."

"I did you wrong and a lot of women wrong because of my baggage. I wasn't going to be trapped and controlled by a woman, and I swore that I would never be like my father. My mother controlled his every move and finally he just became a shell. I had no respect for him. Sabrena, their marriage is what I grew up seeing, so I thought that is what all marriages had to be. I only loved one other woman my whole life, and she was my high school sweetheart. I took the coward's way out and left her at the altar, because I couldn't deal with the possibility of becoming like my father." Steve continued to talk as he stared intently into Sabrena's eyes. She knew that he was baring his soul.

"Sabrena, it gets worse, because I never wanted to feel trapped. I had a vasectomy when I was in my late twenties. I didn't want to be a father, until I met Deena and Renee. Brena, those girls are my life—you're my life, and I can't live without you." Steve took a deep breath and continued. He felt a tear roll down his cheek. He had to tell her everything.

"Brena, I want to come totally clean. I was unfaithful to you with several women. Your accusations have been right most of the time." Steve talked about how empty he felt each time he cheated on her, but there was something in him that wasn't strong enough to just be with her. He poured out his life and his soul to her and felt hot tears of shame flow freely down his cheeks. He still had to admit the heaviest of his sins.

"Sabrena, I did something that I'm so ashamed of. I never told you. No matter what happens after tonight, I just want to come totally clean. I can only pray that you find it in your heart to forgive me." Steve turned and looked intently into Sabrena's beautiful brown eyes.

Sabrena took a deep breath and waited for the confession she knew was coming. She nodded and said, "Go ahead, Steve, I need to know. I need to hear it out of your mouth."

"A few years ago, when you had the STD, I denied having anything and made you feel like it was you. Well, I had been with someone and probably passed it on to you. The same thing with the last time, you were right about that night at the store. I made up the whole story and had been with someone. It didn't mean anything, but I need to just be upfront with you." Steve felt like a load had been lifted from his shoulders. No matter what happened, Sabrena deserved to know the truth.

"What else, Steve! What else did you give me?! What else? Say it, say it!" Sabrena was now hitting Steve on his chest and crying hysterically. "Say it! Say it! It was *you*! How could you do this to me? How could you do this to my girls? How could you? Bastard— say it!" Sabrena's teeth clinched and the room was spinning.

"Sabrena, calm down. I've said it all, there's nothing else. I'm sorry. I know it doesn't mean much now, but I'm sorry. I would've never intentionally given you anything, but I didn't know until you went to the doctor. Baby, please forgive me. We can get over this. It's our past and now we can make a future." Steve tried to calm her down. He'd never seen Sabrena so angry and didn't understand everything she was saying.

"Say it, Steve. Tell me it was you. You did this." Sabrena fell to the floor, crying and rocking herself with her knees in her chest. Steve quickly went to her and put his arms around her.

"Say what, baby? Haven't I said enough? I don't know if you can forgive me, but I'm willing to spend the rest of my life making this up to you. I love you and I love the girls. I want my family back." Steve was overcome with emotion and began to cry silently as he held Sabrena.

Sabrena grabbed his face hard. She forced him to look straight into her eyes and said through gritted teeth, "Say, 'Brena—I'm a ho, I slept around, got HIV, and I gave it to you.' Say that Steve, say that." Sabrena had finally verbalized her secret to Steve and she waited for his response.

"No, baby don't play like that. Nah, nah, don't say that. Don't even play with that. Don't . . ." Steve fell back against the chair's leg, his mind spinning. "Sabrena, are you telling me that you have HIV? Is that what you're telling me? My tests are negative." Steve was totally blown away. "You can't be telling me that you have HIV." Steve didn't recognize his own voice.

"Yes, I'm HIV-positive and I have AIDS," Sabrena said in a whisper as she closed her eyes and continued to rock herself, repeating the words over and over. Steve reached for her, but she pushed him away and screamed, "You don't want me *now* do you? You don't love me *now*, do you? You don't want to *marry* me *now*? Leave me *alone*! *Get out*, Steve, *GET OUT*, GET OUT!"

She didn't know how much time had passed. Sabrena had cried herself to sleep in the corner and jumped as she heard the ringing phone. It was the caregiver, saying she was bringing the girls back to their room. Sabrena ran to the bathroom and washed her face, her head throbbing like never before. She had no idea where Steve had gone. He never even said anything after she told him to get out. She'd pushed him away when he tried to hold her.

He was negative. How could this be? She felt dirty, ashamed, and alone. Damaged goods, as her mother had once called her. But if not Steve, she thought, who? She had to go back to her painful past. She wiped her eyes and prepared to greet her babies. They were the only things that really mattered and their love would outlast any other.

"Mommy, Mommy we had *fun*!" The girls ran in and hugged her.

"Where's Uncle Steve, I have to show him the picture I drew. It's me, you, Deena, and Uncle Steve with Minnie! See Mommy, isn't it pretty?" Renee showed her the drawing, waiting for her mother's approval.

"Yes, honey, it is pretty. Mommy has to go the bathroom, hold on." Sabrena ran into the bathroom. They couldn't see her cry. She pulled herself together and prepared them for bed.

Sabrena felt her body lifting off the bed. She thought she was dreaming, until she felt Steve struggle with the door. The girls were asleep and he'd lifted her out of the bed and was taking her to the living room. She had no idea what time it was.

"Brena, you never answered my question," Steve said, looking haggard, his eyes bloodshot and his breath smelling of liquor.

"What? What question?" Sabrena was shocked that he'd even touched her, and as he kissed her on the lips, she pulled back.

"Baby, I asked you to be my wife. You never answered. You talked about other stuff that is heavy and challenging, but you never answered the most important question."

"Steve, I can't . . . I can't do that to you or anyone. I told you that I have—" Steve stopped Sabrena from talking by kissing her again.

He pulled back and looked into her eyes and said again, "Sabrena Collins, will you be my wife? That's all I want to know. I just want to know if you'll marry me. Later for the rest of this stuff. Will you let me wake up with you in the morning and go to bed with you each night? Will you let me love, honor, and cherish you for better or worse, in sickness and health for the rest of our lives, whether that's a day or a decade? Brena, will you let me love you, hold you, be with you, and take care of you? Will you do the same for me? You're my home." Steve didn't care about his tears now. He had thought long and hard, but there was no alternative for him. He was lost without Sabrena and he needed her to save him from himself.

PART IV

CHAPTER FORTY-FOUR

Sabrena couldn't believe that the summer and fall had passed so quickly. It was nearly Thanksgiving, and since Sabrena hated fighting the crazy Christmas shoppers, she'd already started buying a few of the girls' gifts. She also had to work more hours during the holidays, so she really didn't have the time most people enjoyed. She had more Christmas spirit this year than she'd ever had. Everything seemed to be more colorful, happier, and more joyful. She didn't notice people honking in traffic, but she did notice the clarity of the stars at night. She barely saw angry shoppers, but she noticed a father and son walking hand in hand through the toy store. Things felt right for the first time in a long time. She felt confident and complete.

But not everything was right. A few months earlier, she'd done the unthinkable and tried to contact Carlton. The response was pretty much just as she expected.

"Don't call here. We don't want to hear your voice. We don't want to know about those girls. We don't want to know anything about you or your life," Carlton's mother had hissed into the phone. She was still a witch. Sabrena had called her number, because the old number for Carlton had been disconnected and there was no new public listing. She didn't know if he'd moved his new family, but she'd run out of options. She called his old job and they said that he no longer was with the company. Calling Mrs. Wilson was her last resort and she regretted it before she'd even spoken.

"Mrs. Wilson, I need to contact Carlton. It's an emergency. Now, surely, we can put aside our differences and you can give me a number or give my number to him. Let's be adults. And please keep my children out of it. They don't have anything to do with this," Sabrena said sternly.

"The hell, you say! If you hadn't trapped Carlton by getting pregnant, I wouldn't even know you. You knew that he would do the right thing and you just rode the gravy train. Well, why are you calling here now after all these years? You're divorced, and Carlton moved on with his life without you!"

"Mrs. Wilson, this has never been about you and it certainly isn't about you now. All I want is to speak with Carlton, that's it. Now, you can give me a number or take my number for him to call, but if you hang up without doing one of those two things, I'll call every five minutes until you do." Sabrena had tried to be nice, but Mrs. Wilson had worked her last nerve.

"It will be a cold day in hell before you speak to my son. Leave my family alone! You have done enough, Tramp!" Sabrena's ears rang as the phone was slammed in her ear. A few days later, she tried to call back, but the number had been changed. That was months ago. Now she was ready to face her past, with Gerald by her side. She continued to look toward the restaurant's entrance and finally saw her handsome brother coming toward her.

"There's my baby sis!" Gerald yelled as he grabbed her and lifted her off the floor, twirling her around, as he had for most of her life.

"Boy, put me down. There's more of me to pick up these days," Sabrena said, conscious of her protruding stomach. Dr. Scott said that it was a side effect of the medications. It was a little pouch and no amount of sit-ups was making it go down. Sabrena felt very self-conscious, because the rest of her body was small and her clothes didn't fit right.

"Girl, you still ain't more than a buck thirty-five. How're you? You look good," Gerald said as they sat at the table. "When do I see my nieces?"

"Well, you'll see them tomorrow evening. I needed to have some time with you alone and to ask my Big Bro to go with me on a quick road trip."

"Okay, Sis, but you said that there were some issues that we needed to talk about. What's going on?" Gerald asked, always one to get right to the point.

"Slow down a bit, let's order and chat. How're Sheila and the boys?" Sabrena and Gerald exchanged stories about their families; they talked every week, but they hadn't seen each other in almost a year, so there was a lot to cover. Before they knew it, hours had passed, and they were ready to head out. Gerald had taken a cab to the restaurant, which was near the airport. Sabrena had rented a car and made a hotel reservation in her old hometown. As they got into the car, she began to confide in her older brother.

"Gerald, I need to see Carlton, and that's where we're going."

"Are you kidding? Why? What's going on? All this mystery is making me antsy. What's up?" Gerald knew that Sabrena hadn't talked to Carlton since their divorce.

"Gerald, I need for you to be strong and just listen to me. I need to find him. I'll explain later, but I need to have a conversation. His mother won't give me his phone number, so I have to go. I drove down there already and went to the old house, but he isn't living there. Fortunately, it's being rented out and I got the name of the realtor. After a lot of digging and calling a few old friends, I got the address to where the payments are mailed, but no one could give me the private number. I looked up the address on the tax assessment website, and found that he and his wife Nicole are the owners of the house at the address, so I feel sure that we can find them." Sabrena didn't want to go any further. Now wasn't the time to tell her brother about everything.

"Since when did you become the detective? You know what, people have always underestimated you. You'll get to the bottom of whatever!" Gerald chuckled. "Anyway, all this for an ex-husband. I'll do whatever you need and ain't above putting the man in a choke hold, but I just want to know what's up."

"I wouldn't take your time if I didn't need you. But I'll tell you everything after we finish this." Sabrena turned on the radio and followed the MapQuest directions, and soon they were at the hotel. The city had grown in the last few years, but Sabrena wasn't fooled by the lights and the new paint. This city was full of painful memories and she would be glad to leave tomorrow.

"Are you too tired to go for a ride?" Sabrena asked Gerald, once they got settled in the room.

"Nope, I'm a trooper. With this CIA/FBI type of assignment, I have got to stay on my toes," he answered with a wink. Sabrena threw a pillow at her brother and soon they were headed out. She drove past her old house and got nervous just looking at it. But she reassured herself that, no matter how awful it had been, the past hadn't killed her and had only made her stronger. Sabrena was ready to meet the devil.

Dr. Scott had asked her why she was so intent on finding who had infected her. But even Rach was curious after learning about Steve, whom she'd sworn was the culprit. Sabrena didn't really know, except that she needed to find some closure and move on. She was doing this for her own peace of mind and, while it was painful, she hoped it would also be therapeutic for her. At this point, if Carlton is negative, the only other person could be Francis, and even she couldn't find out any more about him, given his current place of residence.

"That's the house and he's there," Sabrena said as she looked at the address from the other side of the street. She saw a 730 IL BMW in the driveway, black, just as Carlton had always wanted. He'd finally gotten it, and, from the looks of it, it was several years old. She didn't see any other cars in the drive, but there was a two-car garage, so she didn't have any idea if his wife was home or not. She saw a swing set in the backyard and muttered, "He has a swing set for his son. He never let me put one up for Deena, didn't want to mess up the landscaping."

Sabrena was filled with anger as she looked at the house and the seemingly comfortable life that Carlton had made for himself. She quickly drove back to the hotel, determined to come back in the morning. He should be home early on Saturday morning. She was grateful that Gerald was with her.

"Gerald, I need to talk to you about something, but I need for you to be cool about it." Sabrena knew how protective Gerald could be and he did have a temper when it came to his family.

"No problem. I know something is going on and has been for a while. No matter what, I'm here for you," he said as he squeezed her hand.

"Thank you, and I know. You have my back, no matter what. There's no easy way to say this," Sabrena began as she felt her insides start to quiver. She whispered a prayer for strength to herself and then said aloud, "Gerald, about nine months ago, I was diagnosed with HIV and, more to the point, AIDS. I'm doing well now, taking my medications and God knows going to the doctors." Sabrena tried to smile as she grabbed his hands. Gerald looked at her and then looked out the window.

"Sis, why didn't you tell me? *Nine* months and I didn't know? How have you handled this? What are the doctors saying?" Gerald fought back tears as he had a passing memory of Sabrena and he playing tag in their mother's yard. He always would let her catch him, even though he was faster and stronger. He'd looked out for Sabrena, like a sister, but also a daughter. He didn't let anybody mess with his sister. The boys knew that they would be in for a butt whipping if he heard they said anything out of the way, or, God forbid, put their hands on his sis.

He shook his head and whispered, "I can't beat this one." Sabrena hugged him and they reassured each other that everything was going to be all right. He felt that he should be supporting her, but indeed it was Sabrena who was consoling him. Even she was amazed at how strong she'd become over the last few months. Gerald found her strength to be enough to give him hope for her life.

"Sis, you said that you have AIDS. How're you doing? How're you feeling? What are the doctors saying?" They spent the rest of the evening talking about her diagnosis, the prognosis, next steps, and their lives in general. Sabrena would need Gerald's help in talking with their mother, but that would come much later.

They woke early on Saturday and were waiting outside of Carlton's house by 8:30.

"So Sis, this is it. You think that Carlton infected you?" Gerald asked, feeling his muscles tighten. He hadn't slept well at all last night.

"I don't know, but Steve is definitely negative. I saw his results. There is one other person, Francis, who I only was with a few times. But he's now in prison, though, so I can't reach him. Given my time of diagnosis and the fact that I now have AIDS, it's a 50/50 chance that he's responsible," Sabrena said. She took a deep breath and decided she would just go knock on the door. " I just need to know, for me."

Gerald put a hand on her shoulder and said confidently, "What do you want me to do? Are you going to confront him this morning? What's the plan?"

"I'm tired now and I know that finding out who gave this to me doesn't really help my situation. My doctors and Rach all advised me against putting this much energy into it; but I need to know. If I don't find out, well, then it won't be because I didn't try. I still have a lot of anger towards Carlton but I just want to ask him some questions, see how that goes, and put it on the table. I'm strong enough to do that, but I'm not strong enough to do it by myself. He knows that you don't play and I needed my big brother to just be here for support. I also needed to have quiet time with you. I've been trying to tell you for months, but I've never gotten the nerve to spit it out."

Sabrena saw an attractive, slender woman walk out of the house in a jogging suit, a cup in her hand. That was their cue that the house was awake. When the woman had walked back into the house, Sabrena pulled the car into the driveway. Gerald's hand steadied Sabrena as she walked to the door.

"Good morning. May I help you?" The woman said through the screen door. "We don't believe in Jehovah Witnesses, we're Christians." Carlton's wife stood behind the screen door, eyeing them suspiciously.

"We're not Jehovah's Witnesses. My name is Sabrena . . . Sabrena Collins, and this is my brother Gerald." Sabrena noticed the beautiful long eyelashes of the woman and her perfectly rounded face. Her hair was thin and fine like a baby's and was cut in a cute Anita Baker style. She was attractive, but her vacant eyes belied a hollow, superficial inside.

"Oh, I didn't recognize you. You've changed from your pictures. I'm Nicole, but I suppose you know that. What can I do for you?"

"Well, we would like to speak with Carlton," Sabrena said with as much strength as she could muster.

"What? Why are you here?" Nicole asked. Her fake but pleasant smile faded into irritation. A little boy walked to the door and stood behind his mother.

" C.J.," she said to the boy, "Go upstairs and watch cartoons. Mommy will be right there." Nicole opened the door and gestured for them to sit in her living room. Sabrena was impressed. The house was massive, and everywhere she looked, there were family photos, with Carlton at the center of them all, looking as arrogant as ever.

"How can I help you? You come to my home early in the morning, unannounced, and demand to see my husband. You've been divorced for over five years. Why now?" Nicole looked nervous and the tension was rising in the room.

"My sister just wants to speak with him, that's it. Now if you could go get him, we'll be on our way. The car's in the driveway. Is he here?" Gerald asked a bit forcibly.

"No, he's not here, and if you'll excuse me, I need for you both to leave," Nicole said as she stood and smoothed out her pants. Sabrena and Gerald remained seated.

"Do you know when he'll be back? I need to speak with him today. We've driven down and I just have some unfinished business with him. Can you call him or is he traveling?" Sabrena asked, remembering the frequent out-of-town business trips from her years with him.

"Really, I don't have time for this. Please get out before I call the police. I cannot call him and no, he's not traveling. Please leave me and my son alone. He won't be back."

"I know that this house is still in his name. Don't pretend that he doesn't' live here. I don't want anything from him but information. You have all these pictures around, so please don't play like I'm stupid. Where can I find him? Tell me and we'll be on our way," Sabrena said with determination. She stood, but wasn't about to leave without seeing Carlton.

"Carlton told me that you weren't too bright. I see that he wasn't wrong," Nicole said. With venom in her voice, she said, "If you don't get out of my house, I'll call the police and have you arrested for trespassing. Get out and don't bother coming back!" Nicole was visibly shaking at this point.

Gerald touched Sabrena's arm before she could speak and said, "Fine, we'll leave, but we'll be back. Tell Carlton that not only is Sabrena looking for him, but so is Gerald. Tell him that. Come on, Sabrena."

"You can tell him yourself! As a matter of fact—let me give you his number," Nicole hissed as she reached for a pen and angrily scribbled a number on a pad. "Here you go—tell him I said hello!" Sabrena looked at Nicole and felt sorry for her. She was protecting a man who probably wouldn't protect her. The trappings were nice—the car, the house, and the child; the American Dream. Unless you wake up with an arrogant Mama's boy who thinks he walks on water. She and Gerald walked to the door and she glanced at the number to make sure that she could read it.

Written on the paper was Carlton Wilson, permanent number: 1–800–He's in *HELL*. Sabrena went back to the door. Nicole was standing there with tears in her eyes, waiting for her.

"He's dead. He died last year of kidney disease. Please don't come near me, my child, or my neighborhood. I don't want to know you, your two girls, or anything. Carlton didn't leave anything to your daughters and I'll fight you with every bone in my body if you try to take anything away from my son." Nicole was expressionless and as cold as ice as she hissed at Sabrena.

"Nicole, I don't want anything from you or your son. I do want to know if there is anything that you want to tell me about how Carlton died. How did he get kidney disease?" Sabrena asked through the screen door.

"Let's just say, Carlton didn't have diabetes or high blood pressure. He just got it and eventually died. Now if you could please leave, I've said enough." Nicole began to look nervous and she moved to pull the door shut.

"Nicole, did Carlton have AIDS? I just have to know," Sabrena pressed.

Nicole looked off into the distance and spoke quietly to Sabrena almost as if she were speaking to herself. "Carlton did whatever he wanted to do with whomever he wanted. His life was his own; we were always just the ornaments. He never traveled for work, but only for *his* pleasure. He never loved anyone but himself and his mother. He loved her so much that he lived a lie. As wives, we were the smoke screen for his lies. Good-bye." Nicole pulled the door closed and Sabrena closed that chapter of her life.

CHAPTER FORTY-FIVE

"This suit is too tight; the cleaners must have shrunk it," Rach exclaimed. She tried to fasten the waist of her skirt.

"Baby, let me get it—of course the cleaners shrunk it," Barry said with a wink to Sabrena, who was waiting for them.

"Ain't no cleaner shrunk that dress," Steve said. "Ya butt eat too much and you're spreading. You know I'm just gonna tell you the truth. I hope ya'll ain't having kids. Barry, it's over for you after that." Steve helped Sabrena put on her sweater. He was careful to open the arm hole so that her ring wouldn't snag it.

"Steve, that little pebble of a diamond isn't going to do anything to that sweater. You really need to get glasses with your old self. You act like you gave her the Hope diamond. That's called a chip, baby, a diamond chip!" Rach fell over laughing, as did the rest of the room. Rach and Steve still went at it, but now a friendship had grown between them.

"Brena, you shouldn't be laughing with her. I gave you that ring. She has some nerve to talk about a diamond chip; your ring could eat hers for dinner. Talkin' bout my ring. Barry's cheap tail didn't put out the dollars like I did. But then again, Rach, you should be happy that he's seen with you in public. By the way, don't breathe—that skirt is liable to pop open at any time." Sabrena smiled as she looked at her friends. She was blessed to have them all. Life was good, her girls were happy, spring was in the air, and she was getting married in two months.

Dr. Scott and Dr. Grier said that she was doing great, her CD4 counts were well over 200 and her viral load was undetectable, zero. Her numbers had been low for over six months. Dr. Grier told her that she no longer fit the criteria of AIDS, but was still HIV-positive. Sabrena was still confused by that part of the process, but she was happy for the good news. She was trying to take her vitamins on a daily basis and was working out a few times a week. Steve was a constant supporter, and, thank God, his tests were still negative. Although she hated medications and Dr. Grier told her they could consider stopping them, she decided to continue for the time being. Sabrena wanted every chance to be well and to live a long life. She had her girls to take care of and, in two months, a new husband. Many would think that she was a fool to be with him, but her heart believed that he now belonged to her and her alone.

She loved Steve with her whole heart and felt his love every day. It was good to feel love back, a new experience for her. She had loved Kevin, her first husband, or rather the man she thought he was. The love for him was that of a young, naïve girl still searching for who she was. Part of her loved Carlton, as much as she hated to admit it. She had loved him and who he projected himself to be. He was bigger than life and she felt that his being with her made *her* bigger, if only for a moment. With Steve, she felt that their relationship had come full circle. They had become one, both with imperfections, but they were together and for the first time her love was reciprocated.

Sabrena didn't care what people thought, she loved him and that was more than enough to conquer their past. Some would say that he was crazy to marry a woman with HIV. They'd talked for many hours about it and Steve would not be deterred. She was his family, his home, and nothing—not even HIV—was going to put him out of his home. She still worried about the intimacy that she and Steve had agreed would wait until they said their vows. She'd talked with Vance and her doctors about her fears. She smiled as she thought of her friend, Vance. He's outlived all of the doctor's predictions. He was slowly exiting this life but he had found peace with his demons and seemed content. Sabrena was happy also, but still had issues, which she was learning to talk about with her support group and psychologist. She knew that between God, her girls, Steve, Rach, Gerald, her mom and her friends, she was gonna make it.

"Come on, let's go. Rachel, *nothing* that you do is gonna make you look better or that skirt fit better. Barry, I'm praying for you, man." Steve laughed at his former nemesis.

"Brena, you'd better get this old fool before I beat him down," Rach said, as she stomped through the door. Sabrena did notice that her hips were wider, but kept that to herself. Barry needed to lay off the cooking for a minute.

CHAPTER FORTY-SIX

Vivian spent her Sunday morning in church with Joseph, but needed to rush home to relieve the Hospice nurse. Her stomach was a bundle of nerves, but her faith gave her strength. She glanced at her husband, whose head was bowed, and she knew that he was praying for his son. Vivian was grateful to God for the miracle of reconciliation and the renewed relationship between Joseph and Vance. At the benediction, she and Joseph scurried out of the church, hoping to go unnoticed.

"Hello, Vivian, Joseph—Wait up!" the pastor called out to them.

"Pastor White, how're you?" Joseph, realizing they'd been caught, stopped and shook his hand.

"I'm fine, but more importantly, how're you all and how is Vance?"

"He's in good spirits, but we know that his time isn't long. He's a strong man, maybe not in body now, but definitely in spirit," Vivian replied, acutely aware of a few of her fellow parishioners coming out and some of her old friends pretending not to see her. Funny, she thought, if Vance had cancer, the missionary society would be over every week, food would come, and they would send a member to sit with him. However, it wasn't cancer, and once her friends and many of her church members heard that he had AIDS, they stopped calling or coming over. A few offered their prayers, and one or two had come by to try to "save him" before it was too late. The message was clear: hate and condemnation.

Her pastor and his wife, Elder Terri, were not like that; they showed love for her family and she would never forget their kindness. While Vivian had her own beliefs, the one that was the strongest was that God is love and that he loves all of his children.

Her baby was dying and she was finally at peace with that fact. He had outlived all of the predictions and that had given the family time to heal its wounds and enjoy their days together.

Vance was tired now, his body was resisting the medications and he had relapsed with pneumonia. They had all agreed to his decision to enter hospice, but it was Joseph who demanded that he stay in their home and that hospice be brought in. He was heavily sedated and on oxygen, knowing he was in the twilight of his life. Vance had told them that his greatest fear was dying alone but that wasn't going to happen. Vivian was there when he came into the world and she would be there to usher him out.

"Pastor White, please keep us in your prayers. We've got to run, God Bless," Vivian cut off Joseph in mid-sentence and briskly walked to the car. The Pastor walked with them.

"We will, Elder Terri and I are praying for Vance and your family daily. We'll stop by again this week." The pastor opened the door for Vivian and hugged her. Vivian felt the love of God and gained strength to keep moving.

"Honey, we have time. Vance will be there, the nurse is going to call us if anything happened," Joseph said as he patted her hand.

"I just need to get home. I want to try to feed him today and I need to be there—today." Vivian had a feeling that only a mother could comprehend: she needed to sit with her son, to see his face again.

CHAPTER FORTY-SEVEN

Sabrena made sure that the schedules for the week were done and that the sales associates were ready for the weekend. She only had a few hours before she needed to leave to meet Vivian and her family.

"Hi, Sabrena, how's it going?" Leigh had wandered over to her department. Sabrena wasn't in the mood for idle chatter or gossip today.

"Fine, Leigh, just busy," Sabrena said without looking up. She continued to rearrange the sales rack and hoped Leigh would go away.

"Are you going to the funeral? I sent flowers, but I don't think I should go. I didn't know him and Vivian has seemed so distant over the last few months."

"Of course I'm going, Vance was a dear friend and so is Vivian. I'll tell her that you sent your regards." Sabrena wanted Leigh to leave before she said anything stupid. With Leigh, that only took a sentence or two.

"It's just so sad, he was so handsome. You would have never known that he would get . . . Well, you know, he didn't look like the type," Leigh said nervously and looked to Sabrena to respond.

"What does the type look like, Leigh? White, black, male, female, junkie, whore, gay, straight, young, old? Tell me, what does it look like?" Sabrena was becoming agitated, but, as her counselor had told her, she needed to stop holding her feelings in.

"Well, I mean, you know. I heard he was gay, so I guess that explains it."

"Leigh, you're not married, right? You're divorced?"

"Yeah, why?"

"Was your husband a virgin when you two got married? Were you a virgin?"

"Sabrena, what does that have to do with anything? No, we got married in our twenties. Of course we weren't virgins."

"Did you or your husband ever cheat on each other?"

"That's really none of your business. What does this have to do with anything?" Leigh's face was turning red and she was definitely uncomfortable. She didn't know where Sabrena was going with her questions, but she didn't like it one bit.

"You're seeing someone new now, right? The guy in men's clothing, right?"

"Yes," Leigh said, suddenly feeling under attack. "You know that, Sabrena. We've been going out for three months."

"Okay, so have you ever been tested for HIV?"

"Yes, for the insurance policy when I first started here. I may not have been a virgin, but I've never done drugs, and I have known everyone that I've slept with well." Leigh really didn't know where Sabrena got off, getting in all her business. She was married now, but she was no saint either.

"You've been here for over four years. You've never been tested again?"

"No, Sabrena. I don't have any reason to be tested. I'm fine. I don't like all these questions or your attitude. I was just asking about Vivian. I need to go back to my department."

"Leigh, you—just like most people, including myself—could be in the same situation as Vance. Don't be so judgmental. Women get AIDS, too—straight women, who sleep with men, one or twenty. You don't have to sleep around, or do drugs. You can just be in love and boom! Your life is rocked. So just watch what you say and how you say it. Instead of spouting a bunch of nonsense, maybe you should educate yourself and your daughter, for that matter. She's a teenager, and she needs to know, as do you." Sabrena turned and walked to her desk, thankful that she had the courage to confront ignorance. But she knew that she was just one person. She grabbed her keys, the poem she was going to read during the service, and walked to her car. She didn't want to be late.

Vivian sat with Sabrena in her bedroom after the service.

"Sabrena, thank you for coming and for being here for the last year. Vance loved you," Vivian said. Sabrena knew it was difficult for Vivian, but admired her friend's ability to hold it together for the service. She also knew Vivian was disappointed that many of their lifelong friends and some family didn't attend the service.

"Vivian, you don't have to thank me—I can't tell you what Vance has meant to me over the last year. He was a great guy and he loved his family. Do you need something? Are you hungry?"

"No, I'm fine. How's Joseph?" Vivian asked, always looking out for someone else.

"He's outside with the family, and some neighbors stopped by."

"Sabrena, it's not supposed to be like this. You have your kids, raise them, and watch them grow. You're supposed to get old and die. They're not supposed to die before you. No matter how much I tried to prepare, I want my son, I just want him. I know it's selfish and that he's not suffering anymore. But I want my Vance." Vivian sobbed on Sabrena's shoulder, which made Sabrena cry, too. Sabrena knew that this day would be hard for her on many levels. There wasn't anything for her to say. All she could do was be the shoulder for her friend. Sabrena and Vivian cried together; they were friends with a shared love for Vance. Vivian wiped her eyes and went to greet the other guests. Sabrena followed.

Sabrena was glad to see Steve walk in the door with the girls. He'd told her he wanted to stop by and pay his respects. She couldn't help beaming as he walked in the door—what a different man. After clearing the kitchen for Vivian, Sabrena prepared to leave with her family.

"Sabrena, stop in here before you go," Joseph called. "I need to give you something." He handed her an envelope. "Vance asked me to give this to you, privately. He gave it to me a few weeks ago. Thank you for everything, especially for being there for Vivian."

After the girls were in bed and Steve had left, Sabrena opened the envelope. She touched her name written in Vance's handwriting and felt fresh tears in her eyes. She recalled the many hours they had spent talking, especially after she confided in him about her HIV status. She didn't know why she told him, but she wanted him to know that she understood. Funny, how things work out, and who God brings into your life. They think that you're helping them, but really they're helping you. She read aloud, but it was Vance's voice she heard:

My Dear Sabrena,

Well, if you're reading this—my journey has ended and a new one has begun. I know that your big, beautiful brown eyes are moist, but I hope your smile is still there. I can't tell you what your friendship has meant to me over the last months and how comforting you've been. I've looked forward to our talks and laughs—you're such a wonderful woman and you deserve all the love and happiness your heart can hold.

Sabrena, my wish for you is to LIVE YOUR LIFE. Don't let this disease end it prematurely. Don't be held captive by the diagnosis—do what the doctors tell you, take your medications, keep your appointments, and stay healthy. However, more than being consumed by your health challenges, live your life fully. Love your girls and spend as much time as you can with them, but also love those around you and allow yourself to be loved. I know you struggled with accepting Steve's proposal and even now keep moving the wedding date. I don't think that he's gonna back down—so you might as well just do it. He's not marrying you out of pity or loyalty—he's marrying you because he sees the great woman you are and loves you, truly loves you.

My dear friend, I wish you could see yourself through my eyes and the eyes of others. You're so strong, so loving and kind—you're a model of a woman in both strength and beauty. I just want you to continue to move ahead, and even with the weight of what you face each morning, with all the pills, lab tests, follow-ups, fears, and yes, sometimes, the shame, try to be positive. I'm gone, but I do believe that one of my "jobs" in my last days was to somehow speak to your soul and help you learn from my mistakes. Don't be like me—in denial and anger for months, which ultimately led to me calling it quits. When I wanted to get back on track, my body betrayed me. The whole drug resistance and all that stuff really was rooted in me not following directions and being angry at the world. My depression and anger made me not take my meds, take them when I wanted, drink too much, and just act like a fool. If my words

*can help you not go down this path, then my life for the
last few months meant something, and was worth it.*

*I want to thank you for friendship, loyalty, and, most of
all, for loving me. I never thought I'd have a "girlfriend,"
but, thanks to you—I did—smile. Take care of yourself and
keep holding up my Mom.*

Love always,
Vance

P.S. You did make sure I looked good—didn't you?

Sabrena wept silently and gently placed the letter in her journal. She
took her medications prior to going to bed and whispered a prayer.
The day had been long and she was exhausted but at peace.

Dear God,

*Thank you for life, health, and strength. Thank you
that you knew how all this would turn around even when I
doubted you. Thank you for Vance, and please comfort
Vivian, Joseph, and his family. Lord, even me—comfort me.
I loved him and believe he was an angel that you sent to me
during my time of greatest need. Father, please keep me
healthy and strong. Give me wisdom, knowledge, and
understanding to face each day. Bless my babies. Amen.*

CHAPTER FORTY-EIGHT

Rach couldn't believe what Dr. Scott had told her. How could this happen to her? What was Barry going to say? There was only one thing to do now, and that was to find her best friend. She walked into the women's department looking for Sabrena, not certain about what she would say when she found her.

"Hey Rach, what are you doing here? Are you ready for your cruise?" Sabrena was marking down the swimsuits and other summer items for the last sale of the season. She was glad Vivian was back and she could cut back on some of her hours.

"Bre, can we go have a soda or something?" Rach looked dead serious and Sabrena became worried. They went to the food court and had milkshakes.

"Okay, enough mystery. What's up?" Sabrena asked.

"I just saw Dr. Scott."

"You didn't tell me you had an appointment. I have to see her in two weeks. How's she doing? What did she have on today?"

"I know fashion is important, but let's focus. It's about *me* right now—come back, come back to me!"

"You started it," Sabrena said, not knowing if Rach was as serious as she looked or as silly as she sounded. "Okay, I'm sorry. Are you all right?"

"Well, yes and no—I mean I'm okay, but she . . ."

"She what? Rach, what's up?"

"Girl, I'm pregnant—it wasn't planned and I don't think I'm ready," Rach said, looking down at the table.

After all the drama that had happened since her visits to Dr. Scott's office, Sabrena could do nothing but throw her head back and laugh at this news. "Congratulations! Who knew you had an egg left!" Sabrena hugged her friend. "Don't worry, you'll be fine. If you can handle Deena and Renee, you can handle little Sabrena. That *will* be her name, of course, if she's a girl."

But Rach wasn't laughing. Her face was totally serious. She said, "No, I'm not like you. I'm selfish, spoiled, and I don't want to be a wife *and* a mother right now. Marrying Barry was hard enough. I just don't know. What if, what if I screw them up?"

"Look Rach, one thing I know is that you have a good, big heart, and booty—just kidding. For real, children are a blessing from God and He has a way of stretching your heart more than you ever know. Do you love Deena and Renee?"

"Of course, what do you mean? You know that those girls are my heart. If I can just pull Renee out of her shell a little more, it's on." Rach smiled as she thought of Sabrena's daughters, her god-daughters.

"Well, if you have that much love and make all the sacrifices that you do for them and me, imagine when you have a baby who looks like you and Barry. It's going to be fine. You'll make a wonderful mother. Rach, I've known you forever, and believe me, this is good. How are you gonna tell Barry?"

"I have no clue. Don't tell Steve! His big mouth will say something to Barry before I do." Rach was amazed that she actually liked Steve these days. She'd never thought that men could change, but he had blown her theory out of the water. She would never tell him that, but she was glad that he and Bre were engaged. She was ready to stand with them.

Sabrena stopped by the grocery store to pick up some food for dinner and was surprised to see Steve getting ready to leave.

"Hey Honey. I thought you got off at six tonight."

"No, I have an appointment and need to run a few errands, so I'm leaving early," Steve said, trying not to give too many details; he was smiling.

"Oh, okay. Come by the house for dinner. I'm cooking. Where's your appointment?"

"Ms. Collins, soon to be Mrs. Addison, can't a man have a bit of privacy? It ain't any of your business." Steve tweaked Sabrena on the nose and winked. In the past, she would have been suspicious about another woman, but now Sabrena completely trusted Steve. He really was a changed man, dedicated to her and to the girls. Sabrena was blessed to have him and she knew that she was a blessing to him.

Sabrena phoned her mother. The girls were spending their last few weeks before school with her, and Sabrena wanted to catch up with them.

"Mom, how're the girls? Are they behaving?"

"They're Grandmommy's little angels. Lord, if you and Gerald had been this good, I wouldn't have so many gray hairs."

"Well, good. Can I speak with them?"

"Nope, they're at the pool with the church summer school program. I'll have them call you when they get in. Enough about those rascals, Sabrena. How're you doing? Are you taking care of yourself?"

Jennifer Collins knew she wasn't the world's greatest mother. She'd been hard on Sabrena. She believed Black women needed to be treated hard, so they would grow up strong and not die from broken hearts. Her grandbabies, on the other hand, weren't hers to raise, so she'd leave the discipline to Sabrena and just spoil Sabrena's and Gerald's kids rotten.

She'd worried about Sabrena and her health since she and Gerald flew out to tell her, together. That's how she raised them, to look after each other and take care of each other, especially since that no count daddy of theirs left them. She'd made some arrangements for the girls, and taken out another insurance policy for Sabrena. If anything happened, she would be there for her daughter.

"Mom, I'm fine—doing good and feeling good. Are you going to be able to come in for the wedding? It's just going to be a very small wedding at my church, but Gerald is gonna give me away."

"Of course I'll be there. I have already bought two hats—one for the wedding and one for Sunday. Look, I gotta go. My babies will be home and I need to have their dinner ready. I'll have them call when they get settled. Bye, now."

"Bye, Mom." Sabrena smiled as she hung up the phone. They hadn't quite worked up to saying "I love you" yet, but Sabrena marveled at how life had a funny way of working out. She never would've imagined that her mother would be supportive, but, since the day Sabrena told her about her diagnosis, she had been.

CHAPTER FORTY-NINE

Sabrena had worked all morning baking the cupcakes for Renee's class. It was her tenth birthday and she wanted chocolate cupcakes with sprinkles. For some reason, Sabrena couldn't find the sprinkles she'd bought to top them and asked her husband to run home with another pack.

When Steve came in, sprinkles in hand, he offered to take the cupcakes to school for her. Sabrena was having more headaches and had gotten sick several times the day before.

"No, I'm fine. I'm going to take these and come home. Can you pick up the girls this afternoon? We have to be at the skating rink by six for the party." Sabrena knew she'd need another nap before going out that evening. She also wanted extra time to rearrange her braids so her hair didn't look so thin and to put on extra makeup to cover the dry patches on her face. She had what Dr. Scott called seborrhea. She called it dry, flaky, monster skin. It had taken her an hour and a half to begin to look decent this morning. The cream that she was using wasn't really helping, nor did the thick foundation that Rach had bought for her. Sabrena tried her best to look "normal," so that when she went to Renee's school, no one would make any comments that could get back to her girls.

"Sure, I can pick them up, and I'm actually going to drive you to drop these off. We aren't arguing about it at all. I don't like you driving, especially with all the dizzy spells," Steve said defiantly. He made a mental note to call Dr. Grier. As he opened the refrigerator, he saw the box of candy sprinkles sitting next to the milk. Sabrena was becoming more forgetful. Her vomiting had increased, too, but she wasn't taking the medication for nausea, because it made her too sleepy to help the girls with their schoolwork. As she covered the cupcakes, he silently took her keys into the bathroom and removed her car key. He couldn't take the risk of letting Sabrena drive alone until he talked to Dr. Grier.

"Baby, put on a light coat. It's cool out." Steve watched Sabrena walk unsteadily back to their room. It looked like all her energy was gone. He pulled out a coat and helped her put it on. Although he wanted her to stay home, he knew he couldn't win that argument.

"Okay, are we set for the skating rink?" Sabrena asked. "Steve, we have to be there by six. Can you pick up the girls?" Her head was throbbing, but she didn't dare tell Steve.

"Yes, honey, we'll be fine," Steve said. He was used to her repeating herself.

"How do I look? Am I decent? Can you tell?" Sabrena posed in front of him.

"You look beautiful. I like the braids," Steve said. "You look fine. Just hold onto me so that you don't get dizzy." Steve knew that Sabrena was going to need more sleep before the party. He wished she would stay home, but there was no way that she was going to miss Renee's birthday party.

"Who's picking up Dad from the airport?" Sabrena asked as they drove. She thought of her new relationship with her father and smiled at the thought of seeing him again.

"Barry is gonna pick him up and he'll come right to the party," Steve said.

"Okay, I need to change the sheets on the bed in the guest room. I also need to stop by the store and pick up some things for dinner tomorrow."

"Sabrena," Steve said, turning to look at her. "I already changed the sheets and Rach is bringing over dinner. God knows I hope she's buying it and not cooking it." Steve laughed aloud, joined by Sabrena. They reached the school and parked the car. Sabrena glanced in the rear view mirror, before setting out. She took a deep breath and mustered up enough energy for a smile for her daughter and the other kids in her class. She took Steve's arm and, together they walked into Renee's classroom.

CHAPTER FIFTY

As she walked into Sabrena's hospital room in the late afternoon, Dr. Scott asked, "Mr. and Mrs. Addison, how are you? Dr. Grier told me he'd admitted you, Mrs. Addison. How're you feeling?"

"Oh, I'm okay. He said I would only have to be here for a few days. I need to get home," Sabrena said. "I have to get my girls ready for Easter." Sabrena smiled at Dr. Scott and noticed she looked bigger than usual. Maybe it was because she didn't have on the white coat.

"Well, I think you need to concentrate on getting better and resting," Dr. Scott said, sitting down next to her patient. Dr. Grier was taking care of Sabrena during this hospitalization, but Dr. Scott wanted to come see her for herself. She reached out and took Sabrena's hand. Steve quietly left the room. Dr. Scott was glad for the time alone.

"Mrs. Addison, it's been a long road. How're you really?"

"I'm okay, Dr. Scott. I just can't get it all together and am falling a lot," Sabrena smiled weakly. Her vision was blurred, but she was able to look down and see Dr. Scott's low-heeled suede pumps. "Nice shoes, as always."

"Thanks. We all have our addictions, Mrs. Addison. Mine is stress. I have a copy of your living will. We talked about it a few months ago, but, I need to be honest with you, I'll talk to your husband and Rachel, as well, but you're getting worse. The toxoplasmosis is spreading in your brain, and the medication isn't working as well as Dr. Grier and I would like. It's dangerous for you to be alone. The nausea and vomiting can be somewhat controlled with medications, but you have to take them. You're severely dehydrated, and that just makes everything worse. You understand what I mean?" Dr. Scott fought hard to hold back her tears. She felt especially close to

Sabrena, who was just a few years older than she. It could very well be herself lying on that bed.

"You know, Doc, I understand what you and Dr. Grier are saying. But I need you to listen to me. I have a few more things that I need to do. My oldest, Deena, is graduating from elementary school in a few weeks and I have to be there. I have to . . . there's no choice. I'll talk about other stuff after that, but I have to see my baby graduate." Sabrena looked at Dr. Scott, but felt the room spinning again, a state that was almost becoming normal to her. She closed her eyes and drifted to sleep. It was if she were no longer in her body but rather looking down on herself.

She had what they called Toxo, a fungus that was growing in her brain. It made her have headaches, get dizzy, and vomit. She was also losing her memory bit by bit and was tired all the time. She had stopped working several months ago, after having PCP pneumonia and being in the hospital on and off for weeks. She was fortunate to have disability coverage and was grateful Ms. Bernadette had helped her with all of that through the years. She didn't want to be more of a burden to Steve and her family. She knew what the prognosis was, that she was dying, and that there was little else the doctors could do. Her body was just giving out. She prayed for more time, but she knew the end was coming. She was glad she had done her will and even her living will early on, because she knew her judgment was too clouded to do it now. Attorney Octavia Roberts had continued to give her advice, and even completed the adoption papers for the girls.

She and Steve had talked about everything and she was comfortable with her decision. After Deena's graduation, she would go into hospice care. Dr. Grier advised that she enter hospice, and Sabrena was familiar with their care because of how they'd taken care of Vance. She'd already met her hospice nurse and caretaker, introduced them to the girls, and felt comfortable. She didn't want to be a burden to Steve or any of her family, but they insisted that she stay at home. Her mother was coming in two weeks and was going to stay with them until. . . . Rach was going to take the girls when things got really bad, because Sabrena didn't want them to have bad memories of her and her dying. She wanted them to remember her living. She had written enough letters to fill a journal for each of them and had put some things in a keepsake box. Steve knew when to give these things to them.

Sabrena worried about both the girls, but especially Renee. She was so quiet and kept things inside. Deena was outgoing, but also very passionate and wore her feelings on her sleeve. Sabrena had already taken them to see a counselor, and Rach agreed that she would be personally responsible to get them grief counseling when the time came. She needed her girls to be strong, and while she knew they would miss her, she needed them to keep moving, to grow into the women she was teaching them to be. Sabena had worked hard to prepare for them, even on her salary without a college degree. She had saved for them, and, over the years, increased her insurance policy. When the time came, they would be able to go to any college they chose, and have some money to make down payments on their first homes. She knew that their father, Steve—the only one they'd really known, who was now their legal father—would always take care of them and would never let them forget her.

"Mrs. Addison, I'm going to let you rest. I'll be by tomorrow," Dr. Scott said. She stood and turned to walk out the door. Sabrena was able to see her profile.

"Dr. Scott, when are you due?" Sabrena smiled at her lovely doctor and was glad to know that she was having a child.

"Oh, in four months." Dr. Scott smiled at Sabrena. "I hope that I can be half the mother you are."

"You'll be great. Just ask Rach. She's a new woman." Sabrena smiled as she thought of her godson, Thomas. She laughed sweetly until she began to cough, and the impact of her illness became real once again. She silenced her cough and whispered, "Dr. Scott—you know, all I ever did—all I ever did was love a man." Sabrena closed her eyes and both women shed silent tears.

EPILOGUE

Steve waited for the home health agency to come and remove the hospital bed and wheelchair. Sabrena had been so organized. She'd gotten her clothes ready to go to the House of Ruth, a shelter for battered women, and they were picked up right after the funeral.

The house seemed cold to Steve, even though it was late summer. The girls would be back at the end of next week and he would go with Rachel to get their school clothes. It was up to him and Rachel to take care of them.

He was grateful that Gerald had taken the girls with him for a few days after the funeral. The change would do them good and they could hang out with their cousins. Rachel had dropped off his mother-in-law at the airport the night before, and he was glad she made it home. Gerald had taken their father and Sabrena's half sister to the airport the day after the funeral. Steve was glad that Sabrena had spent time with them during the last year. He would make sure that his daughters knew their aunt and grandfather.

Steve was still sleeping on the couch and using the guest bathroom. He couldn't bring himself to sleep in their bed or even use the bathroom that he had remodeled for her. He felt tears well in his eyes again as he walked into the bedroom and sat on the side of the bed. What was he going to do without his wife? How was he going to keep getting up and going through life without her smile, her love? Where would any joy come from? He knew he had to be strong for his daughters, but who was going to be strong for him? No matter what, he would be there for Deena and Renee. He was healthy and strong. Steve wasn't going to let anything prevent him from raising his daughters. He pulled the drawer out and opened his pill box. He had to stay healthy and strong for them. He was going to be around for a long time.

Keep reading. The best is yet to come!

FROM THE AUTHOR

It is my hope that you enjoyed my first novel, *All I Ever Did Was Love a Man*. I'm honored that you took the time to read to the very end. This book was born out of my passion for health awareness and education and I pray that it has touched your mind, body, and soul. For those of you wondering, this story is loosely based on a wonderful woman who touched my heart and changed my life during my first years as a resident physician. However, this is indeed a book of fiction, and all of the names have been changed. I like to think of the characters as a collage of people that I've known and continue to meet.

While I wrote the book to entertain my readers and invoke a variety of emotions, the following pages are the most important in the entire book. Although we all love a good novel, a good laugh and cry, at the end of the day the best novels have taught us something either about ourselves or the world at large. *All I Ever Did Was Love a Man* was created solely for you and the millions of people who are at risk for HIV/AIDS in the world. I'm hopeful that as you read about Sabrena, her friends, and her family, you saw some of yourself or your loved ones. Are they so different from you and me? Sabrena is just a woman, one who loved and needed love returned. Her friends and daughters needed her and, yes, even with all his flaws, Steve loved her. Sabrena was confronted with many of the trials we face, but her ultimate challenge was to live, put one foot in front of the other each day, and finally to die with dignity. It is a journey that we're all on, and our history is being written each day.

The face of HIV/AIDS is one that looks back at you every morning: the young, the old, the middle-aged, the rich, the middle class, the poor, the African American, the Hispanic, the Caucasian, the gay, the straight, the promiscuous, the serial monogamist, the married, the single, the boyfriend, the girlfriend, the drug addict, the alcoholic, the Christian, the Jew, the Muslim, the agnostic, the educated, the illiterate, the laborer, the doctor, and someone who has a story similar to yours or your family's.

Unfortunately, certain groups are disproportionately affected by this disease. However, be clear that every life is worth saving and that HIV/AIDS knows no color or gender. African-American women are experiencing increased rates of HIV/AIDS, primarily due to transmission from infected males. While it is true that many of the men who are infecting women are bisexual males, or men having sex with men, don't believe all of the hype. A large portion of the men who are infecting women are heterosexuals who are promiscuous now or have been in the past, or are intravenous drug users who are unknowingly or, God forbid, knowingly passing on the virus. This is just the story of one segment of the population. There are many more examples of how this disease continues to spread.

As a health professional with a passion for health education, my heart grieves for all the lives affected by this disease. While it is true that there are newer medications which can make a tremendous impact on the lives of people with HIV, the message must remain that, in 2005, there still is no cure. Therefore, we must spread the message of prevention, early detection, and comprehensive and accessible treatment. Have you been tested? Should you be? What about your spouse? These are the questions this book was written to answer.

If you're living with HIV/AIDS, I offer you hope. Listen to the poignant words of Vance, as he pleads with you to follow your doctor's advice, take your medication, and most importantly live your life to the fullest. No matter where you are in your diagnosis, there is hope. Where there is breath, there is life, and where there is life, the rivers of hope run freely.

I challenge each of my readers to keep reading. The next few pages very well may save your life. Further, I ask that you pass this book and its messages on to loved ones near and far so that we can continue the dialogue. Book clubs, reading groups, churches, and community groups provide an open forum for discussion, and I hope you'll use this book as your launch pad. I look forward to hearing how you talk about Sabrena's story and I welcome the opportunity to hear stories of your own struggles and achievements. Ultimately, Sabrena's is a story of triumph, for even in death, she's touching our very souls.

Sharon Denise Allison-Ottey

THE REAL STORY
HIV/AIDS 2005

The following information was provided by the Centers for Disease Control (CDC) National Center for HIV, STD and TB Prevention, Division of HIV/AIDS Prevention, unless otherwise noted. (See http://www.cdc.gov/hiv/dhap.htm)

A GLANCE AT THE HIV/AIDS EPIDEMIC

HIV/AIDS Diagnoses

At the end of 2003, an estimated 1,039,000 to 1,185,000 persons in the United States were living with HIV/AIDS [1]. In 2003, 32,048 cases of HIV/AIDS were reported from the 33 areas (32 states and the U.S. Virgin Islands) with long-term, confidential name-based HIV reporting [2]. When all 50 states are considered, CDC estimates that approximately 40,000 persons become infected with HIV each year [1].

By Exposure

In 2003, men who have sex with men (MSM) represented the largest proportion of HIV/AIDS diagnoses, followed by adults and adolescents infected through heterosexual contact.

EXPOSURE CATEGORIES OF ADULTS AND ADOLESCENTS
WHO RECEIVED A DIAGNOSIS OF HIV/AIDS, 2003

Males
No. = 20,153

Females
No. = 8,733

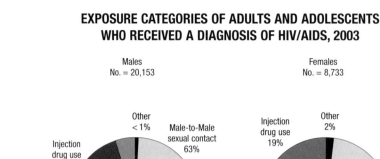

Other
< 1%

Male-to-Male
sexual contact
63%

Injection
drug use
14%

Heterosexual
contact
17%

Injection
drug use
19%

Other
2%

Heterosexual
contact
79%

No. = 131,886

Note: Based on data from 33 areas with long-term, confidential name-based HIV reporting.

HIV/AIDS includes persons with a diagnosis of HIV infection (not AIDS), a diagnosis of HIV infection and a later diagnosis of AIDS, or concurrent diagnoses of HIV infection and AIDS.

By Sex

In 2003, almost three quarters of HIV/AIDS diagnoses were made for male adolescents and adults.

SEX OF ADULTS AND ADOLESCENTS
WHO RECEIVED A DIAGNOSIS OF HIV/AIDS, 2003

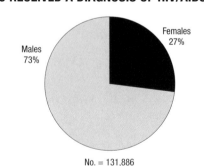

Females
27%

Males
73%

No. = 131,886

Note: Based on data from 33 areas with long-term, confidential name-based HIV reporting.

By Race/Ethnicity

Persons of minority races and ethnicities are disproportionately affected by HIV/AIDS. In 2003, African Americans, who make up approximately 12% of the U.S. population, accounted for half of the HIV/AIDS cases diagnosed.

RACE/ETHNICITY OF PERSONS (INCLUDING CHILDREN) WHO RECEIVED A DIAGNOSIS OF HIV/AIDS, 2003

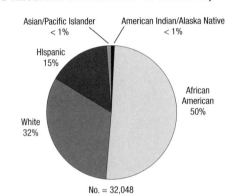

No. = 32,048

Note: Based on data from 33 areas with long-term, confidential name-based HIV reporting. Includes persons of unknown race or multiple races.

Trends in AIDS Diagnoses and Deaths

During the mid-to-late 1990s, advances in treatment slowed the progression of HIV infection to AIDS and led to dramatic decreases in AIDS deaths. Although the decrease in AIDS deaths continues (3% decrease from 1999 through 2003), the number of AIDS diagnoses increased an estimated 4% during that period [2].

Better treatments have also led to an increasing number of persons in the United States who are living with AIDS. From the end of 1999 through the end of 2003, the number of persons in the United States who were living with AIDS increased from 311,205 to 405,926—an increase of 30% [2].

ESTIMATED AIDS DIAGNOSES, DEATHS, AND PERSONS LIVING WITH AIDS 1998–2002

	1999	2000	2001	2002	2003	Cumulative Through 2003
Estimated AIDS diagnoses	41,356	41,267	40,833	41,289	43,171	929,985
Estimated AIDS deaths	18,491	17,741	18,524	17,557	18,017	524,060
Estimated persons living with AIDS	311,205	334,731	357,040	380,771	405,926	NA

NA, not applicable (the category Estimated persons living with AIDS is cumulative)

References

1. Glynn M, Rhodes P. Estimated HIV prevalence in the United States at the end of 2003. National HIV Prevention Conference; June 2005; Atlanta. Abstract 595.
2. CDC. HIV/AIDS Surveillance Report, 2003 (Vol. 15). Atlanta: US Department of Health and Human Services, CDC; 2004:1–46. Available at http://www.cdc.gov/hiv/stats/2003surveillancereport.pdf. Accessed March 16, 2005.

HIV/AIDS AMONG AFRICAN AMERICANS

The HIV/AIDS epidemic is a health crisis for African Americans. In 2001, HIV/AIDS was among the top 3 causes of death for African American men aged 25–54 years and among the top 4 causes of death for African-American women aged 20–54 years. It was the number 1 cause of death for African-American women aged 25–34 years [1].

Cumulative Effects of HIV/AIDS (through 2003)

- According to the 2000 Census, African Americans make up 12.3% of the U.S. population. However, they have accounted for 368,169 (40%) of the 929,985 estimated AIDS cases diagnosed since the epidemic began [2].

- By the end of December 2003, an estimated 195,891 African Americans with AIDS had died [2].
- Of persons given a diagnosis of AIDS since 1995, a smaller proportion of African Americans (60%) were alive after 9 years compared with American Indians and Alaska Natives (64%), Hispanics (68%), whites (70%), and Asians and Pacific Islanders (77%) [2].
- During 2000–2003, HIV/AIDS rates for African-American females were 19 times the rates for white females and 5 times the rates for Hispanic females; they also exceeded the rates for males of all races/ethnicities other than African Americans. Rates for African-American males were 7 times those for white males and 3 times those for Hispanic males [3].

RACE/ETHNICITY OF PERSONS WHO DIED WITH AIDS, 2003

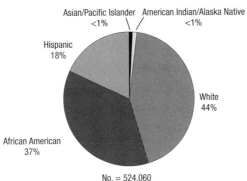

No. = 524,060

Note: Includes U.S. dependencies, possessions, and associated nations.

AIDS in 2003

- African Americans accounted for 21,304 (49%) of the 43,171 estimated AIDS cases diagnosed in the United States (including U.S. dependencies, possessions, and associated nations) [2].
- The rate of AIDS diagnoses for African Americans was almost 10 times the rate for whites and almost 3 times the rate for Hispanics. The rate of AIDS diagnoses for African-American women was 25 times the rate for white women.

The rate of AIDS diagnoses for African-American men was 8 times the rate for white men [2].

- In the United States, 172,278 African Americans were living with AIDS. They accounted for 42% of all people in the United States living with AIDS [2].
- Of the 59 U.S. children younger than 13 years of age who had a new AIDS diagnosis, 40 were African American.

RACE/ETHNICITY OF PERSONS GIVEN A DIAGNOSIS OF AIDS, 2003

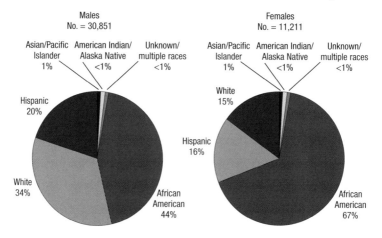

Note: Based on data from 50 states and the District of Columbia.

Does not include U.S. dependencies, possessions, and associated nations or persons whose state or area of residence is unknown.

HIV/AIDS in 2003

- African Americans accounted for 16,165 (50%) of the 32,048 estimated new HIV/AIDS diagnoses in the United States in the 32 states with confidential name-based HIV reporting [2].
- A study of people with a diagnosis of HIV infection found that 56% of late testers (that is, those who received an AIDS diagnosis within 1 year after their HIV diagnosis) were African American [4]. Late testing represents missed opportunities for preventing and treating HIV infection.
- The leading cause of HIV infection among African-American

men was sexual contact with other men; the next leading causes were heterosexual contact and injection drug use [2].

- The leading cause of HIV infection among African-American women was heterosexual contact; the next leading cause was injection drug use [2].
- Of the 90 infants reported as having HIV/AIDS, 62 were African American [2].

TRANSMISSION CATEGORIES OF AFRICAN AMERICANS GIVEN A DIAGNOSIS OF HIV/AIDS, 2003

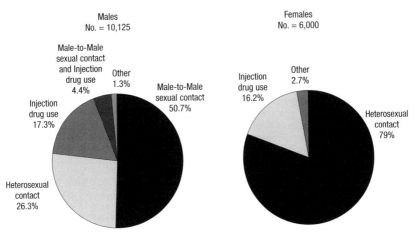

Note: Based on data from 32 states with confidential name-based HIV reporting.

Source. MMWR 2004; 53:1106-1110.

RISK FACTORS AND BARRIERS TO PREVENTION

Race and ethnicity are not, by themselves, risk factors for HIV infection. However, African Americans are more likely to face challenges associated with risk for HIV infection, including the following.

Partners at Risk

African-American women are most likely to be infected with HIV as a result of sex with men [2]. They may not be aware of their male partners' possible risks for HIV infection such as unprotected sex with multiple partners, bisexuality, or injection drug use [5]. According to a recent study of HIV infected and non-infected African-American men who have sex with men (MSM), approximately 20% of the study participants reported having had a female sex partner during the preceding 12 months [6]. In another study of HIV-infected persons, 34% of African-American MSM reported having had sex with women, even though only 6% of African-American women reported having had sex with a bisexual man [7].

Substance Use

Injection drug use is the second leading cause of HIV infection for African-American women and the third leading cause of HIV infection for African-American men [2]. In addition to being at risk from sharing needles, casual and chronic substance users are more likely to engage in high-risk behaviors, such as unprotected sex, when they are under the influence of drugs or alcohol [8]. Drug use can also affect treatment success. A recent study of HIV-infected women found that drug users were less likely than nonusers to take their anti-retroviral medicines exactly as prescribed [9].

Sexually Transmitted Diseases

The highest rates of sexually transmitted diseases (STDs) are those for African Americans. In 2003, African Americans were 20 times as likely as whites to have gonorrhea and 5.2 times as likely to have syphilis [10]. Partly because of physical changes caused by STDs, including genital lesions that can serve as an entry point for HIV, the presence of certain STDs can increase one's chances of contracting HIV by 3- to 5-fold. Similarly, a person who is coinfected has a greater chance of spreading HIV to others [11].

Denial

Studies show that a significant number of African-American MSM identify themselves as heterosexual [12,13]. As a result, they may not relate to prevention messages crafted for men who identify themselves as homosexual.

Socioeconomic Issues

Nearly 1 in 4 African Americans lives in poverty [14]. Studies have found an association between higher AIDS incidence and lower income [15,16]. The socioeconomic problems associated with poverty, including limited access to high-quality health care and HIV prevention education, directly or indirectly increase HIV risk. A recent study of HIV transmission among African-American women in North Carolina found that women with HIV infection were more likely than noninfected women to be unemployed, receive public assistance, have had 20 or more lifetime sexual partners, have a lifetime history of genital herpes infection, have used crack or cocaine, or have traded sex for drugs, money, or shelter [16].

References

1. Anderson RN, Smith BL. Deaths: leading causes for 2001. *National Vital Statistics Reports* 2003;52(9): 27–33. Available at http://www.cdc.gov/nchs/data/nvsr/ nvsr52/nvsr52_09.pdf. Accessed December 23, 2004.

2. CDC. *HIV/AIDS Surveillance Report, 2003* (Vol. 15). Atlanta: US Department of Health and Human Services, CDC; 2004:1–46. Available at http://www.cdc.gov/ hiv/stats/2003sur-veillancereport.pdf. Accessed February 2, 2005.

3. CDC. Diagnoses of HIV/AIDS—32 states, 2000–2003. *MMWR* 2004;53:1106–1110.

4. CDC. Late versus early testing of HIV—16 sites, United States, 2000–2003. *MMWR* 2003;52:581–586.

5. Hader S, Smith D, Moore J, Holmberg S. HIV infection in women in the United States: status at the millennium. *JAMA* 2001;285:1186–1192.

6. CDC. HIV transmission among black college student and non-student men who have sex with men—North Carolina, 2003. *MMWR* 2004;53:731–734.

7. Montgomery JP, Mokotoff ED, Gentry AC, Blair JM. The extent of bisexual behaviour in HIV-infected men and implications for transmission to their female sex partners. *AIDS Care* 2003;15:829–837.

8. Leigh B, Stall R. Substance use and risky sexual behavior for exposure to HIV: issues in methodology, interpretation, and prevention. *American Psychologist* 1993;48:1035–1045.

9. Sharpe TT, Lee LM, Nakashima AK, Elam-Evans LD, Fleming P. Crack cocaine use and adherence to antiretroviral treatment among HIV-infected black women. *Journal of Community Health* 2004;29:117–127.

10. CDC. *Sexually Transmitted Disease Surveillance*, 2003. Atlanta: US Department of Health and Human Services, CDC;

September 2004. Available at http://www.cdc.gov/std/stats/ toc2003.htm. Accessed February 2, 2005.

11. Fleming DT, Wasserheit JN. From epidemiological synergy to public health policy and practice: the contribution of other sexually transmitted diseases to sexual transmission of HIV infection. *Sexually Transmitted Infections* 1999;75:3–17.

12. CDC. HIV/AIDS among racial/ethnic minority men who have sex with men—United States, 1989–1998. *MMWR* 2000; 49:4–11.

13. CDC. HIV/STD risks in young men who have sex with men who do not disclose their sexual orientation—six US cities, 1994–2000. *MMWR* 2003;52:81–85.

14. US Census Bureau. Poverty status of the population in 1999 by age, sex, and race and Hispanic origin. March 2000. Available at http://www.census.gov/prod/ 2003pubs/c2 kbr-19.pdf. Accessed January 3, 2005.

15. Diaz T, Chu S, Buehler J, et al. Socioeconomic differences among people with AIDS: results from a multistate surveillance project. *American Journal of Preventive Medicine* 1994; 10:217–222.

16. CDC. HIV transmission among black women—North Carolina, 2004. *MMWR* 2005;54:89–93.

17. Trubo R. CDC initiative targets HIV research gaps in black and Hispanic communities. *JAMA* 2004;292: 2563–2564.

FREQUENTLY ASKED QUESTIONS ABOUT HIV/AIDS
What is HIV?

HIV (human immunodeficiency virus) is the virus that causes AIDS. This virus may be passed from one person to another when infected blood, semen, or vaginal secretions come in contact with an uninfected person's broken skin or mucous membranes.* In addition, an infected, pregnant woman can pass HIV to her baby during pregnancy or delivery, as well as through breast-feeding. People with HIV have what is called HIV infection. Some of these people will develop AIDS as a result of their HIV infection.

---

* A mucous membrane is wet, thin tissue found in certain openings to the human body. These can include the mouth, eyes, nose, vagina, rectum, and opening of the penis.

What is AIDS?

AIDS stands for Acquired Immunodeficiency Syndrome.

Acquired—means that the disease is not hereditary, but develops after birth from contact with a disease-causing agent (in this case, HIV).

Immunodeficiency—means that the disease is characterized by a weakening of the immune system.

Syndrome—refers to a group of symptoms that collectively indicate or characterize a disease. In the case of AIDS, this can include the development of certain infections and/or cancers, as well as a decrease in the number of certain cells in a person's immune system.

A diagnosis of AIDS is made by a physician, using specific clinical or laboratory standards.

Where did HIV come from?

The earliest known case of HIV-1 in a human was from a blood sample collected in 1959 from a man in Kinshasa, Democratic Republic of the Congo. (How he became infected is not known.) Genetic analysis of this blood sample suggested that HIV-1 may have stemmed from a single virus in the late 1940s or early 1950s.

We know that the virus has existed in the United States since at least the mid- to late 1970s. From 1979–1981, rare types of pneumonia, cancer, and other illnesses were being reported by doctors in Los Angeles and New York in a number of male patients who had sex with other men. These were conditions not usually found in people with healthy immune systems.

In 1982, public health officials began to use the term "acquired immunodeficiency syndrome," or AIDS, to describe the occurrences of opportunistic infections, Kaposi's sarcoma (a kind of cancer), and *Pneumocystis carinii* pneumonia in previously healthy people. Formal tracking (surveillance) of AIDS cases began that year in the United States.

In 1983, scientists discovered the virus that causes AIDS. The virus was at first named HTLV-III/LAV (human T-cell lymphotropic virus-type III/lymphadenopathy-associated virus) by an international scientific committee. This name was later changed to HIV (human immunodeficiency virus).

For many years, scientists theorized as to the origins of HIV and how it appeared in the human population, most believing that HIV originated in other primates. Then in 1999, an international team of researchers reported that they had discovered the origins of HIV-1, the predominant strain of HIV in the developed world. A subspecies of chimpanzees native to west equatorial Africa had been identified as the original source of the virus. The researchers believe that HIV-1 was introduced into the human population when hunters became exposed to infected blood.

What causes AIDS?

AIDS is caused by infection with a virus called human immunodeficiency virus (HIV). This virus is passed from one person to another through blood-to-blood and sexual contact. In addition, infected pregnant women can pass HIV to their babies during pregnancy or delivery, as well as through breast-feeding. People with HIV have what is called HIV infection. Some of these people will develop AIDS as a result of their HIV infection.

How does HIV cause AIDS?

HIV destroys a certain kind of blood cell (CD4+ T cell) which is crucial to the normal function of the human immune system. In fact, loss of T cells in people with HIV is an extremely powerful predictor of the development of AIDS. Studies of thousands of people have revealed that most people infected with HIV carry the virus for years, before enough damage is done to the immune system so that AIDS develops. However, sensitive tests have shown a strong connection between the amount of HIV in the blood, the decline in CD4+ T cells, and the development of AIDS. Reducing the amount of virus in the body with anti-retroviral therapies can dramatically slow the destruction of a person's immune system.

How is HIV passed from one person to another?

HIV transmission can occur when blood, semen (cum), pre-seminal fluid (pre-cum), vaginal fluid, or breast milk from an infected person enters the body of an uninfected person. HIV can enter the body through a vein (e.g., injection drug use), the lining of the anus or rectum, the lining of the vagina and/or cervix, the opening to the penis, the mouth, other mucous membranes (e.g., eyes or inside of the nose), or cuts and sores. Intact, healthy skin is an excellent barrier against HIV and other viruses and bacteria.

The most common ways that HIV is transmitted from one person to another are the following:

- Having sex (anal, vaginal, or oral) with an HIV-infected person
- Sharing needles or injection equipment with an injection drug user who is infected with HIV
- From HIV-infected women to their babies before or during birth, or through breast-feeding after birth.

HIV can also be transmitted through receipt of infected blood or blood clotting factors. However, since 1985, all donated blood in the United States has been tested for HIV. Therefore, the risk of infection through transfusion of blood or blood products is extremely low. The U.S. blood supply is considered to be among the safest in the world.

Some health care workers have become infected after being stuck with needles containing HIV-infected blood or, less frequently, when infected blood comes in contact with a worker's open cut or is splashed into a worker's eyes or inside the nose. There has been only one instance of a patient who was infected by an HIV-infected dentist.

Which body fluids transmit HIV?

These body fluids have been shown to contain high concentrations of HIV:

- Blood
- Semen
- Vaginal fluid
- Breast milk
- Other body fluids containing blood

The following body fluids may also transmit the virus to health care workers:

- Fluid surrounding the brain and the spinal cord
- Fluid surrounding bone joints
- Fluid surrounding an unborn baby

HIV has been found in the saliva and tears of some persons living with HIV, but in very low quantities. It is important to understand that finding a small amount of HIV in a body fluid does not necessarily mean that HIV can be *transmitted* by that body fluid. HIV has *not* been recovered from the sweat of HIV-infected persons. Contact with saliva, tears, or sweat has never been shown to result in transmission of HIV.

Can I get HIV from kissing?

On the Cheek:
HIV is not transmitted casually, so kissing on the cheek is very safe. Even if the other person has the virus, your unbroken skin is a good barrier. No one has become infected from such ordinary social contact as dry kisses, hugs, and handshakes.

Open-Mouth Kissing:
Open-mouth kissing is considered a very low-risk activity for the transmission of HIV. However, prolonged open-mouth kissing could damage the mouth or lips so that HIV could pass from an infected person to a partner, entering the body through cuts or sores in the mouth. Because of this possible risk, the CDC recommends against open-mouth kissing with an infected partner.

One case suggests that a woman became infected with HIV from her sex partner through exposure to contaminated blood during open-mouth kissing.

Can I get HIV from getting a tattoo or through body piercing?

A risk of HIV transmission does exist if instruments contaminated with blood are either not sterilized or disinfected or are used inappropriately between clients. CDC recommends that instruments that are intended to penetrate the skin be used once, then disposed of or thoroughly cleaned and sterilized between clients.

Personal service workers who do tattooing or body piercing should be educated about how HIV is transmitted and take precautions to prevent transmission of HIV and other blood-borne infections in their settings.

If you are considering getting a tattoo or having your body pierced, ask staff at the establishment what procedures they use to prevent the spread of HIV and other blood-borne infections, such as the hepatitis B virus. You also may call your local health department to find out what sterilization procedures are in place for these types of establishments.

Can I get HIV from casual contact (shaking hands, hugging, using a toilet, drinking from the same glass, or the sneezing and coughing of an infected person)?

No. HIV is not transmitted by day-to-day contact in the workplace, schools, or social settings. HIV is not transmitted through shaking hands, hugging, or a casual kiss. You cannot become infected from a toilet seat, a drinking fountain, a door knob, dishes, drinking glasses, food, or pets.

HIV is not an airborne or food-borne virus, and it does not live long outside the body. HIV can be found in the blood, semen, or vaginal fluid of an infected person. The three main ways HIV is transmitted are the following:

- Through having sex (anal, vaginal, or oral) with someone infected with HIV
- Through sharing needles and syringes with someone who has HIV
- Through exposure (in the case of infants) to HIV before or during birth, or through breast-feeding

How long does it take for HIV to cause AIDS?

Prior to 1996, scientists estimated that about half the people with HIV would develop AIDS within ten years after becoming infected. This time varied greatly from person to person and depended on many factors, including a person's health status and health-related behaviors.

Since 1996, the introduction of powerful anti-retroviral therapies has dramatically changed the progression time between HIV infection and the development of AIDS. There are also other medical treatments that can prevent or cure some of the illnesses associated with AIDS, though the treatments do not cure AIDS itself. Because of these advances in drug therapies and other medical treatments, estimates of how many and how soon people will develop AIDS are being recalculated, revised, or are currently under study.

As with other diseases, early detection of infection allows for more options for treatment and preventative health care.

How can I tell if I'm infected with HIV? What are the symptoms?

The only way to know if you are infected is to be tested for HIV infection. You cannot rely on symptoms to know whether or not you are infected with HIV. Many people who are infected with HIV do not have any symptoms at all for many years.

The following **may be** warning signs of infection with HIV:

- Rapid weight loss
- Dry cough
- Recurring fever or profuse night sweats
- Profound and unexplained fatigue
- Swollen lymph glands in the armpits, groin, or neck
- Diarrhea that lasts for more than a week
- White spots or unusual blemishes on the tongue, in the mouth, or in the throat
- Pneumonia
- Red, brown, pink, or purplish blotches on or under the skin or inside the mouth, nose, or eyelids
- Memory loss, depression, and other neurological disorders

However, no one should assume they are infected if they have any of these symptoms. Each of these symptoms can be related to other illnesses. Again, **the only way to determine whether you are infected is to be tested for HIV infection.**

Similarly, you cannot rely on symptoms to establish that a person has AIDS. **The symptoms of AIDS are similar to the symptoms of many other illnesses.** AIDS is a medical diagnosis made by a doctor based on specific criteria established by the CDC.

What are the different HIV screening tests available in the U.S.?

In most cases the EIA (enzyme immunoassay), performed on blood drawn from a vein, is the standard screening test used to detect the presence of antibodies to HIV. A reactive EIA must be used with a follow-up confirmatory test, such as the Western Blot, to make a positive diagnosis.

There are EIA tests that use other body fluids to identify antibodies to HIV. These include:

- Oral Fluid Tests—oral fluid (not saliva) is collected from the mouth, using a special collection device. This is an EIA antibody test similar to the standard blood EIA test and requires a follow-up confirmatory Western Blot, using the same oral fluid sample.
- Urine Tests—use urine instead of blood. The sensitivity and specificity (accuracy) are somewhat less than that of the blood and oral fluid tests. Reactive test results must be confirmed with a blood-based Western Blot.

Home testing kits:

- Can be purchased in most pharmacies and via the Internet and involve no actual testing of the blood by the person using the kit. The only "at-home" components of the testing process involve the collection of a small sample of blood using a finger stick and the receipt of the results over the phone. First, the blood sample is mailed to the manufacturer for a standard EIA test. The consumer must call a phone number several days later to receive the results and be offered the choice of speaking to a trained counselor. A positive result must be confirmed with a blood-based Western Blot.

Rapid tests:

- A rapid test is a screening test that produces very quick results, in approximately 20-60 minutes. In comparison, results from the other more commonly used HIV antibody screening test, the enzyme immunoassay (EIA), are not available for several days to a few weeks.

Both the rapid test and the EIA look for the presence of antibodies to HIV. As is true for all screening tests, a reactive rapid HIV test result must be confirmed with a follow-up confirmatory test before a final diagnosis of infection can be made.

How long after a possible exposure should I wait to get tested for HIV?

The tests commonly used to detect HIV infection are actually looking for antibodies produced by an individual's immune system after exposure to HIV. Most people will develop detectable antibodies within two to eight weeks (the average is 25 days). Ninety-seven percent will develop antibodies in the first three months following the time of their infection. In very rare cases, it can take up to six months to develop antibodies to HIV.

For information on where to find an HIV testing site, visit the National HIV Testing Resources web site at http://www.hivtest.org.

Where can I get tested for HIV infection?

Many places provide testing for HIV infection. Common testing locations include local health departments, clinics, offices of private doctors, hospitals, and sites specifically set up to provide HIV testing. To find a testing site near you, visit the National HIV Testing Resources web site at http://www.hivtest.org.

Between the time of a possible exposure and the receipt of test results, individuals should consider abstaining from sexual contact with others or use condoms and/or dental dams during all sexual encounters.

It is important to seek testing at a place that also provides counseling about HIV and AIDS prevention. Counselors can answer any questions you might have about risky behaviors and ways you can protect yourself and others in the future. In addition, they can help you understand the meaning of the test results and describe what HIV/AIDS-related resources are available in the local area.

Consumer-controlled test kits (popularly known as "home test kits") were first licensed in 1997. Although home HIV tests are sometimes advertised through the Internet, currently only the *Home Access HIV-1 Test System* is approved by the Food and Drug

Administration. (The accuracy of other home test kits cannot be verified.) The *Home Access HIV-1 Test System* can be found at most local drug stores. The testing procedure involves pricking a finger with a special device, placing drops of blood on a specially treated card, and then mailing the card in to be tested at a licensed laboratory. Customers are given an identification number to use when phoning in for the results. Callers may speak to a counselor before taking the test, while waiting for the test result, and when the results are given. All individuals receiving a positive test result are provided referrals for a follow-up confirmatory test, as well as information and resources on treatment and support services.

If you would like more information or have personal concerns, call CDC-INFO 24 Hours/Day at 1-800-CDC-INFO (232-4636), 1-888-232-6348 (TTY), in English, en Español.

If I test HIV negative, does that mean that my partner is HIV negative also?

No. Your HIV test result reveals only *your* HIV status. Your negative test result does not indicate whether or not your partner has HIV.

HIV is not necessarily transmitted every time there is an exposure. Therefore, your taking an HIV test should not be seen as a method to find out if your partner is infected. Testing should never take the place of protecting yourself from HIV infection. If your behaviors are putting you at risk for exposure to HIV, it is important to reduce your risks.

Not having (abstaining from) sex is the most effective way to avoid HIV. If you choose to have sex, use a latex condom to help protect both you and your partner from HIV and other STDs. Studies have shown that latex condoms are very effective, though not perfect, in preventing HIV transmission when used correctly and consistently. If either partner is allergic to latex, plastic (polyurethane) condoms for either the male or female can be used.

What if I test positive for HIV?

If you test positive for HIV, the sooner you take steps to protect your health, the better. Early medical treatment and a healthy lifestyle can help you stay well. Prompt medical care may delay the onset of AIDS and prevent some life-threatening conditions. There are a number of important steps you can take immediately to protect your health:

- See a health care provider, even if you do not feel sick. Try to find a health care provider who has experience treating HIV. There are now many medications to treat HIV infection and help you maintain your health. It is never too early to start thinking about treatment possibilities.
- Have a TB (tuberculosis) test. You may be infected with TB and not know it. Undetected TB can cause serious illness, but it can be successfully treated if caught early.
- Smoking cigarettes, drinking too much alcohol, or using illegal drugs (such as cocaine) can weaken your immune system. There are programs available that can help you reduce or stop using these substances.

There is much you can do to stay healthy. Learn all you can about maintaining good health.

Not having (abstaining from) sex is the most effective way to avoid transmitting HIV to others. If you choose to have sex, use a latex condom to help protect your partner from HIV and other STDs. Studies have shown that latex condoms are very effective, though not perfect, in preventing HIV transmission when used correctly and consistently. If either partner is allergic to latex, plastic (polyurethane) condoms for either the male or female can be used.

Men on the Down Low

What are the origins of this term *down low* and what does it refer to?

The most generic definition of the term *down low*, or *DL*, is "to keep something private," whether that refers to information or activity.

The term is often used to describe the behavior of men who have sex with other men as well as women and who do not identify themselves as gay or bisexual. These men may refer to themselves as being "on the down low," "on the DL," or "on the low low." The term has most often been associated with African-American men. Although the term originated in the African-American community, the behaviors associated with the term are not new and not specific to black men who have sex with men.

What are the sexual risk factors associated with being on the down low?

Much of the media attention about men on the down low and HIV/AIDS has focused on the concept of a transmission bridge between bisexual men and heterosexual women. Some women have become infected through sexual contact with bisexual men [1]. However, many questions have not yet been answered, including:

- Are more cases of HIV infection in women caused by sexual contact with bisexually active men that by sexual contact with men who inject drugs?
- Are bisexually active men more likely than other groups of men to be infected with HIV?
- What proportion of HIV-infected men who have sex with male and female partners identify with the down low?
- Do men on the down low engage in fewer or more sexual risk behaviors than men who are not on the down low?
- Do people, other than bisexually active men, who do not disclose their behavior to sex partners, identify with the down low?

What are the implications for HIV prevention?

The phenomenon of men on the down low has gained much attention in recent years; however, there are no data to confirm or refute publicized accounts of HIV risk behavior associated with these men. What is clear is that women, men, and children of minority races and ethnicities are disproportionately affected by HIV and AIDS and that all persons need to protect themselves and others from getting or transmitting HIV.

Reference

1. CDC. HIV/AIDS Surveillance Report, 2003 (Vol. 15). Atlanta: US Department of Health and Human Services, CDC; 2004:1–46.

FREQUENTLY REPEATED RUMORS ABOUT HIV TRANSMISSION

I got an e-mail warning that a man, who was believed to be HIV-positive, was recently caught placing blood in the ketchup dispenser at a fast food restaurant. Because of the risk of HIV transmission, the e–mail recommended that only individually wrapped packets of ketchup be used. Is there a risk of contracting HIV from ketchup?

No incidents of contamination of ketchup dispensers with HIV-infected blood have been reported to CDC. Furthermore, CDC has no reports of HIV infection resulting from eating food, including condiments.

HIV is not an airborne or food-borne virus, and it does not live long outside the body. Even if small amounts of HIV-infected blood were consumed, stomach acid would destroy the virus. Therefore, there is no risk of contracting HIV from eating ketchup.

HIV is most commonly transmitted through specific sexual behaviors (anal, vaginal, or oral sex) or needle sharing with an infected person. An HIV-infected woman can pass the virus to her baby before or during childbirth or after birth through breast-feeding. Although the risk is extremely low in the United States, it is also possible to acquire HIV through transfusions of infected blood or blood products.

Did a Texas child die of a heroin overdose after being stuck by a used needle found on a playground?

This story was investigated and found to be a hoax. To become over-dosed on a drug from a used needle and syringe, a person would have to have a large amount of the drug injected directly into his or her body. A needle stick injury such as that mentioned in the story would not lead to a large enough injection to cause a drug overdose. In addition, drug users would leave very little drug material in a discarded syringe after they have injected. If such an incident were to happen, there would likely be concerns about possible blood-borne infections, such as human immunodeficiency virus and hepatitis B or C. The risk of these infections from an improperly disposed of needle, such as that described in the story, are extremely low.

Can HIV be transmitted through contact with unused feminine (sanitary) pads?

HIV cannot be transmitted through the use of new, unused feminine pads. The human immunodeficiency virus, or HIV, is a virus that is passed from one person to another through blood-to-blood and sexual contact with someone who is infected with HIV. In addition, infected pregnant women can pass HIV to their babies during pregnancy or delivery, as well as through breast-feeding. Although some people have been concerned that HIV might be transmitted in other ways, such as through air, water, insects, or common objects, no scientific evidence supports this. Even though no one has gotten HIV from touching used feminine pads, used pads should be wrapped and properly disposed of so no one comes in contact with blood.

A *Weekly World News* story claims CDC has discovered a mutated version of HIV that is transmitted through the air. Is the story true?

This story is **not** true. It is unfortunate that such stories, which may frighten the public, are being circulated on the Internet.

Human immunodeficiency virus (HIV), the virus that causes AIDS, is spread by sexual contact (anal, vaginal, or oral) or by sharing needles and/or syringes with someone who is infected with HIV.

Babies born to HIV-infected women may become infected before or during birth or through breast-feeding.

Many scientific studies have been done to look at all the possible ways that HIV is transmitted. These studies have not shown HIV to be transmitted through air, water, insects, or casual contact.

I have read stories on the Internet about people getting stuck by needles in phone booth coin returns, movie theater seats, gas pump handles, and other places. One story said that CDC reported similar incidents about improperly discarded needles and syringes. Are these stories true?

CDC has received inquiries about a variety of reports or warnings about used needles left by HIV-infected injection drug users in coin return slots of pay phones, the underside of gas pump handles, and on movie theater seats. These reports and warnings have been circulated on the Internet and by e-mail and fax. Some reports have falsely indicated that CDC "confirmed" the presence of HIV in the needles. CDC has not tested such needles, nor has CDC confirmed the presence or absence of HIV in any sample related to these rumors. The majority of these reports and warnings appear to have no foundation in fact.

CDC was informed of one incident in Virginia of a needle stick from a small-gauge needle (believed to be an insulin needle) in a coin return slot of a pay phone. The incident was investigated by the local police department. Several days later, after a report of this police action appeared in the local newspaper, a needle was found in a vending machine, but it did not cause a needle-stick injury.

Discarded needles are sometimes found in the community outside of health care settings. These needles are believed to have been discarded by persons who use insulin or are injection drug users. Occasionally, the "public" and certain groups of workers (e.g., sanitation workers or housekeeping staff) may sustain needle-stick injuries involving inappropriately discarded needles. Needle-stick injuries can transfer blood and blood-borne pathogens (e.g., hepatitis B, hepatitis C, and HIV), but the risk of transmission from discarded needles is extremely low.

CDC does not recommend testing discarded needles to assess the presence or absence of infectious agents in the needles. Management of exposed persons should be done on a case-by-case evaluation of (1) the risk of a blood-borne pathogen infection in the source and (2) the nature of the injury. Anyone who is injured from a needle stick in a community setting should contact a physician or go to an emergency room as soon as possible. The health care professional should then report the injury to the local or state health department. CDC is not aware of any cases where HIV has been transmitted by a needle-stick injury outside a health care setting.

APPROVED MEDICATIONS TO TREAT HIV INFECTION

Information from AIDS Info, A Service of the U.S. Department of Health and Human Services (www.aidsinfo.nih.gov)

Anti-HIV (also called antiretroviral) medications are used to control the reproduction of the virus and to slow the progression of HIV-related disease. Highly Active Antiretroviral Therapy (HAART) is the recommended treatment for HIV infection. HAART combines three or more anti-HIV medications in a daily regimen. Anti-HIV medications do not cure HIV infection, and individuals taking these medications can still transmit HIV to others.

Here are the anti-HIV medications approved by the U.S. Food and Drug Administration (FDA):

CLASS			
GENERIC NAME	**BRAND AND OTHER NAMES**	**FDA APPROVAL MANUFACTURER**	**DATE**

Nonnucleoside Reverse Transcriptase Inhibitors (NNRTIs)
NNRTIs bind to and disable reverse transcriptase, a protein that HIV needs to make more copies of itself.

Delavirdine	Rescriptor, DLV	Pfizer	April 4, 1997
Efavirenz	Sustiva, EFV	Bristol-Myers Squibb	September 17, 1998
Nevirapine	Viramune, NVP	Boehringer Ingelheim	June 21, 1996

Nucleoside Reverse Transcriptase Inhibitors (NRTIs)
NRTIs are faulty versions of building blocks that HIV needs to make more copies of itself. When HIV uses an NRTI instead of a normal building block, reproduction of the virus is stalled.

Abacavir	Ziagen, ABC	GlaxoSmithKline	December 17, 1998
Abacavir, Lamivudine	Epzicom	GlaxoSmithKline	August 2, 2004
Abacavir, Lamivudine, Zidovudine	Trizivir	GlaxoSmithKline	November 14, 2000
Didanosine	Videx, ddI Videx EC	Bristol-Myers Squibb	October 9, 1991 October 31, 2000
Emtricitabine	Emtriva, FTC, Coviracil	Gilead Sciences	July 2, 2003
Emtricitabine, Tenofovir DF	Truvada	Gilead Sciences	August 2, 2004
Lamivudine	Epivir, 3TC	GlaxoSmithKline	November 17, 1995
Lamivudine, Zidovudine	Combivir	GlaxoSmithKline	September 27, 1997

CLASS			
GENERIC NAME	**BRAND AND OTHER NAMES**	**FDA APPROVAL MANUFACTURER**	**DATE**
Stavudine	Zerit, d4T	Bristol-Myers Squibb	June 24, 1994
Tenofovir DF	Viread, TDF	Gilead Sciences	October 26, 2001
Zalcitabine	Hivid, ddC	Hoffmann-La Roche	June 19, 1992
Zidovudine	Retrovir, AZT, ZDV	GlaxoSmithKline	March 19, 1987

Protease Inhibitors (PIs)

PIs disable protease, a protein that HIV needs to make more copies of itself.

Amprenavir	Agenerase, APV	GlaxoSmithKline, Vertex Pharmaceuticals	April 15, 1999
Atazanavir	Reyataz, ATV	Bristol-Myers Squibb	June 20, 2003
Fosamprenavir	Lexiva, FPV	GlaxoSmithKline, Vertex Pharmaceuticals	October 20, 2003
Indinavir	Crixivan, IDV	Merck	March 13, 1996
Lopinavir, Ritonavir	Kaletra, LPV/r	Abbott Laboratories	September 15, 2000
Nelfinavir	Viracept, NFV	Agouron Pharmaceuticals	March 14, 1997
Ritonavir	Norvir, RTV	Abbott Laboratories	March 1, 1996
Saquinavir	Fortovase, SQV Invirase	Hoffmann-La Roche	November 7, 1997 December 6, 1995

FUSION INHIBITORS

Fusion Inhibitors prevent HIV entry into cells.

Enfuvirtide	Fuzeon, T-20	Hoffmann-La Roche, Trimeris	March 13, 2003

FINAL TIPS FROM THE AUTHOR AND FRIENDS

TALKING WITH YOUR DOCTOR OR HEALTH CARE PROVIDER

One very important aspect of this book was the relationship between Sabrena and her doctors. It was important for me, the author, to highlight the need to talk and ask questions during your visits. In this story, we saw Sabrena struggle with this, and, indeed, she didn't like doctors at all. However, Dr. Scott and Dr. Grier talked with her, versus talking "to her." The communication was a two-way street. That is my hope for you, whether it is HIV/AIDS, high blood pressure, depression, diabetes, or any medical condition. Dr. Scott gave Sabrena a brochure with questions that she should have answered with each of her visits. These questions, called Ask Me 3, can help with your interactions with your healthcare provider, as well as with understanding your health. The information is provided by the Partnership for Clear Health Communications, and can be found at **www.askme3.org.**

ASK ME 3

Every time you talk with a doctor, nurse, or pharmacist, use the **Ask Me 3** questions to better understand your health.

1. **What is my main problem?**
2. **What do I need to do?**
3. **Why is it important for me to do this?**

WHEN TO ASK QUESTIONS

You can ask questions when:

- You see your doctor, nurse, or pharmacist
- You prepare for a medical test or procedure
- You get your medicine

VITAL TIPS FOR YOU AND YOUR FAMILY:

- Write down your questions before your visit with any health care provider.
- Write down all of your medications and take the list with you *each* time you go to any of your health care providers and the pharmacy. This includes over-the-counter medications, herbal products and remedies, minerals, and vitamins.
- Talk to the pharmacist about your medications and try to use the same pharmacy for everything. This includes over-the-counter-medications, herbal products and remedies, minerals, and vitamins.
- If you have a problem or experience any unusual symptoms with taking medications or following your health care provider's instructions, *call your provider*. Do not just stop medication without calling or seeing a health provider within 12-24 hours after stopping the medication.
- *Take your medications just as your doctor has prescribed them.* (For instance: One tablet a day does not mean one tablet when you feel like it.)
- Throw out expired medications, ointments, and other products.
- Do *not* take any over-the-counter medications without your doctor's knowledge, especially if you have a medical condition that is being treated with medications. This is especially important for persons with high blood pressure, diabetes, HIV/AIDS, depression, glaucoma, heart disease, arthritis, lupus, or other conditions.
- If you are uncomfortable with any diagnosis or treatment plan, ask for second opinion.
- Keep a medical history file that contains all of your current and past conditions, test results, and family history.
- Take time to share information with your family about the

medical conditions that "run in your family." Assign a medical historian and if possible keep online and in print.
- Live, Laugh, and Love; all have been shown to be great *medicine* for the soul!

Photograph by Jacqueline Hicks, Fond Memories

Sharon Denise Allison-Ottey earned her medical degree from East Carolina University School of Medicine and completed her residency in Internal Medicine and Fellowship training in Geriatric Medicine in Baltimore, Maryland. She is a proud alumna of North Carolina Central University, where she earned dual bachelor's degrees in Biology and Chemistry, and minored in Physics, African-American History, and English with honors. The author is a health educator and the Director of Health and Community Outreach Initiatives with the COSHAR Foundation, a non-profit organization with a mission to impact the health of the world, one community at a time. She is a researcher with numerous scientific publications and awards. She is considered an expert in doctor-patient communications and health literacy, as well as women's health with a special emphasis on minority women. She is a dynamic speaker who motivates, empowers, and is able to address a variety of issues in a colorful and meaningful manner. She is a member of several professional, civic, and community organizations.